"A whopping good read . . . Fast-paced, exciting, nicely detailed, with some innovative touches."

—Elizabeth Moon, Nebula Award–winning author of
Crown of Renewal

"Shepherd delivers no shortage of military action, in space and on the ground. It's cinematic, dramatic, and dynamic . . . [He also] demonstrates a knack for characterization, balancing serious moments with dry humor . . . A thoroughly enjoyable adventure featuring one of science fiction's most interesting recurring heroines."

—Tor.com

"A tightly written, action-packed adventure from start to finish . . . Heart-thumping action will keep the reader engrossed and emotionally involved. It will be hard waiting for the next in the series."

—*Fresh Fiction*

"[*Daring*] will elate fans of the series . . . The story line is faster than the speed of light."

—*Alternative Worlds*

"[Kris Longknife] will remind readers of David Weber's Honor Harrington with her strength and intelligence. Mike Shepherd provides an exciting military science fiction thriller."

—*Genre Go Round Reviews*

"'I'm a woman of very few words, but lots of action': So said Mae West, but it might just as well have been Lieutenant Kris Longknife, princess of the one hundred worlds of Wardhaven. Kris can kick, shoot, and punch her way out of any dangerous situation, and she can do it while wearing stilettos and a tight cocktail dress. She's all business, with a Hells Angel handshake and a 'get out of my face' attitude. But her hair always looks good . . . Kris Longknife is funny and she entertains us."

—*Sci Fi Weekly*

"[A] fast-paced, exciting military SF series . . . Mike Shepherd has a great ear for dialogue and talent for injecting dry humor into things at just the right moment . . . The characters are engaging, and the plot is full of twists and peppered liberally with sharply described action. I always look forward to installments in the Kris Longknife series because I know I'm guaranteed a good time with plenty of adventure."

—*SF Site*

Kris Longknife
UNRELENTING

Mike Shepherd

ACE BOOKS, NEW YORK

ACE

An imprint of Penguin Random House LLC
375 Hudson Street, New York, New York 10014

KRIS LONGKNIFE: UNRELENTING

An Ace Book / published by arrangement with the author

Ace mass-market ISBN: 978-0-425-27737-9

PUBLISHING HISTORY
Ace mass-market edition / November 2015

PRINTED IN THE UNITED STATES OF AMERICA

10 9 8 7 6 5 4 3 2 1

Cover art by Scott Grimando.
Cover design by Diana Kolsky.
Interior text design by Kristin del Rosario.

Penguin
Random
House

Kris Longknife
UNRELENTING

1

Admiral Kris Longknife bent over the toilet and explosively lost her breakfast.

Damn! I've never had battle jitters this bad.

Done, she twisted around to the sink, ran some water, and washed out her mouth.

And had to bolt for the toilet again as her stomach decided it was not done with her yet.

Double damn!

NELLY, IS THERE A FLU BUG GOING AROUND THE FLEET? Kris asked her personal computer.

Nelly, much upgraded since she was given to Kris in preschool, was plugged directly into Kris's brain while riding at her collarbone, so, even though her mouth was otherwise occupied, Kris could pose the question.

KRIS, THERE IS NO STOMACH FLU REPORTED. THE WATER USAGE IN THE HEADS IS WITHIN ONE PERCENT OF NORMAL SO IT IS VERY UNLIKELY THERE WAS SOMETHING WRONG WITH LAST NIGHT'S SUPPER. YOU, HOWEVER, ARE AT DOUBLE, NO, TRIPLE NORMAL, Nelly pointed out, as the toilet flushed for the third time.

Again, hoping she was done, Kris did the mouth-rinsing thing.

Her stomach stayed quiescent.

Kris stood, adjusted her shipsuit, with its epaulets showing the stripes of a full admiral, and turned to face her next battle.

No wonder she was nervous: This battle was the craziest she'd ever tried. She was risking two-thirds of her fleet to take out the assassins of the mountain, as Vice Admiral Yi of Earth named them, the kamikaze base, as Vice Admiral Miyoshi of Musashi called them.

Whatever you called them, they'd been launching ships, ships that built up to a good fraction of light speed as they shot through jump point after jump point before slamming themselves into the Alwa system and heading straight for the planet.

So far, Kris's fleet had blasted every alien suicide ship, but Kris was tired of playing defense, holding a line where one failure meant the death of millions of humans and their Alwan allies.

For the first time, Kris's fleet was taking the offensive.

Kris had pulled two of her task fleets, better than two-thirds of her entire force, away from Alwa. The one task fleet left defending Alwa included the First Battle Squadron. It had followed Kris into hell and paid a steep price to get back, returning so bent and busted that the superintendents of the repair yards had taken one good look and suggested the ships be scrapped.

The frigates' Smart Metal™ had been drained into holding tanks. Their reactors and lasers were in the rework facilities. Once recertified for space, they'd be issued to merchant ships. The crews were now waiting for the yards to spin out new ships to bear those proud names.

Kris prayed that the ships following her this time would return in better shape.

She hoped, but only time . . . and the coming fight . . . would tell.

For one thing, Admiral Yi's Third Fleet, half of her attack force, was somewhere out there, heading into the target system from one jump while Kris's Second Fleet stood by to enter from another.

And Yi, being from Earth, had an attitude toward all colonial bumpkins.

No wonder my stomach has a problem. It's just one of many today.

Peace made with her now-empty stomach, Kris turned for her flag plot. She had a battle to win.

2

"**You** okay?" Major General Jack Montoya asked. As Chief of her Royal Security Detail, Commander, Ground Forces Alwa Defense Sector, and, oh, right, husband, he was very good at reading her moods.

"I'm fine," Kris lied.

Jack's smile told her she wasn't fooling him.

"I got a bad feeling about this," he said, but he drew close to whisper it in her ear.

Kris made a face, half between a grin and a scowl, and left it to the others in flag plot to decipher. If they wanted to take it as old friends, or newlywed private chatter, that was their problem.

"I hope Yi doesn't think his newfangled armor is magic," Kris whispered back.

There was no smile in Jack's scowl.

"Yi does seem to think he's got the Shield of Great Worth or something," Jack said.

No question, the three squadrons of ships from Old Earth had arrived with something special for armor. For several centuries, quantum computers had been slowing light and storing it for a bit. First they'd managed a few seconds, finally a whole minute. Computation at the speed of light needed this ability to store quanta of the stuff to make a 1 so the absence of it could be a 0. From time to time, someone with gold braid on their coat would wonder about using this technology to freeze a laser beam for enough time to tame it, but the problems of corralling something with that much energy had defeated them.

Those problems, and the short duration of the only two major dustups humanity had had in the last hundred years:

the Unity War, and the Iteeche War, had made for no major advances in the age-old race between arms and armor.

Some Earth lab, however, must have gotten lucky because even as Earth's Navy started spinning out the new Smart Metal™ frigates, they were coating them with doped crystals that could handle hits from powerful laser weapons.

Thus, twenty-four Earth-built frigates joined Kris's command with their hides gleaming like diamonds.

That was the other aspect of Smart Metal™: Your ship didn't have to stay the same, day in and day out. If there was no threat, you could set Condition Able and turn your warship into a nice, comfortable place to live. When you needed to do some fighting, you set Condition Zed and shrank your "love boat" down into something small, hard to hit, and deadly.

In the case of Admiral Yi's ships, it took a bit longer to rearrange the light-stopping crystals, but it was worth it.

Kris had reorganized her fleets around the new ships, their armor, and their 22-inch lasers. She would have preferred assigning one of the Earth squadrons to each of her three fleets. Instead, she'd let Vice Admiral Yi on the *George Washington* keep two of his new squadrons. The combat-experienced Rear Admiral Bethea led the big cats of BatRon 4 from her flag on the *Lion*. Untested Commodore Michelsen commanded the Scanda Confederacy's BatRon 6 from his flag, the *Odin*.

Kris led the First Fleet. To Commodore Cochrane's borrowed Earth squadron with their 22-inch lasers and innovative armor, Kris had added BatRon 8's Sharp Ones commanded by Admiral L'Estock on *Battleax*.

Admiral Hawkings on *Renown* had BatRon 2, but his task force was missing BatRon 1. In place of it, Kris had borrowed the inexperienced but big-gunned frigates of Yamato's BatRon 9 under Commodore Zingi on the *Mikasa*. That gave Kris twenty-four of the new 22-inch-gunned war wagons and eight of the 20-inch frigates. They had seemed huge just a few months ago.

Yi's four squadrons were evenly divided between frigates armed with 22-inch and 20-inch lasers. Kris expected no problem from that.

Admiral Kris Longknife glanced around her flag bridge.

On any other day it would be her day quarters, but today it was a battle station for her and her key staff.

Her desk had moved itself back against the wall, leaving more room for a conference table. Around it sat Kris's staff. Beside Jack was Commander Penny Lien-Pasley, her intelligence officer. At her elbow was Iizuka Masao, Musashi Navy Intelligence, and, hopefully, more to Penny. Between the two of them they knew everything there was to know about the alien space raiders.

Unfortunately, that was way too little.

Also around Kris's command table was Jacques la Duke who had done the workup on the alien psychology. He'd also spent a rough week living among them . . . and lived to tell of it. His wife, Amanda Kutter, Kris's chief economist, wasn't needed for this battle, but she was there at his elbow.

"Alwa's economy will do fine without me, assuming a poor crop next month doesn't throw the whole mess into famine," Amanda had told Kris, and stalked aboard the *Princess Royal* right behind Jacques.

Kris had shrugged; she wasn't letting Jack out of her sight any more than she had to. She was in no position to lecture another woman.

Also added to Kris's key staff was Admiral Furzah of Sasquan. A six-foot-tall talking cat, she had all the loving nature of the felines of Earth, which was to say she was as bloodthirsty as they came. Back on her home world, she'd commanded atomic weapons and used them on her country's enemies.

Kris shivered to think of such ferocity. She was none too sure how much she wanted these cats loose in space, but the admiral had more combat experience than most aboard the *Princess Royal*, and her knowledge of her people's battle lore was only matched by Nelly's computer memory of man's inhumanity to man.

Kris hoped this team would help her make the best of the coming fight.

Kris's staff had expanded beyond those present. John Longfeather, an Alwan Rooster, had joined Kris for logistics. He'd been with the humans since he'd walked into town as little more than a chick and demanded to learn what they knew. He'd been headed for Granny Rita's government until Kris mentioned her need for admin help, and the old commodore smiled. "Have I got a Rooster for you."

Kris's new chief of personnel was also an Alwan, though she was an Ostrich, Betty Strongleg. She'd helped organize Ostriches for Defense before the last attack and also came with Granny Rita's approval.

Kris was an admiral now, commanding three fleets, and her staff was bound to grow. Those two, however, were doing their work back on Cannopus Station, far from this fight.

Kris eyed the screens lining the walls of her flag bridge. They showed the readiness of her fleet and what was happening in the target system.

Four squadrons of frigates swung at anchor in matching pairs a good seventy thousand klicks back from the jump point. The frigates were big and deadly, but it was the armored merchant cruiser *Mary Ellen Carter* that held pride of place at the moment.

The *Carter* was right up at the jump point, drifting in space, and projecting probes through the jump that let Kris know what was happening on the other side. The *Carter*'s crew were all volunteers. They'd be the first to know, and maybe the first to go, when things got interesting.

The feed from the *Carter* showed things that Admiral Kris Longknife did not like. Maybe her stomach knew what it was doing when it threw up her toenails.

Yi was not following her battle plan.

There were three jump points in that system. One Yi had just brought his fleet through. The second Kris guarded and expected the hostiles to flee through . . . and right into her waiting arms.

And, as luck would always have it, there was a third. That jump was way over on the other side of the system. Still, if Yi gave the alien space raiders half a chance, they might decide for the running fight. They outnumbered Yi's thirty-two ships by five to one with massive four- to five-hundred-thousand-ton ships, not to mention a monstrous base ship the size of a moon.

There were a couple of dozen small suicide ships as well,

but those carried no lasers. A few that had gotten through to the Alwa system had lobbed atomics at Kris's fleet before they'd been blown to dust.

If the Earth admiral had followed Kris's plan, he would have spread his four squadrons out in a loose square and swept toward the aliens at a measured pace, letting his longer-ranged lasers burn any alien ships that came to meet him.

Kris expected the aliens to fall back and withdraw into her system, where she would slice and dice them as they came through the jump, then use a few Hellburners to club the base ship into submission or oblivion—their choice.

To date, they'd always chosen oblivion.

That was the plan. But Kris had learned early that no battle plan survived contact with the enemy. Apparently, plans survived even less when implemented by a hubris-loaded idiot.

Sixteen ships now charged out in front of the other sixteen, accelerating at three gees rather than one.

"Five will get you fifty the lead ships are Yi's," Jack whispered softly to Kris.

"No bet," Kris said, eyeing the rough readouts. The probe through the jump point had a very thin bandwidth. She could tell where the reactors were. She could make out the difference between the huge reactors that powered an alien warship and the smaller power plants of the human frigates. Beyond that, not so much.

For the ships in her fleet, Kris's battle boards showed full status. For the ships in the other system, Kris could only guess which frigates were which. Rear Admiral Bethea had fought with Kris before. Kris trusted her.

Vice Admiral Yi was a totally different can of worms.

Assuming Vice Admiral Yi had his task force out front, he seemed way too eager to match his ships with their 22-inch lasers and special armor against the aliens. Rear Admiral Bethea's sixteen ships had armor that only last year had been considered top-of-the-line. Her 20-inch lasers had been the same, but now fell forty thousand kilometers short of the longer-ranging 22-inchers.

Kris ground her teeth as a dish of thirty massive alien warships charged Yi. As they came in range, he killed half, but the others soon closed the distance and were slashing at his ships with more lasers than any ship had a right to own. The alien lasers had a shorter reach than the humans', but they had plenty of them.

Yi's warships would be glowing like stars as their unique armor caught the lasers, slowed them down, distributed them along the hull, then radiated them back into space.

"I think the fribbing stuff just might work," Admiral Furzah purred. Nelly's translator could handle most of what she said. Some things Nelly just didn't bother converting.

For a moment, Kris held her breath. More alien ships blew away into gas.

Then one, two, three Earth ships exploded in rapid succession.

The alien dish was gone, but so were three Earth ships.

Four more dishes of alien warships were coming up quickly.

"Flip ship, you damn bastard," Kris snapped through gritted teeth.

Yi couldn't have heard her, but the logic of her position was unarguable.

The survivors of the two Earth squadrons flipped ship and decelerated until Admiral Bethea came up even with them. Now they formed a square of squadrons.

Now they took the aliens under fire at long range and blew them away while the aliens' lasers could do them no harm.

Gradually, the Earth squadrons cooled. Maybe Vice Admiral Yi would live long enough for her to give him the first major dressing-down of her short Navy career.

Taking a deep breath, Kris took her seat at the foot of the table, the place that gave her the best view of the screens. On them, the alien dishes began to wilt as they took hits they could not reply to. A few ships put on extra gees, trying to close the distance.

They died.

A few of the speedsters, likely armed with atomics, shot out. They were vaporized.

Someone decided they'd had enough. The dishes began to fall back.

"Well, it seems that the first phase of our battle is over," Kris said. "Anyone want to guess what the alien Enlightened One will do next?"

Kris's eyes polled those around the table. The only consensus was a shrug.

3

In the target system, the situation continued to develop with the momentum of molasses in January. Now, all but a handful of alien warships had interposed themselves between their mother ship and the attacking human frigates.

Four dishes of thirty huge warships engaged each of the four squadrons of six to eight frigates. It was a running gunfight, with the frigates gunning for a change and aliens running.

Lately, the aliens had taken to installing rock armor on their ships. These seemed to have it even thicker. Still, most of their armor was at the bow, and they were running. Their huge rockets and reactors could not be armored.

So the aliens tried variations on the retreat theme. A few ships would charge the frigates. Despite their layers of basalt-rock armor, they'd burn, usually sooner, sometimes later. Some would even get within range of Yi's battle squadrons. Yi would have to slow his squadrons down, sometimes even flip ship to bring his stern batteries to bear.

The alien ships died, but Yi was slowed, maybe even damaged.

While the humans were thus engaged, the rest of the alien fleet racked up maximum acceleration toward the nearest jump.

Which was what Kris wanted. She was the bear waiting behind that jump with open jaws.

While the main battle raged with its ebb and flow, a couple of dozen warships escorted the lumbering alien base ship toward that jump.

"Nelly," Kris said, "give me an estimate for when the base ship will reach the jump. Match that with the rate at which their battle line is giving ground to Admiral Yi."

"The base ship should be in a position to come through the jump in four hours. What's left of the alien battle line should arrive an hour later. I will start a countdown when the base ship gets closer."

"Thank you, Nelly." One of the few nice things about Nelly's present state of intelligence and human interactivity was that she had given up the need to be accurate to the thirteenth decimal place. Now she settled for approximates like any sane person.

Kris tried to tell Nelly when she did well. There were *enough* times when she didn't.

Once more, Kris eyed the screen that showed the jump. There was the *Mary Ellen Carter*, the biggest blip on the screen. There were plenty of other blips. Four even showed on the gravity sensors.

Four Hellburners were arrayed around the rear of the jump point. That was one of the few nice things about the jump points; if you went in with a certain vector with respect to the center of the galaxy, you came out on that vector.

There was no question, the alien base ship would come out pointed in Kris's direction.

That meant that the dormant Hellburners and 12-inch antimatter torpedoes would be aft of the target, just where Kris wanted them.

Still, when should she pull the *Carter* back from the jump?

Command decisions. Kris shrugged. *Well, at least I have four hours to gnaw on it.*

Kris made a face at the screen.

"Yeah," Jack said. "I hate it, too. Absolute, gut-wrenching terror is headed our way, but right now it's boring as hell. Would you care for some coffee and a sandwich, Admiral?"

Kris gauged her tummy and found it . . . uninterested.

Now if Jack had offered a quickie, came from the imp side of Kris.

With four hours, it wouldn't have to be so quick, Kris's logical side replied.

Kris had revised her fleet's policy on fraternization. Still, she didn't think even the revised version was that loose.

"No thanks, Jack, I think I'll sit here and mull my options.

Or maybe read a boring report. Anybody have a truly dull report?"

Her team had the good sense to laugh.

Jacques did speak up when things quieted down. "Dr. Meade has finished her analysis of the alien genome." That got everyone's attention. "I won't try to give you the guts of the full report, but the executive summary is that somewhere between a hundred and a hundred and ten thousand years ago, someone did a major rework on their DNA to optimize them all to be slaves."

Kris raised an eyebrow. "And we saw what those 'slaves' did to their masters."

Everyone around the table except the cat admiral had seen the planet reduced to rock, and she had seen the pictures.

"So how'd they manage to get back at their masters?" Jack asked, ever a Marine.

"Your guess is as good as the doctor's," Jacques said. "Throughout our history, there have been slave uprisings. What you do to most, even nearly all, doesn't mean you've done it to every last one. Moreover, what you did last century might not be working next century. Don't you love mutations?" the anthropologist said.

"No plan is perfect," Kris said, with a grimace toward her own screens, where her plan was now, finally, playing out.

Though not entirely to expectations. A batch of the fast movers tried to drop below and come at Vice Admiral Yi's squadrons from the rear. A division from Scandia, *Odin*, *Thor*, *Loki*, and *Frigga*, dropped out from Admiral Bethea's task group to chase them down and destroy them.

The alien commander chose that moment to have a half dozen of the big boys charge the human line. They died, but the humans shot their forward batteries empty. Then all four of the alien dishes charged.

It got frisky for a bit as some aliens went in faster than others. They died but bought time for others to get closer. Admiral Yi flipped his ships, fired the aft batteries, boosted up his deceleration . . . and danced away from the onrushing fleet.

That bought the aliens space and time, but in the end, Yi

reorganized his ships and began the slow process of herding the aliens toward the jump.

"That was why I didn't give you an exact estimate," Nelly said. "You can say what you want about those bug-eyed monsters of yours, Kris, but they are wily."

"And there are a whole lot of them," Penny whispered.

Kris winced; each alien warship had a crew of least a million. The base ship could have as many as 50 billion aboard.

No, we don't want to grapple and board with one of those monsters.

The room fell silent as that image invaded everyone's mind. Kris moved to break it before they all froze in place. "Does Doc Meade think she can do anything about this genetic modification?"

Jacques shook his head. "It's more than a simple medical lab on the tip of the spear can handle. She suggests we transfer some of the aliens who followed you home back to human space."

That got a well-needed chuckle from the staff. Jack had led a boarding party that had confronted an old alien woman who'd shouted her defiances, then tried to take her own life and have the dozen or so children with her do the same.

Sleepy darts had put a stop to that madness.

The alien woman's ragings had helped the pacifists among the Alwans come to terms with the realities of what faced them. Meanwhile, the alien kids were having a ball watching cartoons and learning computer games.

I bet the Enlightened One didn't see that one coming, Kris thought with a grin. He, always a he among these people, called the shots and led a massive and compliant people in a galaxy-wide search for life, any life, and the never-ending work of murdering it.

Not on my watch you won't, Kris had sworn. Today was just another day on the job.

The key staff gnawed on that for a while, then Amanda brought up the present production plans from the plants and fabrication facilities on Alwa's moon. This raised the effort to fabricate laser armor and spin out big frigates with 22-inch lasers from the yards.

People talked of many things, but always with one eye on the screens.

"Those aliens are desperate," Jack muttered. "Desperate people do desperate things."

Right about then, the aliens did something very desperate.

4

Nelly was the first to spot a change. "Kris, three of the aliens' fast movers have taken off for the other jump point at 3.5 gees."

The screen of the other system now showed a wedge of ships moving away from the battle, headed for the distant third jump.

"I wonder what that's all about?" Kris said.

"Maybe someone wants to hedge their bet on this fight?" Jack offered.

"Or get a better view of what happens next," Jacques put in. "The jump may just be in the direction they're headed. It will give them a better view around their own battle line."

"And what will that battle line be doing?" Kris muttered.

Yi had let his ships get a bit close to the alien dishes. Maybe they'd slowed down, and he hadn't noticed. Now twelve ships flipped around and leapt toward his squadrons at 2.5 gees acceleration, the max the huge warships could handle.

Four of them paid immediately for their folly, but the others kept coming, and another four took off, replacing the initial four

"Kris," Nelly reported, "something is happening around the rest of the alien dishes. I'm getting bits of radar reflection off some things. Not much, and it comes and goes. I'm getting nothing on the electromagnetic spectrum."

"Mines?" Kris said.

"I can't say with any certainty," Nelly said.

"We've left mines behind when we were running," Jack pointed out.

"They never have," Penny said.

"They've never been the ones running before," her friend Masao added.

The two intelligence officers nodded.

On the screens, the fight got messy as Admiral Yi back-pedaled to open the range, then turned and began mopping up the aliens that had caused all the trouble. The alien dishes used the distraction to put on maximum gees for the jump point.

Most of the sixteen ships that surged at Yi's fleet did the usual when they were hit hard and falling out of the assault. If their own reactors hadn't torn them apart, they dropped their containment fields and let them eat their ships, annihilating ship and crew in one giant conflagration.

Today was different. Three of the ships were hit, disabled, and left drifting in space.

"Kris, small vessels are departing the disabled ships," Nelly reported.

"Small, as in lifeboat size?" Kris answered, incredulously.

"Kris, they are larger than the small lifeboat we saw once."

"Hold it," Penny said. "These folks have been launching suicide ships at Alwa, and now some of them want to surrender?"

"You think it's a ruse?" Masao asked at Penny's elbow.

"Would you put it past them?" Penny answered, another question stacked on top of the others.

"I wouldn't," Jacques said, looking grim.

Kris shook her head. "Yi's got to spot this himself. I will not give away this ambush to do his thinking for him."

Vice Admiral Yi appeared to be aware only that he was way out of range of the main enemy force. He put on three gees to close the distance. Two of Bethea's ships, *Puma* and *Loki*, accelerated with the rest of the fleet on a course that would take them awfully close to the tumbling alien ships and their growing sphere of putative "lifeboats."

Nothing happened, and Kris was about to breathe a sigh of relief, when dozens of the "lifeboats" slammed into high-gee accelerations toward the frigates. The humans' secondary batteries snapped out, vaporizing a dozen of the alien boats.

But more were attacking. Scores of tiny specks now charged the frigates. Their skippers took defensive actions, even using the main batteries to swat at the assailants. More died, but those left were getting close.

In a final surge, a handful of the tiny ships closed on two of Bethea's ships. Three boats closest to the two frigates exploded.

"Atomics," Nelly reported.

One ship continued on its way, out of the wave of atomic fury . . . for a moment. Then it seemed to cave in upon itself. Survival pods zipped from the ship. Most got far enough. Many did not.

The reactors lost their containment, and the ship disappeared in a glowing cloud of dust that itself quickly vanished.

The other ship did better; it limped out of the battle line and slowly fell behind. It joined up with a smaller blip on Kris's screens to comb the space around the other kill. The two set about collecting survival pods.

The rest of Admiral Bethea's two squadrons opened fire with their 5-inch secondary batteries on anything in the space ahead of them.

"All the shooting ships are Bethea's," Nelly said. "The Earth squadrons appear to be taking the time to catch their breath."

"Damn," escaped Kris's lips. In the last battle, she'd done to the aliens just what it looked like they were doing to him.

"Damn," Jack repeated. "Didn't Yi read the report on how we won the last battle and how there were three ships studying our tactics? Three ships that got away."

The anthropologist Jacques shook his head. "Yi doesn't strike me as a man who sees the need to learn anything new. Certainly not from Rim rats. How did Earth ever give him command of a fleet of new ships that would need to fight a new way?"

"I think it's safe to assume," Penny said, "that he's the best they have."

"I'd hate to have the worst," Kris muttered.

Third Fleet was coming up on the area Nelly suspected was mined. Now, even Yi's ships were shooting at the space ahead of them.

There was a blinding flash. A huge one. Then another, and three more in rapid succession.

"More atomic explosions," Nelly reported.

"God help them," Penny said.

One of Yi's ships was caught between two explosions. A moment later, it converted to an expanding ball of gas.

Another ship was close to an atomic mine. It lost acceleration, tumbling in space.

Now all the human ships had cut their acceleration and were devoting all their weapons; main and secondary, to sweeping the space in front of them.

More explosions went off as someone made the decision to use them before they lost them.

And the alien fleet flipped ship and charged in.

Maybe Yi's sensors had been damaged by the atomic explosions. Maybe he couldn't see what was happening. What was clear was that he was drifting in space with no weigh on, no way to jink his ships, and a whole lot of enemy charging down his throat.

Worse, the alien base ship had flipped as well and was now headed for the battle scene.

Yi's ships were from Earth. They had new, bigger lasers. They had new, fancy armor. What they didn't have was Hellburners that could rip apart moon-size mother ships.

Just exactly how Yi would handle being caught between a base ship and a lot of angry monstrous warships would be anyone's guess.

Kris wasn't ready to see how he'd guess.

"So much for my battle plan," Kris snapped, and made her decision as she did. "Admirals Hawkings and L'Estock, take your squadrons through the jump. L'Estock, have Earth's BatRon 12 lead the way. Hawkings, the Wardhaven division of BatRon 2 will go last after they retrieve the deployed Hellburners."

"Understood," quickly answered her.

The Hellburners were a uniquely Wardhaven weapon. *Renown*, *Repulse*, *Royal Sovereign*, and *Resolute* all had headed toward this fight with two aboard. Four had been deployed as mines; four had been held in reserve on the ships as weapons for the final *coup de grace* for the base ship. Now it would take time for them to retrieve the deployed mines.

Exactly how the "R's" would close on the alien base ship

with all its lasers firing was a question Kris desperately needed an answer for.

Kris's staff headed out on the double to get themselves into high-gee eggs, something that wasn't on the schedule for another hour. Jack pulled Kris's chair back, and whispered, "After you, my love."

Kris would have loved to give him a kiss, but they were already overdue for those eggs.

"Captain Gathmann," Kris called as she raced into her quarters, already unzipping her shipsuit, "Take us through the jump right at the end of Commodore Zingi's BatRon 9."

"Aye, aye, Admiral."

Jack was just helping a naked Kris into her egg, him already naked as well, when the *Princess Royal* suddenly lost all sense of down. The high-gravity station eggs fit the Sailor like a second skin. With the ship maybe making four gees and going every which way to jink out of laser fire, you didn't want anything between your skin and your second one. Buck naked was the uniform of the day in an egg.

Around Kris, her fleet was slipping their moorings and pulling away from the ships they'd been paired with as they prepared to depart the anchorage. That meant ships went every which way and, if you weren't holding on to anything, so did you.

Kris's egg held her tight, and used its Smart Metal™ to secure it to the Smart Metal™ deck. Jack, however, was a good meter away from his egg; his only hold was on Kris's shoulder.

She grinned like a loving wife, and motored her way over to his egg so he could secure himself in it before the ship accelerated away, and there was a down to fall into.

"Thanks," Jack said. "You're a good egg."

"Bad joke," Kris said, and headed back to her flag plot as soon as Jack was halfway in his egg.

The attack was already under way. The screens showed the *Saladin*, the last of BatRon 12, disappearing through the jump just as Kris did her check. L'Estock's flag, the *Battleax*, led the eight ships of the Sharp Steel Squadron toward the jump.

The *Princess Royal* was moving, along with Commodore Zingi's BatRon 9 from Yamato, to be next into that bit of roiling space that let them jump from one star system to the next.

Then the universe farted.

No sooner was the *Grenade* through than the jump did a boogaloo.

One moment the jump was there, the next . . . it wasn't!

Kris knew these things could happen. It had happened during the Unity and Iteeche Wars, sometimes at the worst of times.

She knew it, but it had never happened to *her*!

Now it had.

It took everything she had not to dash onto the bridge of the *P. Royal* and demand that they find where the jump had wandered off to. The jumps orbited several suns; some six or even eight. The influence of all of those suns decided how any one jump behaved.

Most of the time, they docilely followed their own way around any one sun. Sometimes, for no apparent reason that we humans had figured out . . . they jumped tens of thousands of kilometers.

"I got it," was shouted loud enough from the *P. Royal*'s bridge for Kris to hear.

"Where?" from the captain was not quite as loud.

"There."

"Pass it to the squadron flag."

"They got it, too," and the squadron suddenly jerked to three gees and took off for the new jump location, twelve hundred kilometers away.

It took some smart ship handling to accelerate at three gees for six hundred klicks, then flip ship and decelerate at the same hard pace to arrive at the jump as close to dead in space as possible.

Kris spent the time hardly breathing. No doubt, captains, navigators, and helms personnel were chewing nails at a dangerous rate.

Coming to a dead stop with no collisions had to be a minor miracle of naval proportions. Then, as if they did this every day, each of the Yamato frigates followed the *Mikasa* placidly through the jump.

And the *Princess Royal* brought up the rear, following *Toikiwa*.

Kris checked her boards. The frigates from Lorna Do were right behind them. The "R's" from Wardhaven had collected their Hellburners and were already doing a hell-raising three-gee acceleration for the new jump location.

A moment later, Kris got her first good look at the battle in the targeted star. Her boards filled up with data, encrypted and sent via tight beam at the jump nearly five minutes ago from the ships of the Third Fleet and their fight.

Kris's boards showed ships in the red and getting worse.

5

During their planning, Admiral Yi had repeatedly warned Kris that she was dividing her forces. He'd charge into the system using one jump while she would lurk on the other side of the one they intended the aliens to flee through.

Kris had countered that the aliens would find themselves split as well, with half on her side of the jump and half fleeing from his forces on the other.

Admiral Furzah had named several battles won when a force found itself engaged while straddling a river. Nelly had matched the feline admiral example for example.

It had almost been funny, but it had ended Yi's objections to her orders.

Now, Kris was in the system and all the surviving aliens were between her and Admiral Yi.

In theory, the aliens were in a perfect position to divide and conquer. In reality, they were in a world of hurt.

Only a dozen or so ships stood between Kris's fleet and the huge, unarmored, but way-too-armed alien mother ship.

Kris had never attacked one of those monsters without some dirty, sneaky, or underhanded trick up her sleeve. But then, Grampa Trouble always said the only fair fight was the one you lost.

Now, with the alien base ship open to her attack, Kris was left struggling to come up with a good way to clobber the damn thing.

If she assaulted the base, they'd throw the whole fleet at her. The odds were only four to one, but they'd be desperate to defend the base ship with their women and children. The crews of alien warships were a sixty-forty split, with males dominant. No doubt, the base ship was skewed the other way around, if not more so.

Kris's flag plot filled up as her staff rejoined her, now in their eggs and ready for the fight. They silently studied the battle readouts from all of her ships as Kris did the same. Finally, full information was coming in on what she'd seen dimly through the jump.

Of Admiral Yi's sixteen super frigates, the *Lincoln*, *Lenin*, *Clemenceau*, *Chairman Mao*, and *Togo* were gone. The *Bismarck* was trailing, well behind the line. Bethea had lost the *Heimdallr* and *Loki*; with the *Puma* out of the line and trailing as well. The remaining twenty-three showed plenty of damage to their weapons, reactors, and hulls as their displays glowed red on Kris's screen.

At the moment, Yi was slowing but holding his fleet in good order.

That left the aliens free to turn on Kris.

"For what we are about to receive may we be truly grateful," Kris muttered.

"Amen," Penny added.

At the moment, Kris's fleet was scattered, thanks to the jump's meandering.

"Admiral L'Estock, kindly re-form your ships into a square while at the charge. Three gees acceleration toward the enemy base ship, if you will," Kris ordered.

"Aye, aye, Admiral," came back at her quickly, followed by orders for BatRon 12 to keep up its advance at 3 gees and BatRon 8 and 9 to join using up to 3.5 gees.

Kris felt a kick in the rump as the *Princess Royal* responded to his orders.

Behind her, Hawkings's BatRon 2 began jumping into the system, the Lorna Do warrior class first and in line, followed by the Wardhaven "R's" in a somewhat disorganized flow.

Ahead, the base ship went to a full 1.25-gee acceleration as it fled toward its returning dishes while the thirty-odd ships that had been a close escort charged in open ranks at the onrushing humans. While most were holding at 2.5 gees, a few were edging up close to three.

"Nelly, project the enemy course."

The main screen revised itself to show red lines pulsing toward her own blue lines. A green arc showed when the human ships would be in range to open fire on the charging alien warships.

The fast-moving aliens would be in trouble. The entire three squadrons of human frigates could slash them to bits.

Then the main alien force would pass quickly through the one-way killing zone, and Kris's forces would find themselves in range of the massive broadsides the aliens so loved.

Things would get rough then.

"Nelly, I want to try something."

"I'm all ears."

Kris shared her idea with Nelly and her key staff. Nelly made the plan appear as squiggles on the main screen. Kris listened as Jack, Penny, and Masao gave their thoughts, then Nelly revised the display.

When Kris was satisfied, she began to issue orders.

6

"Admiral L'Estock, this is Admiral Longknife. I am taking tactical command of First Fleet," Kris said tersely. Admiral L'Estock was a good administrator, but he'd never commanded a fight. This battle, Kris's command could not afford any first-timer mistakes.

Any more of them.

"Aye, aye, Admiral, you have command," came back just as tersely. Combat was only moments away; there was no time for niceties.

"Three ships are out in front," Kris said. "BatRon 12, you will take the one to our right. Eight, you have the left one. Nine, take the middle. We will engage them as they come in range with a single shot from each ship's bow batteries. I want to know how strong their rock armor is. Understood?"

"Aye, aye," came back from her squadron commanders.

"Hawkings, hold fire on your 20-inch frigates. I'm holding you in reserve for the next echelon."

"Understood, Admiral, I'm reserve when I come up." The four "R's" armed with Hellburners were just catching up with the Lorna Do division, which still trailed the rest of the fleet. Kris was making a virtue of necessity. Only time would tell if it was a true virtue.

The enemy's thirty-two ships had lost cohesion in their mad charge for the newly arrived humans. Three were out in front. Six more were in a loose line some ten thousand klicks behind them. Fifteen formed what was left of the dish some twenty thousand kilometers behind them while a trailing eight who had either been out of position or were having engine problems were scattered in twos and threes over the next twenty thousand kilometers.

That was it. Thirty-two huge, overgunned warships scattered along a fifty-thousand-klick approach charged hell-bent for Kris's throat.

So what else is new?

The first three ships were approaching the maximum range, two hundred thousand kilometers, for the new 22-inch lasers on the frigates.

"Begin Evasion Pattern 1. Fire one round per ship," Kris ordered.

The eight ships in each squadron hit their targeted ship.

The warships lit up as rock melted away and spewed flaming droplets out into space and down their sides.

They kept coming.

"Engage your ship with your full forward battery," Kris ordered.

Now five big lasers reached out from each frigate to slash into the racing enemy. Pinned by forty big guns, the alien ships bent, folded, and blew as lasers blasted through rock to slash stressed hull-strength members or pierced into reactors and their containment gear.

In the blink of an eye, where three ships had been was a long trail of fire, gas, and wreckage.

But six more were closing fast.

"Flip ships," Kris ordered, and her gut did a twist as the *Princess Royal*, still under way at three gees, did a one-eighty in space.

"Slow to one gee. Engage hostiles by divisions with aft batteries."

Despite the egg's protection, Kris felt thrown forward as the ship slowed drastically. Still, her boards showed all twenty-four ships emptying their four aft lasers at the six onrushing aliens.

Those six aliens were taking only about a third as much fire as the first three. Worse, two of the targets managed to put the wreckage of the first ships between them and their antagonists.

Three aliens blew up. While one staggered forward, the other two were coming on fast and eager.

But Kris's ships had shot themselves empty. They needed

time to recharge their lasers. Seconds ticked past as the aliens closed.

Kris could have accelerated away from the onrushing aliens. But that would have put herself farther from the huge base ship. If she took too long to reach it, the other ships would be back.

Kris accepted the risk and held to one-gee deceleration while the aliens rushed at her with all the energy their reactors could generate.

Previously, the aliens had demonstrated that their lasers were good out to 120,000 klicks.

Today, they opened fire at 160,000 klicks.

Their lasers were weak. Their power attenuated. Still, the engines on the *Mandela* and *Saber* took hits. Their course went wild, and jink patterns failed for a full two seconds.

They took more hits.

Per Kris's standing orders, both ships went to three gees and pulled away from their tormentors.

"Flip ship," Kris ordered. "Engage the closest targets with three lasers per ship by divisions."

The division commanders called "Right," "Left," "Middle," and in a moment, the three ships died.

That left Kris counting the seconds as the largest alien group closed. Her ships were heading at them at only one-gee acceleration, but the others were as close to 2.5 gees as they could manage.

Kris kept one eye on the reloading process for her ships' lasers and the other eye on the closing aliens. It looked like the aliens would be in maximum range for a full two seconds before Kris would have a forward salvo ready.

"Go to Evasion Pattern 3," Kris ordered. "Prepare to engage targets by two-ship sections with fire from forward batteries, then flip ship and fire aft batteries. I will then order a three-gee deceleration burn to keep the aliens in our range and us out of theirs for as long as possible."

"Aye, aye," came back at her on net from her admirals and commodores. On her battle board, the name of each ship blinked as the captain acknowledged the message.

"Fire," Kris ordered.

Twenty-two frigates emptied their forward batteries at fifteen big alien warships.

Or that was the plan. Actually, it was more like ten.

Just as they came into range, the alien commander must have ordered evasion maneuvers. Maybe he didn't, but eight of his ships did it anyway. The evasion wasn't nearly as good as Nelly would have designed, but it threw off frigates that weren't expecting any.

On top of that, there was the confusion created by having sixteen two-frigate sections firing at fifteen ships. Worse, two sections were down to only one ship. Several aliens were not targeted.

"Flip ships," Kris ordered. "Commodores, correct your ship assignments. Fire aft batteries when ready."

The squadron commanders reallocated targets among their sections and fired. The huge aliens took more hits this time, but the aft batteries were only four guns strong.

The aliens just kept on coming in their ragged formation.

"Up deceleration to three gees," Kris said. "Execute Evasion Plan 6. Deploy chaff."

Around Kris, her ships went into a wild dance of up, down, right, left as they jumped up to three gees deceleration, then dropped to one. To complicate fire control solutions more, they popped chaff, shooting tiny balls of iron, ice, and flares out the way they were going just as they changed direction.

They needed the wild jig. The aliens were just coming into their new, extreme range, and had too many lasers firing into the general space around their dancing target. They missed a lot of shots, but they had so many lasers sweeping the area where Kris's ships were that some had to connect.

The *Caesar*, *Asama*, and *Broadsword* took hits on their rocket engines. This time their captains were ready. As soon as one engine's power skewed, they countered with corrections to their other rockets as well as boosting their ships to a full 4.5-gee deceleration.

None ran into any more lasers than they would have as they dropped away from the battle line.

Kris was in a tough fight.

"Flip ships," Kris ordered. She'd have to be a fool to keep

her vulnerable rear with its rocket engines and reactors where the hostiles could get at them.

The ships flipped. Now armored bows took the light hits from the attenuated alien lasers. It was bad, but acceptable.

Better yet, the *Mandela* and the *Saber*, repairs made, were coming back into line.

Kris measured the seconds as the forward batteries edged toward full.

"Kris, I've evaluated the evasions the aliens are using. It's a simple algorithm. I think I can forecast where they'll be next."

"Feed it to the targeting computers, Nelly."

"Done," her computer reported.

"Fire forward batteries," Kris ordered.

Fifteen alien ships burned as twenty-one frigates hit them hard. Two exploded. Fire from others slackened, but the range was closing, and the alien lasers were taking bigger bites.

The Smart Metal™ hull of the *Princess Royal*, like all the other non-Earth frigates, was a honeycomb of metal and cooling reaction mass under a thin covering of reflective material. It spun around the ship to spread out any hit while the reaction mass around a hit bled into space, carrying away heat as well as causing the laser beam to bloom and lose power.

Damaged frigates took on a halo.

The Earth frigates were a different story. Now they fairly glowed as they took in the laser hits, slowed the light down, spread it out along the entire length of their armor, and reflected it back into space.

Earth's BatRon 12 had led the way through the jump. It was always closest to the enemy. Now the thirteen aliens concentrated on the seven Earth frigates. They made them glow.

But they did not make them explode.

Kris watched her board. The Earth frigates' armor wasn't even into the red yet.

"We've got to keep our nose to the foe," Jack whispered.

"And the Earth squadron out front," Kris agreed.

The forward batteries were recharging. The aft batteries in Kris's fleet were coming up on full as they crossed the hundred-thousand-kilometer range.

That also put the trailing 20-inch frigates of Hawkings's BatRon 2 in range.

"Forward squadrons, prepare to flip ships and fire aft batteries. You will flip back, bow toward the enemy as soon as your aft batteries are empty. BatRon 2, fire your forward batteries at the ships you identify as least damaged, then flip and fire aft lasers. You will also flip back and offer the enemy your bows."

Ships' names blinked acknowledgments as Kris finished.

"Flip ship. Fire," Kris ordered.

The slaughter among the onrushing alien ships was brutal, but they gave as well as they got.

Thirteen big warships took fire from twenty-nine frigates. Actually, a full thirty-two as the damaged frigates flipped and contributed their recharged forward lasers as well.

Eight of the five-hundred-thousand-ton alien ships dissolved, wrecked by their own acceleration or eaten by the plasma in their own reactors. One ship actually bent along its middle, then broke in half. Another ship seemed to burn from the inside, gutting itself before the inrush of vacuum could dowse its own fires.

Most just exploded into gas as reactor containment vessels failed and sun-hot plasma was released to incinerate flesh and steel.

Eight ships died, but the other five just kept coming, firing whatever lasers they could still bring to bear.

Hawkings immediately flipped his eight ships and fired their aft batteries at the five survivors. One blew, but the others kept racing at Kris.

Kris's ships had to take it. Tests had shown that they couldn't feed all the power into a single capacitor and get one laser ready ahead of the rest. No, they might give three priority, but only at a ten-percent penalty.

Kris had weighted the options and established the fleet doctrine. Charge the entire forward battery. Charge the entire aft battery. Only under unusual circumstances charge three guns ahead of the rest.

Kris considered the present circumstances and shook her head.

The two fleets rushed at each other. Behind this fight, the

monstrous alien base ship fled at 1.14 gees toward the third jump.

No way you're going to make that, Kris swore.

Beyond that, the survivors of the ships that had fought Yi were also bearing off to connect with their mother ship. Yi's ships had time to mend and make repairs. They were now back to yellow or green on their boards although Kris counted five that were trailing the rest of the fleet. Seven destroyed, five too damaged to pursue. That left Yi with only twenty ships. The ten surviving 22-inch war wagons were closing with the retreating aliens, nipping at their heels, but from an extreme range of 180,000 klicks.

Admiral Yi's secondary batteries were also sweeping the space ahead of him for those troublesome mines.

Admiral Bethea had pulled her two BatRons off a bit, as if to get well ahead of the aliens on their flight to the third jump point. With the speed of her frigates, no doubt Bethea could put herself square in their path and make them come to her as she fired and retreated, fired and retreated.

The humans had shown the aliens that chasing us was a bad idea.

Kris turned back to her own battle.

First Fleet might have lost a ship if the five alien ships had concentrated on a single frigate.

Instead, the aliens seemed mesmerized by the glow from the Earth frigates. What fire they had, they concentrated on them. The ships took their hits, absorbed them, and radiated them back into space.

The five Earth ships showed hull damage as their crystal armor heated up. Kris had suggested to Yi that his ships might benefit from a layer of honeycomb cooling under their crystal belt. He'd declined, with his usual attitude that seemed to say nothing good could come from the Rim worlds. *He* was of *Earth*.

Kris had chosen not to make it an order. She wasn't all that sure that the ships could be redesigned. Certainly not in the time before she ordered this operation.

Without orders, the secondaries opened up on the alien ships as the range closed to less than fifty thousand kilometers.

The forward batteries were over half recharged.

At this range, even a half-strength laser would be deadly.

"Prepare to fire forward batteries," Kris ordered.

Ships blinked back their reply.

"Fire," Kris almost whispered.

One hundred and ninety-two lasers reached out at reduced strength for the four surviving warships.

They vanished in hellish blazes.

"We got a problem," came from the commander of BatRon 12.

"Report," Kris said.

"There's a lot of crap showing up on my sensors. I think they seeded the space behind them with whatever those mines were that hit Admiral Yi so badly."

"I think you're right," Kris said. "Captains, have your secondary batteries take on anything close to your ships."

Again, ships blinked their acknowledgments.

Then something exploded close on to the *Longbow*.

"There's a whole lot of this crap," Admiral L'Estock reported. "And some of it's moving."

"Nelly," Kris said.

"I'm taking a feed off the *Princess Royal*'s scientific sensors," Kris's computer reported. Most of the ships had sailed without their science teams, leaving them behind to explore Alwa and its star system. Kris had insisted on having at least a team aboard her flag. She also had Doc Meade to offer her expertise if they had a chance to talk to some real-live aliens.

Now her boffins were passing along information that Kris could hardly believe.

A picture appeared on one of Kris's unused screens. It showed a tiny spacecraft. A rocket motor, a small crew compartment that appeared to hold a single alien, and a big bulge in front that Kris suspected was explosives, maybe atomics.

Kris was not shocked.

She *had* been shocked when the aliens started hurtling ships into the Alwa system, intent on crashing the planet and killing people by the hundreds of thousands, if not millions. Possibly even rendering the planet uninhabitable.

"How can any living person do that?" Kris had asked. Then Nelly answered. Kris got a lesson on Kamikazes and

Jihadist suicide bombers and others from Old Earth's bloody and dark history.

Admiral Furzah had added examples from Sasquan history. "Do not mistake my meaning," she added. "We consider those who resort to this as fools. They have never won a war, but they have certainly made their mark on our history."

Now Kris saw space between her and the monstrous alien mother ship littered with these tiny weapons, propelled by hate and guided by a living mind.

"Kris, some of the ships are larger," Nelly reported. "I think there is room for two, maybe three. It is possible that these carry the outlawed atomic weapons."

Outlawed by humans. Not so outlawed by these bug-eyed monsters that looked just like us.

"Nelly, warn the fleet. Get the big ones before they get you."

"Warning sent, Kris."

A loose cluster of three alien ships were coming in range, hurtling themselves like some bug to a flame. Kris ordered her ships to take them out, and they vanished under a hammering of full frontal fire.

Next, two came in range. Kris flipped ship just long enough to obliterate the pair.

Forward batteries were reloaded when the last three rushed to their deaths.

Kris scowled and ordered an end to the massacre.

"Whether they come at us in full ships, or in tiny, sentiently guided mines, they die," Jack whispered.

Now that part of her problem was done. She had ten minutes to destroy a base ship before its bloodthirsty brood came howling back, screaming for Kris's head.

"How the hell do you destroy an alert and fully armed base ship?" Kris asked no one in particular."

Still, Admiral Furzah attempted a reply. "It is like, what do you call that animal? A porcupine. Sharp spines everywhere."

"Only these spines are lasers," Jack added.

"Yes," Kris said, and considered her next major challenge.

7

"**Squadrons**, flip ship and come up on 4.5 gees deceleration slowly. Let me know if battle damage causes you trouble."

At 3.5 gees deceleration Earth's BatRon 12 had a hard time keeping their overheated crystal armor from sliding off their hulls. Kris reduced them to 3.35-gee deceleration.

The *Asama*, *Broadsword*, and *Saber* hollered uncle around four gees. Kris detached them to proceed independently. She ordered all the separated ships to aim for well out on the mother ship's base course.

They decelerated with their vulnerable sterns to the alien base ship through a loose cloud of intelligently guided mines. They fishtailed a bit, opening up their amidships secondary batteries to pop the bits and pieces of murderous crud. Occasionally, a denser cloud would require short, low-powered bursts from the aft main battery.

Still, *Longbow* suffered a near-miss atomic and had to slow down.

Kris had twelve of the large 22-inch frigates, as well as all eight of BatRon 2's 20-inch war wagons and the *Princess Royal* as she matched course and speed with an alien mother ship the size of a small moon, still 180,000 klicks out.

"Nelly, send to the alien. 'Enlightened One, you and all your black hats will die. Give up your arms, and I will let you live. Admiral Longknife sends.'"

"I have sent it, Kris, using what we know of their language."

"BatRon 8 and 9, let's back up my surrender offer with a full broadside. Pick a target on that monster and make it vanish."

"Kris, we really ought to concentrate on what will do the most damage," Nelly said.

"Yes, we will," Kris answered, "but not right now. Let's scourge him a bit before I go for blowing him to bits."

"Psychology, huh?" Nelly asked.

"Just plain human orneriness," Jack put in.

"It's gotten us where we are today," Kris pointed out.

"How long do you plan to be ornery before we slice some serious chunks off that ship?" Nelly asked.

Kris sighed. So long as the ship had rocket power, it could keep up its flight. If she cut the huge bell-shaped rockets off its aft end, would that end the run, or just allow them to douse the reactors back there and become a whole lot harder to blow up?

Kris posed the question and got half her human staff in favor of destroying the rockets. The other half, Jack included, proposed delaying that until they could get some antimatter torpedoes into the reactors and turn them loose to rip the ship apart.

Admiral Furzah voted with Jack.

It didn't matter.

A number of Kris's captains had taken it on their own to aim for the rocket engines that dominated the aft end of the huge, thick ellipsoid. The moon-size ship's dash through space took on a distinct shimmy before it settled down at a steady .97-gee acceleration.

A moment later, its acceleration fell off significantly.

"They've dumped reactor cores and closed down half their engines," Nelly reported.

"All ships, prepare to flip ship," Kris ordered. "Aim your aft batteries at the rear of the base ship. Reactors are our target."

Ships blinked on Kris's board.

"Flip ship now. Fire."

The *P. Royal*, having been up-gunned only to 20-inch lasers, did not join the shoot.

"We hit three, maybe four reactors," Nelly reported. "However, they seemed to have dumped alternating reactors so one wild wave of plasma is not washing over and tripping the next one. Oh, now they're dumping all reactors along the aft end of the base ship. Kris, the alien is just coasting."

"That may make her an easier target," Jack said.

"I don't think so," Nelly said. "They've just put a spin and rotation on the ship, Kris. It will be hell on whoever isn't tied down aboard it, but it will be hell to target any specific point on its surface or inside."

"And, no doubt," Jack drawled, "their Enlightened One is ensconced in the safest place on that rock, waiting for the fleet to come and save his skin."

"It will be a cold day in hell when that happens," Kris said, and did a new count on the ships charging back from their fight with Admiral Yi. The aliens were down to sixty-three. No, make that sixty-two as another ship bloomed into a colorful flower of hot gas and bits of wreckage.

Kris eyed the clock; she had eight minutes. Time for thirty salvos from her frigates. Maybe less.

"Nelly, do you know where the reactors were on that wrecked mother ship we examined?"

"Yes, Kris."

"Send that data to all ships. Close into one hundred and twenty-five thousand klicks and aim for the reactors that power all those lasers."

Nelly sent the data, and the frigates began circling the base ship, keeping up their jinking while doing it. Kris had been surprised once today by longer-range lasers.

As they closed to Kris's ordered range, she gave her next order. "Skippers, I want to slice that big, ugly melon. Aim your batteries for the same spot on the ship. I want it drilled right down to the reactors. Understood?"

The message boards blinked acknowledgment.

"Fire at will," she ordered.

Ships flipped to present their forward batteries. The lasers showed nothing as they departed the ships, but showed brightly as they sliced into the spinning ship. Several skippers managed to walk their fire across the twisting ship, keeping the heat on one place for an entire broadside.

"How'd you do that?" on net got a quick reply. When the aft batteries were brought to bear, each frigates' fire was much concentrated.

"Nelly, why didn't you suggest that?" Kris asked.

"Nobody asked me, Kris, and it didn't occur to me that you humans would need help tracking such a slow-moving target. Sorry."

BatRon 12 joined the shoot two minutes into it. It fired its aft lasers on the approach, flipped ship, and cut power, then fired the forward lasers. Another flip, and they were decelerating toward the base ship as they recharged. They repeated that maneuver twice before they were circling it, firing with the rest of Kris's ships.

Moments later, the rest of the cripples joined up and got into the shoot.

The monster burned under their fire, but it was a huge monster, and there was a lot of it to burn.

Then a reactor cut loose. Its plasma vented through the hull, incinerating everything along the way. That had hardly died down when another of the two hundred or so reactors along the centerline of the base ship also let loose its plasma to burn its way to the surface.

"BatRon 9, fire one antimatter torpedo per ship, if you will."

"On their way, Admiral," Commodore Shoalter answered.

Before they crossed the hundred-thousand-klick line, lasers reached out to burn them.

We don't use the Hellburners yet.

Thirty-two ships blasted away at the rolling hulk. Volley fire was gone. Every second a couple of ships would fire either their forward or aft batteries. Among Shoalter's squadron from New Eden, the ships organized themselves into pairs, aiming for a single place on the mother ship.

That quickly caught on. Now, with ten or so lasers piercing the hull at or near the same place, the pace of reactors losing containment went from occasional to frequent.

The boffins on the *Princess Royal* had applied Nelly's map of potential reactor locations and were now running them through their sensors.

Reactors were quickly located, identified, and targeted.

The base ship was blasted to hell.

Kris ordered a volley of antimatter torpedoes. Several almost made it to the base ship.

It looked desperate for the aliens, and the ships that might give them respite were still four minutes away when desperation gave rise to a new choice.

The alien moonlet began to pop out tiny pups.

"Are those survival pods?" Penny asked.

"Sorry, Penny," Nelly said. "Those are more of the suicide boats to attack us."

"Nelly, warn the fleet. Suiciders coming our way. Engage them with secondary when they come in range."

"There are a lot of them, Kris," Amanda said, speaking for the first time that day. "Do you think we can get them in time?"

"We'll see." Kris said, and kept one eye on the approaching dishes, the other on the blasted and bludgeoned base ship. Maybe it was time to try some more antimatter torpedoes.

"BatRon 2, will you have a go at the bugger with one torpedo each?"

"On their way, Admiral," and another eight ripped away and headed in.

Two hit.

"All ships, prepare to launch six torpedoes. Hawkings, have your four 'R's' ready to add a Hellburner to each volley. Skippers, warn your gunners to not hit our missiles. Stand by," Kris said. "Ripple launch antimatter torpedoes . . . now! Launch Hellburners . . . now!"

The missiles took off toward the base ship about the same time that the 5-inch secondary batteries took on the approaching suicide craft. Human missiles screamed away at ten gees acceleration; their suicide boats were barely making three gees, though they had had more time to get up to speed.

One suicider turned abruptly and crashed into a torpedo. That caused a huge explosion.

Several more small craft tried the twist. None succeeded. A few came apart as the radical turn bent, then broke the hull.

"They can't turn," Nelly reported. "Though those were pretty hard turns," she added with a sniff.

Every surviving laser on the base ship came to life as if their very life depended upon it. It did. The antimatter torpedoes did a jig of Nelly's design, as did the Hellburners. But the antimatter torpedoes were coming in faster and dancing harder. The alien targeting computer must have mistaken the Hellburners for underperforming torpedoes.

Some torpedoes were hit. No Hellburner was even grazed.

Torpedoes began to hit, taking great chunks out of the alien base. Lasers hit where the rockets didn't.

Then the Hellburners buried themselves in the alien ship and just kept going.

At the tip of the missile was a small chip off a neutron star. A chip weighing fifteen thousand tons! It hit with all the momentum a rocket powered by the antimatter annihilation of lead grains could impart.

That momentum carried the chip deep into its target.

Then the antimatter gun bathed the chip off the neutron star with antihydrogen.

And the whole thing went to pieces.

And the ship did, too.

Four Hellburners slammed deep into the alien planetoid before beginning their final annihilation. All ended up close to reactors.

The moon-size ship began to explode from the inside out.

Kris grinned. No doubt, the Enlightened One had located himself somewhere deep inside, safe from everything but a rampaging bit of neutron star.

The ship split apart as its own twisting and rolling sent one chunk in one direction, another in a different one. Lasers continued to engage late torpedoes as they ripped into the revealed innards of the ship.

Now laser fire from the frigates hacked huge chunks off the wreck.

No one's going to salvage this one, Kris thought.

The slaughter continued, but Kris chose to rethink her strategy for the small attack rockets when one of them blew up with atomic force just short of her line of circling frigates.

"All ships, accelerate away from the small attack boys at two gee. Concentrate all fire on them."

It was fine to slice and dice a monstrous alien base when you had all the time in the world. It would be a shame to lose a ship after she'd won the battle.

Frigates changed course as main and secondary batteries played over the approaching wave of little boys.

One more exploded in an atomic ball of fire, but most vanished away with neither a bang nor a whimper.

Kris ordered her squadrons to re-form and prepare to receive the closing alien warships. She'd won this battle, but she could still lose ships and lives. She'd manage what was left at arm's length.

It turned out that she didn't have to.

Four ships broke away from the oncoming ships, heading for the third jump. The others began to blossom into huge balls of fire and gas as their captains took counsel with despair and gave their ships back to dust.

"L'Estock, take your least damaged ships and pursue this last bunch," Kris ordered.

"With pleasure. Do you want me to pursue the ones that left earlier?"

Kris weighed the last three against the need to get all her ships back to Alwa. There was also the matter of what surprises the fleeing ships might leave in their wake.

"You should be able to get these four without having to follow right behind them and dodge any nice presents they leave. Get them and follow us home."

"Aye, aye, Admiral, and may I say, as one who's just fought his first battle, it was a pleasure to serve under you."

"You may, but don't tell my husband," Kris said, and immediately regretted letting her mind dash off to that gutter.

Still, the net seemed to enjoy the joke, and Jack was grinning as she turned back to him.

"May I help you out of your egg, Admiral, my love," he said.

"Please do," Kris said.

8

Next morning, with no battle to worry about, Kris found herself again bolting from the wardroom to dash for the head in her quarters.

What she'd just put in her tummy came right back up. Explosively.

NELLY, THERE HAS TO BE A FLU BUG OR SOMETHING, Kris said as she heaved more fine food into the toilet.

SORRY, KRIS. NO BUG. WE GOT RID OF THE BUGS THAT ARRIVED WITH THE NEW SHIPS WITHOUT A SINGLE OUTBREAK. NO FOOD POISONING EITHER. I RAN A CHECK ON EVERYTHING IN THE MESS YESTERDAY, AND IT'S ALL UP TO SPECS.

IN YOUR INFINITE SPARE TIME WHEN WE WEREN'T UP TO OUR NECKS IN PEOPLE WANTING TO KILL US, Kris thought sourly.

YES, Nelly answered. She said nothing more. She didn't need to.

Kris scowled through her tormented stomach. *Of course Nelly can fight a battle and check on chow's safety. She's a computer.*

Kris stood, rinsed her mouth out, then bent over as more breakfast explosively departed.

DAMN IT, NELLY, WHAT'S WRONG?

AH, KRIS, WHEN WAS YOUR LAST PERIOD? was almost in a whisper.

The question alone was enough to make Kris's stomach lurch.

THINGS HAVE BEEN A BIT TENSE OF LATE. THEY'VE BEEN KIND OF SCANTY.

HOW SCANTY?

Kris didn't answer her computer. The last one had only required one pad, and hadn't had that much to show.

I CAN'T BE PREGNANT, NELLY, I JUST GOT MY BIRTH-CONTROL IMPLANTS REPLACED LAST MONTH, Kris thought, her hand going to her arm where the implant site was still a bit sensitive. It and the place where the old implants had been removed.

It was Navy policy, long before Kris joined, and certainly before Kris modified the fraternization regs, that every female recruit was issued birth-control implants. Every three years, like clockwork, they were replaced.

Kris had just entered her seventh year of service. She'd been issued new implants during her physical.

I CAN'T BE PREGNANT, Kris repeated.

ALLOW ME TO APPLY LOGIC TO THIS SITUATION, Nelly said in her oh-so-reasonable voice.

Kris scowled. Nelly could come up with such a reasonable computer voice.

WE HAVE NO FLU BUG. THERE IS NO CHANCE OF FOOD POISONING. YOU CAN'T BE PREGNANT. YOU ARE THROWING UP YOUR TOENAILS IN THE MORNING BUT ENJOYED THAT FINE VICTORY DINNER LAST NIGHT IN THE WARDROOM WITH NO PROBLEM.

MORNING SICKNESS CAN COME AT ANY TIME OF THE DAY, Kris shot back. I READ THAT SOMEWHERE.

"Stipulated," Nelly said from Kris's collar.

Kris took another try at rinsing her mouth. This time her stomach allowed her to finish and walk the few paces to her bed and collapse on it.

Puking was hard work.

"Now, Kris, when all the possible answers to a problem have been exhausted, it's time to look at the impossible options, no matter how unlikely."

"I'm not pregnant."

"So, could you have an ulcer? All your jobs could give a marble statue an ulcer."

Kris could only sigh at that. As Commander, Alwa Sector, she was in charge of the fleet. As Viceroy of King Raymond I of the United Society to both the humans and natives on

Alwa, she had to juggle political issues. And, as if that weren't enough, as senior executive officer of Nuu Enterprises in the Alwa system, she bossed a major proportion of the economic life of the place. Enough that she usually had the other corporations in line, too.

"I guess I could have an ulcer," Kris agreed.

"However, I know for a fact that if you were to present yourself to Dr. Meade with these symptoms, she would send you home with a pregnancy test. What do you say I order one and you show up with it already done tomorrow when you see the good doctor?"

Kris frowned at the overhead. *It looks like I'm going to have to pee on one either way.* "Nelly, can you get me a pregnancy test without everyone in the fleet's knowing the admiral is taking one?"

"The fleet's betting pool has Abby and Sergeant Bruce as the first likely to pop out a kid. You and Jack are down the list at five."

"There's a betting pool on that?"

"Kris, there's a betting pool on everything, including when I'll go on strike for a decent paycheck."

"Nelly!"

"That one I started myself. I bet I won't. You'd be surprised at who's betting against me."

Kris decided she wouldn't.

"Well, can you get me the test without anyone's knowing?" Kris repeated.

"I can arrange to have a test sent to Abby."

"My maid is not on the ship, Nelly. She's busy being Pipra Strongarm's right arm." Kris liked the sound of the joke. Abby hated it, but she was becoming a very good expediter and problem solver for Pipra.

"Yes, Kris," Nelly said in her remember-I'm-a-computer-and-nowhere-near-as-dumb-as-you-humans voice. "I'll backdate the order to before she left and have it handled as if it had been lost in processing. When it gets here, you can intercept it and misappropriate it to your own evil ends."

"The end involved is not evil," Kris growled.

"Yes, I know. Jack really likes that end of you."

"Enough with the dirty jokes, Nelly. You order the test, and I'll take it. You make sure I have an appointment early tomorrow with Dr. Meade."

"Is ten hundred soon enough?"

"Eleven hundred would be worse, nine hundred would be better."

"She's handling a batch of sprained backs, ankles, and other infirmities of the flesh today. You really did honk the fleet around, Kris. The first appointment she has tomorrow for a routine problem is 1000 hours."

"If I'm pregnant, it will *not* be a routine problem."

"But you can't be pregnant," Nelly jabbed back.

"I'm fingering your OFF button," Kris growled.

"No you aren't, at least physically. I can see you from the emergency power-and-surveillance system."

"You're using the emergency-surveillance system in my bedroom!"

"Only now because it's an emergency when you threaten to turn me off."

"Enough of this," Kris said, coming to her feet. "What's my day look like?"

"Bad and likely to get worse."

"I hate it when you try to fake it as a seer."

"Who says I'm faking?"

9

Nelly was not a false prophet. Kris's day did get worse. With the fleet making only a single gee as it accelerated toward the jump point, Nelly had laid in a course for home that involved one big and one normal jump, so at least it was comfortable.

The message traffic alone could well give Kris an ulcer.

Admiral Yi sent a full report on the battle that in no way jibed with what Kris had seen through the probe. If she was to believe it, the alien warships could now make 3.5 gees, and that was how his fleet had been shot up.

A second report, PRIVATE AND PERSONAL—FOR LONG-KNIFE EYES ONLY, arrived from Admiral Bethea. It pretty much verified what Kris herself had watched through the probe. To that, she added that Admiral Yi had sent to the fleet before they jumped into the system that he would fight the battle as he saw fit and not by any plan drawn up far from the fight that was likely obsolete before they jumped in.

He had also informed the fleet that he opposed evasion plans of any kind since they only ruined a frigate's firing solutions.

Bethea had tight-beamed to her squadrons not to dump their evasion plans. They'd need them quick when the shooting started.

Kris checked on the recording of the battle. Admiral Bethea's task force had been jinking as they came in range of the hostile. Yi's task force of Earth frigates had not.

Kris found herself looking forward to a "Come to Jesus" meeting with Yi, as Grampa Trouble would call it. But that, or any other meeting, would have to wait until they got back to Alwa.

Meanwhile, Kris would contemplate the question. Could she relieve an Earth admiral and ship him down to run the bird-guano mine on Alwa?

There were plenty of other matters for Kris's attention. The crystal armor had not done as well as advertised. She was, however, no expert in warship design. She signed off on a report from the squadron of Earth-designed frigates in her own fleet and made a bet with herself that she'd see nothing of the sort from Yi.

She won.

Nelly was right about the bumps and sprains among some of her fleet. Most were on the ships getting their first taste of battle. They'd learn, and, hopefully, pass the experience on to the next batch of new arrivals.

Kris was going through her reports, signing or initialing as required, when a small delivery robot rolled in and reported it had a package for Abby Nightingale.

Kris signed for it, and Nelly immediately wiped that from its tiny memory. Someone had drawn an empty-headed-looking smile on the thing. It bobbled off, happy as a clam, leaving Kris to meditate on the small package in her hand.

Jack stayed busy during the day; they met for supper. The *Princess Royal* was back to Condition Able, or as some called it, Love Boat. For the fight, the ship had been small and tight, with as much of the Smart Metal™ as possible shipped out to the hull to form a honeycomb of metal and cooling reaction-mass to soften the damage from laser hits. Now, the nice Smart Metal™ had been pulled back into the inside of the ship, allowing for broad passageways, spacious rooms, and a wardroom that could have passed as a fine restaurant on Earth. In place of a few long tables, where everyone sat elbow to elbow, the room was populated with tables for two or four, and couples were dining by candlelight, or at least a very good imitation.

"Did you do this?" Kris asked Jack.

"The President of the Mess made the call though I will admit to suggesting something like it. We faced death and smelled its stinking breath. After something like that, people need to celebrate life."

That was one of the reasons Kris had chosen to loosen the

regs on fraternization aboard ship. Some brilliant person back in human space had shipped a lot of young people off to the other side of the galaxy. They'd been chosen for their flexibility when ships started hard evasion maneuvers and for their lack of attachments in human space.

Oh, and because they were smart.

Being smart, it took them about five minutes to realize that having a nifty app to move Smart Metal™ around on their jobs also let them make doors in their rooms to next door. Attachments formed with the speed of hydrogen mixing with oxygen.

Back in human space, people could be reassigned to other ships or to base facilities. Here, Kris had almost no base facilities, and her ships had to be ready to fight at a moment's notice.

She could not reshuffle her crews constantly.

So Kris decided to treat her crews like grown-ups. What you did on the Navy's time was the Navy's business. What you did on your own time was your business if it didn't get carried back to Navy time.

There had been some restrictions. No dating across the officer-enlisted barrier without permission. No dating more than two ranks or rates up or down. Again, permission could be granted for exceptions, but they were looked at real hard.

Admiral Kitano had already relieved one captain for cause while Kris was out traipsing around the galaxy. Kris had endorsed the relief and assignment to the bird-guano mine. An enlisted young woman should not have to tell her captain no more than once.

Kris had not had to make more than one example.

So, there were a lot of officers dining as couples. Kris glanced around. Most of the couples were male-female. There were a smattering of single-sex pairs.

Kris wondered about the tables seating four and six. Where they just friends, or were some berthing spaces connected now in larger groups.

I CAN GET YOU AN ANSWER, Nelly offered.

IT'S NONE OF MY BUSINESS, AND YOU ARE DEVELOPING A DIRTY MIND, NELLY.

NO DIRTIER THAN YOURS.

Jack picked that moment to start making gentle circles on Kris's palm. He did that when she'd wandered off someplace on business or otherwise. It usually brought a smile to her face and her attention back to him.

It worked tonight.

"I've got plans for this evening," Jack said.

"And I'm so glad you do, my husband."

10

Next morning, Kris waited until Jack was in the shower before she pulled the pregnancy test out and did her thing on it.

It was pink. As she counted to five, it turned blue.

Kris's mind spun.

She pulled the instructions out and read them again . . . slowly. Then read them again. The words seemed to spin around in front of her. She could make no sense of them.

Finally, she put one finger over the writing and read it one word at a time.

Pink was negative. Blue was positive. Blue meant you were pregnant.

Congratulations, the instructions said.

"You going to join me in the shower?" Jack asked.

"Yes. Just a second." Kris wiped down the test and slipped it back into the box it came in and the box back into her purse. She went through the necessary actions step by step. That was what she always did when she was in a fight.

Only I'm not in a fight. I'm pregnant!

The test has a .5-percent error rate, some part of her warned.

Yes, yes, yes, another part of her answered as she slipped into the shower.

Jack greeted her with a kiss and began soaping her front.

Kris smiled back at her husband and relaxed into the sensuality of his touch.

Careful, girl, or you'll be late for chow.

Who cares? I'll just throw it up again.

You going to tell him? brought Kris's wandering mind to a halt.

No. Not now. Not until Doc Meade says it's for real, not 99.5 percent likely.

Kris washed Jack down, then rinsed him off. Sadly, he was in full business mode, and they were not late for breakfast.

She again had to dismiss herself from breakfast to hurriedly deposit her meal in the toilet.

Jack flashed her a worried look, but she managed a smile and an "I'm fine" lie that he usually accepted at face value if not as fact.

Ten hundred hours could not come soon enough.

The nurse took Kris's vitals and accepted "intestinal distress" for a reason for the visit.

Doc Meade didn't keep Kris waiting. She arrived in full professional mode. "Tummy problems, huh. You ever had this before?"

"No, and I only have it in the morning," Kris said, and removed the pregnancy test from her purse.

"Hmm, I knew one of those had gone out. I figured it couldn't be for Abby. I should have figured that only Nelly could jigger my system."

"Thank you," Nelly said.

"Blue, huh?" the doc said, looking at the test results, then asked, "Your last period?"

"Fifteen days ago. Scanty as to be nearly nonexistent."

"And I take it that you and Jack are still acting like newlyweds?"

"Horny newlyweds," Kris said.

"I didn't know there were any other kind," the doc said with a smile.

"I had my implants replaced last month," Kris said, fingering the three lumps on her arm.

"Yes," the doc said, looking at her med reader. "Right on time. Those things have about one failure in a million."

"It would be a bitch if I was that millionth," Kris said.

"You can't be the millionth," Doc Meade said. "We've had three pregnancies reported in the fleet this week. One the week before."

Kris frowned. "Once may be an accident. Two is bad luck. Three or more is enemy action," she quoted the old military axiom.

"We've got something just like that in the medical profession. Well, let's get some blood work and see if that test is accurate."

Kris waited while blood was taken. It was sent off to the lab with no name on it and a *Rush, we want this five minutes ago* note.

It was back before Kris and the doctor could adjourn to the office.

"Yep, you're the fifth pregnancy in the fleet. I wonder how many more we'll have."

"This is going to be a problem," Kris said.

"Between you and Jack? He does want kids?" The doctor paused. "Oh, do you want children?"

"Of course I do. I mean, yes, I think." Kris sputtered to a halt and frowned. "I really hadn't given a lot of thought to it. I had the implants. We're out here with a fight coming at us every second of the day or night. Kids were something to think about later. Maybe. I guess."

"You and Jack did discuss kids before you married?" the doctor asked.

Kris thought long and hard. "I think we may have missed that part."

"So, you've got a lot of talking to do tonight," Doc Meade said.

"And I've got a fleet to run with five pregnant women in it, including the Admiral Commanding."

"Hmm," the doc answered. "It is a discharge offense to remove your implants and get pregnant without authorization."

"So, where does that leave us five? Did any of us have our implants removed?"

"Not a one."

"Have you studied these implants? Did we get a bad batch from the factory?"

"I don't know. What with you pregnant, I'll need to remove the implants. You've got enough hormones coursing through your system without tossing in more."

"Do you keep track of these implants? Is there any chance that we can identify the bad batch and get them out of fleet distribution before there are too many more of these 'little surprises'?"

"Let's get you back to a room and see what we can see."

Five minutes later, Kris was lying down on a table with an anesthetized arm. A nurse was standing by as Doc Meade removed the first implant. "Get me the number on that joker."

The nurse put the strip under a magnifier and read out a number.

"Hold it. That batch was issued three years ago. Maybe more. That number has got to be wrong."

Doc Meade did her own eyeball check. "Damn, that's the number."

With a frown, she went back to Kris's arm, made a second small incision and withdrew the next implant strip.

The nurse eyed the strip, and turned to the doctor. "This number is not in sequence with the first."

In a blink, Doc Meade was looking over the nurse's shoulder. "Double damn," she breathed.

"What's this sequence of which you speak?" Kris asked.

"You get three implants, each numbered. Almost always one right after another. There's a chance the batch can get mixed up a bit in the machine that puts them in three-strip packets, but they're always the same in the first five or six numbers. This one is way off."

"And the third is?" Kris said.

Doc Meade removed the third and, instead of handing it off to the nurse, walked it over herself, set it down, and eyed it.

"Totally different batch," she said. "Three different batches, all from three years ago. Kris, my good Admiral, this is no accident. This is sabotage."

"Damn," Kris whispered.

11

How do you tell your husband you're pregnant?

Kris tried to remember what it was like in the Longknife household six, nine months before little Eddy was born. She was four. She remembered nothing.

Okay, how do I tell my husband he's going to be a daddy? He wants this baby, right?

Kris's internal dialogue stumbled. *I want this baby, don't I?*

Kris's empty tummy grumbled, no answer to her question, but it pointed in a direction. On the *Wasp*, she'd call him up and invite him to lunch at the Forward Lounge. There he could have a drink. He'd think nothing of her having something nonalcoholic. There she could let him in on her little secret.

That was getting bigger by the day.

But the *Princess Royal* had no bar aboard, and it was very likely that the next *Wasp* would be a dry ship as well. Third *Wasp* in less than that many years.

You're hard on ships, kiddo.

Kris had to admit that she was. But that was another problem. For now, she had a different one.

KRIS, I COULDN'T HELP BUT LISTEN IN. YOU'RE THINKING VERY LOUDLY, Nelly said.

SORRY. WAS I BOTHERING YOU?

NO, BUT YOU KNOW, I COULD TURN YOUR DAY QUARTERS INTO A VERY NICE PLACE TO SHARE A CANDLELIT DINNER WITH JACK.

WHERE WOULD WE GET THE FOOD?

KRIS, MOST ADMIRALS HAVE THEIR OWN MESS FOR THEM AND THEIR STAFF. I COULD EASILY ARRANGE FOR THE WARD-ROOM TO DELIVER. THEY HAVE A FEW STEAKS LEFT OVER

FROM OUR VICTORY DINNER. I THINK I COULD GET YOU AND
JACK TWO WITH ALL THE TRIMMINGS.

COULD YOU?

I'VE ALREADY ARRANGED IT.

AND MY DAY QUARTERS?

WAIT UNTIL YOU SEE WHAT I'VE DONE.

WELL, SINCE YOU'VE ARRANGED IT, TELL JACK I'D LIKE
TO SEE HIM IN OUR QUARTERS IN A HALF HOUR.

HE SAYS HE'LL BE THERE.

*Now, how to let him know. Hmm, maybe if I dress the
part, I won't have to tell him.*

Major General Jack Montoya opened the door to his
wife's day quarters and came to a complete stop. Dead stop
one might almost say.

He did not recognize the place.

In place of the usual spartan walls and furniture that
made clear that his wife was business with no frills, the place
looked like some quiet little hideaway.

The walls were made out like adobe, and there were red
roof tiles. Flowering plants circled the wooden roof sup-
ports. The deck had been made into flagstones of several
colors in a pattern that delighted the eye.

In the middle of all this, Kris sat at a wooden table.

He had to look twice to notice the table. Kris was wearing
the white negligee that he'd bought her the last time they
were dirtside on Alwa. The two thin straps allowed for a
truly plunging neckline. Made of hand-tooled lace, it let her
lovely skin play peekaboo with his hungry male eyes.

While the guy part of his brain lapped all this up, the
major general section was hammering alarm bells.

WHAT'S UP? Jack asked Sal, his computer and one of Nelly's kids.

I DON'T KNOW ANY MORE THAN YOU DO, BOSS. MOM'S BEEN
OFF-LINE TO THE REST OF US KIDS FOR MOST OF THIS MORNING.

Throwing caution to the wind—*who do you trust if you
can't trust your wife?*—Jack stepped into this illusion and
crossed quickly to seat himself across from his wife.

"Am I overdressed or underdressed?"

"You're perfect, as usual," Kris said.

"What's that I smell?" Jack went on, filling the silence until Kris chose to let him in on what was actually coming down here.

"I've ordered dinner from the wardroom. May I serve you?"

"Please."

Jack hadn't noticed the serving cart from the wardroom, now it moved out of the shadow of Kris's wooden desk and came to the table. Nelly magic, no doubt.

Kris uncovered two plates, deliciously smelling of steak, potatoes, and sautéed vegetables, all likely from the larder of the newly arrived Earth fleet. The next crop wasn't due until after they got back.

Kris returned to her seat, and they cut into their steaks. Jack saw red as he cut. "Perfect," he said.

"I'm glad you like it. Nelly oversaw its cooking."

"Thank you, Nelly." *Now just what is a wizard of a computer doing in the kitchen?*

Down boy, this is her show. I have a real strong suspicion that the best thing a husband can do is let the lady play this exactly how she wants to.

I just hope she's not about to announce she wants me to move out. Or add some third to the bedroom. Jack made sure his internal turmoil didn't show on his face.

Two bites later, Kris paused with a fork just short of her mouth. "We never talked about children back when we were thinking of tying the knot. How many kids would you like? Someday, I mean."

While one part of Jack's brain did a quick threat analysis of where this conversation was going, the simpler part of him answered her. "I come from one of those large Catholic families. There were four of us, a brother and two sisters. I know you grew up with just your brother."

"There was Eddy for all too brief a time," Kris pointed out, still chewing that bite she'd used to cover her question.

"I figured two, maybe three kids."

"Two point five. That .5 kid would need real love," Kris said, with an imp of a smile that he loved.

"No doubt my wife will find all the love in her heart that any of our kids needed," Jack said, smiling his love back.

They took another bite. As Jack chewed, he took in his wife. She was lovely. Lovely as she always was. She was also troubled. Taking extra care not to narrow his eyes into an inquisition, he studied her not as a loving husband but as a fellow soldier.

His eyes came to rest on her upper arm. There was a small bandage there. He knew every square centimeter of her. His hands had often roved that arm.

There should have been the three small ridges of her birth-control implant there.

What had been there since the first time he saw her bare arm was missing.

Jack took the information in and held it, NO ACTION TAKEN.

Kris finished chewing her latest bite and swallowed. She looked at her plate for a long moment, then said, "Jack, what would you say if I told you I was pregnant?"

Jack was up out of his chair in a heartbeat. A moment later, he was pulling her from her seat, lifting her up off the deck, and swinging her around, the two of them sharing a laugh of pure joy.

Jack measured the swing as a three-quarter circle and had his wife back down on the deck before he banged her knees against her chair.

"Pregnant? As in baby on board?" he asked.

"As pregnant as a girl can be," she assured him, then buried her head in his chest.

He hugged her and felt her tremble in his arms.

And then the second string of thoughts caught up with him. *How could she be pregnant? How will the fleet take to a pregnant admiral? Oh hell!*

He held her close and waited for his wife, his admiral, to say whatever she wanted to say.

"Jack," she said to his chest, "I've so looked forward to that moment when we could start a new life between us. That choice that *this* moment a child begins. I'm sorry this got taken away from us. My new birth-control implants were sabotaged."

"Sabotaged?" he whispered back.

"Yeah. Dr. Meade, the fleet surgeon, will be looking into

it as soon as we get back to Alwa. I'm the fifth gal having this conversation with a guy."

Jack examined several answers, and settled on, "Oh."

There was silence between them. Jack feared to taste it. Instead, he tried something else. "You know those two days we managed to get away to Joe's Seaside Paradise?"

"Yes, they were wonderful, as always."

"Weren't they in about the middle of your cycle?"

"You keep track?"

"I'm a husband, of course I keep track."

"Of when I'm about to get bitchy, when my cycle's about to start?"

"No, of that great time in the middle of your cycle when I can really send you up the walls."

"Oh." She paused for a moment. "Yes, I think you might be right. We were there in the middle of it all."

"Well, officially, I'm declaring one of those wonderful times the occasion when we started this darling child."

"Yes, I think that might be the time," she said, wistfully.

"Honey, have I made a mistake?" Jack said, his gut suddenly going cold. "You know I'm Catholic, but I know you were raised a lot less religious. Is this pregnancy a problem for you? Do you want to do something?"

Kris pulled away from him. His heart about broke in two until she looked up at him.

"Oh, no, Jack. This little one and I have become great friends in the last few hours. You needn't worry. No, I may have some problems with some sand-for-brains subordinates, but you are going to be a daddy, and I am going to be a mommy."

That required a second swing around. He got them out into the middle of the room so he didn't have to cut this one short.

The swing around ended in a kiss, and that ended in dinner getting cold.

A long while later, Kris Longknife and attached forces looked into her husband's eyes. "Thank you, Jack."

"For what?"

"For being you. For marrying me. For giving me this little bundle of problems."

"It will be a problem," Jack agreed. "Isn't pregnancy a discharge offense?"

"Removing your birth-control implants without authorization and getting pregnant are grounds for dismissal from the service. It takes both actions to earn that discharge. Neither I nor any of the other gals in this predicament removed our implants. They were sabotaged by a person or persons unknown. And when I get my hands on that one or many, I intend to hang them from the highest yardarm."

"None of your ships have yardarms," Jack pointed out.

"I'll have Nelly program the Smart Metal for one just to throw a rope over."

"But they made you a mommy."

"Okay. I'll thank them first, then hang them."

"That sounds like a plan," Jack said, and rolled out of bed. "We've still got a bit of the workday left."

"And I am the admiral," Kris sighed as she rolled off the other side.

"See you tonight," Jack said.

"You bet. We're not practicing anymore, but you have to come visit your little one."

"I plan to visit every chance I get."

12

Sometime during the night, they made a fast passage through their intended jump point. This time, it didn't move. This put them only one jump out from Alwa if they took it nice and easy. The fleet had flipped under its sleepy midnight watch and begun a deceleration. They'd had to up it to 1.16 gees to make the next jump dead slow.

Kris had ordered it, and it was made so.

Through all this, Kris slept soundly in her husband's arms.

The flag comm unit dispatched a message to Alwa not to panic, it was their defenders returning home. Kris expanded the routine message to include a list of lost and damaged ships with orders for the yards to make ready to receive the bent and busted and make them whole. Kris also appended a commentary on the performance of the crystal armor in the fight along with a request for yard personnel to put their heads together and figure out a way to improve it.

Kris did this hard day's work as she slept. In the morning, she went down what she'd accomplished while she dreamed and wondered why she wasn't more exhausted.

Then again, she did feel tired.

She'd have to mention that to Doc Meade at 1000 hours.

She didn't get a chance to mention any of her concerns, at least, not at first. Doc Meade was hopping mad.

"There are now twenty-two of you ladies-in-waiting," the good doctor snapped at Kris as she came into her office.

"Twenty-two!"

"Yeah, I finally got a report from the Third Fleet's chief medical officer. They've had eleven report pregnant. All in Bethea's squadrons, as you'd expect, although Yi seems to think it shows the Earth's superior virtue. Anyway, that man has ordered the Medical Officer to prepare orders for the women to be dismissed from the Navy way the hell out here or have an abortion, with a strong emphasis on the abortion option."

Now Kris saw why the normally placid doctor was about to explode.

"I was planning on having a 'Come to Jesus' meeting with our Admiral Yi. I now see that it's likely to take a meeting with Jesus, Mary, Moses, Mohammed, and Buddha."

"For Yi, you might want to add Confucius," the doctor added. "And maybe the devil himself."

"I think I'd rather throw in the devil's wife," Kris said. For a moment the two of them just looked at each other. Then the doc started laughing, and Kris joined in.

"Well," Doc Meade finally said, "I can see that pregnancy has not affected your sense of humor. Any other complaints?"

"I don't seem to have my usual oversupply of energy," Kris said.

"Sorry, the little one there and your support equipment are drawing heavily on your energy supply. You'll just have to make adjustments, Admiral. Like take a nap after you hand that bastard Yi his cohones."

"I'll make sure to save enough to rip him a new one," Kris assured the fleet doctor. "Now, that done, can you tell me how the search for the saboteur is going?"

"I'm pretty sure it's no one with this fleet. Likely it's someone safe back on Cannopus Station. Can you remember anything about the woman who inserted your implants?"

"I admit I took the process for pretty routine and was otherwise occupied with plans for this little sally." Kris stared at the overhead and tried to see herself a month or so ago.

"I see the nurse vaguely. Hold it, did you say woman?"

"Yes, I always have a woman insert the birth-control implants. Call me old-fashioned and maybe a bit sexist, but I don't see that as a man's job."

Kris eyed the doctor. "A man did mine," she said evenly. "Impossible."

"And it's impossible that I'm pregnant," Kris said, dryly.

"I'm getting tired of impossible things," the doc said, scowling.

"That's the way I remember it. I don't remember the guy's face, but he was most definitely a guy."

"A guy," the admiral said softly. "That may narrow down our search parameters. Access to the expended implants before they're destroyed. Access to the new implants somewhere in the supply chain, and"—she eyed Kris—"the ability to get aboard the flagship, access the medical section, and insert himself into your medical procedure."

"Going face-to-face with me sounds like a stupid stunt," Kris said.

"Stupid stunt, yes," the doc said, "but maybe a very necessary bit of defiance. We'll have to let him tell us when we catch him, now, won't we?"

"To my face," Kris growled.

Matters progressed in their usual fashion as the fleet slowed. The next day, they jumped into Alwa system. A message was waiting from Admiral Kitano, whom Kris had left in charge. There had been no surprises from the alien, but there was activity along their most distant warning pickets. The new *Wasp*, third of that name of late, was about to commission. Did the admiral expect to transfer her flag to it?

Oh, and there were a number of pregnant woman in the Second Fleet. Admiral Kitano would like to discuss that matter with Kris.

Kris sent back the count that First and Third Fleets were up to and asked Kitano what her count was. It totaled out at seventy-two, one Admiral, Her Royal Highness, Kris Longknife, included.

"I think I'll keep *Wasp* as my flag and let you have *Princess Royal* back," Kris sent. "See if you can arrange for some kind of Forward Lounge on the new *Wasp*, will you?"

13

Kris and Jack marched for the pier where the new *Wasp* lay. Admiral Kitano joined them as they went by the New Eden squadron. She'd had her flag on the *Banshee*.

"Congratulations on another victory," Kitano said.

"It's either victory or death," Kris said.

"Yes. What a bunch of hardcases. Were they actually blowing themselves up even before you took them under fire?"

"Afraid so. I'd blown away their mother ship. I guess they didn't want to live without their Enlightened One. Crazy," Kris said, shaking her head.

"Can I talk to you about our epidemic of pregnancies?" Kitano said. "I can't tell you how embarrassed I am to have it on my watch."

"Didn't you get the word?" Kris said, as they crossed the brow to the *Wasp*. They paused in their conversation as they rendered honors to the flag and the OOD, then continued forward. "We had more pregnancies in First and Third Fleets."

"You did!"

"Yes, it seems someone sabotaged the recent implants that were installed."

"Sabotaged! Who the hell would do that?"

"I don't know. Maybe Granny Rita really wants more great-grandkids," Kris offered.

"You're not pregnant!"

"Yep," Kris said, not even turning to make a memory of Kitano's expression. "I'm one of the lucky seventy-two."

"Damn!"

"Any chance you're one of us lucky sisters?" Kris asked, now looking at Kitano.

"No way, José," the admiral said. "In case you hadn't

noticed, I'm sleeping with the chief engineer on the *Princess Royal*."

Kris called up a picture in her mind. "Lovely woman."

"Yep, so there's very little chance that either one of us will be reporting to sick call pregnant."

"Gosh, and I thought the same."

"Occupational hazard when you keep one of those guys around."

"One of many," Kris agreed.

They'd arrived at the nonairtight doors to the Forward Lounge. Jack did the gentlemanly thing and opened them for the two women who outranked him.

Kris paused, both to take in the new, yet familiar sight, and to listen. Yi had the floor. Or more correctly, Admiral Yi of her Third Fleet and until recently of Earth, was shooting his mouth off.

A glance told Kris that her instructions had been followed. The new Forward Lounge was small, just big enough at this moment for a large flag meeting. Three groups of tables formed a U shape. Seated across from each other were First and Third Fleets' vice admirals, task force rear admirals, and squadron commodores. Each admiral was allowed some key staff. Kris noted that Admiral Yi had expanded his table to include quite a few staffers.

Second Fleet under Vice Admiral Miyoshi was between them. That was not an accident; Kris had ordered it that way.

She expected trouble before this meeting ended.

What she was hearing told her the trouble had started before the meeting even got under way.

"This fraternization rule of *yours* is really something," Yi was saying. "I got three guys and one gal shacked up together. I got one collection of six rooms joined together. At least that's three guys and gals each, though what they're doing, I have no idea. Guys and guys. Gals and gals. Bethea, I don't know how you handle all these," he said, turning to his own subordinate.

Rear Admiral Betsy Bethea of Savannah had been placed under his command. Kris had hoped he might learn from her experience out at the far end of the galaxy. From the results of the recent battle, he clearly had not. From his yammering, he hadn't learned much of anything for a very long time.

"I wouldn't know, Admiral Yi. I don't concern myself with my crews' *voluntary* living arrangement," Betsy Bethea answered coolly.

"Oh, the tigress has claws," he said, giving her a sideways compliment since her squadron was known as the big cats from the names they sported. "If you'd paid better attention, maybe your ladies wouldn't be all knocked up. None of my Earth girls are."

"I had heard the pregnancies were a result of sabotage," Betsy Bethea snapped back.

"Sabotage my eye. They just want out of this man's Navy, I tell you. What you want to bet me that not one of them gets an abortion, so they can stay with the fleet."

Behind Kris, Jack cleared his throat. Admiral Miyoshi turned and shouted, "Atten'hut," as he jumped to his feet. The room was only slightly behind him at coming to attention.

Kris left the room standing as she marched to the front where her table had been reserved by Penny and Masao. Though she knew her face was in a deep glower, she let her gaze wander around her commanders. Most met her eyes evenly.

Admiral Yi seemed intent on studying the table in front of him.

"As you were," Kris said. Her commanders sat. She stayed standing.

"For the record," Kris began, voice hard as flint, "each of the Sailors still had her birth-control implants in place when they reported to sick call and yielded up a positive pregnancy test. I know this because I have been in touch with the senior surgeon of the fleet." Kris paused before adding, "And because I am one of those pregnant."

"Jesus, Mary, and Joseph!" was just one of the louder expletives that greeted that announcement.

"Somehow expended implants were substituted for new ones and reinserted into women. Senior Surgeon Meade is investigating the handling of both used contraceptive implants and the new ones to find out how they could have been mixed up. Under normal handling, there is no way that could have happened. Any questions?"

"So what are we going to do with all these pregnant women,

Admiral?" Yi put in without being recognized. "My wife is a real bitch when she's knocked up, and her hormones start yo-yoing all over the place."

"I suspect I could be a real bitch in your presence under most any circumstance," Betsy Bethea said, under her breath. Well, not so much under her breath. It carried around the entire room and drew smiles from First and Second Fleet, as well as her own commanders in the half of Yi's fleet that she led.

Yi shot her daggers.

Bethea buffed her nails and seemed to miss his look.

"As you were," Kris said, and the room sobered. "The pregnant women will decide how they will go forward," Kris said curtly. "There. Will. Be. No. Command. Involvement. In. That. Decision. Do I make myself clear?"

"Yes, ma'am," came back at her from all. Except Yi.

"Admiral Yi, do you have something to say?"

"No, ma'am. I understand, ma'am. But may I ask how we are going to handle this? Space is dangerous. Radiation. All kinds of stray particles. I understand most Navies send their women dirtside for their own protection."

"My Granny Rita was commanding a cruiser when her first child was still being weaned. I understand she was pregnant with her second while commanding a ship in space and didn't give up the conn until quite late. Our senior fleet surgeon is looking into making adjustments to some ships to handle these problems."

"Any adjustments are going to cost weight," Yi countered. "You're the one saying all the time that we have to be ready to bounce our ships all over the place. You add weight, and you aren't nearly as nimble," could be taken several ways.

"I expect to concentrate the pregnancies in two or three ships, Admiral. None in your fleet, I might add. My flagship, *Wasp*, will be one of them. Now, are there any further questions on this matter? If not, we have a major battle to review and lessons to learn."

Even Yi seemed out of barbs.

"Asshole," Jack was heard to mutter, as Kris sat down.

She placed a restraining hand on his arm. Then agreed softly. "Yes, I believe he is."

14

Matters did not get any better as the meeting turned to the battle.

Admiral Yi stood and gave his battle report . . . of how he saw it.

Kris let him finish, then asked, "Did you bring any recordings from your battle boards?"

"No, the original data was lost due to a failure on the part of a technician while archiving the databoards, ma'am."

Kris would have preferred to be addressed as admiral, but she'd let that slide. For now. For a moment, she considered calling on Admiral Bethea to provide any readouts from her battle board, but that would only further poison the atmosphere between them.

"Nelly, please play back the Third Fleet's battle with the main enemy force as you recorded it."

"Yes, Admiral," Nelly said, and the take from the jump probe filled the screens behind Kris's table.

"Where did you get that?" Yi exploded before she was well started. "It's all a lie. You can't know what was happening in the system before you jumped in."

"Before we deployed, I told you that I had a probe that could look at the other side of the jump. I told you that I would use that feedback to decide when to intervene in your battle. Don't you remember my telling you that?"

"You said something like that, but I just figured you were blowing smoke up my ass. No one can see what's on the other side of a jump."

"No one from Earth," Bethea whispered to the commodore from Savannah who had taken over her squadron upon her promotion.

"You really didn't think I could see that you were ignoring my battle plan, did you?" Kris said evenly.

Yi turned beet red but risked no answer.

"Admiral Bethea, do you have better data on the initial contact with the alien?" Kris asked.

Yi's subordinate task force commander glanced at her boss. He did not meet her eyes. "Yes, Admiral Longknife. I do have a full readout from my battle board. Shall I put it on screen?"

"Please."

The admiral turned to one of her subordinates, who placed a fist-size unit on the table in front of him. Behind Kris, the screens lit up with a display of what the target system had looked like when Third Fleet arrived.

The screen advanced quickly. The frigates accelerated away from the jump at the one gee Kris had ordered. Around the mother ship, a dish of thirty warships formed up quickly and charged for the humans at two gees while others formed into four dishes and began a more sedate one-gee acceleration on an attack vector.

The replay moved the ships rapidly across the system as the two forces rushed to contact.

Suddenly, the sixteen Earth-built frigates slammed into a three-gee charge, Yi's flagship, the *George Washington*, slightly ahead of the rest, leaving the task force from Savannah and the Scanda Confederacy behind them.

"Pause," Kris snapped, and the screen froze. "Admiral Bethea, why did you fail to accelerate to match the other half of Third Fleet?" Kris asked.

"I received no orders to do so, Admiral Longknife," was terse to the point of sharp.

"Interesting," Kris said. "Admiral Yi, would you care to share with those present the basis for your deciding to split your command?"

Around the room, there were soft snickers. Yi had spoken long and often on his opinion about Kris dividing First and Third Fleets for this operation.

"I saw an opportunity to inflict a decisive defeat on a portion of the alien fleet. Once I demonstrated a clear superiority, I expected the fight would go out of them." The words sounded worn and overpracticed.

Apparently, Admiral Yi had gotten nothing from the reports Kris sent him. Reports that showed the aliens never let the fight go out of them. Kris considered pointing that out but settled for, "Continue the playback."

The two forces, thirty aliens and sixteen humans, came together at a blinding-fast rate. Yi's task force opened fire at two hundred thousand klicks. The aliens had to take it; fifteen exploded under the blaze of the humans' forward and aft batteries as Yi's ships quickly flipped and emptied all their guns at the onrushing warships. Then they flipped again, providing their heavily armored bows to the fire of the surviving aliens.

Those fifteen ships hurtled into range of their own lasers while the Earth ships were recharging their lasers. Now the alien slashed out at their tormentors. Each reached out with more lasers than Kris had ever been able to count.

As one, the Earth-built squadrons began to glow as their new armor took in the lasers' beams, slowed them down, then redistributed them along the hull to radiate back into space.

"Pause," Kris ordered. "Admiral Bethea, did you get readouts of the damage to the Earth task force?"

"No, Admiral Longknife, my battle boards showed me only the damage to my own task force. However, the display combines not only radar reports but also infrared measurements. The other task force was glowing red-hot from the enemy fire."

"Thank you, Admiral. Continue the display at real time."

The action continued apace, then the fire from the alien ships changed. Someone got smart. The fifteen ships concentrated their fire on only three of the humans.

Suddenly, *Abraham Lincoln*, *Clemenceau*, and *Mao Zedong* became the center of every alien's fire.

The infrared readout showed them going from hot to blazing to gone.

The other ships of the Earth task force had reloaded. In rapid succession, they fired. Another twelve alien warships vanished.

Of the surviving four, at least two were hard hit. They did what they could, all concentrating on the *Togo*. It glowed and blistered off some of its armor, but it held together long enough for the other ships to recharge their guns and wipe out the last survivors of the first alien formation.

Yi's ships now flipped and decelerated to form up with Bethea's task force as it came up even with them. Together, they engaged the four alien dishes as they came in range.

Kris noted how *Togo* stayed in the firing line rather than fall back, out of harm's way, so it could be repaired to fight another day. Apparently, Yi had a different attitude toward this long war than Kris did.

The rest of the battle proceeded as Kris would have had it. The aliens were scourged at long range as Third Fleet first fell back in front of it, then followed as the alien commander chose to withdraw. They witnessed the attack of the suicide boats, including the ones that slipped through with atomics to destroy the *Loki* and severely damage the *Puma*. Unlike Admiral Yi, the experienced Admiral Bethea had her wounded cat fall back into reserve. That saved the *Puma* to straggle home and fight another day.

At one point, the aliens made a thrust toward the second division of BatRon 11. Since it was already weakened by the loss of the *Clemenceau* and *Moa*, the aliens concentrated their fire on the crippled *Togo*, and another ship was lost. Kris noticed what looked like life pods spewing from the burning hulk of the *Togo*.

"Pause again, please. Are those survivors and did we collect them?"

Yi said nothing. Bethea stepped in. "I had the *Regulus* converted to an armed merchant cruiser." An isolated dot well behind the battle line flashed red. "She collected life pods from *Loki* and *Togo*. We recovered about half their crews. Likewise when we lost *Lenin* and *Heimdallr* to mines. Unfortunately, the alien lasers were pretty heavy around the earlier three ships when we lost them. We only got two or three survivors from each."

"Thank you, Admiral," Kris said. She had specifically ordered that each fleet have some rescue ships with them. The *Mary Ellen Carter* had been ready to do that service for the First Fleet. At least Bethea had seen to it that the Third Fleet had such aid.

Kris examined the facts of the fight, and her options. It was never easy to relieve an officer, but it was worse to let other commanders see an officer fail . . . and get away with it.

NELLY, EXPAND THE FORWARD LOUNGE SO THE OFFICERS PRESENT CAN GET A DRINK. WE DO HAVE SOMETHING TO DRINK, DON'T WE?

YES, KRIS, THE BAR ISN'T UP TO MOTHER MACCREEDY'S STANDARDS, BUT THEY CAN CUT THEIR THIRST.

THEN RAISE A WALL BETWEEN THIS AREA AND THE REST. A CLEAR WALL.

NO. I'LL NEED SOME PRIVACY.

As Kris and Nelly spoke, the Forward Lounge expanded, tables and chairs appeared, and a wall rose behind those attending this meeting, a wall with a wide double door in it.

"I need this room. Why don't you get some coffee, or something stronger," Kris said to her officers.

All of them began to stand up.

"Admirals Yi and Bethea, please stay."

Yi eyed Kris as he retook his seat.

"Save me some coffee," Bethea said as she sat back down.

YOU WANT ANY OF US TO STAY? Jack asked for Kris's staff.

NOPE. I EITHER DO THIS ON MY OWN, OR I CAN FOLD AWAY MY FOUR STAR FLAG, Kris answered.

Her staff joined the others headed for the door. While there were plenty of backward glances from the other officers, there were only small, firm smiles from Kris's staff.

15

As the door swung closed behind the last officer, Kris stood.

"Admiral Yi, your performance in this recent operation leaves a lot to be desired."

"I commanded Third Fleet. I fought that battle the way I saw fit," he shot back.

"You lost six ships. First Fleet lost none."

"If the enemy had reacted in a rational manner, the defeat of their first task force should have routed the rest and sent them streaming for the jump and into your arms," he spat back.

"I gave you reports on all the battles we've had with these bastards. Did you study any of them?"

"I looked them over," Yi said, again not meeting her eyes.

"It's clear to me that you learned nothing from them," Kris snapped.

"Every battle is different," Yi shot back.

"Enough of this. You failed to follow direct orders. You suffered casualties you didn't need and that we can't afford out here at the hind end of nowhere. I am relieving you of command of the Third Fleet and returning you to your permanent rank of rear admiral. I will leave you in command of Task Force 7."

"You can't do that. Earth gave me command of its ships. I was kind enough to let you detach one squadron from my command to reinforce your weaker US ships. I could have objected, but I didn't. Still, I command *all* Earth ships."

"But you will not command one of *my* fleets," Kris growled.

"I will command *all* Earth ships, then," Yi said, stubbornly. "Those are my orders."

"Are they? Nelly, put up Rear Admiral Yi's orders."

His orders, signed by the president of the Earth Union, appeared on the screen.

"Let's see now," Kris said, as if she didn't remember every word. "You will report to Commander, Alwa Defense Sector. You will place your command under her and conform to her lawful orders," Kris read slowly. "That seems pretty straightforward to me, and very much identical to all the other ships seconded to my command. Rear Admiral, I now order you to attach the remnant of BatRon 10 and 11 to Vice Admiral Miyoshi's Second Fleet. Do you have any questions?"

"No. Are we done here?"

"Yes."

The former fleet commander bolted for the door.

Admiral Bethea breathed a sigh of relief as the door clicked shut behind him. "I can't tell you how grateful I am to be out from under that man's thumb. Thank you, Admiral."

"You're welcome, but don't get too grateful just yet. I'm giving you Third Fleet, but I can't give you much in place of Yi's Task Force 7."

"There's not a lot left of it."

"Yes, but it has that nice, new armor, and those nifty 22-inch lasers."

"I think I can make due just fine with what I've got. You didn't do too bad fighting with the old armor and 20-inch lasers. Good Lord, just a few months ago we figured 18-inch lasers were God's answers to desperate Sailors' dreams."

"Well, I'll pull the Fourth Task Force out of Miyoshi's fleet. The New Eden squadron at least has 22-inch lasers although you'll have to make do with the Esperanto League's hippie dippy division."

"I think the Hispania division will more than make up for them, and I really think the Esperanto frigates have more fight in them than their names imply."

The two shared a smile.

"Nelly, make the wall disappear. Tell Jack I'd like some coffee."

"Coffee, Kris? How do you think that little one will take to the caffeine?"

"It's so little," Kris whimpered.

Betsy Bethea laughed. "My mom used to remind me that she went nine months without a drop of anything but water. 'You owe me,' she'd say."

Kris sighed and glanced at her flat midriff. "Nelly, tell Jack I want a big glass of water. With ice. Plenty of ice. I feel this sudden need to chomp on someone. I mean something. If he doesn't want it to be him, he better get me ice."

"He says it's on its way."

Across the room, Jack was already behind the bar and holding aloft a very large glass. Even across the room, Kris could hear the tinkle of ice as he filled it. Done, Jack quick marched for her.

"Nelly, could you get Admiral Miyoshi?"

"He's on his way," and the commander of Kris's Second Fleet was on his feet and trailing Jack for Kris's table.

"Pull up a chair," she told the fleet commander.

As Miyoshi sat, he raised an eyebrow. "Does this mean what you are going to tell me is likely to knock me off my feet?"

"Only if you have good sense," Kris said.

"Oh, good, then I can stand. No one with good sense follows a Longknife. Certainly not all the way to the other side of the galaxy."

The two enjoyed the laugh. Then Kris got serious.

"I've relieved Rear Admiral Yi of command of Third Fleet," Kris said bluntly.

"You could do nothing else," the Musashi admiral agreed. "His performance was, ah, extremely unsatisfactory."

"However, I've chosen to let him remain in command of Task Force 7."

"Hmm," was all he said.

"And I'm moving the Seventh to your fleet."

"Gods help me with a kami like that one beside my hearth," the fleet commander said.

"He has a point that Earth gave him command of its ships."

"One can only wonder why?"

Kris raised both eyebrows in agreement with the question. "Admiral Bethea will command Third Fleet. I'm giving her your Task Force 4.

"I will miss the Esperanto bunch. They throw great parties. Did you know, their ships are not nearly as dry as ours?"

"No I didn't, and I'm sorry about pulling them out of your fleet." Kris took a deep breath, let it out, and dumped the full extent of her possible problem on her old friend. "If Yi continues to not follow orders, keep me informed. I will beach him. He is in line to replace the guy who couldn't take no for an answer bossing the guano mine."

"Where will you send that one?"

"Maybe I'll give him command of a canoe, out where the big 'eats everythings' swim." Together they laughed at the image of a canoe in waters where the big ones swam and anyone in less than a six-hundred-ton, harpoon-rigged trawler was at risk of their lives.

Levity done, Kris surveyed the room. Yi was absent, but most of the rest seemed ready to get back to work. Kris used a spoon against her water glass to summon them.

"Commanders of Task Force 7 should join Admiral Miyoshi at his table. Commanders of Task Force 4 will be in the Third Fleet under Admiral Bethea. Nelly, cut paperwork for my signature fleeting her up to Vice Admiral."

"It's waiting on your desk as I speak, Admiral Longknife," Nelly said. Do I HAVE TO SAY ADMIRAL LONGKNIFE EVERY TIME?

ONLY IN MEETINGS WHERE I'VE JUST BROKEN A VICE ADMIRAL, Kris said, and tried to hide the grin from this sidebar.

"I think we've learned our lessons from this last dustup," Kris began. "The enemy is not dumb. They learn fast, and they can adjust their tactics in only seconds when we confront them with surprises. They also have a few surprises of their own," Kris noted. "We may have to double our secondary batteries to handle their small suicide boats."

"Admiral Benson is working on that in the yards," Admiral Kitano said. "He was quick to point out that need after reviewing your after-action report."

"Good. Now that you have the floor, Admiral Kitano, why don't you fill us in on what the little bug-eyed monsters have been up to while we were off having fun?"

Admiral Kitano stood, and the screen behind Kris changed to show the picket line around Alwa. Every system within ten or twelve jumps had a large, low-tech but very effective buoy at every jump. They would report any ships entering that system.

No doubt, the picket at the used jump would be blown away by the alien. However, across the system, another buoy would take note of that, record data on the ship that did it, and pass through the jump to send that message streaming back, buoy by buoy, to Alwa. It might take a week to reach Alwa, but the data would arrive ahead of any attack.

"We've lost some outer buoys," Kitano reported. Several green dots began blinking red. "They were simple pop-and-duck-back raids. We seem to have as many system freighters as we need, at the moment, or at least Pipra assures me we've met demand. I've turned the *Kamoi Maru*, *Activity*, and *Cherry-leaf* into buoy tenders. They've got enough power to run away from most, and a few 20-inch guns to handle anything they can't run from. They should have the buoys replaced in a week and add another layer out."

The room nodded along with the benign report, but there was a clear feeling that there was another shoe to drop.

"Then there is this system," Kitano said, and a yellow dot began blinking red.

"It's a truly worthless system. A red giant, two white dwarfs, and a neutron star doing their own dance around each other. What planets have survived are either way-out gas giants or barren rocks. The system, however, has eight jumps into it."

The admiral paused. "Our scientists guess that what we have here are two star systems that collided after the three alien races that built the jumps set their initial jump maps up. Whatever the reason, you can go a lot of places from this place, and some of them allow you to jump over the nearest systems."

"That could be a problem," Kris said.

"Yes," Kitano said. "Two buoys in this system have been shot up. We got fingerprints on the ships that did the shooting. They were both different."

Any boredom that might have been nibbling at the attendees fled.

"Three ships observed the last attack on Alwa," Kris said. "By any chance, can those two ships be matched to any of those three?"

"Six massive reactors on one. Just eight giant ones on the

other. Yep, they likely were scouting for two different base ships."

The aliens seemed to hold to a single design involving huge to the point of not quite ridiculous . . . at least to human minds. All the alien bodies that Kris's boffins had sampled DNA from showed they had started as a pretty homogeneous group some hundred thousand years ago. They'd branched off from there over the years.

If Kris understood the bragging that the aliens did in their horror collection of trophies from murdered planets that she'd discovered in a pyramid, there were at least forty base ships now going about the galaxy, striving to exterminate all living things not of their flesh.

There might be as many as fifty.

With the latest operation, Kris had destroyed three.

That left a lot out there, and, if the ravings of the old woman Kris had captured in the Sasquan System were to be believed, the flame had been sent to all the ships demanding they join in exterminating Kris and her ilk.

You do good at a hard job, you get an even tougher one for your reward.

So long as they are sniffing around on this side of the galaxy, they aren't finding humanity or the Iteeche.

Kris knew her job. Everyone here was a volunteer.

Hopefully, Kris Longknife would figure out a way for them to survive their job as the stalking horse for one hell of a monster.

And I'm going to do this while my body concentrates on what evolution has made my most important traditional contribution to the human race—producing a healthy child.

Oh, joy.

16

The meeting broke up shortly after that with orders to expand the picket line past the huge system the aliens seemed interested in. Captain Drago walked in quickly as the admirals and commodores were leaving. Most of those in the know stepped aside for the flag captain. He might be only a captain, but they knew he pulled more than his weight. A lot more.

"How's the new ship?" Kris asked.

"Much like the old one. Oh, Admiral Benson asks that we go easy on the old girl. Or young girl. He'd dearly like to replace some of our other lost ships rather than keep replacing your flagship."

"No doubt you will keep that in mind the next time you get her all dinged up."

"Per your orders, Your Highness."

"That's hitting below the belt." Of all people, Drago knew how much Kris hated being "Your Highnessed."

"Does Benson think he's got the new crystal armor right?" Jack asked. Kris could count on him to think of her safety first, second, and last.

"Yes. I'm taking the *Wasp* out tomorrow for a test. We'll let the new *Endeavor* plunk away at us with her 5-inch battery for a bit. If everything works, we'll back off and let her hit us with her old 18-inchers. If they don't faze her, we might let L'Estock have a shot at us with a battery of 20-inchers."

"Don't get carried away," Kris said. "We can't afford to put you back in the yard. We got dinged and broken ships from this latest shoot. And we need to redesign the armor backing for the Earth ships with crystal armor."

"They can use the same design the *Wasp* has backing up her crystal belt," Drago said. "I told those Earth skippers that they were way too optimistic about heat transfer, but would they listen to one of us hicks from the Rim?"

"They'll listen now," Jack said.

"Who's next on my list of torturous meetings?" Kris asked.

"Pipra just came aboard," Drago said.

"Pipra Strongarm is waiting in your day cabin, Kris," Nelly reported. "Your desk and other personal items have arrived from the *Princess Royal*. Oh, and Dr. Meade wants to know when you will have time for her today."

Kris sighed. It had been easy to find time for the doc on the ride back. Hell, Kris had even considered taking up knitting little booties, only to discover there was no yarn aboard.

With a smile, Kris went to do what Longknifes always did.

What they had to do.

17

"I hear you're pregger," Pipra said the moment Kris walked into her day quarters. "Are congratulations in order, or are you going to take care of this problem?"

"Is the news all over?" Kris tried to growl, but she was grinning too much. "And I will be taking very good care of this little problem for the next couple of months until I can drop him or her in daddy's hands and let him try his hand at taking care of the little stinker for a while."

"That's the attitude, girl," Pipra said, poking the air with her fist.

"So, if it's not too much of an invasion of privacy, how many unplanned pregnancies are there on the civilian side of things, and what are the chances of your joining me among the plural?"

Pipra made as if to watch fast balls whizz by her head at light speed. "You slipped two by me real fast, didn't you, mother?"

"A gal can try."

"There's no chance of my joining you. I was part of a five-person S group before I decided to seek my fortune all to hell and gone. They bought out my share, and I used it to buy shares in several of the fabricators we brought. Just as soon as your gorgeous genius Amanda can figure out how to make money here that you can take to a bank, I'll be rolling in the dough, assuming we haven't run the fabs down into wreck and ruin. That reminds me, we need a sinking fund to recapitalize our industrial assets. Admittedly, that's hard to do when we can't figure out how to capitalize anything. Which brings up that thing we're not permitted to talk about?"

"Hold it, Pipra, you danced right by the question I most

wanted answered. How many unplanned pregnancies among the industrial workers?"

"None."

"None?"

"Yep, no planned pregnancies. No unplanned ones, either. And to answer your next question, we brought our own medical facilities and supplies and, so it appears, the problem is totally Navy."

"That's interesting," Kris said. NELLY, PASS THAT ALONG TO DOC MEADE.

DID IT BEFORE YOU ASKED. SHE SAYS IF YOU DON'T DROP BY HER PLACE BEFORE THREE, SHE MAY HAVE SOMEONE FOR YOU TO TALK TO.

TELL HER I'LL BE THERE.

"Yes. Isn't it," Pipra said. "Now about the unmentionable."

The unmentionable was a weird plant found in a couple of rivers on the South Continent. It traveled. Sometimes at an amazing speed in water. It did photosynthesis, so biologists agreed it qualified as a plant, but it could identify predators and make tracks for the other side of the pond. And if the pond dried up, the things had been seen inching their way toward the nearest water.

Its power source was mitochondrial DNA that made human adrenaline seem tame.

What the boffins were excited about was hitching these organelles to nanos as fuel sources. Kris had lost nanos during strong winds. She would have killed for what this little bugger could do to turbocharge the microcosmic world.

"We should be getting our first shipment off to human space soon," Kris said. "The new *Endeavor* is out of the yard. I'll need to check on the new *Hornet*."

Kris had been hard on ships named *Hornet*, much like she'd been on *Wasp*. On her third in the last three years. The *Endeavors* had gotten off easier—or harder, depending on your perspective. Only one busted, but that in less than a year.

"As soon as they're ready to go, I'll send them on their way with a full load of plants and plenty of seeds."

"You going to send anyone home that wants to go?"

"No," Kris said, bluntly.

"A good idea," Pipra agreed, "although I must tell you, the word is getting around that there are ships going back. If you don't do it quickly, you may have a problem on your hands."

"And I don't have problems already?" Kris said, dryly.

"More tomorrow than you had today," Pipra offered.

"No doubt. Now, talk to me about boring production statistics."

The meeting went two hours as they weighed the different demands for production. The Alwans like human tech: TVs, computers, now, even electric cars. Oh, and electric egg warmers. The more of them, the better.

Egg warmers, under the eyes of old birds, left the younger Alwans free to participate in the growing high-tech economy. While the old birds complained and grumbled about changes they didn't like, more of the younger ones were galloping off into the future with both feet.

Or, better said, plowing ground with new farm gear.

Kris had discovered, as more ships arrived with hungry crews to feed, that both the native Alwans and the humans were on the edge of starvation. If the crop next month was as good as promised, Kris might not have to worry so much about where her fleet's next meal came from.

However, until the harvest was in safe storage, Kris worried.

For two hours, they juggled production of Smart Metal™ for warships, properly balanced with electronics and weapons. But the electronics had to be taken out of the stream of gizmos the Alwans wanted. Maybe Kris needed less of the Smart Metal™?

Besides, she didn't have a lot of spare Navy to crew more ships. In this war, when ships blew up, raw plasma left few people alive to find their way into survival pods.

However, some Alwans were taking to space, and fighting, with a passion. Especially the Ostriches. Unlike the Roosters, they liked nothing better than a good fight.

How many trainee Ostriches could Kris risk among her crews in order to spread her human Sailors out over more ships? Assuming the yards could turn out more ships.

Kris knew that logistics was a brutal science. How did you get the right stuff to the right place in the right amount at just the right time so that the want of a nail didn't cost you a ship or a battle? Kris now played this game with wild abandon.

Her hand went unbidden to her tummy. There was a tiny life growing there. If she blew it, that life might never get a chance to laugh at her mommy's silly face or feel Jack's warm hug.

Kris suppressed a shiver and went back to listening to Pipra. The CEO of Nuu Enterprises in the Alwa system forced herself to listen closely to every word from her executive officer. It sounded like Pipra had a good plan. A well-balanced plan.

But would it be the right plan?

Kris struggled with this new demon and refused to blurt out her new fear. There was a lot more to being a mother than just growing a child.

Kris was exhausted by the time Pipra closed down her computer, and said, "Gal, you look tired."

"Doc Meade tells me I won't be my usual peppy self for a while."

"Well, it makes me glad I don't have to worry about your problem."

"Oh, I've had one person tell me she was safe. You have a girlfriend?"

"Not at the moment. I keep hinting to your Abby that she and her Marine could join my new S family. There are only three of us, and we gals would like another boy to avoid monotony. However, your friend is a head case. I don't know of a woman more averse to jumping the broom or doing anything else to tie a knot, but she sure is doing a good imitation of monogamy with that big fellow."

"To each their own," Kris said. Nothing Abby did surprised Kris.

Kris let Pipra let herself out, finding it amazingly hard to get to her feet.

She did manage to walk herself into her quarters. The bed looked so good.

I can lie down for just a few minutes.

In a moment, Kris was out like a light.

18

KRIS, ARE YOU AWAKE? brought Kris back to a wakefulness that was not her friend.

WHO WANTS TO KNOW? had a strong hint they would pay for the question with their life.

JACK. HE SAYS PHIL TAUSSIG WANTS TO CHECK IN WITH YOU, BUT I TOLD HIM YOU WERE TAKING A NAP.

"I'm not anymore," Kris said, and rolled herself off her bunk. She managed to stumble to the sink and get a drink of water. It tasted delicious.

Holding on to the sink for support, she glanced around her quarters. They looked about the same, even to the door leading to her maid's quarters. "I wonder if Abby will even have space aboard," she muttered groggily.

"Why shouldn't I?" Abby said from the door to Kris's day quarters. "Just 'cause you got a brat in the oven, am I suddenly unwelcome?"

"Never," Kris said, actually managing to crack a smile at the woman her mother had hired to wash her hair and see that she made it to balls on time. "I just figured you were having too much fun being a woman of business to have any time for little old me."

"Old, I might agree with," Abby grumped in her usual merry way, "but you've been six feet of trouble since I first saw you. You planning on having your next meeting in those rumpled whites?"

Kris glanced down at her uniform. Clearly, whites were not meant to be the uniform of the nap. At least not and be worn to the next meeting.

"Could you get me a new set of undress whites?" Kris

said. "No need to have all that fruit salad to see Phil and Doc Meade."

"Can I tell Phil that you're accepting gentleman callers?" Nelly asked.

Kris wondered what obsolete fiction Nelly was studying now, but answered, "Yes," as Abby dug out a new pair of white slacks and a short-sleeve white shirt. "Tell him to give me five minutes to recover from a little nap, and I'll be human."

"They're on their way," Nelly reported.

Abby, in her own inimitable way, got Kris presentable and even human in time to meet her husband at the door between their day and night quarters. He gave her a kiss.

"Can an old friend give his pregnant friend a hug, even if she is the boss?" Phil asked.

"So long as you do it where I can see it," Jack growled, but through a delightfully possessive smile.

Kris opened her arms, and Phil engulfed her in a hug. "Hey, if pregnant women get hugs like these, I could get to like this," Kris said.

"Can I ask when baby's due?"

"Not for a long time. With luck, you can get gone and back and still have time to hold my hand while shouting 'breathe,' or 'push,' or whatever I'm supposed to do."

"Don't they have machines that can take over the hard part?" Phil asked. "My wife used one the one time I hung around a bit to do the service required."

"That's something she needs to talk over with Doc Meade," Jack said.

"I will. I will," Kris insisted. "It's just we've been a bit busy in our meetings trying to figure out why seventy-two of us are in this state without getting proper Navy authorization."

"God forbid that anyone do anything without proper Navy authorization," Phil drawled.

They shared the laugh at that.

"So, you're ready to run the alien gauntlet back to human space?" Kris asked. Unspoken was her requirement that if the aliens caught this tiny force, and somehow managed to overpower them before they could run away, Phil would see that his reactor lost containment and that his ship, and all in it, were burned to atoms.

"I want to run the *Hornet* and *Endeavor* out to the asteroid belt for a shoot tomorrow to see if those old 18 inch lasers on the *Endeavor* and the banged-up 20-inchers on the *Hornet* are still good."

"I hear you're going to take a few potshots at the *Wasp* while you're at it."

"No way to prove the armor works but by hitting it."

"I seem to remember there used to be proving grounds where they'd do that without putting a ship at the end of the gun," Kris said.

"There were," Nelly put in.

"But here we do things fast and cheap," Phil said, "and don't worry. We'll be gentle on Captain Drago. First sign of any shortcomings with the crystal stuff, and it's back to the yard for him."

"Well, I'd like to get you on your way before I have too much trouble. You're supposed to be a secret, but news of just about anything leaks out around here like a sieve," Kris said, resting a hand on her midriff, which was still quite flat, thank you very much.

"A day trip out, another day to load supplies. We've already taken on board some of that stuff we don't talk about. Hard to believe that could change everything."

"I'm also sending you as many of the alien tribe as want to see our world," Kris said. "They and the rabid old hag that just screams that we're all going to die ought to be an overnight sensation back home."

"Can I keep her asleep for most of the trip?" Phil asked. "She is one angry old biddy, and she really gets her jollies telling us what they're going to do to us vermin for having the gall to fight back and kill them instead of dying quietly."

"Sorry, Phil, but Doc Meade says it's not good for the old woman's heart to spend it all drugged and off her feet. She needs to exercise."

"So she gets it screaming at her guards. Okay, I'll arrange the guard shift so they only have to put up with her awake once. It will make for a fast trip."

"Fast out and fast back. Is that what you and O'dell want?"

"I've got a few of the crew who are talking of staying, but I'm thinking of asking Bahati to come out here. Alwa's a good place, plenty of open space. Some Ostrich folks say we can homestead there. I think Bahati would love some land around her and the family. Her folks have settled a half dozen planets in the last twenty generations."

"If you can talk her into it," Kris agreed, wondering why anyone would take the risk. But then, now that we knew about the aliens, humanity had been at risk for a hundred thousand years and not known it.

"Now, I've got to see what Dr. Meade is up to," Kris said. "I'll be there to wish you and your crew Godspeed when you shove off," Kris assured her old friend. He and his crew had saved her life. But then, she'd come back to save them.

That was the Navy way. You stood by your friends and didn't keep count of who was up or down in the saving of each other's neck business.

With an informal salute, Phil was on his way.

"Do you think Doc Meade has her hands on who took this little choice out of our hands?" Jack asked when they were alone. "I'd love to know what he thought he was doing. I might even get it out of him if he is reluctant to talk. Please, dear God, make him reluctant to talk."

"Down, Marine. I get first go at the bastard although it's kind of hard to be too angry. I'm starting to like this little hitchhiker."

"Who said I don't love the little one?" Jack said. "I just have to wonder who thought it would be a great idea to take the consent out of childbearing."

"Okay, Marine, if you promise to be nice, and hand me the brass knuckles when I ask for them first, you can accompany me to the good doctor."

Together, they set out to see what they could see.

19

A young junior officer was just leaving as they arrived, a firm and resolute look on her face. She saluted Kris without showing any signs of recognizing her.

Clearly, her gaze had gone someplace else.

As Kris settled into Doc Meade's office, she asked, "That young officer. Is she okay?"

The good doctor shrugged. "As good as any young person is who has just made one of their first grown-up calls."

"Oh."

"She's the first of you seventy-two to choose to end her pregnancy."

"Is there anything I should know?" Kris said.

"No. No, there was no command influence involved. I would have had your Nelly drag you out of any meeting if I thought there was. It's the usual story. A relationship went sour. She asked to be reassigned off the *Fury* and arranged the exchange herself. She's a very capable young woman. She's just learning a lot of lessons harder than she should have had to."

Kris nodded. Jack made her decision easy. This could have been a whole lot worse.

"Oh, I have a question," Kris said, remembering. "I was talking to a friend, and he mentioned that his wife used a mechanical womb, what do you call them?"

"Uterine replicators," the doctor provided. "I take it Admiral Yi's bad-mouthing his wife hit too close to a mark."

"I'm not sure. It would be nice, if it is not too late, to move baby into one of them. I imagine Granny Rita would love to babysit one."

"It was too late a year ago," the doctor said flatly.

"Huh?"

"When the fleet sailed from human space, we didn't carry any of them. You young women were all on implants, remember?"

"Right, and I don't know that I would have authorized it if someone had asked to have her implants removed."

"None have. These women know where their duty lies."

"Yes," Kris agreed. "Have you found anything out about that?"

"Yes, but in a minute. Let's finish this thought. Nelly, could you make a uterine replicator out of Smart Metal?"

"I have the specifications," Nelly said. "It shouldn't be too hard to spin one out," came across far too vague for Kris's likes.

"Nelly, you don't sound too sure of yourself," Kris said.

"It's not the machine itself. Making one is duck soup. It's the supplies."

"The consumables," Doc Meade put in. "Proteins, enzymes, specially manufactured hormones. Things that you're knocking together in that miracle of a body you were issued at birth, Kris, and that you've spent the last fifteen years since puberty practicing how to make."

Kris nodded, suspecting she knew what would come next, but still she said, "Nelly, if I made your number one priority making them, how long would it take you to produce these 'consumables'?"

"Kris," came out actually sounding pained. "I'd have to make stuff to make stuff to make stuff, and that assumes I could find the basic feedstock on Alwa. There's no bet that I could. If I got lucky, I'd say we could have some ready in six to eight months."

"Just in time for me to pat your little darling on her rump and see how big a yelp she'd give me," Doc Meade said.

"Is it going to be a girl?" Jack asked.

"Don't know yet," Doc Meade said, "but I figure a gal has a right to hope for a cute little girl until science proves otherwise. You got a problem with that, General?"

"Not at all. A cute little miniature of my wife would be a great end to this journey we're on."

Kris smiled at Jack. She'd figured him to want a boy. It was great to be on this journey with him. And in the end, this little one had likely already made up his or her mind. What would be would be.

"So, this will be a body birth," Kris said with finality. "How do we make this a safe journey? Doc, do you plan to beach every one of us seventy-one?"

Dr. Meade returned Kris a puzzled look. "Your Granny Rita spent the first six months of Alnaba's gestation walking the bridge of her battlecruiser. She called to make sure I knew that."

"She knows already!" Jack said.

"I suspect she knew the night we started this bit of fun," Kris said, patting her belly.

"She told me great-grandmothers have a way of knowing," the doc said, "the old liar. Anyway, we have better ways today to harden our ships against the background radiation of space than back then. Sailors rarely get cancer. What we don't have is the ice cladding of the old battlecruisers. Two meters thick will stop a lot of high-energy heavy particles. I'm thinking of reassigning my ladies-in-waiting to two or three ships and having them given an old-fashioned ice cladding. I've already talked to Captain Drago, and he's game. He's kind of excited, what with his new reactors, new lasers and all the rest."

Kris didn't doubt that the old sea dog was delighted with the new *Wasp*. Of course, if she loaded it down with several thousand tons of ice, it might wallow a bit, but it wouldn't likely be any worse than the recent *Wasp* with two Hellburners aboard or the older *Wasp* expanded to handle containers for five hundred Marines and scientists.

"We'll tackle that problem tomorrow," Kris said. "Now, what about the guy who put the bum implants in my arm?"

"As I told you," Doc Meade said, "I'm old-fashioned. It just seems to me that a woman should have a woman installing her birth-control implants. It avoids some male coming up with bad jokes at moments like those."

"A guy wouldn't do that," Jack said.

"You'd be amazed at some of the off-colored jokes I've heard," the doc answered back.

Jack retreated into silence.

"Well, whether I'm sexist or not," the doc continued, "my

policy seems to have given us a clear red light where you're concerned. That and the logistics of how this all is possible. Rudo, come in here for a moment, will you?"

A young woman nurse came in. Her white nursing togs were striking against her ebony skin. Kris hadn't met many people who still showed such strong evidence of roots to Earth's old Africa.

"Tell this nice future mother what you found out about the other misused implants."

"Yes, Doctor. Good afternoon, Admiral," she said, giving Kris her full Navy due even if the doc was reluctant to. "This is one of the packets the birth-control implants come in," she said, holding up a clear plastic container. Kris could distinctly see the three strips inside.

"The packet has a number on it that matches the number on the first strip. Each of the three strips has its own number, in sequence, from the first to the last, although sometimes the loading process back at the factory gets the strips out of order. Still, they're supposed to be one, two, three, or nine, zero, one. You get the idea?"

Kris nodded.

The woman sighed. "Good practice requires that the nurse check each strip to make sure the numbers match."

Rudo paused for a moment. "I'm sad to report that good practices have not been followed. Nurses always check the first one. Many check the second strip. When questioned over the last few days, everyone I talked to admitted to not bothering to check the third one. It didn't seem like a problem," came out with a bitter twist.

"Every one of the pregnant women presented with two effective strips and a third that had been issued three years ago, removed and, somehow made its way back into a new-issue packet."

"Someone knew about the actual practice and took advantage of it," Kris said.

"Yep. But that someone also had to have access to the expended ones on their way to disposal as well as the new packets. He'd need to check the packets out, take them to someplace safe and carefully remove the third strip, replace it, and reseal the packet so that no one would notice it had been tampered with," Doc Meade said, temper growing with each word.

"I'm guessing there aren't many men who meet that requirement," Kris said. "I'm also guessing that he wasn't really risking much when he took the chance of installing my implants."

Doc Meade's scowl was dark. "We could have caught him. We didn't."

"That's water under the bridge," Kris said. "However, has everyone who got shortchanged on her newly issued implants gotten pregnant?"

"No. We're running every woman who got new implants through sick bay. It seems that over half of those with one bum implant have not gotten pregnant. It was just the luck of the draw it seems."

"But not for me."

"No. He made sure that you were totally unprotected."

"You're seeing that those women get effective implants." The doctor nodded. "Good. I've taken care of my responsibilities as the fleet's admiral. Now, *I* want to meet this man. Do you have him in custody?"

"The Marines have him in a lockdown on the station," the doc said. "Chief Warrant Officer Mugeridge serves in the Naval Supply Corp. He was trained as a nurse but went into supply when his knees went out and he couldn't stand eight straight. We thought we were being nice to him. By the way, he came out on the *Constellation* with Lieutenant Commander Sampson. They go way back. He paid her quite a few visits while she was recuperating from that brain surgery. Right about the time he was hatching this plan."

Kris groaned. "I should have sent the *Conny* back with the king. Her skipper has been just one problem after another, and now this."

"No good deed goes unpunished," Jack drawled.

"Good deeds had nothing to do with it," Kris said. "I lusted for another ship with 20-inch lasers. It seemed like a good idea at the time."

"Shall we go stationside and see what this bastard has to say for himself?" Jack asked.

"Hell, yes," Kris said, then rethought herself. "Will there

be a court-martial? Do I need to avoid any appearance of command intervention?"

Doc Meade shrugged. "I was planning one, but it doesn't have to come to that. I could just terminate his warrant and send him dirtside. I suspect he'd have a hard time finding a job down there. Most likely, he'd end up shoveling bird guano in the mines right beside his good friend Sampson. We could do it with a court-martial or the other way. Either way, he ends up the same place."

"Fill out the paperwork to terminate his warrant," Kris snapped. "Jack, let's go talk to this ass."

20

Kris and Jack were quick marching for the detention center on Cannopus Station when they came to a roaring halt.

"Hi, honey child. When you going to bring that baby to see Granny?"

At "honey child," Kris froze. *Nobody* talked to her like that. Fortunately, "granny" got added before Kris exploded.

"Granny Rita?" Kris said, turning to see her great-grandmother hurrying to catch up with her. "What are you doing on my station?" Kris would tackle that life-and-death issue before she tried to get a handle on this sudden twist in Granny Rita's attitude toward her Viceroy.

"I caught one of your shuttles," the old lady said, beaming proudly.

"Didn't I tell you that you were grounded? No shuttle-assisted suicide," Kris pointed out, all the time noting that granny looked rather well.

"You didn't actually send me for a flight physical, so I am not officially carried in the log as grounded"—the old gal grinned even wider—"and I am not anywhere near to dead, just in case you haven't noticed."

"You are looking surprisingly well," Jack said. "Last time you were fresh out of a shuttle, there was a distinct green to your gills."

"I don't have gills. I'm not an Iteeche," the old Iteeche fighter snapped. "That rejuvenation clinic dirtside has been doing wonders for us old codgers. I suspect I'll be ready to fly my own shuttle up here about the time that baby makes her bawling appearance. Maybe change the first diaper myself."

"Nelly, see that Granny's authorization to operate shuttles is canceled and logged."

"Krr-i-sss," sounded like Nelly really was pained, caught in the bite of the line between two Longknifes.

"Jack, you log the change and see to it that one of your sergeants walks the change through the system."

"Yes, my love," made it clear that it was the husband obeying, not the Marine major general.

"Oh, bother," Kris snapped. "Granny, promise me and my baby that you will not try honking a shuttle around in space, no matter how frisky you feel after a rejuvenation session."

"For that great-great-grandkid of mine, I'll promise. Not for you, miss prissy pants, but for that little one I want to see married off to a man as fine as her dad."

"Thank you," Jack said.

"Now, where are you two off to like a herd of turtles?" Granny Rita demanded.

"To have a few choice words with the guy who sabotaged my birth-control implants," Kris said.

"While I can't complain about the results, I do have a few quibbles with a Sailor that doesn't do his job," the old commodore said through a stormy frown. "Lead on, McDuffy, and damned be he who gets in my way."

So it was that three of them charged into Cannopus Station's brig. A gunny pointed them at a door, not a word said.

Jack opened it, and two very angry ladies stormed in to face a man cuffed to a table.

Mugeridge apparently had been rousted out early that morning; he had a day's worth of stubble on his chin. He also hadn't been given a lot of time to dress; he looked to be in yesterday's uniform. His shirt was unevenly buttoned. He looked a mess, but, to Kris's minor surprise, the Marines had not used undue force.

"You," he spat. "I should have known a whore like you couldn't pass up the chance to gloat. A knocked-up whore, no less."

"Since my husband knocked me up, I don't think that word applies."

"You turned this whole fleet into one big whorehouse."

"As your friend Sampson told me every chance she got."

"It's true. Here we are out in the middle of nowhere, bug-eyed monsters all around, and you let discipline go to hell with everyone sleeping around."

Kris knew this train wreck was not going anywhere good, but she couldn't look away or keep her mouth shut.

"So you took it upon yourself to render the women of this command less than combat-ready."

"Somebody had to do something. No one will follow a knocked-up admiral. You'll have to surrender your command to someone who knows how to fight a fleet."

"In case you didn't notice, Mugeridge, my command has blown away three of those monstrous mother ships. We must have killed close to two hundred billion of them. I know very well how to command a fighting fleet."

"Whore," was his answer.

Kris had had enough, but she had a cruel streak in her. Instead of turning on her heels, she stayed to tell him his fate. "Warrant, your services are no longer required by this fleet. Effective immediately, you are out of a job. Sergeant."

Kris didn't have to raise her voice. Gunny had followed her into the confinement cell although she had kept well out of the way.

"Ma'am."

"See that this man is on the next shuttle down. You will remove his manacles when he is dirtside and send him on his way."

"Yes, Admiral Longknife."

Mugeridge blinked several times, not following where this was leading.

"Dirtside, if you don't work, you don't eat. Good luck finding a job," Kris said, knowing her smile was pure evil.

"You ain't gonna have no such luck in my town, sonny boy," Granny Rita put in.

"What do you mean?" the former Navy warrant got out, real fear finally replacing the smug gloat he'd had for his pregnant admiral since she stormed in.

"What I mean is that no farmer has a job for you," Granny Rita snapped. "No Alwan will have one for you, either, not when the word gets out what you did here, asshole. Your next meal will be a long time coming."

He swallowed hard, dawn coming up like thunder. "You can't let me starve."

"I would," Granny said. "I've let bad apples like you starve in my day, but my kid here is too kindhearted. No, she's got a job for you."

"A job?" didn't sound too happy.

"Yep," Kris said. "Right beside your old buddy Sampson, shoveling bird shit."

"You can't do that to me."

"I can and already have," Kris said. "Gunny, this man is yours to transport."

"Yes, ma'am," she said.

Then Mugeridge lost it. The stream of invectives and downright nasty words started low and got louder by the second.

"Shut your mouth before I shut it for you," Gunny growled.

He kept right on going, now screaming. His language ended with a whoof as Gunny buried her fist in his stomach just about the time Jack closed the door behind Kris and Granny Rita.

"I hope that kid just keeps making it harder on himself. I surely do," Rita said through tight lips.

"He hasn't shown much good sense so far," Kris agreed. They took the elevator down and stepped out onto a crowded A Deck.

"Hey, I told you I seen that Princess Longknife. There she is."

Kris found herself facing a crowd, growing by the second, as there were more shouts of "There she is!" and "She's got to listen to us."

21

NELLY.

JACK'S ALREADY ORDERED OUT THE GUARD.

A man stepped well into Kris's comfort zone, and shouted, "You got to listen to us. Even a Longknife can't ignore us."

Jack made to shove him back, but Kris rested a restraining hand on her husband's arm. This crowd looked ugly. Anything might set it off.

Granny Rita, however, was an elbow of a different gender. The old lady stepped forward, rested a hand on the man's shoulder, and just kept on walking.

So the guy took two paces back, giving Kris some breathing room.

"What do you want to talk to me about?" she said, in her most reasonable voice.

"You got some ships headed back to Wardhaven."

"I don't usually comment on operational security," Kris said, still reasonable.

"We know you do," a woman shouted. "It's all over the station. A whole fleet's going back, and not one of us working stiffs got a billet on one."

"I don't know where you heard that rumor. We've got three fleets now and every ship in them is staying right here," Kris said truthfully. The *Endeavor* and the *Hornet* weren't assigned to any fleet.

"Maybe it ain't a fleet, but you got ships going," another man put in.

Kris had taken the time to check out the crowd. There wasn't a Sailor among them. Likely not a yard hand. They were merchant sailors and production workers. Many wore shirts with the insignias of one of the six big corporations that were doing the heavy industrial lifting here.

None had been given a decent briefing about what they were headed into. Not until they ended up in Kris's lap, and she let them in on the secret that they had signed up for ten, fifteen, maybe twenty years on the tip of a spear that might be busted any moment now by a horde of bloodthirsty aliens.

Nope, they weren't happy to start with, and the only thing that had keep them from downing tools and striking was the knowledge that they were all, from Kris Longknife down to the least of them, in the same boat.

Now they'd heard that the case might be different for some, and the herd was angry.

Kris pitched her voice to carry. "I am ordering two ships back to human space."

"Yeah," "I told you so," and "Son of a bitch," seemed to be the general reply.

"They are carrying some of the alien people that we have found as well as scientists that I have ordered home to share the results of their study of the aliens and the unique assets of the Alwa system. I am ordering them home with the expectation that they will build a fire under the folks back there to get more stuff out here."

"Fat chance," along with other nastier responses met that.

"The skipper of both ships intend to bring their ships and most of their crew back here. One skipper even wants to bring his wife and kid."

"No way," was the most repeatable response to that.

"I want on that ship," growled the guy who'd first gotten in Kris's face.

"Only those I order go on those two ships, and I'm not ordering you to go."

"You better," was backed up by a balled fist in Kris's face.

Jack moved forward to involve himself, but someone got there first.

"Way, way," an Ostrich shouted as he forced his way to the front of the crowd. As soon as he got there, he bumped chest with the human, knocking him back into those behind him.

"No way. No way," he crowed, and was joined by a female

of his kind. They were bigger and meaner than their mates. She raised a knee menacingly.

Humans had seen those legs kick the head off their prey. The crowd backed up.

Now a pair of Roosters were making their way through the crowd. They were young, the male still had his mating plumage, and the smaller female would not normally have risked herself in a crowded public situation, but she was right behind her male.

"Go way. Go way," the Rooster crowed. "He one ah uh," he said, failing to get the human S sound past his beak. Still, he flapped his vestigial wings, putting on quite a display. From the way the female was dunking her head, she was quite impressed.

The elevator door opened behind Kris, and a dozen Marines deployed in front of their admiral.

The crowd backed up quite a bit after taking one look at their M-6s with sheathed bayonets.

"Gunny, have your crew take a knee," Kris said. Gunny, after giving her one of those glances NCOs give particularly stupid officers, obeyed.

Once the Marines had their weapons pointed toward the deck and were on one knee, Kris shouted, "Now listen to me, all of you. You and the Navy are doing a great job of protecting this planet, and your own lives. I don't know if you heard, but we just got back from kicking some serious alien butt. Those nutcases who have been trying to crash into us or the planet below won't be coming anymore. They're dead. All fifty billion of them. Give or take a few million."

That dry addition got a chuckle out of the crowd.

"Every time they come up against us, we knock them down. We do it with the gear and material you're building here and the reinforcements we're getting from human space."

Kris paused to let that sink in.

"So far, we haven't made any report back. Now I've got a couple of dozen aliens to show them, especially that old coot. I'm sending a ship back with a report on how we're doing. I wasn't kidding you when I said that both ships will be coming back with most of their crews and maybe a few womenfolk."

"No accounting for sense," a woman muttered loud enough for everyone to hear. And laugh at.

"The fleet is staying here. I am staying here," Kris said.

"And I'm stuck here," a guy added.

Now there was a real laugh.

"Sorry, folks. That's the way it is. Besides, now that we know those bastards are prowling around the galaxy, you got to admit, no place is really safer than another."

"And that place has my old lady, so maybe this isn't so bad," got a good laugh.

The crowd began to break up. One woman stayed where she stood. "Is it true you're pregger, Admiral?"

Kris made a face. Were there no secrets around this place? "Yeah. Someone messed with my new birth-control implants. They didn't work. My husband was kind enough to knock me up before we discovered the sabotage."

"Bummer," the woman shouted, as most of the men laughed.

"Let's get you out of here," Jack said.

"But not too far," Granny Rita added.

"Why?" they both said.

"Because I've wrangled you an invitation to talk to the Assembly of Assemblies tomorrow."

"I can't be talking to those birds tomorrow," Kris said, as they walked, under close escort, to *Wasp*'s dock. The Marines stayed alert, but there were no more problems. No doubt people weren't happy, but at least they had the truth and knew the same rules applied to them all.

"The flock of flocks," Granny Rita said, "has been changing a bit. Some of the back-home assemblies have been seeing some rather spectacular shows."

The Roosters among the Alwans did not fight. Instead, they put on wild displays of plumage and arm waving. Whoever put on the best show intimidated the others into surrendering.

"Feathers are really flying. Anyway, a lot of the old birds have withdrawn, and the latest Assembly has a lot of newer, younger birds. I told them you'd just kicked some alien butt, and they want you to show them how you managed it and talk to you about what they can do to get more of those nice things they like. Oh, and help your defenders as well."

"I guess I know where I'll be tomorrow," Kris said, surrendering to her granny.

"And if you can stay down for the night, I know just the place to put you up," Granny Rita said, only a slight leer in her smile.

"Joe's Seaside Paradise," Kris and Jack said in unison.

"You bet."

"Okay, Granny, you win. One night and a bit of lying in the sun won't hurt this girl at all," Kris said. "But I have to be back in time to wish Godspeed to the ships I'm sending back to human space."

"I'll make sure you are," Granny said.

Was there something more there? Kris thought, but Nelly interrupted.

"Kris, Admiral Kitano and your fleet commanders would like to come over for a quick staff meeting. Tomorrow's likely to be busy. Do you have one more meeting left in you?"

"I guess I do," Kris admitted.

"Well, I'll go find a place to lay these old bones down," Granny Rita said as they came to *Wasp*'s brow.

"You can lay them down in a room on board," Kris said, tugging her granny's elbow to drag her aboard.

A few minutes later, the JOOD was taking Granny off to a spare stateroom, and Kris was heading for her own quarters.

Surprise of surprise, her admirals were already there.

"What took you so long?" Admiral Kitano said. "It couldn't have taken all that long to keelhaul the bastard."

"I didn't keelhaul him," Kris said, innocently. "I let him go."

"No!" came in shock from four admirals.

"To shovel bird shit."

"That still sounds too good for him," Kitano said.

"You can ask him in a month. From the paunch on him, he hasn't done an honest day's work in a while."

"Oh," seemed to settle that.

"So, did you come here to see if I was wearing his guts for garters, or is this a real meeting?"

"A real meeting," Kitano said. "You know that *Wasp*, *Hornet*, and *Endeavor* are going out tomorrow."

"Yes," Kris said.

"I'm keeping the First and Third Fleets back to mend and make whole. The yard will take in the worst cases. I know that you likely want Admiral Miyoshi to stay close to ride herd on Yi as necessary."

"Yes. I know you're good, Betsy," Kris said, eyeing her newest fleet commander, "but staring down the man who was your boss last week can get bad in a hurry, for both of you."

"I understand," Betsy said. "It's as much to keep him out of troubled waters as it is to keep me from taking his head off, without proper authorization."

"God forbid we do anything without proper authorization," Kris agreed, dryly.

"Moving right along," Kitano said, "I want to get a fleet of ships out to our friendly, neighborhood ice giant to collect reaction mass. I hear we'll be wrapping a few ships in ice for our not so icy maidens."

"You know, saying such things around your boss could get you in trouble, her being mentally unbalanced due to a physical impairment," Kris said, smiling toothily at Kitano.

"What can my boss do to me that's worse? She's stuck me with this job."

"I see your point," Kris had to agree. "So, who has the water detail?"

"I'm sending Betsy. I know you've transferred the Task Force 4 to the Third Fleet, but it didn't get banged up in the last fight. BatRon 3 and 1, now that the *Constellation*, *Congress*, *Royal*, *Bulwark*, *Resistance*, *Wasp*, and *Intrepid* are out of the yard, would make for a full fleet."

"Obviously, *Wasp* will be otherwise involved tomorrow," Kris said, "but Betsy, you can have the rest."

Kris looked around the table and saw only happy faces. "If we're done, I'm about dead on my feet." The other admirals stood and headed for the door. Jack looked ready to order in a crane to haul her to bed.

"Kris," Nelly said. "I've got a request for one more meeting."

"Who dares risk my wrath? Or exhaustion. Exhausted wrath."

"Abby says that Pipra, Jacques, and Amanda need to talk to you. All four."

Kris let out a sigh. "They know where I live."

"They're outside the door, dodging admirals."

"Bring them in."

"I understand you got hit by a flash mob of unhappy workers," Pipra said as soon as she was in the door.

"Hello. Come right in. How's your day been? Had anything interesting happen to you?" Kris said, not making it sound at all jolly.

"Folks, I think she's warning you that she ain't happy, and we better make this fast," Abby said.

"But I'm trying to make it fast," Pipra said.

"Yes," Kris said, in full tired, "I got mobbed by some workers who'd heard a whole fleet of ships were leaving them here while they got to go home. Idle rumors seem to know no limits."

"That's what happens when you let rumors be the only information people get," Jacques put in. "It's human nature."

"And I got a lot of human nature telling me it's past my bedtime," Kris said.

"So you set them straight," Pipra said. "Those two ships leaving aren't a secret anymore."

"If they ever were," Kris agreed.

"Would you please make an address to, how do you Navy types say it, all hands, telling everyone what you told those few?"

"In God's name why, Pipra, and does it have to be right now?"

"Yes, it does," Abby said. "There're all kinds of different versions making the rounds of what you said, only one or two of them even slightly related to what I think you actually did. You either get the real skinny out now, or you may not have a production force to wake up to tomorrow. Hell, I don't know, even some Marines are wondering what's happening for real."

Kris closed her eyes. After two deep breaths, she stared at the corner where her overhead included an emergency security camera. "Nelly, can you focus that thing on me without showing too many of my worry lines?"

"I have it filtered very nicely."

And Kris gave the closest thing she could to a decent repeat of what she'd told the threatening mob. It didn't sound nearly as nice without the asides the workers provided.

Kris finished with a smile.

"There. Does that do it?"

"Good enough considering you're a Longknife," Pipra said, and stood. "Let's get out of here, folks. I've see volcanos less urgent to blow."

"Good," Kris said, as the four fled her presence.

"Nelly, do I have another meeting?"

"No, Kris."

"Jack, could you please carry me to bed."

Her husband swooped her up in his arms and carried her off to bed. Sadly, she was asleep before he got her shoes off, much less her panties.

23

Kris came awake slowly the next morning. She was still in the bra and panties from the previous day. She took a deep breath and enjoyed the thought of having nothing immediate to do.

Oops, she needed to get off *Wasp* before it sailed and down to another meeting, this time with the birds.

After reviewing her To Do list, Kris found that she just could not engage her motivator, not if it involved getting out of bed and waiting to upchuck her breakfast.

"You awake?" Jack asked.

"Who wants to know?"

"Give me a second." In a moment, Jack appeared around her side of the bed with a small plate of crackers and a glass of milk.

"Where'd you get those?" Kris said, reaching tentatively for a cracker. Somewhere she'd heard something about crackers, but maternity was an unknown land around the girls she'd known since high school.

Sex. They knew plenty about that. Or at least claimed to. What occasionally happened next? Not so much.

"I remembered my dad bringing mom crackers and milk during her last pregnancy. So I had Sal do some research."

"We all helped," Nelly put in.

"What don't you know? Crackers and milk before you get out of bed helps keep morning sickness at bay. That and getting up slowly, just like you're doing today."

Jack grinned at her. She gave him a death's-head grin back.

"Oh, and ginger cookies help, too. Word is Cookie will bake you up a batch for tomorrow morning. Granny Rita sent him a request for you."

"And all the other pregnant women, I hope," Kris said. It was nice to have Jack and be adopted as *Wasp*'s pregnant-admiral mascot, but all the other gals deserved a helping hand, too.

They couldn't have Jack, but anything less was open for discussion.

"You decent in there?" came in Abby's anything but dulcet tones.

The door opened before they could make a reply and in walked Abby with something smelling of heaven on Earth.

"What is that?" Kris cried through joy as her tummy rolled over and purred.

"Cookie's patent-pending ginger cookies," Abby announced.

Jack grabbed for the blanket. He was in yesterday's undershorts.

Abby waltzed over to within reach of Kris. Like a four-year-old, Kris grabbed one for each hand before taking a bite out of one. Her tummy purred and purred.

"Leave the plate, Abby," Jack said, "and leave. I am not decent."

"Maid rules," Abby said, giving Jack a good leer.

"Leave, Abby," Kris said, and reached for the glass of milk Jack was holding in the same hand as the blanket.

"Hey, this is nice and chilled. How'd you manage that, Jack?"

"Nelly installed a small refrigerator last night."

"Just the right size for a glass of milk," her computer told Kris.

"More things we have to share with all the mommies-to-be," Kris said.

"We can talk about this at the next staff meeting," Jack said. "Now shoo, Abby."

Abby shooed herself, with many an enthusiastic backward glance, and Jack waited while Kris finished her four ginger cookies.

"I can't believe I'm saying this, but when's breakfast?"

"You want it before or after we shuttle down to the surface?"

"Oh, decisions," Kris said. "How about I decide while we take a shower. While you and Sal were doing all this research about the care and feeding of a pregnant wife, did you come across anything about sex?"

"I'll tell you all about it in the shower. Remember, the *Wasp* is sailing early, and your Granny Rita arranged for an early meeting with the birds, so if you have any complaints, you can file them with anyone but me."

"Hmm," Kris said, and eagerly followed Jack to the shower. *After all, once I'm pregger, I can't get any more pregnant.*

24

The Assemblies of Assemblies was held in the same plaza, but Granny Rita was right, the plumage of the elders was a whole lot younger. There was actually a leader of the assembly, for the first time in years, and he called them to order on time.

Human time. A clock had been added to the plaza. Several of the birds had watches of their own.

The elders listened as Kris walked them through this battle. She did her best to avoid highlighting any of the places where her battle went sideways. The Alwans didn't seem to have a problem with Admiral Yi's charging the alien line. That was what hunters did to their prey.

That some of the hunters paid for the charge didn't draw a second glance.

Kris hoped these birds fit nicely into reactor watches or laser battery positions. With this kind of attitude, it would be a long time before she let one on the command deck of a ship

The briefing was just ending when Pipra joined them. As soon as she did, the leader thanked Kris for her report, and the discussion took a hard turn, straight to production and the rewards for participating in it.

Kris sat ignored as Pipra went over what they'd talked about the previous day. In the end, Pipra put their production plans for the next six months to a vote, and the Alwans gave it a resounding "Aye."

"So that's why you wanted to see me yesterday."

"Yep, I didn't want to suggest anything to these, ah, folks, without your approval," Kris's private-sector subordinate grinned. "Ain't it great when a plan comes together?"

"Ain't it nice when we know enough to have a plan?" Kris shot back.

"Yes to all."

As the meeting broke up, several Alwans came by to compliment Kris on her egg and how good it looked. Since she had no egg for them to look at, she accepted their praise with an appropriately metaphorical smile.

Soon enough, she and Jack were in one of the new electric cars, headed for Joe's. The car cut the drive time in half, getting them to their cottage soon enough to enjoy fish sandwiches before a stroll to the beach.

The excuse of lying in the warm sun allowed them to shed their uniforms and every other stitch of clothing.

They were otherwise occupied when the dinner bell rang, but they managed to get in a quick shower. Kris settled for one of Jack's lavalavas covering her from breasts to well above the knee. Jack wore his lavalava lower.

They got to the restaurant before the "total nudity not allowed" brigade to find that their usual table had been reserved.

And expanded into something that could seat six couples and have room left over for Kris and Jack. At least Kris assumed they were couples.

Each of the young women seated in the six chairs to the right and left of the empty seat at the head of the table were pregnant, from ready to pop to just starting to show a bit maybe (so don't risk asking).

Six guys were seated to the left and right of the empty chair at the foot.

"Hi, cuz," one gal shouted cheerfully at Kris. "We saved you a seat," and pointed at the vacancy at the head.

"You might as well settle down here with us, you poor bastard," one of the guys said with a big grin, and pointed to Jack's empty place.

With a shrug for Jack, Kris went where she was pointed.

"In case you haven't figured it out, this is all Granny Rita's idea," one moderately pregnant gal in a minimum bikini bottom said. Most were in the skimpy bottoms, except for one in a muumuu and the youngest-looking one in shorts. Whatever their bottoms bared, their tops were supported with solid bras.

"Granny figured you didn't want her telling you about anything," the youngest girl piped in.

"So we got delegated the job of letting you in on a few secrets about what lies ahead," put the older woman who looked ready to pop. "And since this is my fourth and Alanda's first"—the youngest one, hardly pregnant, blushed to be pointed out—"we figured we might have a pretty good idea of what you'd want to know and actually know it."

"And we're here to tell Jack that his job is to listen a lot," the older of the guys said.

"And give good foot massages," two of the older women put in, to which two of the older men gave long-suffering nods of agreement.

Kris took her seat at the head of the table but held up a hand to postpone further chatter. "I do have one question of my own before you start answering questions I don't even know to ask," she said into the silence. Well, near silence, the youngest gal seemed to have a case of the giggles at the idea of being asked a question by the famous, or infamous, Kris Longknife, battle admiral et al.

"And what might that be?" one of her older cousins asked.

"How did I get demoted to 'honey child'? Am I going to have to put up with that kind of stuff for nine months from Granny Rita?" Kris asked.

"Yep," "Pretty much," and "Get used to it," answered the question. "Even I," one of the older women said, "get 'demoted' every time I get pregnant to girl-child so-called endearments for the whole nine months."

"Does she baby talk the kid?" Kris asked.

"No, she treats the newborn tiny ones just like they're uniform tall," the other older cousin said. "I don't get it either: baby talk to us moms, but straight talk for the toothless young'uns."

Kris shrugged. "So I better get used to being everyone else's Viceroy but Granny Rita's honey child."

"Or baby cheeks,"

"Or worse," the youngest tossed in. "Suddenly, I'm honey bear pumpkin. What's a pumpkin?"

The look on the young woman's face was such a delight

that everyone laughed, even her, after a perfectly timed pause.

With that, Kris began to get from five of Granny Rita's great-great-granddaughters and one great-great-great-granddaughter, Alanda, the straight dope on impending motherhood. As soon as Alanda got her own question in.

"You look awful young to be just a great-granddaughter," Alanda gushed. "My great-granny is a great-granddaughter of the commodore."

"When you've got a filled-up world, Alanda," one of the gals on her fourth birth pointed out, "people are a lot slower to have kids. We're lucky."

Kris allowed that Alanda was lucky while doubting Mother would agree.

What Kris discovered over the next two hours was . . . confusing. Take morning sickness. Please. Just take it somewhere far away from Kris.

"I'm on my fourth pregnancy. I've got four kids, and I've never been sick one morning," one said.

"Thank your lucky stars, Belinda. I was sick every day for nine months with my first. At least this second one is letting me have some decent mornings since I started my third trimester."

Granny Rita might have intended to help Kris, but the conclusion she arrived at as dessert was served was that every pregnancy was a voyage of discovery for mom and tadpole. What would come, would come, and you just better enjoy the ride.

That was what Kris shared with Jack as she lay in his arms much later.

"That was what the guys basically told me, too. Stay close. Don't get scared by it all and run away, and most of all, love you no matter what kind of mood you're in."

"Mood I'm in, huh?"

"Their words, not mine," Jack assured her, hand held up in surrender.

Kris sighed. "I don't want to agree that Admiral Yi can be right about the time of day, must less about the moodiness of pregnant women, but Jack, I may need your help if I start to, ah, I don't know. Let my hormones affect my command decisions."

"That's a mighty tall order," Jack said.

"I know. I'm asking you to tell me when I'm around the bend and don't realize it. Right?"

"It sounds that way to me."

"Well, try to help me on that, will you?"

"I'll try."

"Then kiss me, and hug me, and let's see if we can go to sleep or someplace else again."

"Hmm," Jack said as he kissed her.

25

"**Are** you awake, dear?" from Jack woke Kris next morning.

Without opening her eyes, she took stock of her situation. She was snuggled warmly under a thin blanket, but she could feel a cool morning breeze playing on her face. What she couldn't feel was Jack in bed beside her.

She checked her tummy. It was unhappy but not yet in full revolt.

"Do I have to wake up?" Kris asked.

"No, but the milk might get warm. Nelly can't make a refrigerator out of the wood of this bungalow."

Kris risked opening one eye. Jack was standing across the bed from her, a tall glass of milk in one hand and one of her favorite sticky buns in the other.

"I might be willing to face the morning," Kris admitted, risking reaching for the milk. She took several swallows; her tummy seemed more content with its fate. Jack broke off a bit of roll and handed it across to her. She tasted it.

"This is different."

"What with a herd of future moms here, the cook made up a batch of buns with less refined flour and more natural folic acid."

"You mean the cook has nice buns in the oven, huh," Nelly said.

"Bad joke, Nelly," Kris said.

"But a good one," Jack added.

"Bad enough to be good," Nelly observed. "No wonder you humans go crazy so easily. You live halfway there already."

"Another good one," Jack said.

"Don't push me," Kris grumbled, but was starting to feel

more human. Jack handed her more bits of her breakfast, and she washed each bite down with more milk.

"You don't look green," Jack said, hopefully.

"I don't feel all top o' the morning either," Kris mumbled back.

"I'll get you another bun," Jack said. The one he returned with was less sticky but had nuts and raisins on it. Kris allowed that he was earning extra husband points for remembering what breakfast buns she liked. He allowed that he hoped to be rewarded for it in the not-so-distant future.

"I wouldn't bet money on that," Kris said, but found herself almost smiling. She did feel nearly human.

Kid, you better have a lot of nice smiles for your mommy. I'm putting up with a lot while you're my involuntary passenger. But Kris found herself smiling as she thought it.

Jack invited Kris to the beach. He collected several towels and other gear. Kris found all she had to do was carry herself. Herself and the sunny-side ups on her chest that were suddenly painful.

Kris found a bra and put it on. It seemed ridiculous to walk around wearing only a bra, so she scrounged up a string bottom and added it to her ensemble.

At the water's edge, she found Jack laid out on a towel, another one spread out beside him. He glanced up.

"Yes, I know I'm overdressed. But suddenly I've got two very touchy girls. Don't even look at them too hard. They hurt."

"The guys warned me that the view might be great but it could be 'look but don't touch' at times."

"Today's one of them," Kris said as she settled on the towel beside him.

The sun was barely up. The morning mist was cool. Kris closed her eyes and listened to the lapping of the water, the calls of the birds.

"On mornings like this, it's hard to believe that anyone would want to destroy it all."

"Fear can do that to people."

"Yes," Kris sighed.

For a long time, she just lay there, enjoying being alive.

"Do you feel like you're going to be a daddy?" she finally said to break the silence.

"Why? Aren't you feeling like you're going to be a mommy?"

Kris winced. "Every morning I can't help but feel all mommy-to-be. No, that's not right. Every morning, I feel sick. Like I ate something I wish I hadn't. That is not the same as feeling in my bones that I'll be the mother of some cute new life eight months from now. Different thing entirely."

"Yes," Jack said.

Water lapped their feet. Somewhere, a bird skimmed the water and splashed as it caught a fish. Kris listened to the flapping of its wings as it climbed up. She opened her eyes in time to see it settle on a treetop nest, call its delight, and begin feasting on its catch.

Kris blinked as the thought took her. She'd just watched something die so that something else could live. Even here, in her private paradise, there was death.

Death so that life could continue.

Different from death so that senseless fears could be placated.

She shook herself; she didn't want to think about that today.

Jack reached across to take her hand. "Something wrong?"

"No. Yes. I don't know," Kris said in rapid succession. She sighed and began again. "I want to think about what it means to have this surprise on board. What it means for you and me. Instead, I see a bird catch a fish, and I'm thinking about bug-eyed monsters who want to kill everything."

Jack nodded but said nothing. For a long time, Kris listened to the ocean, trying not to think that something as eternal as the sea might be emptied into space to satisfy some ancient fear. The sun warmed her. The birds continued their song.

Kris held on to the moment with her fingernails and willed everything else to go away.

She heard Jack moving beside her but did not open her eyes. He began to massage her right foot.

"I'll give you thirty minutes to stop that," Kris said.

"Forty-five," Jack countered.

Kris smiled. "I don't think you've grasped the concept of negotiations, love."

"I think your concept of 'stop' needs some analysis," came right back at her, but with too much of a laugh in it to be called snappish.

"Oh"— Kris sighed—"just keep that up."

"Most definitely."

Kris luxuriated in a human's touch. Jack's touch. Her husband's touch. The father of her child's touch. Deep breaths came in and deep sighs went out in time with his gentle rubbing of her feet, playful strokes up her ankles.

"Will I be a good mother?" Kris found herself asking. Not sure who she was asking even as the words came out.

Jack seemed to mull the question over for a bit. Not too long. Not too short. "Are you a good naval officer?"

"I like to think I am. I try."

"Are you a good fighting captain?"

"The king seems to think so."

"I'd say several billion aliens are dead proof of that," Jack quipped.

"You have a point. You do have a point," she said, suggestively.

"You don't get that until I get a few answers," Jack tried to make it sound like a grumble, but there was way too much smile behind it.

"But I asked the first question. What do you mean, you want answers?" Kris said.

"You give me my answers, then I'll give you yours. Fair trade."

"It seems out of step. Ooh, right there, do it some more," Kris said, losing any thoughts to the feel of Jack's strong hands working the kinks out of her feet.

"Can you think of anything that you've set your mind to that you've been bad at?" Jack said, but his hands went back to the arch of her left foot and did that thing he did.

"I got relieved of my first command," Kris pointed out.

"You know as well as I that the whole screwup was a political move against your dad. And you went right back, took command of the whole shebang, and blew away six battleships with a splinter fleet."

"And got a lot of people killed," Kris added.

"And saved a planet," Jack insisted on pointing out.

"Okay, I can't think of anything that I really have done poorly," Kris admitted. "Even when the dice are loaded, I seem to pull a boxcar out of them."

"That's my gal," Jack said, and spent a full minute on Kris's left ankle.

"So you say I'll be a good mother if I only set my mind to it."

"No doubt in my mind."

"But what if everything else I have to do gets in the way?" Kris almost broke into a scream, the fear wanted out so badly.

"How many hats do you wear?" Jack said. "Assuming you wear anything at all."

Kris liked the sound of that, and the quick trip his fingers made up her leg to the soft flesh of her thighs.

"Hmm, I like that."

"Answer my question." Jack was counting her toes as if playing with piggies going to market.

"Okay, okay, I wear three hats. And I assume you asked because you think I can wear four just as easily."

"You've juggled three hats very nicely. Yes, I assume that you can add a fourth and do it with just as much panache. You going to tell me why I'm wrong?"

Kris found her hands involuntarily coming up to rub her eyes. "I don't know. I guess so. I want to be a good mother. Heaven knows, I've seen enough bad ones. I don't remember any that I really would want to be like."

"Gramma Trouble?" Jack said.

"All I've ever known her as was Gramma," Kris pointed out. "I guess her kids turned out okay, but they weren't in my circle of friends. And before you say Granny Rita, remember, I've never known her as mother either, and Grampa Al is not a good recommendation for her mothering skill set."

"But what about the gals we had supper with last night?"

Kris sighed. "Good point. So, are you suggesting we raise our kids on this side of the galaxy?"

"Did I hear kids? Are you carrying twins?"

"I don't know. Isn't it too early to tell? And besides, this little one is going to have a brother or sister to boss around just like Brother did me."

"No only child?"

"Yep."

"So you're already thinking of how you'll be a good mother, huh?"

"Point, set, and match. Okay, husband, and daddy, I'll do my best and you'll do your best and I'm sure we can corral several other folks on the *Wasp* to help us all do our best."

"And if not, we can send home to Wardhaven for the best nannies in the business."

"Oh Lord, should I tell Phil to bring some nannies back with him? Good God, they don't even know we're married, and we're asking for nannies."

"That's sure to get the word out."

"Speaking of out, isn't it about time for you to drop in and visit baby?" Kris cooed.

"Is the best mommy this side of the galaxy inviting me in?"

"The best mommy in the galaxy desperately wants you in."

Jack's fingers began to gently explore the soft flesh of her thighs and pass beyond. Kris felt her passion kindling into flame.

She heard the shot, a large-caliber round from the sound, just as it plowed in a few inches beyond her shoulder, showering sand in her face.

26

"What the . . ." Jack snapped, but Kris was already rolling away from the shooter's direction. In a second, she balled herself up and shot to her feet, racing for the cottage.

The second round missed, but she could feel its hot passage on her back.

She zigged away from the direction the fire seemed to be coming from, counted off the time it would take to work the bolt of one of the new hunting rifles they'd issued to both hunters and the home guard, then zagged.

Again, the shot missed.

"Damn this sand," she muttered as she zigged.

Jack was up with her now, staying on the shooter's side. Long ago, he'd sworn to take a bullet for her. Now he was putting his body between her and whoever this whack job was.

Kris zagged. Jack was a bit slow to follow her.

"Damn," he muttered,

"Damn why?" Kris said, again zigging.

"It's just a flesh wound. Keep running. You can kiss it and make it well when we're in the cottage."

Kris didn't zag when the time came, but crouched low and kept running.

This time the bullet went over her head . . . by a couple of millimeters.

"Talk about parting your hair," Kris muttered, and slammed into the door of the bungalow.

Its latch gave way, splintering, and she and Jack were inside.

"Where's a med kit?" Kris demanded.

"There isn't one," Jack shot back. "Get down and into your spider silks," he ordered.

"You too," Kris ordered back.

"After I teach that bastard to keep down," Jack said. He had his service automatic out of the closet and went to crouch next to the nearest window. Aiming high, he snapped off four rounds as fast as he could work the trigger, then dropped and rolled over to the door.

Three quick rounds splintered the wall below the windowsill.

Jack stepped back, into the shadow behind the wide-open door, and put another four rounds downrange. Then he rolled back as two more shots answered him.

"He'll have to reload. The magazine on those .30 caliber rifles we're making only holds five rounds. But they've got stripper clips to reload fast."

Kris finished pulling on her spider-silk bodysuit. It took her only a second to retrieve her own automatic from the back of her uniform pants. Automatically, she checked her load, switching from sleepy darts to kill-you rounds without a thought.

She came up beside Jack. "I'll cover while you get in your spider silks. You're wrong, that 'graze' on your shoulder is bleeding bad."

"You'll still kiss it, won't you?" he said with one of his lopsided grins, but he said it as he went to dig body armor out of his side of the closet.

Kris grabbed Nelly from where she'd left her in a bowl, both to keep sand out of her computer and to let herself have a few uninterrupted minutes with Jack. Staying low and well back in the shadows, she moved across the room to get a look out the other window. She saw the beach with her abandoned towels, water, and beyond that, the headlands that sheltered this bit of paradise from the vicious critters in the ocean deeps.

Of a shooter, she saw nothing.

Kris plugged Nelly into her socket at the back of her head.

"Thank you, Kris, for finally remembering me. Might I inquire as to what is happening?" was pure sarcasm.

"We're being shot at," Kris snapped.

"I wondered why your heart rate was so elevated. Usually you wait for it to slow down before coming back in after making love to Jack."

"This morning never got to that point," Kris growled.

"How tacky of the shooter to interrupt you," Nelly continued in her biting vein. "I am attempting to get situational awareness."

"Wait until the bastard shoots at us again," Jack said, struggling into his tight spider silks.

"How many rounds were fired?" Nelly asked with maddening calm.

"Ten," Kris and Jack said as one.

"Then the shooter is likely out of ammunition," Nelly said.

"Out?" Jack demanded.

"Most civilian hunters are only issued two stripper clips," Nelly said. "The gun stolen last week from one hunter's home had only two clips with it. I suspect we now know where the rifle went."

"Why didn't someone tell me we had a rifle missing?" Kris demanded.

"We were kind of out of pocket and busy with other matters," Jack said, now grabbing his own Sal and putting on his skull harness. "Two more went missing last night," he added.

"I think our local problems just took a whole new turn for the worse," Kris said.

"Very likely," Nelly agreed, dryly.

Jack came up next to Kris. Both stayed in the shadows.

"Can we call for backup?" Kris asked.

"I've already got a fire team of Marines heading this way as fast as their electric cart will take them," Nelly said. "Is that okay with you, General?"

"How many trails are there off that headland?" Jack asked.

"Only one," the computer answered.

"Tell them to head for the trail. And be careful. How many rounds went missing with those other two rifles?"

"Ten rounds each."

"Thank heavens for small favors," Kris said.

"Or tight policies," Jack added.

"You safe in there?" was shouted in the voice of the resort's owner.

"Pretty much," Jack answered.

"I have a rifle, single-shot, black powder. I'm coming in, if it's okay with you two."

"Move fast, and don't point the rifle at anyone I know," Jack answered.

A moment later, Joe joined them. He ran fast and low and kept his long rifle pointed mostly at the ground.

Inside, he handed the weapon off to Jack.

"I thought I heard two kinds of shooting going on," he said, glancing at their service automatics.

"These are too short-ranged to hit much of anything that far away, but they can sure scare a first-timer who doesn't know better," Kris said.

Jack took the long rifle and edged closer to the door; his eyes squinting as he studied the tree-covered point.

"You think whoever this was isn't a hunter?"

"It's a long shot from that point," Jack said. "I'd have gotten closer, but he shot ten rounds and only grazed me."

"Oh," the proprietor said, spotting the blood dripping down Jack's back. "Let me get you our first-aid kit."

"You sure you want to risk going out there?" Kris said.

"I came in and didn't get shot at. I'm willing to try going back for some bandages." With no further discussion, he dashed out the door and was gone.

As Joe had predicted, no one shot at him.

"The Marines are at the crossroads where the road goes here or to the point. They're starting up the other road," Nelly reported.

"I think they can forget it," Kris said.

"Yeah," Jack agreed.

"Oh," Nelly said. "Is that a boat?"

"Yep," Kris said, "and it's heading across the bay for the mainland. Nelly, do we have any assets that can stop that boat?"

"Sorry, Kris. All the aircraft are out on survey work, and none of them are armed, anyway. Same for the boats. Nothing is in port or heading back in."

"Everyone is busy putting food on the table," Kris said, dryly.

"Pretty much," Nelly agreed.

"It may be time for Alwa to get a police force that is good for more than collecting drunks and breaking up domestic disturbances," Kris said. "Nelly, contact all the usual folks on Alwa, we need a meeting of the colonial establishment pronto."

Kris eyed Jack's wound. "And a doctor waiting for us just as soon as we get back into town."

"It's just a flesh wound," Jack insisted.

"I'll tell you that when I get one."

"I truly intend to never let you."

"We'll see about that."

27

The drive back was as fast as Kris could make the electric car go. Jack's "flesh wound" was bleeding through the bandage Joe had put on it.

Still, Jack did what he needed to do. The Marines reported finding the place the shooter had used. He'd policed up his brass but left an empty stripper clip. They also found where he'd tied up the boat.

Jack called up a team to find the boat. A search along the shoreline identified several small craft. None had rifles in them or showed evidence of a weapon. That left the local volunteer constabulary walking the beat looking for a colonial or Alwan toting a rifle.

They stopped four coming back into town with one of those elephant-size things towing a cart with a half dozen large hunks of dead meat. A check of their ammunition allotment and the hits in the targets showed only two rounds not accounted for.

With dead ends everywhere, Kris appealed to a higher authority. "Captain Drago."

"Yes, Your Highness?"

"I've been shot at," Kris said, without preamble.

"Well, Alwa's been a bit slow, but I see it's caught up with every other planet you've visited."

"Thank you, Captain. Could you get a longboat full of forensic investigators, US and Musashi, down here pronto? What we're facing is beyond the locals' toolkit."

"They'll be on their way. Expect them in, ah, about an hour. As luck would have it, we just passed over you a while ago."

"Just get them down here. Oh, and the best surgeon you can lay your hands on."

"Surgeon. Why?"

"Jack has a 'little flesh wound' that won't stop bleeding."

"It's not bleeding much," Jack shouted to get on net.

"He's not looking at it. I am."

"So you stopped one in the back, big fellow?"

"I was between her and the shooter," Jack answered back.

"You think this wound will need more than the local saw-bones can handle?"

"He's my Marine boss, husband, and father of my baby. I want him with a good arm when it comes to changing messy diapers."

"Most certainly, Your Highness," Kris's flag captain answered with too much of a laugh behind it. "Doc Meade has been notified and has a team moving."

That left Kris trying to get a few extra volts out of her car's batteries.

It was the longest hour of her life.

As Haven came in sight, a Marine on an electric bike was waiting for her.

"He's signaling you to follow him," Jack said, far too weakly for Kris's tastes.

She did. Haven had a hospital; she'd just never made its acquaintance. She followed the cyclist right up to the emergency room door.

Doc Meade was waiting for her. "We've got to quit meeting like this. If it's not one of you, it's the other," she said, but a young male doctor was already pulling Jack's spider silks down and examining the wound.

"Just a flesh wound," Jack insisted.

The young doctor's, "Yeah, right," didn't sound at all right to Kris.

She made to follow Jack into the emergency room, but Doc Meade intercepted her. "He's the best cutter we've got. If I stop a bullet, I want him working on me," she said, and steered Kris into the waiting room.

Kris let herself be steered but let her annoyance show. "If he's so good, why are you here?"

"Admiral, I'm here to keep you out of the operating room," the doctor said, with more than a bit of twinkle in her eyes.

"Am I that obvious?"

"Yep."

"Am I that much of a problem?"

"Oh, yes. You're the admiral, and you're a Longknife. It doesn't come any worse. Now, I see a posse coming. My guess is they're for you. Why don't you mosey along and do some admiral and Longknife stuff and let us do our doctoring stuff?"

Kris turned to follow the good doctor's glance. Granny Rita, Ada, and a small collection of colonials and Alwans were heading in from one door. From the opposite direction came Penny and Masao with Brigadier Hayakawa of the Musashi Marines and now Jack's deputy commander.

Kris sighed. "Doctor, you tend to your knitting, and I'll tend to mine."

In a moment, Kris was surrounded by a tidal wave of concerns. Half about Jack. The other half centered on the shooter.

Kris raised her arm for silence and, surprisingly, got it.

"Is there a conference room we can take over?" she asked.

"Follow me," Ada said, and everyone did. Down the main hall, up a flight of stairs, and around another turn took them to a large room decked out with training aides. Several tables accompanied by uncomfortable-looking chairs faced a blackboard.

"Form the table in a square," Kris said, and willing hands quickly made it happen.

"Choose anyplace you want," Kris said when it was done, and she found the Navy and Marines at her elbow, Ada and her people filled up two sides, and Granny Rita, Iago, and an Alwan Kris couldn't remember meeting sat with her.

"Now, for the record and my sanity, will someone let Dr. Meade know where we are so when they are done using Jack for a cross-stitch class, they can tell me. We Longknifes are known for juggling a lot, but they've got a very big part of me, and I want to know everything as soon as they know it. Okay?"

Iago bolted from the room.

"Okay," Kris said, taking over the meeting by the simple step of not sitting down when the others had. "I see three problems. Someone tried to kill me this morning and did wing

Jack. Who did it? Why? How do we catch them and bring them to justice?"

That got nods around the tables. Kris went on.

"Second, rifles are being stolen. Who's doing it? Why? How do we recover what's gone missing and how do we keep any more of our hard-won goods and gear from walking out?"

That drew grim looks.

"Lastly, I've been saying that the times, they are a changing here on Alwa. Are we now witnessing changes that we don't want? Are they out of our control? Are they taking us down a rabbit hole that we don't need to see the inside of?"

"Yeah," Granny Rita said.

"The first two are practical problems," Kris said, finishing up. "The last one represents a major difference in philosophy between us and some people. Ada, are there colonials in that possible camp, or is it just Roosters?"

"You sure it couldn't be some of your dragooned workers up topside?" Granny Rita put in. "Remember, Admiral, you've already had one mutiny from that Sampson woman, and I was there when some really disgruntled folks backed you up against the wall demanding passage home. Sometimes, we command types make pretty harsh demands on folks and expect them to deliver. I know. I done that in my misspent youth."

Kris could only shrug at the question. "It's possible. I don't see that we have a lot of choices in the matter. If we want to keep breathing, both us and the Alwans *have* to keep fighting."

"I don't think Granny Rita is saying that we should stop fighting, Viceroy," Ada put in. "I am wondering if we are maybe feeding the cow too little for all the milk, or defense, we expect it to produce."

"You too, Ada?" Kris said, raising an eyebrow.

"I don't know why someone took a shot at you and hit Jack instead," the colonial prime minister was quick to say. "Whoever did it is not talking to you, to me, to anyone. I'm just wondering if we're pushing everyone too hard to get ready for something that isn't here. That for now, isn't even on our radar."

Kris scowled at the woman.

Ada did not give ground. "I mean, three times you fought

them. Three times you beat them. We have only the ravings of that old woman that more are coming. Can't we celebrate? Throw a party or two? I'm just asking."

"And if she's asking," Penny put in, "some folks must be way past asking. Closer to demanding."

"Have you picked up anything?" Kris said, turning to her intelligence officer.

"Kris, I haven't been listening for anything, so, of course, I haven't picked up anything. Maybe I should have brought Amanda, or Jacques, or Pipra. They're more likely to have their finger on the pulse of civilian things."

"And you, Ada?"

"I know our folks have been working nonstop since your ships showed up in orbit. Working nonstop and without much of a beer ration. Don't get me wrong. We're eating better than we have in anyone's memory. We look to eat a whole lot better in a few more weeks. I sure want to throw a harvest festival when we're done. We're working harder, sunup to sundown on more things than I ever thought we could. Yes, folks are tired. Dog tired."

She paused to take the measure of her subordinates. "We can't tell you how grateful we are that you've thrown back one attack on our star system. That you've gone out and stopped those damn suicide attack ships. Don't ever fail to hear our thank-you in there, but Kris, you're driving my folks mighty hard. I suspect you're driving your industrial workers hard. Could it be possible that you're driving even your Sailors and Marines too hard?"

"You saying one of them shot at me," Kris growled. Then answered her own question. "No, if a Marine got his sights on me, I'd be dead."

Granny Rita accepted that answer with two raised eyebrows.

Kris scowled. "I thought we just had an agreement with the Alwans on the six-month plan for their work and their rewards."

"No, Kris," Granny Rita said, "they accepted what you promised them. There's a big difference. You offered them more nice stuff. They accepted. Would they like to have even more nice stuff? You didn't ask them that."

Kris swallowed her scowl. "No, I didn't."

Ada turned to Kuno, her coordinator for Mining and Minerals. "What are you hearing from our friends among the Alwans?"

Kuno paused before saying, "They're grateful for the rewards they can earn. But they do think we're skimping on the rewards and asking a lot for what we give them. They know a lot of production goes to the Navy. I don't know how they know it, but they do. The ones that have been with us for a generation or three tell me that the Roosters just out of the trees are lazy and want too much for too little work. No question in their minds about that. Still, I've had at least one of them ask if they aren't sucking hind teat. Strange phrase for a bird, but I'm sure they picked it up from some human, no doubt," he said, eyeing Granny Rita.

"No doubt," the old girl said, as innocent as a former Longknife could manage.

"We know there is all-out opposition among some of the older birds. Even among the new-line birds, there are a lot of undercurrents out there, and they haven't been looked at." Kuno took a deep breath. "I'd say we've got some issues that we need to look at real hard in the coming months if we're to hold everything together."

He turned to one of the Alwans at the table, but she was carefully keeping her eyes on the table, obviously uncomfortable in the presence of human disagreement. And clearly uncomfortable with our way of handling it.

Kris wanted to spit out, "If we're going to still be here, we better reinforce the fleet," but she held her tongue. The cow analogy was a good one. You could only get so much milk out of one of those things. When she'd campaigned for Father in the farm belt, she'd been shown one, and even given a chance to milk it.

She still had nightmares about that.

The basic point was clear. She had to feed them if she wanted to get anything back. And maybe she was being too stingy.

Kris sat down. "Okay, you have my attention. I see that we need to examine our distribution of production again, but first, can we look at the two initial problems I identified? Who took a shot at me? Can we capture them? Who is stealing weapons, and how do we stop that loss?"

"I think we can definitely do that," Ada said.

Beside Kris, General Hayakawa breathed a sigh of relief as they got down to practical matters.

28

An hour later, General Hayakawa was smiling as orders went out to recover all rifles and store them in four armories around town and the colony. Marines would be in charge of securing the weapons lockers and would use all available tech to see that the weapons stayed put.

Which wasn't to say that anyone who wanted to couldn't go hunting—they just had to sign for the rifle and the ammunition, and had to turn it back in when they said they'd be back.

"That's a good idea," Anyang, the man coordinating Public Safety, said. "If any of our hunters get lost or run into major trouble and miss their return date, we can turn out the guard for them. I've been worried about folks going deeper into the woods. Game's starting to get scarce close to the settlements. We're going to lose a hunting party sooner or later. This might make it later."

"Will we have any problems with this change?" Ada asked.

"No," Anyang said. "The three guys who had their rifles stolen took a lot of ribbing, and no one wants to be the next joker to have his gun stolen. If we have problems, I'll let you know."

"Admiral," General Hayakawa said, "I've got a report from the forensic teams that went over all the boats that were tied up along the shore."

"All the boats?" Ada said.

"There were only five, ma'am, that the shooter might have used," the general answered. "Four are clean. The other has gun residue on it. There is strong evidence that a fired rifle and spent brass were in it sometime today, but no longer."

"So someone walked away with a rifle," Kris said. "How's the search gone?"

"Not well, Admiral. The boat was anchored off the beach a bit. Whoever was in it swam ashore. Likely, the rifle was deep-sixed while your shooter was crossing the bay. No one was seen around the harbor with a weapon."

"So someone, human or Alwan, used the rifle, dumped it, and walked away whistling," Kris said.

"Yes."

Kris turned to Ada. "Do Roosters swim?"

"Yes," she said.

"Damn," Kris said.

Kris was mulling that brick wall over when the door opened and Dr. Meade led one pale-looking major general into the room.

"Jack!" Kris cried and was on her feet and rushing for him.

And came up short. His shoulder was well bandaged. His left arm was tied tight across his chest.

"I'd hug you, but I don't know what's safe," Kris said.

Jack offered her his right hand, pinky finger out. Kris wrapped her hand around it.

"Just a little flesh wound," she grumbled.

"Compared to worse wounds," Jack said weakly in his defense.

"He'll mend," Dr. Meade said. "I'd recommend light duty for a couple of weeks. Knowing you jarheads, I hope my admiral, his wife, can sit on him for at least a couple of days. I would strongly suggest no shuttle flights for three days. You pop that open, and you could bleed out before they docked on Cannopus Station, General."

"I hear you," Jack grumbled.

"Someone else is grounded with me," Granny Rita chortled.

"So, what's going on here?" Jack said, moving slowly to take the seat next to Kris's. Her team rearranged themselves; General Hayakawa dismissed himself to work. Kris quickly brought Jack up to speed on the first two of her issues. The third took a bit more time.

"Have I got this right?" Jack said. "One nutcase takes a shot at you, and you're ready to rework all your production priorities?"

"Pretty much," Kris agreed.

"Can we have this room for a few minutes?" Jack said.

Granny Rita was on her feet in a blink. "Let's let these two talk a bit. Isn't there a coffee machine somewhere? I could use a cup of bad joe."

Following her, the rest filed out of the room.

"You think I'm doing this wrong?" Kris asked.

"I'm not sure. Damn, they got painkillers in me, and my head is all full of wool. No, Kris, I'm not saying you're wrong, I'm just wondering if you're right."

"Isn't that the same thing?"

"I hope not. But tell me, were you willing, before the shot, to change production?"

Kris didn't shoot back a quick response, but instead stood and paced back and forth behind Jack for a long minute. She was still pacing as she spoke.

"I know I've been pushing hard for more ships. Hell, Jack, we lost seven ships and have two that just barely made it back. Those need to be fixed. I was also wondering if the crews of the ships we recovered might be augmented with Roosters and Ostriches. That's how desperate I am to grow the fleet."

Kris came to a sudden halt. "Back on the beach, when I was worried I couldn't be a good mother, you said I'd done good at every job I've done in the Navy."

"Yes."

"I can get pretty fixated on the problem at hand. I think that's part of the Longknife thing."

"I think so, too," Jack agreed. "But now you're wearing three hats."

"Four," Kris shot back, resting a hand on her stomach. "Four," she repeated softly.

"Is your fear for baby pushing you more to defense?"

"I don't know," Kris said. "I thought I was already so prodefense that I couldn't get any more."

Kris thought back over the last session she'd had with Pipra on production goals. "I wasn't any more prodefense than usual," she whispered half to herself.

"But you're rethinking this all because someone took a shot at you. Or because someone got a hit on me?" Jack asked.

Kris reached out for Jack. He offered his little pinky finger. Kris's caressed it softly . . . and went back to pacing.

"I've known since we started that these folks are having a tough time swallowing what's coming at them. Hell, back in human space, my father and King Ray felt they had to sugar-coat the alien space raiders and were doing a whole lot of nothing until Musashi came up with the idea of smaller, cheaper frigates rather than battleship fleets. Maybe I haven't noticed it enough, but most people really hate wars."

"Strange, that, it's been in all the history books, or didn't you read them?" Jack said, that grin out to play.

"Maybe I skipped those sections," Kris said. *Maybe I did.*

"And this morning's coitus interruptus on the beach has given you a new insight."

"The only thing I wanted was you," Kris growled.

"Don't change the subject," Jack growled right back.

Kris came back to him and moved her chair so she could sit facing him. "I've got a problem that is so much bigger than any I've ever seen in my life. Any I ever thought I'd face in my life."

Jack nodded along as she spoke.

"King Ray didn't think this one through," she said. "If the aliens take this planet and know anything about DNA, they'll know we don't belong here. We have no DNA roots among the plants and animals here."

"Yes," Jack agreed. "Instead of us decoying the aliens into thinking they'd destroyed their problem root and stem, they'll know we're just a forward defense."

"So, how do I get the most defense out of this place, both for Alwa, and humans and Iteeche?"

Jack shook his head. "It all depends. If they're coming now, we need all we can patch together. If we're in this for the long haul . . ."

Kris let the pause grow long between them before saying, "Yeah."

"You got to pay your money and take your chances."

Kris took a deep breath. "And for that I need to talk with Pipra and maybe the shipyard superintendents."

"You got to go topside to wish Phil Taussig a good voyage," Jack pointed out.

"Or to ask him to delay so a few lucky raffle winners can ride along with him."

Jack raised his eyebrows at that.

"Yes, I'm even rethinking that."

"Order, counterorder, disorder," Jack offered the ancient military maxim.

"But wrong is wrong, and being bullheaded about being wrong only makes it a whole lot worse."

"Talk it over with Pipra, maybe Amanda and Jacques. Get everyone you trust involved."

"That's what I plan to do," Kris said.

29

The shuttle ride up was lonely without Jack. Worse, Kris couldn't use it to plan. Whatever she was about to do had to be done on the basis of what she learned in the next couple of meetings. So much depended on her getting it right.

And there was no way she'd know if she'd gotten it right until all hell broke loose. Or the aliens proved a no-show.

Kris examined whose input she needed now. "Nelly, tell Pipra we've got a full-up production review. She can bring along anyone she wants. Get ahold of Admirals Benson and Hiroshi. Throw in Amanda and Jacques."

Penny, Masao, and General Hayakawa were in the seats around her.

"Oh, right. Nelly, I may not be as strong for Alwa Defense Sector as I need to be, me wearing all my hats."

"All four of them," Nelly put in.

Kris's grimace had nothing to do with the gig's boost. "Yes, all four. Tell Admiral Kitano I want her there, and she needs to bring anyone she thinks is strong on fleet mobilization and growth. Does she have anyone involved in integrating the Roosters and Ostriches into ship billets?"

"Where are you going to hold this, Kris? The Forward Lounge?"

"I don't think so, Nelly. Our discussion is likely to spoil a lot of peoples' appetites. No, use my day quarters on the *Wasp*. Oh, include Captain Drago. He's been with me since the start. If anyone can call horse pucky on me, he's the man to do it."

"I've informed him, and I'm shrinking your and Abby's quarters down to Condition Zed size so you can have the largest possible room."

"Are you getting RSVPs with others attached?"

"Yes. Several have asked me just what sort of meeting this is, and I've given them a brief of what you said to the colonials. There are a lot of extras."

"A real zoo?"

"No, Kris. A lot of folks that know something you might need to know. Kris, there's one person you haven't mentioned. Admiral Furzah. She had good input into the most recent battle but also knows how to keep her mouth shut."

"You want to add her?"

"Yes. I also think it would help for her to see how we make critical, maybe life-or-death decisions."

"Add her. Sit her next to Jacques. He can answer any cultural questions."

"Done, Kris."

The admiral's barge docked directly to *Wasp*. Kris walked quickly to her day quarters; Nelly had outdone herself. Kris's space was a no-nonsense, ready-for-business conference room. How she'd stored the desk and comfortable couches and chairs away was anyone's guess. The room was cleared of distractions . . . the screens now displayed a penthouse view of a city in late afternoon, with sunset not far off.

"Nice, Nelly. Very nice."

"Thank you, Kris. Your attendees are arriving. Guests or victims?"

"Stakeholders," Kris said. "Folks who have a very big stake in what is about to happen. Nelly, could you get Ada on the line for this?"

"I advised her of the meeting. She has several of her staff waiting. I can hook them into the meeting and put them on the far wall's screen."

"Do it."

And Kris found herself looking down the table at a table with Ada at its head and most of her key staff, humans and Alwans, even Granny Rita. Thank heavens, Jack was also included.

"Nelly, rearrange the tables. Include the colonials as equals."

It was quickly done. "Thank you, Viceroy," Ada said.

"Smart kid, even if she is one of mine," Granny Rita mumbled.

"We'll know how smart I am when we've beaten off the next alien raiders," Kris said.

People began to arrive. Nelly raised name tags on the table to show those intended for the head table.

Pipra arrived first and took the side closest to the door. She had Abby at her elbow as she began assigning her people to their seats. "Nelly, I brought a few extra. I don't know if we'll need their input, but I'd like to have them hear what I hear. Could you raise some chairs against the wall behind me?"

Nelly did, and more people found seats.

The Navy began to file in while Pipra was finishing with her mob. No, concerned parties. Not mob, because the Navy had just as many people following in the wake of Admirals Kitano, Benson, and Hiroshi.

Nelly created seats against the other wall without being asked.

Kris took her seat at the center of the top of what was now a U. Penny and Masao were on her right, Amanda and Jacques on her left. General Hayakawa and Captain Drago had the corner next to Masao; Admiral Furzah was at the other end next to Jacques.

Kris cleared her throat. "As you all likely know, someone took a potshot at me this morning. We've known for some time that we had problems incorporating all our effort into a single initiative to save Alwa from the alien raiders. I thought I was doing a decent balancing act between guns and butter. This meeting is to examine those assumptions and see if we need to make some changes."

Kris paused. No one at the table or along the walls seemed surprised. No doubt, Nelly had briefed them well.

"As Captain Drago can attest, this is not the first planet where someone has taken a shot at me."

"So very not the first," the captain muttered under his breath, for all to hear.

The tension in the room softened as they enjoyed a chuckle.

Kris waited for the chuckle to run its course. "I have been told that you can't get milk from a cow if you don't feed it. I've also thought that it would be nice if we had more cows. Lurking in the background, of course, is a rather murderous bunch of aliens who can't wait to serve the cow up for steaks."

Now Kris got her own dry chuckle from the room.

"So, if no one has more metaphors, shall we discuss our challenges? Ada, would you like to start?"

"You could have at least warned me I'd be first on the hot seat," Ada said, taking a deep breath. "We've known for a long time that some of the older Roosters don't like what our Viceroy is doing. We've put up with their obstruction, and it's gotten worse. Was the shooter some Rooster of the old line? Possibly. Are some of the colonials worked to the bone and wishing for a day off? No question about that. Me, I'd love to let off a bit of steam. I'm really looking forward to one hell of a harvest festival with plenty of beer."

She paused. "But all the problems aren't down here. That Commander Sampson managed to talk a crew into hijacking a freighter and making a run for it. I'm told that someone sabotaged your birth control. It seems to be that we've got a whole lot of problems. Are they each different and need to be solved differently? I don't know. What I do know is that I'm glad you're finally getting all this out in the open."

Ada leaned back in her chair, her piece said.

"Kris, are we looking at reducing our readiness?" Admiral Kitano said, jumping in.

"We're examining our posture," Kris said. "Can we maintain the present level of effort for the long haul? Could we get something better if we did something different? Is this a zero-sum game, or can we get more cows so we don't have to demand so much from the one we have? No, Amber, I'm not saying we reduce our readiness. We have to be ready to fight at a moment's notice. My question is this. Can we get more if we take a longer perspective? How much would a long haul cost us in the short haul?"

"I could be wrong here," Pipra said, "but don't you have to quit milking a cow if you want to breed it. And while it's got a calf, don't you have to let it at the milk. Course, once the calf is weaned you can go back to milking the cow and then, once the calf is big enough to have a calf of her own, you got two to milk."

"Your point is well taken, even if that's not how it works," Kris said, "and no, Nelly, I don't want to know how dairy farming works."

"But I could tell you," Nelly said, with a sparkle in her nonexistent eye.

"She has a point," Admiral Benson said. "We could divert production from the fabricators, mills, and foundries on the moon to making more fabs, mills, and the likes. Then we'd have double the production."

"Assuming I could find double the workforce," Pipra pointed out.

"I've found Ostriches and Roosters who can work well in my yards," Admiral Benson put in.

"There are Roosters who have been with us for three generations down here," Ada added. "They're providing technical support to your scientists. I think a couple have qualified for copilot slots on their aircraft. They *want* to pitch in more. They're the third generation working with us, and I find it hard to tell them from humans in many ways."

The three Roosters sitting at Ada's tables ducked their heads. Kris wasn't sure if that was agreement, embarrassment, or "Hell yes, we're as good as any human." Kris suspected it was time to find out.

"Okay," Pipra said. "I've heard this and that about this meeting, but I still don't know why we're here. Admiral, Viceroy, whatever, what do you want from us?"

"Pipra, you're a civilian, call me Kris," Kris said, then took a deep breath. "We can argue philosophy until we're blue in the face. What matters is what comes out of the fabricators on the moon. I want to know what that looks like depending on which option I pick. How many guns would we get on a policy that maximizes butter? Do we have enough of a market for all that butter? What does it cost in guns and butter if we get the cow pregnant with a new fabricator? Two, three new fabricators? Do we need new reactors? The Alwans want things. What could we offer to the Sailors and Marines, fab workers and asteroid miners that would make them happier to be here and maybe more productive workers? And yes," Kris growled, "in the end, I always come back to more production. That's just the way it is. Okay?"

Pipra lit up with a huge smile. "Then I think we all want to hear from Abby," she said, and swept her hand around to the woman at her right elbow.

30

Kris found herself grinning as she eyed her former maid. They'd come a long way from the afternoon Kris found Abby standing on the stairs of Nuu House, newly hired by Kris's mother. And fired by Kris three times in the first hour of their acquaintance.

That was one of those fond moments that changed Kris's life.

Though it had taken a while to become apparent.

"As some of you know," Abby began, "I've spent too damn much of my life around one of those damn Longknifes."

That got a laugh.

"I knew this moment was coming, knowing what I know of Kris Longknife, and I've been putting all my spare time, what this young woman beside me allows, on just this issue of options. I have a spectrum of options ready for your review."

The view of the sunset vanished, to be replaced by three sets of charts: red, yellow, and green.

"Red maximizes defense. Yellow maximizes consumer goods. Green grows our industrial base. I think I got the color scheme easy to remember."

That got nods. Abby might have gotten more, but most folks were craning around to get a better view of the charts.

"Now, before you all go yapping about all the leftovers hanging out of each of the three options, I know none of these three is the best way to go. All have a lot of unused resources hanging fire. The real issue isn't guns, butter, or growth, but the balance between the three that uses as much as we can produce."

Kris squeezed her eyes closed. *I used this woman to wash my hair!*

And to keep my sorry ass in one piece more times than I want to admit, another part of her pointed out.

Kris opened her eyes to see the charts spreading apart on the screens. An orange chart formed between the yellow and green. A turquoise one sprouted between the green and yellow. Both of these two compromises went long and used finer print. A few of the folks in chairs against the walls stood to get a better look.

"When you balance any two against each other, you get a better use of resources."

"Mata, show them the seventh seal, I mean seventh option."

"Yes, Madame," Abby's computer said, and the six charts spread out to make room for a black one in the middle. It filled about a third of the screen space, even with tiny print.

"This is by no means a final plan," Abby said. "It's got too many places where some experts need to look them over and make a good, solid, human call. No offense meant to Nelly or her kids without whom this whole exercise would have taken years and probably not been finished in our lifetimes, right, Mata?"

"So true, Abby."

"You didn't pull this out of a steamer trunk, did you?" Kris asked Abby.

"I pulled this out of my own little head, Baby Ducks, my head and a lot of time from Nelly's kids."

"And you didn't tell me, Nelly?" Kris said.

"You weren't asking. I didn't know that you humans would ever ask. We had time on our hands, and it was a fun exercise in iterative planning," was Nelly's answer.

Kris chose silence as the better part of valor.

Now people were crowding around the walls, studying the options. Dirtside, Ada must have had some screen available because her people were now crowding around something off to the right.

"Let me see if I can do this," Nelly said. You could almost see her tongue working as she attempted something.

"What kind of 'this' are you up to?" Kris asked.

"Well, I can make clear Smart Metal." Suddenly, the top of all the tables turned into what looked like a centimeter of clear glass.

"Now if I can do this," Nelly said, and numbers and words appeared etched in the glass. In a blink, the etchings filled in with black, duplicating the black option on the screens.

"That wasn't so hard," Nelly said.

"But on the screen, people can move things around," Mimzy said at Penny's collarbone. "What if they want to change a column? Move it over?"

And a column of numbers on the table changed and moved over to the next apparent page.

"But what if I want to change my options?" Kris said. "For example, what if I want to double Slow Light Crystals production to armor the ships I've got?"

On the table, the production of Slow Light Armor doubled, and that immediately worked back through the production figures and forward to show the yards taking on more work.

"Very good," Kris said.

"Only if every table has one of my kids working it," Nelly said, with a distinct sniff.

"So Abby hangs around her table, and Penny goes over to the Navy side," Kris said. "And you, Nelly, stay with me."

In a moment, each of the tables became a work in progress.

"I hope someone's saving all of these options and changes somewhere," Captain Drago said, coming up on Kris's elbow.

"You're grumpy as ever when you see computers doing good," Kris said.

"I just don't want them doing all this good and it getting lost when someone sneezes."

"We're backing all this up," Nelly said. "We'll want you humans to look at some of our assumptions. For example, when we flowed extra crystal armor through the system, we made assumptions about how much time the yards need to coat a frigate with the stuff. That alone is a major process. I think our estimate is within ten percent of actual, but until a yard has done its own estimate, it's a . . . what do you call it?"

"Guesstimate," Admiral Benson said, coming up on Kris's other side.

"I know, but I wanted to emphasize it. It's just a guess until you do the full estimation job," Nelly said.

"Hmm," Benson said. "Now, about that armor and our

workload, Admiral. We've got more work than you've been led to believe."

"Admiral, it's been a really bad day," Kris warned. "Please don't make it worse."

"Sorry, but here it comes. That armor the Earth yards slapped on their frigates. It ain't nearly as good as advertised."

"No surprise there, I saw three ships that thought they were invincible blown out of space. What's the problem?"

"What is it ever? Poor quality control. The front of that armor is level. Mirror flat. The back of the armor, not nearly so much. It seems that the crystal filaments they made don't grow exactly to ten centimeters. They vary from 98 to 102 millimeters. It's the mess behind the armor that transmitted heat directly into the ship's skin."

"So that's what killed them," Drago said.

"In spades. Our fabricators have better quality control than Earth's. Our actual filaments are anywhere from 99 to 101 millimeters, give or take a few nanometers, if you follow my meaning. We'll have all the armor for one ship use one length filament. Another use another selected batch."

"So one ship may have 99 millimeters, another 101," Kris said.

"Something like that. We've still got the problem of bolting the armor onto the hull. I'm really thinking of nuts and bolts as much as it hurts me to use technology that ancient." Benson's face actually looked pained.

"We need something," Kris said. "One of the Earth ships in my BatRon 12 was sloughing off its armor at high-gee acceleration. We can't have that."

Pipra came up now on Captain Drago's blind side. "I hate to tear my CEO away from such fun discussions of how to blow shit up, but I need her thoughts on how to grow more fabs this year so she can have more fun stuff to blow shit up with next year."

"Just a second, Pipra. Admiral Benson, is there any chance you could sort out the Earth crystals and standardize the length of the filaments?" Kris asked.

He was shaking his head before she finished. "The stuff is fused together. No way can we separate it."

"So, we figure out a way to cool the hull behind the armor and try to keep the Earth ships out of any really hot spots," Kris said, dryly.

"It looks that way."

"I'd love to be there when you tell Admiral Yi about his little problem," Kris said.

"You want me to save you a seat for the show?" Benson asked.

"Yes, but no thanks. I have too much business to allow me that pleasure. Now, Pipra, what do you have in mind?"

"I need workers. Despite what some people think, nothing gets made without workers supervising the fabs. Don't walk away, Admiral Benson," she said, reaching across Captain Drago and Kris to nab the admiral's elbow. "You said you had some Roosters and maybe even some Ostriches who might be good with machinery."

"Yes, for my sins, I did let that slip out," the admiral allowed.

"Well, some of my folks want to take the Ostriches up on the land grants they talked about giving us humans if we'd just settle in their areas. I don't know why they want us. Maybe they think that just being close to us, the Roosters have somehow gained on them. Anyway, I got folks who would love to settle some of those 144-hectare land grants, but they're all working their asses off, twelve hours a day, six days out of seven. You know what I mean."

Kris allowed that she did.

"Heaven knows why everyone wants land, but folks do. At least a lot of my assembly-line folks dream of having their own farm or something. So . . ."

"You want those land grants," Kris said.

"Oh yeah, but that's just the first part. Folks need time to live on that land. They need homes. I don't know if manufactured homes are good enough for them, but even those involve a lot of stuff. To tell you the truth, this has all just been a lot of dreaming about castles in the air, so I don't really know what they'd need to make a go of it."

"Let's pass them along to some real colonists," Kris said, smiling at the dirtside team.

"But even before we do that," Pipra put in, "they have to have some time off. If you're doing twelve on and twelve off, you got just enough time to get some chow and some sleep before you're back on the job. With one day off a week you can't do much more than roll over in your bunk and go back to sleep."

"Now I'm seeing why you grabbed my elbow," Admiral Benson said.

"Yeah. With one of your locals shadowing one of my experienced hands, we might be able to change our workforce to twelve and twelve for a week and then a week dirtside. What do you think?"

"It would be a start to get locals working on the moon when you get some more fabs," the admiral said.

"I'm thinking that," Pipra said, "and maybe with all the automated farm equipment we've shipped dirtside, we can get some colonials up here, too."

"And if my yards aren't spinning ships out that we don't have Sailors to crew, we could put some of my skilled technicians down in your moon fabs, mills, and foundries."

"That's what I'm seeing," Pipra said.

"Somebody tell me that getting colonials and Alwans up on the moon, supporting production, will be a good introduction to their becoming reserve Sailors on the ships I hope to get next year, or year after next," Kris said.

"If we do this right, you'll have them sooner," Benson said.

"Okay, let me sashay over to the colonials and see what they think about this," Kris said, and, taking Pipra and Benson by the arm, she walked them down the room to where Ada was busy with her team.

"Ada, have I got a deal for you," Kris said.

The colonial first minister looked away from a screen Kris could now see and smiled. "I was expecting you. Have you seen how this Black Plan is changing?"

"Nope, I've been up to my burning ears in people talk. People and Alwan talk, that is."

"Yeah. I figured as much. There's no way for the folks you have up there to handle all that's showing up on this plan."

"Can you spare us some of your more technically inclined colonials and Alwans?" Kris said, going straight for the heart of things.

"You're going to use us as some sort of Christmas turkey, stripping the meat off and leaving just the bone, from the looks of it," Ada said, not at all happy.

"That isn't the way I'd put it," Kris said.

"How would you put it, then?" Granny Rita came into the conversation, clearly supporting Ada.

"If we're willing to increase butter so that there are more goodies for everyone dirtside," Kris said, holding up one finger, "and we're willing to make all this butter available for people willing to work on our growing, high-tech economy, I'm thinking that there's a lot more turkey meat to go around, and no one gets left with the scraps."

"No turkey has four legs," Baozhai from the treasury pointed out.

"No, but if we have twice as many turkeys on the table, you do have four legs," Kris countered.

"The Green Plan," Ada said.

"The Green Plan rolled into the Black Plan," Kris said. "If we can grow the base, we can get more of everything for everybody. More Red. More Yellow. Who knows, maybe we can keep the Green side growing, too. But we need people for all of this. People willing to learn how to make the things we all want. We can't drive the manufacturing side with just the people they have."

Kris paused for a moment, then glanced at Pipra. That was enough encouragement. She took up the tale of her over-worked crews who needed some serious downtime. Preferably down on the planet in dirt they could call their own.

"I was wondering when that would come up," Ada said.

"Do you have a problem with a second center of human presence on Alwa?" Kris asked.

Ada made a worried face. "I don't know. From what I hear, the land down there is just begging for a plow. I expect some of our youngsters will pack it in and head down there. I'm not sure how their folks will take that. Kids are a built-in labor force for farms."

"Things are changing," Kris said.

"So you keep telling me," Ada answered. "I've seen what happens to old birds that get in the road to stop it. I never thought I'd be one of 'em."

"There are a lot of changes coming," Pipra said. "If you think you have it bad, imagine me and mine trying to see that everyone gets all the lollipops they want for the work they're doing for this princess, or admiral, or whatever hat she's wearing today."

"We'll need to juggle a lot," Kris said.

"The harvest will come in next week. Thanks to all the nice gear King Raymond sent, it won't be the backbreaking work that takes every last person every last moment of daylight. I never thought I'd say this, but I can get a few kids moving up to your fabs even now. And some Roosters. Some have been with us since we arrived and are comfortable with our tech. Which isn't to say any of us are up to the tech level you are. It's up to you to see that they don't break anything."

Now it was Pipra's turn to make a face. "Yeah. I hear a lot of talking, but whether it's just pie in the sky or will deliver the goods on schedule is another matter."

"No time like the present to find out," Ada said.

"I'll leave you all to figure this out," Kris said, and slipped out of the circle.

This is delegation, right?

She rambled up the other side of the table to where Abby stood watching others make changes to the Black Plan. Someone would do something, it would cascade up and down the visible plan. People would study it critically, then either cancel it, or look for another one.

This was happening on all three sides of the table as well as both wall screens.

"Are these connected?" Kris asked Abby, waving at the tabletops and walls.

"Nope. Each group is doing its own thing. Maybe in the end they'll all have the same plan. Or maybe they'll be way off. Then we'll look at the different ones and see what we like and don't like. Either way, we win."

"Hmm," Kris said.

"Not bad for a maid, don't you think?"

"Not bad for a hotshot production expediter," Kris said. "I knew you had it in you. You had to pull all those things I needed out of those steamer trunks just when I needed them."

Kris enjoyed a smile at fond, if desperate, memories.

"I had a lot of help figuring out what went into those trunks," Abby allowed.

"But you were the one that did it in the end."

"I guess so. Oh, sorry I wasn't there this morning to get a shot at that shooter."

"Jack and I were hardly dressed for company," Kris said, trying not to blush.

"Compromising positions do leave you open."

"I wasn't compromised. I was with my husband."

"You managing?" was so vague a question that Kris needed time to think on it.

"I am," Kris finally said. "And those that don't like what I'm doing can take a long walk out a short airlock."

"That's the spirit."

"So, are things as hard as Pipra says they are among the workers?"

"Maybe worse," Abby said. "You and her can live in your own little world of charts and reports. I got to go out and talk to the worker bees. They got a problem, I get sent to see it in the flesh. I get to share their coffee breaks with them. I like this job. Get to meet lots of interesting people, people you're driving mighty hard, Kris."

Now it was Kris's turn to make a pained face. "And if the bug-eyed monsters show up tomorrow?"

"We'll be in trouble," Abby admitted. "But if they don't show for a couple of months, you might well be doing their job for them."

Kris gave Abby the look she reserved for Commander Sampson and her ilk.

"No, I'm not talking mutiny or open rebellion. But I am talking folks who are dog tired and need a rest. Or folks that are nose up against the candy-shop window and feeling locked out. You've got so much change coming at these people that it's a crapshoot as to where it all falls apart first, second, and last, Kris. You need to get out more."

"The last time I was out of my bubble, I got shot at."

"Yeah, but maybe if you'd been out of your bubble a month ago you'd have spotted this problem sooner and headed it off at the pass."

Kris shrugged. "Not too long ago, I was chasing down

Sampson, fighting the remnants of the bug-eyed monsters we beat the first time, and making friends with our fine feline friends."

"So your problems have to stand in line, and some of them get pissed and cut to the front."

"Cutting I don't mind. Shooting, that's another matter," Kris said with a dry chuckle.

"Yeah," Abby agreed.

After a few quiet moments, Abby went one way to tell a production type that his latest change was boneheaded. Kris kept moving, smiling encouragement and doing her best not to get drawn into any of the arguments raging around the screens and tables. Any hope that all of these efforts would end in one harmonious plan was rapidly going up in smoke.

Kris found Admiral Furzah at her elbow.

"This is an interesting development," she said.

"Interesting in what way to you?" Kris asked.

"Many of my people, not all, I assure you, and maybe fewer of late, but many of my people would have used the shooting incident to land the warriors. Your Marines. Land them and take control of the situation with force. You, instead, seek to calm the fire by feeding it. Interesting."

"We have found that landing the Marines often has the effect of tossing gasoline on the fire. Instead of making it smaller, it makes it huge. Haven't you found that out?"

"Yes, we have. That is why I say that fewer would do that of late. Even we warriors, at least we older, grayer warriors, have noticed that."

"What I am attempting to do here is to smother the fire. To take its air away."

"But do you have time for that?"

Kris scowled. "That is the problem. But if we keep driving the worker bees to produce but give them little honey, they get less interested in their work. They make mistakes. Maybe intentionally. More likely just from exhaustion."

"Yes. It is interesting that our greatest powers now are the ones that looked to their industry and their people more than just building up their warriors. Now they have more people, more industry, as well as more warriors. Strange how that happened," the feline said slyly.

"Yes. They took the time and now they have the power. Now, if the alien space raiders will just leave me time for this."

"Yes, that is the heart of the problem."

Kris continued to rove the room. She had hoped that the plan would come together. Instead, the discussions in the room drew more heated. She actually had to impose herself between two women before they came to blows. Then two men.

"Okay, we've done enough for an afternoon," Kris announced to the room. "Let's take a break. Go to your own corners. I mean that. Those of you having problems with others, get out of each other's sight. There are plenty of places to eat on the *Wasp* and the station. Get out, get some food in you. We will continue in three hours. Next time, we'll use the Forward Lounge."

I THOUGHT YOU DIDN'T WANT TO SCARE THE DINERS, KRIS.

I DON'T, NELLY. YOU'LL JUST HAVE TO COME UP WITH A CLOSED OFF, SOUNDPROOF ROOM IN THE LOUNGE.

YES, KRIS.

31

So Kris found herself going to supper in the *Wasp*'s wardroom, and being followed by half the Navy from the meeting.

"Kris, we've got to talk," Admiral Kitano said.

"I'm next," Admiral Benson added.

"I guess that makes me last," Captain Drago said.

"You'll all wait while I get a message off," Kris snapped.

"I'll get you something to eat," Captain Drago offered, and led the other flag officers off while Kris settled at a table.

"Nelly, get me Phil Taussig."

"Phil here," came a moment later. "We're about to shove off. You're going to miss telling us good-bye."

"Can you stand down?" Kris asked.

"You don't want us gone?"

"Sorry, but I may be asking you to take the lucky winners of a raffle contest for a few slots home."

"I heard you'd been shot at and were rethinking things. I didn't know it would impact me."

"I'm afraid it does."

"Okay, I'll tell folks to stand down and give half the crew shore leave. How long do you think this will take?"

"A couple of days, maybe," Kris admitted. "I'm putting several things on the table. If I'm lucky, you may become a whole lot less appealing. I won't know until a few of my chickens come home to roost."

"I like my chicken fried," Phil said. "If you're done, I got some fast shuffling to do."

"Longknife out," Kris said.

Captain Drago returned with a salad, of the sort that relied heavily on Alwa leafy greens, nuts, and berries. He also had a tall glass of chocolate milk.

"You are a darling," Kris whispered, reaching for the milk.

"So I've been told," the *Wasp*'s skipper said with a smile, and headed back to get himself something. Admirals Kitano and Benson settled in on either side of Kris.

"Kris, you've got to put a stop to this," was Kitano's opener.

"Why?" Kris said, getting a nice forkful of greens headed for her suddenly ravenous tummy.

"We've lost another buoy at that crazy system. Three of the eight are gone."

"When did this happen?"

"Likely a week ago, but I only got the word as you were closing down that meeting. I figured I should tell you first rather than dump it out there in front of everyone."

"Thank you," Kris said. She munched her salad as she mentally called up the system. Four suns in crazy orbits. Several dead, rocky planets in the middle of that mess. Several huge ice and gas giants well back from the suns following totally weird orbits. Why would three aliens take a sudden interest in that system?

A rallying point, she thought, answering her own question.

Ice giants provided plenty of good reaction matter. Likely some had interesting moons. Just what a space rover might call a rich environment.

"Do we know the type of ship and reactors that dropped in?" Kris asked Kitano.

"The sensor people just finished analyzing the data," Nelly said. "The signature of the ship matches the third ship that was observing our last system battle."

"Likely all three have agreed on where to get together to gang up on us," Kitano snapped.

"Likely," Kris agreed, munching more of her salad.

"So?" Kitano left hanging.

"So, we still don't know if this is an advanced guard or just scouts. Nelly, all three were single ships, am I correct?"

"Yes, Admiral. Three ships of three different patterns."

"We need to know more about them and about that system. Nelly, how long will it take a base ship to get to us from there?"

"Do we assume single jumps through twelve systems or a faster approach?"

"Can they go faster?" Admiral Benson asked.

"Two-gee acceleration and 20-rpm spin can get them here in five jumps," Nelly said.

"Hmm," Kris said. This just got more and more complicated.

"Admiral," Kitano said. "We can't ignore this."

"I'm not ignoring it. I'm thinking." Kris took another bite of greens and found it surprisingly tasty. Since Cookie had set himself up at a restaurant on the station, that couldn't always be said of wardroom meals.

Captain Drago returned with an interesting dinner. It looked like liver and onions, but it smelled like nothing Kris could remember. She chose not to ask any questions.

"How are you liking Cookie's salad?" Drago asked, opening his napkin.

"This salad is from Cookie's place?" Kris said.

"He knew you were having a bad day and sent over the salad just for you."

"Nelly, send Cookie a thank-you from me."

"Done. He says great. He'll try and have more salads for you whenever you're on board. He says he can do it if I'll just give him some advanced notice."

"Nelly!" Kris said.

"You like the salad, don't you?"

"Yes," Kris had to agree.

"So much for operational security," Admiral Kitano groused.

"My neck is stuck out as far as yours," Nelly pointed out. "I know when to keep my mouth shut and when I can trust people to make a salad and keep their mouths shut."

"I side with Nelly on this one. If I can't trust her to protect me, whom can I trust?"

"Why do I feel like I'm being ignored?" Kitano asked the overhead.

"I'm sorry you do," Kris said. "I'm not ignoring you, I'm thinking about every word you said while minor things keep my mouth moving on things I don't have to think about. Now, what do we know about that system?" Kris said, eyeing her chief subordinate.

"Not a lot," Kitano admitted.

"So, let's change that. Please send a force out there to support our survey and buoy tenders. Survey the system in depth and outpost it for at least three more systems out."

"And that would do what for us?" Kitano asked.

"It would give us more warning when the base ships start moving in, assuming that is the whole idea here. I'm betting that they won't just show up in system, form up together, and start sweeping in toward us. If I'm reading the way those 'Enlightened Ones' work, they are pretty much gods in their own domain. Put three of them in the same system and there's going to be fur that needs petting, and heaven help the one that pets the other one wrong."

"You're guessing," Kitano pointed out.

"Yes," Kris said, taking another forkful of greens, this time with extra berries mixed in. "Yes, I'm guessing, but I've been to their holy of holies. I've read the brags they post and the snide remarks some ships add to others' boasts. I don't think these folks play well together. They don't have to."

"What if the three we're facing are children ships?" Admiral Benson asked. "Spawned off the same mother ship?"

Kris tried munching her salad and chewing her lip at the same time. Fortunately, one was figurative. "I don't think so. At least one of the warships had eight reactors. Even the two that had six reactors had different signatures from them. No, I think we're dealing with those that just happen to be in the area." Kris eyed her supper guests. "Tell me, did any of you settle down right next to your folks?"

"We're on the other side of the galaxy, for Pete's sake," Amber Kitano said.

"I rest my case. Some 'Enlightened One' gets his own ship, he's going to go in the opposite direction from the old mother ship."

"You betting the farm on that?" Amber said.

"As has been pointed out, I can't keep people on the edge of terror every minute of their lives. I've got to let up before they fall apart. Or start shooting at me. I'd rather manage this a bit than have things crumble when I least expect it. If . . . no, when the aliens start causing trouble, we'll change. But for now, we've batted three out of the park. We *will* take a break."

"So we do nothing," Kitano said.

"No. We dispatch Betsy Bethea with Task Force 4 to survey that system."

"Those flakes," Benson put in.

"I don't think the ships from Hispania are flaky. And I think Bethea is perfect to see what the ships from the Esperanto League are good for. Put them through their paces. Add in the *Kamoi Maru*, *Activity*, and *Cherryleaf* to drop off buoys the next three systems out, and we'll have a deeper picket line. You want to send Bethea her orders, Admiral?" Kris asked.

"Well, it's something. Not enough, but something."

"It gives us more time to get ready when things start going to hell," Kris said.

Amber settled down to attack her hash and beans. Kris eyed Admiral Benson as if to say, *You really want to be next?*

"Bad day. Maybe I ought to come back tomorrow."

"You think it will be better? Especially if I don't have Jack to bring me milk and toast in bed before I get up?"

"Hmm, you have a point. Okay, can I protect some of my work bosses from being hijacked by Pipra's moon factories? If they start offering land grants, I'll have my own people grousing."

"So we offer them land grants, too."

The retired and unretired admiral rubbed the stubble on his chin. "I'll have to figure out a way to let folks have time off dirtside. I've been working two shifts, ten hours a day, six days a week. I've brought in Alwans to work with my crew, Learn the ropes as it were. I expect I'll lose a lot of them to the moon," he said slowly, thinking it through as he spoke.

"How much will you have on your plate if we cut back ship work?"

"But you said you wanted to up armor all your ships."

"I didn't say I wanted it tomorrow."

"Good point. So, I'm hearing you'll get us land grants, too, and put up with one shift a day until things pick up."

"One twelve-hour, seven days a week to be followed by seven days off."

Benson chuckled. "Tough, but there's land in it."

"I'm promising a lot of land. I may need to talk to the Ostriches. Make sure they know what they're getting into. By the way, will any of your crew want into a lottery for a ride home?"

"They knew what they signed up for. I suspect the land and some time to enjoy it will take a lot of the rough out of their backsides."

"You going to offer land to the Sailors, too?" Admiral Kitano asked.

"My first answer is I don't see why not. My second answer is I better talk to some Alwans before I give away their land."

"Kris, how are you going to decide who gets what land?" Nelly spoke for the first time. "Without water, land is worthless."

"Thank you, Nelly, for the complications," Kris said.

"Everything comes with some," Benson said, almost under his breath.

Kris finished her salad and stood. "Well, if you'll excuse me, I'd like to tend to a few personal matters before its back to the Coliseum and the lions."

Her subordinates allowed her to dismiss herself, and she headed back to her quarters. Nelly had managed to return her night quarters to some semblance of their normal size; Kris collapsed on her bed and slipped into a gentle nap.

32

"You awake?" brought Kris awake, muzzy brain and all.

"Is it time?" Kris asked the overhead.

"About that," Abby answered. "You want some milk?"

Kris took a survey of her stomach and found it good. "Nope. Nelly, send a second thank-you to Cookie and tell him that salad was not only good going down, it was nice to wake up to."

"Done," Nelly said.

"He promised me some ginger cookies for tomorrow morning," Abby said.

Kris considered several answers, and decided, "Thank you, Abby, but you don't have to."

"You're my boss, Kris. One of the best bosses I've had in a long line that included a few real stinkers. I like to think of you as a friend as well."

"A friend who owes you her life," Kris added.

"Well, that too. Still, I want to take care of you."

"Thank you. It seems I need taking care of," Kris said, ruefully.

"I don't see a problem with that. How'll you take care of the baby when it comes?"

"I don't know," Kris admitted.

"You'll need a nanny."

"I thought that was one job you'd never want."

Abby dismissed that with a wave of her hand, the one not holding the milk. "Getting that pregnancy notice in my mail raised some strange thoughts."

"Hmm," Kris said. "I haven't approved the removal of any birth-control implants, Abby. I wasn't planning on approving any. You want an exception?"

Abby made a face. "I said I had interesting thoughts, not that I went stone-cold stupid."

The two women enjoyed a laugh.

"On second thought, I'll take that milk," Kris said. It was locally grown, not powdered milk from across the galaxy, and someone had gotten it to just the coolness Kris liked.

"You want a fresh uniform?" Abby asked.

"I guess so. This one went through the wringer before I slept in it."

Her maid helped Kris up, efficiently aimed her toward the shower, left her with a nice fluffy towel, then retreated to get her uniform ready.

Kris showered quickly, toweled off, and felt a hundred years younger. Abby greeted her with, "I got you a clean set of spider silks."

"You think I need them up here on my own ship?"

"This morning, did you think you'd need them down on that beach? Don't lie to me. I've lain on the same beach or one just like it with nothing on but a smile."

Kris slipped into the silks, then into undress whites.

"I have an extension added to the Forward Lounge," Nelly reported. "It's big, walled off from the rest, and has glass-covered walls and tabletops. You should be able to break up into smaller groups."

"Good, Nelly. Do you have enough computing power to run all that glass?"

"I was about to suggest that Sergeant Bruce and Cara attend tonight's planning session as well as keeping Jacques in attendance."

"Do they want to come?" Kris asked both Nelly and Abby.

Abby answered. "Steve will go anywhere I do. He's been getting more interested in what I'm doing. Cara thinks this planning stuff is more fun than computer games."

"It is," Nelly said.

"So you'll have six of your kids there," Kris said.

"Seven. I've talked Chief Beni into coming, or maybe Captain Drago ordered him," Abby said.

"That leaves out only Jack and Professor Labao," Kris noted.

"Jack's Sal is working with Granny Rita and Ada," Nelly

said. "There is no way I'd include Professor Labao. He and my daughter that he only calls 'computer' have gotten quite unmanageable."

"So, you're happy with the attendance?" Kris said.

"Yes."

"Then let's go find some agreement."

"Agreement the Alwans will approve," Abby pointed out.

"You think they'll push for more consumer goods?" Kris asked.

"Wouldn't you if you suddenly saw more available?"

"But they have to earn them. It's only for those working with us."

Abby raised an eyebrow. "You sure some don't see this as their fees for letting us use their land?"

Kris's smile got evil. "How eager are Ostriches for us moving down there?"

"Good Lordie, but I see trouble rising," Abby declared.

Then they walked into the extension to the Forward Lounge.

Nelly had outdone herself. It was spacious, secure, and quiet, although it seemed like everyone was talking at once.

It was also crowded.

Two dozen were in Kris's initial meeting. Fifty plus had returned from supper.

"Nelly, you better double this place," Kris ordered.

In a blink, the room was three times its size. "I think we'll need the extra room, Kris, to keep tempers down."

"No doubt," Abby agreed.

Staff Sergeant Steven Bruce was there on the Navy side. From the looks of it, Admirals Benson and Hiroshi had brought half their estimators. They were intent on hard estimates to rearmor ships as well as feeding in the numbers for repairing those banged up during Kris's last battle.

Even victories had their price.

Pipra had added planners and divided them into three groups: those for building plants, those for supplying the Navy, and those for providing more consumer goods for Alwans, colonials, and workers building their own bit of heaven dirtside.

People moved from one set of plans to another, passing ideas back and forth. Abby went to join those groups; Cara was already with them.

Circulating loosely among them were Penny and Masao, Amanda and Jacques.

Kris headed for Pipra and found Amanda and Jacques joining her as well.

"I've delayed the departure of the *Hornet* and *Endeavor* for human space," Kris said. "I'm willing to organize a lottery for as many as thirty people to return home. They have to know that if the ships are in danger of being taken, they will be blown to atoms."

"Right now, I'm not sure you'd find thirty takers," Pipra said. "Us going to week on, week off and having land to farm or fish or hunt has leaked out with the subtlety of Vesuvius. We've got a call-in show on the moon. They haven't had one naysayer. I never thought you could get everyone on the same page, but this land deal has done it."

Now it was Kris's turn to wince. "You remember, this was just an idea. I'm not totally sure the Alwans who made the offer had the authority to."

"Don't say that too loud. How soon can you flesh it out?"

"Tomorrow, maybe. Nelly, do you have contact with anyone among the Ostriches?"

"No, Kris."

"Can you set up a contact?"

"You might want to talk to Admiral Benson, or maybe Ada," was all Nelly offered.

"I see he's next on my list," Kris said, and turned toward him.

Pipra stayed with her planners; Kris's key staff followed her.

"Admiral Benson, I see you've got reinforcements," Kris said, with just the right amount of smile.

"I figured it's better to have hard numbers. I've put in the honest numbers for repairing damaged ships. We also fed in estimates for applying crystal armor to ships that don't have it. I've even included what it would take to spin out an entirely new crystal armored frigate with 22-inch lasers, assuming we decide to make a few."

"Thank you, Admiral. I'm glad that everyone will be working with real numbers, not wild estimates for the Navy," Kris said.

"Now, about those land grants. The word's out on the shop

floor that they may be coming our way, along with the week on, week off. I have to tell you, morale is taking a skyrocket ride. When do you think we can actually see those grants?"

"I'll be talking with the Ostrich government tomorrow. Next day at the latest," Kris said.

"Good. Good. Now, what kind of prefabs can we have to set up our dirtside homesteads?"

"Talk to Pipra," Kris said, and watched two shipyard superintendents head off to get in her hair.

"Do you see the problems I see?" Amanda asked Kris softly.

"I see all sorts of problems," Kris said. "I've got to get land, but land grants are worthless unless someone can set up a homestead. Every homestead takes consumer goods away from the Alwans."

"I'm glad you didn't miss that. Suddenly, we'll have humans competing with the Alwans," Amanda said.

"Will we get any production out of all these homesteads?" Jacques asked, "Or are these fab workers planning on being gentleman farmers?"

"This will not turn out well," Amanda whispered.

"Not unless we get ahead of this stampede," Kris said.

"I think Pipra is planning on letting the market control all this," Amanda said.

"This market better meet a Longknife's expectations," Kris said, darkly. "Nelly, how's this all going?"

"Kris, I hate to say it but the Black Plan is starting to look more and more like a Turquoise Plan. Plenty of growth for butter, some for industry, not a lot of guns."

"How bad?" Kris asked.

"Something like sixty, thirty, ten," Nelly said.

"That bad, huh."

"Pretty much."

"Okay, Nelly. Please have your kids save all the plans as they now exist."

"Done, Kris."

"Now clear the boards."

"Kris," came in four-part harmony from her staff, with a lone "Done" from Nelly.

"What the hell?" seemed to be one of the more neutral responses around Kris.

Kris let the uproar run for a moment, then said in a command voice that carried, "Now that I have your attention," and the room fell silent.

"Boys and girls," she began in dripping sarcasm. "I gave you free run to see what you would do. I do not find the present trend acceptable. Sixty percent for consumer goods and only ten percent for defense is not what I had in mind when you started this exercise."

"But we need this for homesteads dirtside," came in a plaintive cry from a corner of the room.

"Maybe we need to be clear about those homesteads. They are not dude ranches," Kris said. "I expect those farms to grow food. One person enjoying the good life on their private half-time bit of heaven is not something we can afford—not out here in the dragon's mouth."

Kris glanced around the room. Few met her eyes.

Abby, however, was not one of them. She had a tight smile on her face and was nodding. Once again, Kris's former maid had apparently called the shot.

"Now then, let's start this over again, and let me give you more precise guidance. Defense will be lowered from sixty percent of our effort to thirty. Industrial growth will raise from an anemic ten percent, which was barely enough to provide spares and support infrastructure growth for the colonials, to a solid thirty percent. Consumer goods will stay at thirty percent."

"And the remaining ten percent?" Pipra asked.

"Will be apportioned as best to level out resource usage," Kris said.

"Got you."

"Now," Kris said in her most reasonable, but still Longknife voice, "let's go back to work as adult men and women."

The glass tables and walls came back to life, and people studied them.

Nelly, did you change the plan?

I put them back the way you said. Thirty, thirty, and thirty.

Well done, Nelly and kids.

You're welcome, came in several-part harmony in Kris's head.

Pipra headed in Kris's general direction but made no show of it. Still, she was at Kris's elbow in no time.

"I foresee a problem," she whispered softly when she was close enough.

"I foresee many problems. Which one do you want to talk about?"

"The thirty percent that we were devoting to consumer goods was split fifty-fifty between the Roosters and the colonials. Now we're looking at splitting it three ways."

"No," Kris said, "four ways. Don't forget the Ostriches."

"Damn, four ways?"

"If we move onto Ostrich land, they'll want TVs and commlinks, electric cars and egg warmers for starters."

"That means a drastic drop in goods for the colonials and Roosters."

Oops.

Kris took a deep breath. "So," she said, in her most reasonable, but solidly Longknife legend voice, "how do we solve this?"

Across from Kris, Pipra's eyes went unfocused. Kris waited patiently.

"One of the things that's bugged me," Pipra said softly, "is that we brought a lot of heavy industry. Hell, everything we brought was for heavy production."

"Heavy fabrications to support the fleet."

"Right, as you keep reminding me. Anyway, we've been using heavy fabs to make light consumer goods. That's a poor use of resources. Now, if our initial fab growth was in light manufacturing, just the stuff to make consumer goods . . . ?"

"Are light fabs easier to make?"

"As one is to two," Pipra said.

"So what we really need is the light stuff."

"Exactly, my CEO, Princess, and Admiral."

"Give me a plan that shows a month's worth of growth in light fabricators."

"And those fabs will be a lot safer for rookie Alwans to learn on."

"See, I knew you had it in you," Kris said, smiling as she sent Pipra on her way.

Admirals Benson and Hiroshi were next in line.

"You really want me to cut my level of effort in half?" he asked.

"That's what I said. You've got BatRon 1 back in fighting shape or *Wasp* would be back in your body and fender shops. You've got two badly damaged ships from our last fight to mend. We've recovered enough Sailors from the ships we lost to crew one, maybe two. We'll commission more, but only after we grow some local manpower up to crew qualifications. I don't see Roosters going straight from the trees to a reactor watch. First, they lose their egg teeth on fab work, then we trust them aboard a warship."

"So, this cut in defense is really one step back to take three steps forward," Admiral Hiroshi said through a broad grin.

"I hope for more reinforcements from home, but if we can grow our own, I'm all for it," Kris said. "People fight harder in defense of hearth and home. Let's give them a hearth to fight for."

"I'll ask for volunteers for moon fab duty," Benson said.

"More of the same old same old," Jacques said, as he and Amanda sauntered up.

"Yep," Kris said. "Amanda, what do you think of all this?"

"Economics at its messy best," she said. "I think Jacques is having a field day."

"The human animal howling at its best," he said. "Maslow's hierarchy of needs going full steam ahead. They've got food, water, warmth, and I might add air to the list. Now they want more."

"Despite the fact they may have their throats cut next week," Kris said dryly.

"It's your fault they're less worried about staying alive. You've beat back the bogeyman three times and made it look easy."

"So if I'd lost more ships and had more people killed, I wouldn't be having to put up with this mad dash for the cookie jar."

"Something like that," Amanda said, dimples showing in her smile. "It's all your fault, you damn Longknife."

Kris did a sarcastic bow to the both of them. "Thank you very much. Tell me, Jacques, I delayed Phil's run to human space. How many of our alien friends were planning on taking the trip with him?"

"The crazy bitch was going to be locked away on Phil's *Hornet*," Jacques said. "Strange as it may sound, the bald-headed old woman wants to go. 'To see where the star walkers come from,' as she put it."

Kris felt a chill. "We need to keep her away from the wild woman."

"She's on the *Endeavor*," Amanda answered. "Her and her man."

"They've made up?" Kris asked.

"I don't know if I'd go that far," Jacques said, "but he's not willing to let her walk among the stars without him at her elbow."

"What about the rest?" Kris asked.

"The kids, both the three hunter kids and the twenty kids we saved from suicide, are coming along like rocket cadets. They love their readers, and they're fitting right into school at their age level. Well, math for the older kids is a bit slow, but the kid whose leg you saved is taking to math like peanuts. Lord, is that kid smart with numbers. Several of the younger men have taken to hunting in the deep woods, even using rifles.

"I think that might be why the older folks are more willing to follow the wise woman and the man into the ships and across the stars. They aren't quite fitting into the new hunting scheme of things, and it's rough, eating the younger men's meat. Anyway, we've got six old folks taking the trip."

"I'll get them under way as soon as I sort out everything," but Kris was kept from thinking further on that. Pipra was headed her way with a half a dozen planners in her wake.

"Kris, we need to know exactly what you have in mind for these farms," Pipra said.

"A working farm. Don't any of you know what a working farm looks like?"

The planners looked at each other. From their looks, none had ever done manual labor.

"Don't get me wrong. I've never worked a farm myself," Kris said. "But when I was out in the farm belt campaigning for Father, I never saw a farm with less than four or more hands, usually family, and I never saw a farm that worked one week on, one week off. Haven't any of you talked to Ada and the colonials?"

Silence.

"Okay, crew, what say we walk over there and have a little chat?"

Since no one objected, Kris started walking.

Ada must have seen them coming. She was waiting, Jack at one elbow, Granny Rita at the other.

"Kris, I don't like this new batch of numbers any more than I liked the last," Ada started.

"I didn't think you would," Kris said, cutting her off from a direction Kris didn't want to go, at least not with these witnesses. "But I have a question for you right now. What does it take to run a farm?"

"No good sense," Granny Rita put in. "Desperation. A lot of sweat and hard work, sunup to sundown. Why do you ask, Kris?" was posed with an all-too-knowing grin.

"Well, Granny, some of our fab supervisors up on the moon think it would be restful to get some fresh air, working out in the sun. Some good, old-fashioned back-to-nature relaxation."

"Ha," came from both women. Jack just grinned.

"I take it that you don't see it that way."

"I take it that these fools have never had to farm for their lives," Granny Rita said.

"So, how many hardworking people do you think it would take to manage 144 hectares?" Kris asked.

"I wouldn't try to work that much land without a good-size family," Ada said. "Husband, wife, at least three kids up man- or woman-size."

"And if they were industrial workers?" Kris posed.

"More," Granny said. "I remember how we mucked around when we first landed. We hardly knew what a hoe was, much less which end went into the dirt."

"Well," Kris said, and tried to sound like she was seriously considering the problem, "what if these farmers had the usual modern tools? What might those be anyway?"

Ada smiled. Wickedly. "You mean tractor, plow or roto-tiller, disk harrows, posthole digger, unless they plan to feed anything that wanders by, a mower and rake? They planning on buying all of these up front, collecting them slowly, or maybe sharing them around among a couple of farms?"

"I don't know," Kris said, eyeing Pipra and her crew, trying not to smile.

"I think we may have been overly optimistic," Pipra said. She glanced at her team. As one, they looked poleaxed. "We thought it would be good to do some different work for a change. To have our own land, you know."

"I bet none of you ever farmed a day," Granny Rita said. Heads nodded.

"But the movies about how the landers tamed a raw frontier are always so romantic," Kris said with only a hint of sarcasm.

"For people that never had to lance a blister," Granny added.

"No doubt," Pipra agreed dryly.

"So, are you going to call it quits on this idea?" Kris asked. "Or do we get serious about how we make it happen?"

"What do you think it would take?" a pale, reed-skinny man asked from the back of Pipra's bunch.

"Granny Rita, you're the only one here who's been raised to fabs and done hard sod busting," Kris said.

The old woman eyed the folks through the screen. "You won't have it anywhere near as bad as us. Leastwise, you don't have to unless you make it hard on yourselves. Let's say, for discussion purposes, that you've got 144 hectares with easy access to water. Assuming you can put up a prefab for a roof and some outbuildings to keep the sun and rain off your gear, you've got a good start. A modern tractor can break most ground here with a simple cultivator and tiller. A seed drill can go on for the second pass. Then you got the usual hard work of getting the crop in. Fencing, weeding, not all of which can use the tractor. I say at least four to six willing pairs of hands. Best would be if you had a couple say, family high, off a colonial farm to give you some help doing it right the first time."

"Can they work the farm a week on, a week off?" Kris asked.

"Hell no," Granny shot back.

"So," Kris said, "if our folks have to spend half of every two weeks back on the moon, working a shift, what you're really talking about is eight factory types and two locals."

"Couldn't we just hire a lot of Ostriches to work for us?" came from someone who carefully mumbled it.

"No," "Hell no," and "Don't even think of that," came back from the colonials.

Granny Rita took it from there. "The Alwans are not our serfs. They work side by side with us. You never stand around watching them do your work. Never."

Beside her, several Roosters had come to silently watch the humans talk. Now they were ducking their long necks and flapping their vestigial wings. "No, no," was easy to understand.

"Okay," Pipra said, "bad idea. So our farming needs for anyone crazy enough to think farming is a nice way to relax are likely one-eighth or less of what we were thinking. Could all our people still get the full land grant and maybe only develop one parcel for now?"

"What land grants?" Ada asked.

"I'll talk to you about that in a bit," Kris said.

"Yes, you will," came from both Ada and Pipra, letting Kris know that she was now on several hot seats.

"Do you have enough to go in?" Kris asked Pipra.

"It's a lot more complicated. We'll have to match people into groups. It'll be worse than your damn fraternization rules because anytime there's a breakup, there will be land and property to divide. Hell, I wish I hadn't even raised this idea."

"You think there will be more folks interested in a lottery to go home?" Kris asked.

Pipra shook her head. "No. You're right. We can die there or die here. Maybe we die a bit sooner here, but hell, we got one of those damn Longknifes looking out for us here. Back home, who will we have if the damn monsters show up in the sky? Really, I ask you that."

Kris had no answer. She wasn't sure where her baby would have the best chance to grow up.

Pipra and her crowd moved off, leaving Kris to face Ada's and Granny Rita's glowers.

"Land grants?" Ada said.

"Don't you remember, after the last flock, I mean Assembly of Assemblies, there were Ostriches around offering land, so we could move down to their neck of the woods. Offering land grants. I don't know how it mutated to 144 hectares."

Kris quit talking. The blank faces eyeing her did not encourage babbling.

"Don't you remember anything?" she added. Weakly.

"I don't remember anyone *from* the south empowered to talk *for* the south," Granny Rita said. "Maybe you need to talk to Jacques, but as I remember, the Ostriches aren't any more organized than the Roosters."

Kris turned to Jacques.

He was shaking his head. "I'm afraid I agree."

"So we're talking about castles in the air," Kris said.

"Pretty much," Ada agreed.

"Unless you know something we don't," Granny Rita added.

"I think I need to do my homework," Kris said, and turned to hunt up Admiral Benson.

33

Kris found the good admiral bent over a table, watching as one of his estimators filled in a section of the planning document. If Kris was reading it right, it was a good seven levels below where most of the others were working.

"I wonder how that will effect all the other planners," Kris said.

"Well, they can take these numbers with them to the bank," Benson said, "because I'll bet my pension, what I have of it out here to hell and gone, that those numbers are within .05 percent of dead-on."

"Good," Kris said. "Now, please walk with me."

"By all means," the yard superintendent said.

Kris walked him right out of the annex to the Forward Lounge to a table in the corner. A cheerful barmaid brought two glasses before they even settled in: pale ale for the admiral, tonic water with a twist of lime for Kris.

They smiled a thank-you. As the young woman walked away, Kris said, "Nelly, raise us a wall."

In a blink, they were in a tiny cell. "So, what's the big secret?" Benson asked, sipping his beer.

"I'm not sure we can take that offer of southern land to any bank," Kris said.

"What?" Benson shot back. "All my Ostriches are talking about how things will be when my yard crews set up home down where they come from."

"They are?"

"It's common knowledge."

"Who says?" Kris shot back. "Who has the authority to make such an offer? Nelly, get Jacques in here, pronto."

A minute later, Jacques and Amanda came in through a

door that was suddenly there, and just as suddenly not. The table expanded to make room for them.

"Admiral Benson, please tell Jacques what you just told me."

When the admiral finished, Jacques winced. "It's hard to say how the rules are made down there. With the Roosters, anyone who can put on the best display sets them. For the Ostriches, it's chest bumps. I'm thinking that all the Ostriches we're dealing with have seen the 'chest bumps' Kris gave the aliens and assume that whatever she wants, she gets."

"And?" Kris said.

"And among the Ostriches back home, maybe it's not so much."

"Are you saying I may have to do some chest bumping to get the local leadership's attention?"

"Or kick a head off," Jacques said.

"Or get your head kicked off," Amanda appended. With a smile.

"Don't get me wrong," Jacques quickly added. "I think you can make this happen, but I think you'll need to start from scratch and go from there."

"From the looks of the planning in there," Kris said, "how much time do I have?"

"Very little," Amanda said.

"Okay, Jacques," Kris said. "What connections did you have with their Assemblies of Assemblies?"

"Ah, Kris, they aren't that sophisticated. They're still in their hunter-gatherer phase with some crops they regularly come back to in the winter months. You'll have to talk to a lot of different tribes and get them to, ah, I don't know what the word is, to give you primary use of a certain range of land."

"No concept of land ownership, huh?" Kris said.

"No more than the Roosters."

"How are the colonials getting by with their land use?" Kris asked.

"They got the land no one wanted. And, as we well know, a Rooster can wander anywhere, even in the middle of a road."

Kris winced. "Right." She thought a moment. "Admiral, I need introductions to several tribes. Especially tribes where your workers think we can share land."

"We track tribal connections among workers, both so we

can deliver them back home and to make sure we don't have certain tribes working with others."

"Let me guess," Jacques said. "Some tribes have hereditary head-kicking contests."

"Pretty much. We learned early to keep the two apart both in work details and where they sleep and eat."

"And I missed all this?" Kris said.

"Not something to worry you about. Lord knows, you had enough on your plate."

"I need a bigger plate," Kris muttered.

The admiral took one last pull on his beer. "If you'll excuse me, I need to talk to my Alwan personnel manager."

"Let me know when you have a contact point. I need to make this happen soonest."

The admiral set down his beer. The wall disappeared, and he strode away quickly.

Jacques was just opening his mouth when Nelly said, "Pipra would like you back in the room. They want your opinion on how much farm gear gets charged to the colonial food account and how much counts as consumer goods for the industrial workers."

"God in heaven save me," Kris said.

"See, you get enough problems, and you'll learn to pray," Amanda said.

"But what god will listen to a Longknife's prayers?" Kris said, standing up.

34

The day that had started with her smiling up at Jack and expecting a very pleasant morning, only to be interrupted by rifle fire, was still going strong at 2200 hours. At least it ended with a call to Jack.

"Could you fly down south. Do the scientists have a plane going that way?"

"There's a red-eye that leaves in an hour," Jack told Kris. "I've got Sal reserving space. If I have to, I'll toss someone off."

"Try not to toss an Ostrich off. We might need his vote on this land use permit thing."

"Kris, Admiral Benson wants you to talk to some of the Ostriches he's sorted out. They're in two different rooms to avoid fights. He really wants to get them back to work."

"Sorry, Jack, I have another fire to put out."

"I know, and I have a plane to catch. See you and baby tomorrow."

"Oh, yes," Kris said.

Next morning, two longboats loaded with Marines, Abby, Amanda and Jacques, and a dozen Ostriches were on final approach to the bird-guano mine's landing field. Parked off on the apron waiting was a large, four engine transport. The Marine armored rigs drove off the longboats and right into the transport.

Kris took a walk across the apron to a welcoming committee made up of Jack and Commander Hanson, who now oversaw the shit farm for his crimes.

"We have a minor problem, Kris," Jack said, still bandaged and wrapped but offering Kris a pinky finger for a hug.

"And it is?" Kris said, hugging the one finger.

"Sampson and Mugeridge began a hunger strike yesterday," the former frigate skipper said. "I don't know how they found out that ships were headed back to human space, but they did, and now they're on a hunger strike unless they get a ride home."

Kris shook her head. "Not going to happen. There may be a lottery for a few slots, but those two will not have their names in the hat."

"I'll pass that along to them," Hanson said.

"Would you like to get your name in the lottery?" Jack asked.

"No, sir," he said. "All by myself, I screwed up the best job a man can have, skipper of my own ship. It's hard to believe I was that stupid. Anyway, no, I'm doing good work here. Truth is, I'm hoping that you might find a garbage scow you need a skipper for," he said, nodding toward Kris. "I know I don't deserve it, but maybe the next time you have to put a sub under the ice of that moon to shoot Hellburners at base ships, you'll consider me."

"That was damn near a suicide mission," Jack pointed out.

"I doubt I'll get a better command," the ex-skipper admitted.

"You stay squared away, and I'll think about that," Kris allowed.

"Thank you, Admiral. Now, about my two problem children?"

"Tell them they've still got to produce their work quota. If they die, they can rest assured no one will bother to read their obit. There's no media to carry it. Work and eat. Don't eat, they still work."

Hanson grinned. "My thoughts exactly."

"The plane is loaded, Kris. We're burning daylight," Jack pointed out.

Two days later, Kris was back at the guano mine, waiting while a doctor qualified Jack for a shuttle ride. Commander Hanson asked her how it went.

"We got access to the land. They got rifles and ammunition. Someone took a potshot at me. Pretty much what I expected. How has Sampson been?" Kris asked him.

"Both are still not eating. We rouse them out of bed and

march them off to the digs, but they refuse to work. They just sit there, demanding to talk to you."

"And you'd like me to talk to them."

"No, ma'am. You asked. I'm telling you."

"You can tell them for me that I don't care what they do. They can work and eat or they can sit on a pile of shit and die. Their choice. But they are going to do it here. Nowhere else."

"I'll pass that along," the ex-skipper said.

Kris was back on *Wasp*, had gotten in a long bath with Jack, and was halfway through a nice dinner in the wardroom before a long line of people with business caught up with her.

35

Pipra was first to slide into the seat across from Kris. "I hear you got us some land."

"I got some farmland, yes," Kris allowed. "Have you sorted out who will work it and in what groups?"

"That's been the hot topic the last couple of days. People have been dividing themselves up into eights, tens, twelves, depending on how many friends they can find willing to work with them if they didn't have to. Interesting times we live in."

"And who's willing to farm with you?" Kris asked, knowing there was too much sly in her grin.

"You'd be amazed. Not all of them are guys."

"And what kind of gear are you going to provide these start-up farmers?" Jack asked.

"Carbon-composite homes, steel farming gear, and solar-generated power," Pipra said. "We're knocking out the fab to make them first."

Kris noted Amber Kitano standing in the door of the wardroom. She spotted Kris and headed for her table with only a brief stop at the coffee urn for the essentials of life.

"So, how much land will each of these farming teams have?" Kris asked Pipra. Nelly had already told Kris there wasn't nearly enough land for each worker to claim 144 hectares.

"That depends on what happens up east of Haven," Pipra said.

"East of Haven?"

"About the time you made it known that you were going to set up farms on South Continent, Ada mentioned some nice land on North Continent, just four or five hundred kilometers from Haven."

Kris raised an inquisitive eyebrow.

"Back before we started providing folks with roads and electric rigs to drive on them," Pipra said, seeming to enjoy spinning out this tale, "the colonials thought of spreading out. There's a decent bit of land along a different, nice, wide river. Young Roosters had been walking in from there and asking for work and tech toys. They even offered land where they came from, but it was too far away, what with matters being where they were."

"But nothing is where it was," Kris said.

"Nope. They've got barges to carry loads down Haven's River to the sea and then back up Big River. Overland, it's gone from a two-month, elephant-pulled trek to a day's drive on decent roads."

"And the Roosters would much rather have the jobs and earnings than let the Ostriches take them," Jack added.

"You got it in one. Ada had a team of Roosters and colonials meet with the associations in that area and they've given us a real, honest-to-goodness land grant. We've marked off the land, and we'll own it, under the colonial traditions, not the Rooster way of doing things."

"You going to have someone mention this to the folks I just promised a few rifles and ammunition to?" Kris asked.

"You bet."

"Does this smell as bad to you as it does to me?" Jack asked.

"You offering them whiskey as well?" Kris asked, fixing Pipra with a thunderous scowl.

"No. I'm not that dumb, working with a Longknife."

"Good, because I am the Viceroy of this place, and I will cancel any contract that crosses my desk that takes advantage of the Alwans."

"Can you define 'takes advantage'?" Pipra asked.

"I'll know it when I see it," Kris growled.

"I think I've brought my boss up to date. I better get to work, so I'll have something to brief her on tomorrow," Pipra said, collecting her papers.

"You do that."

"When will the *Intrepid* be back?" Pipra asked Amber as she was leaving.

"When it's back," Kris's senior subordinate admiral growled.

Kris eyed Amber. "The *Intrepid* is bringing in a load of ammonia," she said. "Carbon composites need feedstock."

"But using the Navy?" Jack said.

"You don't think the Sailors and officers are doing their own land-office business?" Amber said. "Kris, you've sent Sailors and Marines down to help the fisheries and farmers. They've gone hunting and done just about anything to keep their minds off the lack of beer. But when the day is done, they haven't got a lot to show for their efforts but some blisters and maybe sunburns. Admiral, your command is very much looking forward to putting down roots on this planet. Of having something to fight for next time they have to fight."

"Be it ever so endangered, there's no place like home," Kris muttered.

"Yes. Phil Taussig tells me he's bringing his wife and kid out here. You think they're going to set up housekeeping in some corner of the station?"

"He talked to you about that?"

"Yep," Kitano said. "He had already looked for some land around the colony. There wasn't any. He's tickled about this Big River thing. They want to name it the Mississippi. It means Father of Waters in some Earth language."

"We may have to ask the Alwans," Kris said.

"Their word for it is just 'big wet' and we can't pronounce it. So, yes, I loaned out a frigate that was already out and passed up a load of reaction mass that I can get next trip." Kitano eyed the economist. "Amanda, you better figure out how to compare Navy pay with industrial pay and who gets to buy what. If my folks can't have an even run at production, I'll demand either a lottery or rationing."

Kris found herself rubbing her eyes, tired already this morning. "I'm thinking lottery, with one ticket for each one in the farming group."

"A ten-person farm get ten tickets. Six people get six?"

"That sounds about right. Each ticket gets one set of farm gear."

"This is going to be a real pain," Jack said.

"And I foresee all kinds of social stress," Jacques tossed in. "There's a reason why we prefer a market-driven economy."

"Don't I know it," Kris said. "My father hammered that into me at his knee, but how do you start a market economy when there's not enough to meet demand?"

"Well, no doubt the fab workers have got a lot more of this thing called money in the bank than my Sailors do," Amber growled.

"We'll work it out," Kris said. "So, Admiral, have you heard anything from that system that seemed to hold the raiders in its thrall?"

"Bethea's headed back. She's done a full survey of the place and dropped off pickets three jumps farther out. So far, nothing to report."

"So we wait," Kris said.

"Hopefully, for the longest time," Jack said.

"Yes," came from everyone around them.

36

So they waited.

Nelly turned part of the wall across from Kris's side of the bed into a calendar, counting down the days until baby's big day. Kris didn't need to be told when her first trimester ended. She woke up one morning with a happy tummy and eager lady bits.

Jack's bones got jumped before he had a chance to make a move for the milk and cookies.

"I take it that morning sickness isn't a problem today?" he said later, looking up at Kris.

"Not today. Hopefully not again, knock on wood," and she tapped his head with her knuckles.

Kris's stomach wasn't the only thing a lot happier. The Local Roots Initiative got off to a good start. As it turned out, it was a good thing they came up with the idea of sending Kris's new arrivals dirtside for some work. A lot of colonials were looking for jobs in orbit.

The farm equipment King Ray had shipped out with the first wave of reinforcements proved sufficient to feed all the immigrants from human space. It was a close run thing, but the crops came in before the food they brought ran out.

The second harvest that year would provide a surplus.

If they kept planting at the rate they were going, they'd be buried under a mound of food.

Three out of four colonials had been working their arms off, trying to raise enough food for all of them. Now, one in ten was enough.

There was a major labor surplus.

So they, as well as Roosters and Ostriches, were hitchhiking rides up to the station looking for work. This might have caused trouble, but a lot of the farm co-ops realized they needed help if they were to make a serious go of it.

"You teach me how to farm, and I'll show you how to keep this dang machine from screwing up," became the contract among a lot of work groups.

It also worked aboard ship.

So things changed faster than Kris had expected. No doubt, there would be pinching and pulling, but for now, there was plenty of goodwill to go around.

Furthermore, no one wanted a ride home. No one except the two that had finally gone back to shoveling bird guano in order to eat.

Kris was ready to send Phil Taussig's *Hornet* and the *Endeavor* on their way. She was walking to the *Hornet*'s berth, when Admiral Kitano buzzed her.

"You about to send Phil back home?" the admiral said.

"Yes."

"How about you and him come to my flag plot instead."

"We got problems?"

"You look at the report and tell me, Admiral Longknife."

Oops. When Kris was Admiral Longknife, there was trouble in the wind.

"Nelly, have Phil meet me at the *Hornet*'s brow."

"He's on his way, Kris."

"You want to tell me what's got Amber's panties in a twist?" Kris asked her computer.

"She got a message from the Beta Jump Buoy in a code I can't easily decipher. You want me to crack it?"

"If you think you can in the next five minutes," Kris said. "Otherwise, we'll know soon enough."

"It's a single-use cipher, and only a few number groupings. I can control my curiosity," Nelly said.

Phil saluted Kris at the bottom of his own gangplank. "I thought you were coming to see me."

"That was the plan. Admiral Kitano thinks you and I need to see something before you shove off."

"Hmm," was all he said. Kitano had been his XO a long two years ago. A lot of water had gone under the bridge since then. Good for her, not so good for him. Still, he was alive and kicking, so it wasn't all bad.

Together, they boarded the *Princess Royal*. In her flag plot, Kris found Amber staring at a screen. It was centered on the system the aliens seemed to find so interesting.

"Trouble?" Kris asked.

"Most likely not immediately," Amber said. "We've lost two buoys, three out from the system. Two of the alien clans look to be headed for that system. If we're reading the reactors right, it's the same two clans headed for the same jumps they used last time."

"Are they bringing the fleet?" Phil asked.

"Not that I can tell. It's one fast scout each. Of course, once it shoots up the next jump buoy, I won't know what's behind him."

Kris gnawed her lower lip. "So we wait, just like we've been waiting."

"We wait," Amber agreed

"You had this in a single-use code," Kris said.

"I don't want every comm watch in the fleet decoding stuff from that system. We've got colonials and even Roosters standing watches. I don't want anyone going all flighty on me."

"Good," Kris said.

"I better be on my way," Phil said. "Nothing's changed. The settlers need reinforcements because the bad guys might be just around the corner."

"True," Kris said, and followed him back to his ship. She wished him and his crew Godspeed before dropping over to the *Endeavor* to wish the same to Captain O'dell and her crew. Since her crew again included both Roosters and Ostriches, human space was in for an experience. O'dell's passengers included six of the older aliens Kris had recruited on the aliens' home world.

With any luck, these aliens might allow humans to dig into their DNA and see how it had been bent to make them better slaves as well as how that might be untwisted. Whether that would make them friendlier was an unanswered question.

Meanwhile, the aliens would keep trying to kill every living thing in the galaxy not of their seed.

And Kris would keep killing them.

What a mess, Kris thought as she went ashore. Even as

she left the docking bay, *Endeavor* was sliding down the pier, on her way to human space or self-destruction.

The aliens would not capture them. All they'd know was that they killed us as we killed them.

Kris patted her still-mostly-flat belly. "Somehow, my darling inconvenience, I will make all this better for you."

37

Months passed. Kris found herself wearing a tent, or feeling like she should be wearing one. *Can't anyone design a comfortable maternity uniform?*

No, Kris, because no woman is comfortable pregnant.

The amateur farmers put in their first crops, and returned sunburned, blistered, but smiling to their ships, fabs, mines and mills. To Kris's surprise, the number of accidents went down, and production went up.

In the fleet, new hands shared the burden with old hands as half the crew went below and a mix of colonials, Roosters, and Ostriches tried their hands at keeping a frigate battle-ready.

Task force commanders exercised their ships with these mixed crews and found them at least minimally acceptable.

"With more practice, they'll do better," Admiral Kitano assured Kris. "We didn't do all that well the first time out."

"We were under the gun then as we are now," Kris reminded herself.

"Look on the bright side. The yards have finished putting the crystal cladding on most of our ships and are now spinning out eight new frigates. That means promotion for our officers and a chance for some of these colonials and birds to try their hands as crew for these new warships."

Kris nodded. On her desk were a hundred suggested names for those eight ships. Popular among them were the whimsical names the yard hands had fought the last time they defended this system: *Proud Unicorn* and *Lucky Leprechaun* had been lost with all hands; *Temptress*, *Fairy Princess*, and *Mischie-*

vous Pixie had likely been snide references to Kris. *Kikukei*, or *Lucky Chrysanthemum*, had been the name the Kuro Docks gave their ship.

Somebody kept sending in *King Raymond I* and *Princess Kris*. Kris kept erasing them. Now *Trouble* was one name she was willing to fight beside, but who would want to fight in a ship with that name?

It was not that Kris was adverse to naming things. She and Jack had gone through a whole bag of baby names. Kris wanted her daughter to be Ruth, after Gramma Ruth, aka Gramma Trouble. Jack's mother's name was Maria, so Ruth Maria it was. Or Mary Ruth if Jack was talking. Kris was willing to make a peace offering to her own mother, so the poor baby's name had grown to Ruth Maria Brenda and Jack always added Anne for Kris and also for Sara Anne, Trouble and Ruth's daughter who had married Grampa Al . . . and paid for that mistake with her life far too soon.

So a girl would be Ruth Maria Brenda Anne.

Any boy would be John Junior for starters. Kris added William for her father. Jack wanted Raymond for obvious reasons. Kris was not about to make the poor child suffer through Terrence, though any son of hers would more than likely be Trouble at every chance.

John William Raymond was it for the boy so far.

Now that Kris was out of the first trimester and her stomach was back with the program, Kris had joined the *Wasp*'s pregnant women's PT program. Every morning, without respite, the twenty-four of them were in the Forward Lounge doing their exercises. The girls were nice, though the first day or two had been a bit quiet. Once they realized the admiral was a woman just like them, with a baby on board, they'd gone back to their chatter and included Kris as well.

It was the first time Kris could remember being "just one of the girls." It was fun. Dr. Meade had arranged for the first birthing class, which gave Kris and Jack a chance to meet the whole bunch together. Most of the future mothers had shown up with a man at their elbow. A few had girlfriends to help them through.

All of them seemed to have no limit to their joy.

Kris remembered one woman and took Doc Meade aside. "The young officer I saw leaving our office once. I haven't seen her aboard."

"No, she exchanged with one of the preggers who needed a billet on *Wasp*."

Kris nodded. It was only human to protect yourself.

But Kris's job was to protect everyone.

And that job started to get serious.

They'd sent Admiral Miyoshi back out to what was being called System X with his BatRons 3 and 9 to replace the jump buoys lost when the two alien ships cruised through three layers of pickets to take a second look at the large system. This time they picketed out four systems.

"That still means it will take four weeks for us to know they'd popped the outer picket. By that time, they'll have gotten all the way into the system and left, if they're doing what they've been doing," Admiral Kitano growled.

"Or have set up shop in that crazy system," Kris pointed out.

"We've got too much lag time in our warning system," Admiral Miyoshi concluded.

"How can we get the word back here sooner?" Jack asked the screen they were all standing around showing System X and environs.

"Have we got some empty supply ships?" Kris asked.

"Most of them are empty," Kitano reported.

"Okay, here's what we're going to do," Kris said. "Admiral Miyoshi, I'd like you to take two of the Marus that came out with Yamato's squadron and merge them into one fast merchant cruiser. I plan to take the 20-inch lasers off the last of your frigates when they come in to get crystal cladding over their armor. I've talked to Admiral Benson about putting 22-inchers on them as well as a fourth reactor to support them."

"Good." Miyoshi grinned happily. "I saved my flagship for last."

"I'll do the same with two of the Blossoms from Earth and leave them standing guard in the first system inward of System X. It has a fuzzy jump. With a bit of acceleration and rpms, they should be able to get a message back to us in only two jumps, a good two weeks before the speed of light will let us get a radio message."

"Ships faster than radios," Admiral Miyoshi marveled. "What will we humans think of next?"

He departed the next day, leaving the *Haruna* and *Chikuma* in the yard for armor and armament upgrades. He was back three weeks later.

"You know, that fast route out is not a bad way to go," he reported to Kris.

Kris nodded. She didn't tell him that she'd gotten the idea in a dream. She was dreaming a lot these days. What was unusual was that she was remembering them. Some were just dreams. Showing up late for formation at OCS . . . in her birthday suit. Others were more challenging, like getting into arguments with Father or Mother and not doing her usual run for her room and slamming the door.

She woke up a lot with Jack holding her.

Kris broached the topic of her active night life with Doc Meade.

"It's not unusual for pregnant women to have lucid dreams," she told Kris. "Mentally, you're working out unresolved issues. Do you have issues with your folks?"

"Doc, I got whole subscriptions with my folks. Lifetime subscriptions."

"Maybe your dreams will find a way to cancel some of those subscriptions," Doc Meade said with a sparkle in her eyes. "After all, you're going to be the mother soon."

Kris found herself taking stock of her life, her command, and her situation. She looked upon her work and found it good. Very good, overall. Things were going so well, she was starting to think that everyone had the right idea. Here was a place to set down roots and relax.

She should have hunted up a sledgehammer to knock on the wood of her desk.

38

The fast routes out and back gave Kris ideas. That and her dreams.

Six months into her pregnancy, she and baby were doing fine. Four months into the Roots Down Initiative came the first harvest. The new farms didn't produce as much per acre as the colonial farms, but the food was a welcome addition.

It was during the harvest festival that Kris announced the names for the new eight frigates. Four were easy. *Furious*, *Enterprise*, *Audacious*, and *Resolute* were the ships that followed Granny Rita into battle for the last time.

Those drew cheers from the colonials.

After long and serious consideration, and letting a lot of people bend Kris's ear on the topic, the other four would be the *Proud Unicorn*, *Lucky Leprechaun*, *Kikukei*, and *Temptress*. The last two had suffered the most casualties in the battle that caused the loss of the first two.

Those drew cheers from the yard workers, both the ones who'd come out from human space and the Alwans who were working beside them now.

"I'll be wanting volunteers for those crews. We plan on a hard and long voyage for them after they shake down."

Kris said no more, but she soon had plenty of volunteers. Apparently, farming wasn't as much fun as getting killed. She explained the mission to the eight XOs who'd earned promotions to skipper the new ships.

"We've pushed the pickets out four jumps from System X. I want a pair of you to anchor just inboard of the third jump point. Keep an eye on the next system. If they try to pop our latest set of jump buoys, you pop them. It's time they learn they can't just waltz back and forth around our space.

However, if a whole alien clan shows up, run for home. Any questions?"

There were none.

Kris had come up with the idea one morning, lying in Jack's soothing arms after a particularly hard dream. In it, she had not run away but had stood, toe to toe with both her mother and father and argued her point home.

Exactly what the point was and what she said had not survived waking. That she woke with her heart pounding had been evident to Jack. He said nothing, just held her.

So her mind had wandered anywhere but back to her family. She'd found herself mulling System X as her heart slowed.

Why not stay rather than run?

What had started as a muzzy-minded question turned into a serious thought and a policy before breakfast.

Why not?

Now Kris sent six newly built ships with the best Alwa had to offer to guard those outposts and bite back when the aliens tried to take a nip.

Whatever happened, it was likely to be interesting.

Two ships stayed at Cannopus Station to relieve the watch and allow a section to come back and resupply. Kris wondered how her plan would survive first contact with the aliens.

She hadn't long to wait.

39

Commander Alex Rogers had come out as the operations officer on the *Repulse* in Hawkings's squadron from Wardhaven. He'd been promoted to XO when his skipper got command of a division. Having distinguished himself in the First Battle of Alwa, he now commanded the Alwa *Resolute*, second ship of that name in Kris's fleet.

Having a fleet made up from many sources meant a couple of duplicates: *Resolute* and *Churchill* so far.

The *Resolute* and the *Audacious* had drawn the C approach route to System X.

At the moment, standing in Kris's flag plot, Commander Rogers looked sure of himself but a bit nervous.

"We had just arrived at the jump from System C3 into C4 when the buoy came through to tell us that Jump Buoy C4c had been popped," he reported, standing not nearly as "at ease" as Kris had ordered.

"We sent the periscope up to the jump, and it identified four fast movers from Wolf Pack Anton coming across the system at 3.25 gees acceleration. Captain Beaudette and I decided to wait for them on our side of the jump. It took them two days to come up to the jump, ma'am. When it was clear they were coming through, we recovered the periscope and made ready to receive them."

"How'd that go?" Admiral Katano asked.

"As good as we had any right to expect. They came through one ship at a time. We stationed ourselves behind the jump so we had a good shot at their reactors. The first three were a bit slow, so we had no trouble firing, flipping, firing, and recharging in between."

Commander Rogers eyed Kris. "We'd been warned to expect them to be shooting at anything and everything,"

"Yes," Kris said.

"Ma'am, they must be getting sloppy. They weren't shooting at all. We got the three of them. Then nothing. So we ran the periscope back through the jump. The fourth was sitting there, waiting for something.

"After a while, it moved around to behind the jump. No doubt, he intended to hit our sterns when we came through. When we didn't, after a long while, it headed back the way it came. We waited until it was over a hundred thousand klicks out, then jumped through and shot out its reactors before it could flip ship and return fire."

"So the aliens will get no report back from that bunch," Kris said.

"Not a peep, Admiral. The rest of the system was cold and empty."

"How did the mixed crew work out for the *Resolute*?" Admiral Kitano wanted to know.

"I couldn't ask for better, Admiral," Commander Rogers answered. "The Ostriches held off doing their chest-bumping thing until after the last alien was dust. The Roosters didn't blanch at the lack of a dance. The colonial kids were delighted beyond words to be serving on a ship just like the old codgers had. Now *they* have tales to tell. The hands you let me bring from the old squadron clicked perfectly. Ma'am, I don't know that all crews drawing one-quarter from each source will work as good as us, but it did for the *Ressie* in this fight."

"Thank you, Commander. Does your ship need any yard time?" Kitano asked.

"No, ma'am. Let me take on some fresh food, and we're ready to head back. The *Audacious* is holding the line alone. We didn't have any trouble handling four ships together, but I wouldn't bet one of us could. You got to hit them hard and fast."

"We've got L'Estock's Sharp Steel Squadron from Pitts Hope heading out to relieve the *Audacious*," Kris said. It had taken a long and difficult talk with her key staff and admirals to get their agreement to send three of her thirteen squadrons out to the picket line.

"You're dividing your forces," Admiral Yi had grouched over and over again.

"They're divided into three clans," Kris had repeated. "They are probing us. I don't want to miss a chance to bloody their nose while we're in the scouting stage of this meeting engagement. Let's use the advantage the periscope gives us for as long as we can."

"Nip their whiskers as they come through," Admiral Furzah had enthused.

With the cat behind her, Kris wondered if she needed to turn around, but the others came along with her.

"Letting them know we aren't just sitting here waiting for them is good policy," Admiral Bethea finally said for all. "We've got enough pickets out around Alwa. We can always fall back using the fuzzy jumps if they switch directions and come at us from somewhere else."

So Zingi got a chance for an independent command, taking his Yamato squadron out to guard the B Approach to System X, while Shoalter's New Eden Ghost Squadron would cover Approach A.

They were just approaching the Alpha Jump out of the Alwa system when the *Temptress*, under the command of Commander Lizzy Chekhov, jumped in ahead of them.

Kris got the report as soon as it came in.

"Three fast scouts from the Beulah Wolf Pack jumped into the next system out when we'd been on station at observation point B4b for five days. We blew them away as they came through the jump into our system. When I left to report, the next system out was empty. Request permission to return to station."

Kris ordered the *Temptress* down to the yards for a quick reduced availability and amended her orders to the battle squadrons going out to send a scout into the next system and see if there was anything the next jump out. "Oh, and picket that system, at least the jump from four out to the fifth they're using. If they keep using the system, we want warning when they head toward our pickets at Four."

"They getting rambunctious?" Abby asked, as Kris enjoyed her lunch that noon. It was nice to eat for two and not have the extra passenger kicking about the chow. Speaking of kicking, the little passenger has taken to fluttering a bit. Jack couldn't feel it, but Kris could.

"Yes, Abby, our aliens are getting a bit rowdy."

"You think it's time to ramp up the Navy's side of production to fifty percent?"

"Don't tell me," Jack said. "You've got a new plan ready."

"Of course me and Mata have a first draft of a revised plan," Abby said. "Every morning, Mata has a revised, defense-heavy production plan ready. I keep telling her no one can read a Longknife's mind. I can never tell if you'll want forty-five percent, fifty, or bigger."

"What are we at now?" Kris asked.

"Thirty-two percent, with the consumer side getting forty-three percent, but that's only because we've got the new light-industry side turning out that stuff. It will be wasteful to cut the civilian side down much more. We've got mostly Alwans and colonials working that side. The new trainees that aren't ready for the heavy side or ship duty."

"You plan it that way?" Jack asked, giving Abby a jaundiced eye.

"No, it just works out. Kids got to start somewhere. Light industry is easier. It's kind of harder to get yourself killed making a TV. Try falling into a vat of Smart Metal. It not only kills you, but ruins that batch. Ugh."

"Has that happened?" Kris asked.

"We had to pull an Ostrich out of a vat. He took it in his head to chest butt with a buddy and bounced harder than he figured. Now they sign a pledge, in blood, not to butt on the job."

"That sounds reasonable," Kris said.

"Even they think so. We run a film of what the Ostrich looked like when we fished him out of the vat. They're cutting their finger before it's finished to seal their pledge paper."

"You tell Pipra that both of you need to stop by my quarters after lunch," Kris said, as Admiral Benson came up behind Abby.

"We'll be there. 12:45 or 1:00?"

"Make it 1400. I may need a nap."

"Or to jump Jack's bones. You don't look tired to me."

"Away with you, Abby, or I'll have you washing my hair again."

Kris's erstwhile maid was out of her seat like a shot. Benson slipped right into it.

"We want to go to two shifts at the yards. Twelve on, twelve off, seven days a week."

"What happened to folks wanting shore time to farm?" Jack asked. He had a pretty big grin on his face, like he knew the answer but wanted to hear it anyway. "We don't want to do anything to damage morale."

"Grubbing in the dirt is great when nothing's happening. Word's gotten out that the aliens are nibbling, and we're blackening eyes. It was real smart of you to put the new ships out on the tip of the spear. Those folks have lots of friends. The *Resolute* was hardly in system before I was getting requests to return to work."

"So nobody really cares about all that farming stuff?" Jack said.

"I wouldn't say that. I think they really like the idea of having a place to call home. Every dude asking to get back on shift was quick to tell me that they had local workers, colonial and bird types, to keep the home fires burning and the crops growing. They care about those farms a lot."

He paused to eye Kris. "They care about staying alive and killing aliens more. Can we build ourselves some real frigates this time for the yard crews to fight?"

"That depends on what goods and gear we can get out of the moon fabs and how long the aliens give us to build ships," Kris said.

"May they give us plenty," Jack prayed.

"Yeah, I know. What do you have in mind?" Kris asked her yard boss.

"Commodore Cochrane of Earth's BatRon 12 asked me if I could double his squadron into a task force. Pedro doesn't care any more for Yi than anyone else. Unlike Yi, he's been letting his crews sign up for homesteads and absorbing colonials and Alwans into his crews. Yi won't allow us to do anything with the twelve ships he's got surviving in BatRon 10 and 11. As Pedro sees it, he can double his ships using half Earth-born crews and the other half locals. With a task force, he'll rank right up there with Yi."

"Couldn't happen to a worse officer," Jack said.

"I'd also like to replace the ships we lost in the first battle," Kris said. "The *Atago*, *Constitution*, *Warrior*, and *Hotspur*. Before we start adding new squadrons, it would be nice to get those squadrons up to full strength."

Benson nodded. "After that, do I get to knock off ten new ships for my shipyard workers to fight?"

"I was hoping to turn all the empty supply ships that weren't running around the system into courier ships. Armed but fast."

"We can do those in our side slips. If I'm going to double shifts, I can handle new construction and conversions. We've got plenty of 20-inch lasers taken off the frigates you've upgraded to 22-inchers. Why don't you let me figure out what I can do? You just tell me what you want."

"Are you going to tell Pipra what you want out of her fabs: reactors, lasers, computers, sensors?"

"If I have to."

"She'll be in my flag quarters at 1400 hours."

"I'll be there," Benson said, and headed off.

"So, are you really feeling in need of some sleep?" Jack asked.

"I've been known to sleep with you, after all is done, and little said."

"You had enough of that salad?"

"I thought you'd never ask."

Jack left half his sandwich on his plate as they hurried out.

40

Kris actually did come awake in Jack's arms. She stretched like a cat. It felt good, and baby didn't seem to mind.

"Thank you," Jack said.

Kris put a sly and satisfied smile on her face. "You want to expand on that a bit? I can think of many things you might be thanking me for. I want to say, 'You're welcome,' for the right one."

"Thank you for not ordering *Wasp* to go chasing out there. Most likely with the A Approach squadron since they're the only one that hasn't had a fight yet."

"I wouldn't have ordered *Wasp* out there alone."

"Thank you."

"I was thinking of taking Hawkings's BatRon 2 along with *Wasp*."

"Kris!"

"Well, I was," she said, pulling the sheet up to her chin. Only when she was in a fight with her husband did she feel a need for something between them.

"But you didn't," Jack said, deflecting himself away from where Kris feared the battlefield would be.

"No, I didn't."

"So, was it the admiral who admitted she needed to be with the main force, or the mother who thinks maybe chasing after every little chance to get yourself killed might be a bad idea?"

Kris chewed on the question. "Could I get credit for all, maybe along with a bit of not wanting to get in a fight with my security chief over what I should do?"

Jack pursed his lips, then licked his finger and made three

imaginary lines in the air. "I think you deserve three atta-girls for that."

"Good. Now, can we get in a quick shower so the evidence of my misbehaving isn't there for everyone to sniff?"

They were showered, dressed, and Kris was at her desk reading reports on production when the next meeting started to form up. Benson arrived first. Granny Rita called from dirtside, and suddenly she and Ada, with a few key staffers, were on the screen at the foot of Kris's table.

"Have my meetings gotten that popular?" Kris asked.

"Has knowing what's happening and what's gonna happen become any less important than it was yesterday?" Granny Rita answered.

Pipra arrived, with a half dozen men and woman trailing her.

"Do I need to add a few more from my shop to keep the sides even?" Admiral Benson growled.

"You got the Longknife on your side," Pipra shot back.

The rest of Kris's staff showed up, thanks to Nelly's notice: Penny and Masao, Jacques and Amanda, even Furzah. Abby sat with Pipra, but it seemed that the only chair for her was at the end next to Kris's side of the U-shaped table.

Somehow, Admirals Kitano and Bethea arrived before Kris started.

I WAS HOPING TO AVOID A ZOO, NELLY.

IT'S A JUNGLE AROUND YOU, KRIS. GET USED TO IT.

Kris began by tossing the ball to Pipra. "No doubt you've heard there's fighting on the picket line. Abby may have told you I'm muttering about upping the defensive level of effort. You may not have heard that Admiral Benson has yard workers volunteering for two shifts a day, seven days a week."

"Yeah, we heard about it," Pipra groused.

"So, what's the answer from manufacturing?" Kris asked.

"How's it going to eat into consumer production for the colonials and Alwans?" Ada injected. "I know you Navy people are smelling the smoke, but not all the folks I got working for me understand matters the way you do. I can't turn off demand like Admiral Benson can turn up production. By the way, you planning on leaving a lot of farmland, goods, and equipment just lying around like a bunch of toys?"

"No," Benson snapped.

"Let me answer that," Pipra said. "I've got the numbers she's worried about."

One screen came to life. "That is what we're producing right now," Pipra said. "We've almost tripled the production of consumer goods. We could do that because the first thing we turned out were light-industry fabs specifically designed to generate consumer goods. You want TVs, commlinks, boats, and farm goods. Have we got them for you? Once we got those fabs up and producing, we reassigned the heavy-industry fabs to grow more heavy fabs. We're up twenty-five percent. But to answer Ada and Granny Ruth's concerns, the light fabs are designed for consumer goods. We can't change them over to heavy industry. Unless you plan to raise an army, those fabs are yours to make all the goodies your people want."

"And if we want to equip an army?" Granny Rita asked.

Pipra made an ugly face. "Why didn't you say that in the first place?"

"Because I'm not all that for it," Ada said.

"Oh," came softly from Pipra. "Which of you is my master?"

"Can we outfit, say, twenty-five thousand colonials and twenty-five thousand Alwans with hunting rifles, light mortars, and recoilless rifles?" the former commodore asked.

"I can ship you the hardware for them. Can you produce the wooden stocks?"

"We can produce them faster if you ship me a couple of small lumber mills and lathes."

"We'll turn them out first," Abby offered. "Fifty thousand rifles, say, two thousand mortars and rocket launchers. That would eat into consumer goods a bit."

"Which will cause me trouble," Ada said.

"But we got plenty of goodies stored in the warehouses," Rita shot back. "It will take a while to work off that inventory."

"We tripled our deliveries of light consumer goods," Abby pointed out. "It can't all have gone out the door."

"Your amateur farmers wolfed down a lot of it," Ada shot back.

"And most of that stuff is being passed along to the colonials and Alwans who work those farms for now," Admiral Benson put in. "Assuming we beat back these damn raiders and there's anyone alive to harvest the food."

"Point well taken," Ada said. "My problem is do I want fifty thousand rifles roaming around my colony when this scare has vanished in my rearview mirror. A few hunting rifles, I have no problem with. A lot of rifles in a lot of hands, some not all that much out of the Stone Age? Good Lord, people, someone could start a war."

Kris could see where this was going. Now she stepped in. "Ada, there are more reinforcements coming out here. Even if the fleet loses a fight, if you hold on for a while, there may be ships swooping in to help you."

"So we *do* need to be ready to have a war down here, huh?"

"I'm afraid so. Now, most of your guns are under lock and key," Kris started, trying to sound oh so reasonable.

"All our guns are under lock and key," Ada corrected.

"So," Kris went on, "if you organize a colonial militia, their weapons can stay in armories when they aren't in use."

Ada made a face. "That's what Granny Rita keeps saying. I wish I could believe her. Those rifles you gave the Ostriches to get land use agreements, I keep hearing that there's trouble down there."

"If there was trouble, I'd cut off their ammo supply," Kris said. She also was hearing things, but so far she hadn't been able to prove it. No settlers were harmed, and the Ostriches insisted none of them had been shot.

You can't solve a problem no one admits exists.

At least there was only so much murder and mayhem they could get into with twenty bullets a rifle per month.

Ada blew out a long sigh. "Okay, ship us the lumber mills. We'll get Roosters operating them and the lathes. I can find colonials familiar enough with rifles to teach other colonials how to make them." She chuckled. "You want to be in the militia, build your rifle first."

Ada eyed Jack. "I'll need more trainers to teach my people, what do you call it, battle craft?"

"I'll give you some," said Major General Montoya, Commander, Ground Forces Alwa Defense Sector, and technically

General Commanding, First Division. It was also the only division.

"But," Jack said, "I'm not willing to give over all my ship Marines."

"How come?" came from Granny Rita.

"The aliens tried something last time. Suicide boats sent at us. Those we handled with our secondary batteries. They also sent single men in rocket-powered space suits. Initially, we thought they were trying to surrender. When we tried to rescue them, they started shooting at us. Either they changed their mind or had something else on their minds from the start. Anyway, we left most of them to suffocate when their air ran out. Most blew themselves up when we pulled back. Any way you cut that deck, they got more wild cards, and we need to be ready. So, no, you can't have too many of my trigger pullers."

"Maybe we ought to be looking to give them some of our troopers," the old commodore muttered to Ada.

"If you don't think much of rifles turning up in the odd places of your neighborhoods, Ada, imagine how little I want dudes shooting off hunting rifles on my ships," Kris said, dryly.

"Don't you just hate messy wars?" Penny said, wryly.

"Okay, folks, you can make policy later," Pipra cut in. "What I'm here to tell you is that I can boost Navy production from its present low of thirty-two percent, which, if I may point out, in actual tonnage of product is only a bit below what you were getting before at sixty percent, to fifty percent in three weeks. Maybe two. That will let us finish all the heavy fabs that we have in the production pipeline."

Pipra studied her readouts for a moment. "That should grow our heavy-production capability a good ten percent more, which will be nice, what with you leaving less than ten percent to us to cover spare parts and other problems."

"If we keep the aliens off your back," Kris said, "you can try another round of starving defense to grow the base. If not, you won't need spare parts because all your problems will be over."

"That is one way of looking at it," Ada said, now taking her turn at dry humor.

That resolved the issues for the meeting, but it rolled on for another hour refining details. Kris got a squadron of armed courier ships: *Mercury, Hermes, Apollo, Sand Piper, Alhatross, Kestrel, Sparrowhawk,* and *Merlin.* Each was two freighters spun into one ship, now with four reactors plus four 20-inch lasers, mounted evenly fore and aft. They'd be stationed well out with the distant squadrons to bring word faster through the fuzzy jumps than it could be passed from one jump buoy to another across systems.

Commodore Cochrane would get his eight new ships, allowing him to command a task force and pin on a second star. His division leader, Captain Yosuf Suluc, would get his own squadron and a commodore's flag. No doubt, Yi would do much gnashing of teeth.

Only when those eight frigates, along with the four Kris needed to replace her early losses were in commission, would the yard supervisors like Benson get to lay down the next eight ships for them to command and crew.

"I think that qualifies as motivation," he was heard to grumble as he passed the word along to the other yard bosses.

It was a good plan. It lasted a whole week. Then the aliens made it obsolete.

41

"Kris, you need to wake up," Nelly said.

Kris didn't want to wake up. She wanted to see how her dream ended.

Kris was in an all-too-familiar position, flat on her back on an examination table. Her legs were up and spread. Only this was not an examination.

It had taken her a while to realize it, but the people busying around her were laying out instruments to perform an abortion on her.

Kris told them, in the most rational words she could come up with, that this was unnecessary. She had everything under control.

They ignored her and kept on laying out huge and horrible metal objects.

Sometimes, the nurse looked like her mom. Sometimes it was Admiral Yi or Commander Sampson. Whoever they were, they would not listen to her.

Even as Kris kept arguing her case, she came to realize that she was not tied to the table. She was free to get up and run for it. She stayed put, doing her best to dissuade whoever it was she was talking to, but in her heart, she'd already made up her mind.

If they picked up one of those horrible things with intent, Kris and baby were off to the races.

They would not take what she was becoming.

Even in her dream, she thought that strange. *It's not my baby they want, it's me.*

Kris struggled to wakefulness without learning the ending.

"Yes, Nelly, what time is it?"

"Way too early, Kris, but the duty section woke up Admiral Kitano, and she thinks you need to see this right away."

"See what?" Jack asked.

"It looks like we have another fast-moving suicide ship coming in, only this one is different," Nelly said.

"How different?" Kris asked as she rolled out of bed.

"They are coming in a lot faster. Faster and wilder. This one jumped into a system only seven out. It managed to skip five systems. The estimate is it's doing four hundred and fifty thousand kilometers and accelerating at 3.45 gees."

"Ouch," Jack said, and pulled on a fresh set of khakis as Kris reached for whites.

Five minutes later, they were in Kris's flag plot staring at a screen showing Alwa's picket system while Admiral Kitano and the duty officer reported from another.

"This report arrived fifteen minutes ago," the duty officer, a young lieutenant, reported. She looked very calm for a JO who'd just woken up a total of seven stars. Nine, if you counted Jack.

"I must point out that this report has been five days, eight hours in transit. It is possible that the suicider could be jumping into our system anytime."

"Nelly?" Kris said.

"I'm working on it, Kris, with *Wasp*'s nav computer. We don't do these kind of jumps, and I don't have this stuff in memory."

Kris raised an eyebrow. Nelly sounded sharp, harassed, and busy. Kris chose to cover another matter. "Kitano, who has jump-point duty?"

"BatRon 5," she answered quickly, then glanced off screen to check herself. "Hispania has the *Libertad* and *Federacion* at Alpha, the *Independencia* and *Union* at Beta Jump. The Esperanto League was scheduled to relieve them next week."

"All of those are 20-inch frigates," Kris said, measuring their 160,000-klick range against this fast move. "Alert the Esperanto League division to get under way immediately, as in ten minutes ago."

Even as Kris was issuing orders, another blip appeared on the picket line. Then another. The last was only four out.

The duty officer's attention was drawn offscreen. "Two more bogeys reported. One is going five hundred thousand klicks. That's got to be wrong—the next is reported at nine hundred thousand."

Kris rubbed her tired eyes. "If it jumped eight systems, maybe more, it would have to be going that fast." Kris really could use some help from Nelly.

"It will almost certainly miss," Nelly reported. "Even if it brakes in that system, it will jump past us," Kris's computer reported. "It's the second one that might be a problem."

"When?" Kris asked.

"A bogey has just entered the system," the duty officer reported, almost as calmly as she likely wanted to.

"Right about now," Nelly said, in a rather tardy answer to Kris's question.

Kris waited to be told how the Hispania frigates had done against the intruder. While this was news to them, the alert frigates had handled this problem several hours ago. Kris tried not to grit her teeth too tightly as she waited for the speed-of-light delay.

The screen beside the multisystem lit up to show only Beta Jump and two frigates anchored to each other. A fast-moving blip shot through the jump at the worst moment. Neither of the ships had its bow or stern on to the jump.

That didn't hold them up. In less than a second, both ships had broken loose from their mooring and were going bow or stern on to the target. Three seconds after the suicide ship showed up, nine lasers sliced into it, hacking it to pieces. The reactor blew, and most of the pieces were caught in a rapidly expanding ball of gas.

"Send a very well done to the *Independencia* and *Union*," Kris said. "Nelly, talk to me about that ship we just blew away."

"This is just a preliminary report, Kris, but the ship seems to have only had one reactor. It was denser than the usual alien ship. It may have had a minimal crew, but we need more data. There were several sensors pointed at that jump, and we're compiling their data now."

"How about the reactor?" Kris asked. "Is it from one of our usual suspects or has a new ship been heard from?"

"The reactor was different," Nelly reported. "Smaller than

what we've seen before. Whether it's a new version of a familiar design, I need more data."

"But the bastards have come up with a new twist," Jack said.

"It sure looks that way," Kris agreed through a yawn. "Now, if there's no more fun for tonight, I'll leave the watch to those who have it and get a few more hours' sleep. No doubt, tomorrow will be another busy day."

"No doubt," Kitano said, and showed no interest in her bed as she turned to her duty officer.

"Nelly, keep up with what's going on, but unless all hell breaks loose, let me sleep."

"Will do," Kris's computer answered, and the screens went dim.

"You that tired?" Jack asked.

"Yes, maybe," Kris said, although another yawn reinforced the yes. "I was having another one of those dreams. Really weird. Now this. I don't know if I want to go back to sleep, but I do know that my people need their sleep, and tomorrow will be soon enough to start ripping up our latest plans and cobbling together the next ones. Hold me. Help me sleep, dear."

He was very good at holding her.

42

Nelly awoke Kris at her usual time. "I'll have a report for you before breakfast, but you might as well shower and dress. There's nothing that can't wait."

Kris headed for the shower after only a quick peck for Jack. She couldn't remember any dream from the second half of her sleep, but something must have been going on. She felt like she'd had more of a workout than a rest.

Jack followed her into the shower this morning, having laid out fresh uniforms for them. Kris dressed as she eyed the screens in her flag plot. There was plenty of activity.

Fourteen bogeys were scattered around the picket line. Nelly had backtracked most to their launching system. Systems. No more than two had come from the same place.

"Have these learned anything from the mother ship we wiped out?" Jack asked, joining her.

"Nelly," Kris said, "any report on the reactors? Is it a single design or are we dealing with several base ships?"

"The reports from the pickets are not as informative as I would like. All the bogeys have a single reactor. It's smaller than the two we put on our freighters. It may not be all that well made. One of the ships exploded as it boosted from one jump to the next."

"Are they shooting out our pickets?" Jack asked.

"No. The one bogey that made it into our system didn't shoot, and I didn't read any lasers or capacitors on it."

"But it's denser?" Kris asked.

"Yes, Kris, denser with one small reactor and minimal life support."

"A crewed suicide rock," Jack said, sipping his coffee.

"Launched from the opposite side of our perimeter," Kris observed, "away from the System X quadrant."

"Yes. It's as if they want you chasing off as far from System X as possible."

Kris shook her head. "I wonder what's happening out there with the three squadrons I sent. We need couriers to get word back fast, and we needed them last week."

"But we need guns at our jump points," Jack pointed out. "And we need to know which of these is the main thrust." He turned to Kris. "Aren't you glad now that you're here and not out there?"

"Yes, love, I'm glad I'm behaving like a good admiral and not having any fun."

"No fun at all?"

"No fun blowing shit up," she said, and gave him another peck for a promise.

Breakfast was soon interrupted. Kris was still going down the steam table and surprised to find the scrambled eggs and ham unusually attractive this morning when Pipra and Abby came in. They made a beeline for her.

"I hear there was fun last night," Pipra said, as Kris gave in to temptation and added the eggs and ham, from whatever source, to her plate.

"If you mean that we have a new wave of suicide attacks coming at us, you're right," Kris said.

"And you want to rework my production plan."

"The thought has occurred to me," Kris admitted.

"When?"

"Can I at least eat my breakfast in peace?" Kris said.

"I warned you she was cranky before she ate," Abby said.

"I'm not cranky, I'm hungry," Kris shot back, but with a smile, or at least an attempt.

"Will nine o'clock be too soon?" Pipra asked.

"Nelly, advise all the usual suspects that we'll be reviewing our situation and its impact on production at 0900 in my flag quarters. Show up if you want to protect your ox from my goring."

"They are informed, Kris."

"Good. Now let me eat."

Abby took Pipra by the elbow, and the two quickly disappeared, though not in the acrid puff of smoke Kris could have wished.

"Kris, does leaving you alone include me?" Nelly asked with amazing deference.

"If it's entertaining, talk to me."

"The data is still preliminary, Kris. It appears the new suicide ships are made to two similar schemes. Lightly crewed, heavily built, but the reactors are slightly different. It could just be the difference in production lines on one ship, but normally an alien base ship always does the same thing the same way."

"That's the way it's been," Jack agreed. "Is there any pattern to the difference? Are we being hit from one section of sky by one type, the other section by the other type?"

"It's still too early to tell, sir. Some of the buoys aren't as sensitive as others. I'm afraid some of our own construction efforts have not been all that standard."

"Well, that's just human," Kris sniffed.

"But it's causing me trouble," Nelly sniffed right back.

"Enough, girls," Jack said. "Is there any way to check this out, Nelly?"

"I expect it will shake out as we get more data, sir."

"How come he gets a sir and I just get lip?" Kris demanded.

"He's a general, Kris. You're just a princess and a pretty poor excuse for one at that, if I may say so."

"I am also the person with her finger on your OFF button."

"You wouldn't dare push it, Kris. Too much is happening that you need me for."

"She has you there," Jack pointed out.

Kris sighed. "Yes, Nelly, you win this one. But when things calm down . . ."

"Kris," Nelly interrupted, "things never calm down."

Jack licked a finger and made two marks in the air. "Two good ones in less than a minute. Nelly, you're magnificent."

"I keep telling you so."

"And she believes it," Kris grouched.

"A bogey just jumped in using Alpha point," Nelly reported. "The *Libertad* and *Federacion* nailed it in two seconds. Kris, there is wreckage this time. Could you have them launch a pinnace to collect it? I'd like to examine it, maybe determine where it came from."

"Magnificent idea, Nelly," Kris said. "Order the *Libertad* to collect any junk they can find and bring it in when they're relieved. Order the *Union* to do the same if they can spot any debris from the first one."

"It is done, Kris."

"Thank you."

"You're welcome."

"Now, girls, isn't it nice to be nice?"

Kris waited for Nelly to respond. It turned into a long wait.

"Well, maybe not," Jack finally said.

Kris had just enough time to check the screens before her meeting began to form. There were now two dozen identified bogeys. Two had blown up. Eight had made jumps that carried them past Alwa. Unless they had the fuel to turn around, they were headed into deep, cold space and a slow, cold death.

"How do they get volunteers for a job like that?" Penny muttered as she joined Kris eyeing the screens.

"You have to indoctrinate people at a very deep level to get this kind of fanaticism," Jacques said, joining them. "They've got a very closed system, both in fact and fiction. What the Enlightened One says is the way it is, and there's no way for a reality check."

"So we provide the reality," Kris said.

"Yes," the anthropologist said, as Amanda came up beside him.

"You going to redo the economy again?" she asked Kris.

All Kris could do was shrug. "It sure looks like our summer vacation is over, folks. What's it look like to you?"

"A long, cold winter," Jacques said.

Admiral Benson showed up with Admiral Hiroshi of the Kure Docks on one elbow and a newcomer on the other. "Kris, may I introduce Admiral Ellen Tirpitz, supervisor of Gosport Docks. She came out with Admiral Yi from Earth."

Kris knew that the Earth fleet had brought its own port. Gosport Station was trailing Cannopus by fifty clicks, and Admiral Yi had made it into a private fiefdom. Kris had chosen to let that happen rather than risk a break with Earth. That

Admiral Tirpitz had chosen now to show up with Admiral Benson suggestèd that Yi's hold on Earth's assets was now tenuous.

"I'm glad to have you here," Kris said, shaking Tirpitz's offered hand.

"Glad to finally be making your acquaintance. Marty here has been telling me how he's putting his yard to a lot more use than taking dents out of ships. I'm looking forward to trying a few new twists of my own."

"Good," Kris said. "There are a lot more twists and turns headed our way."

Kris noted that Nelly had been expanding the U-shaped table and Kris's day quarters as the size of the meeting grew. Kitano had brought the other two fleet commanders, Admirals Miyoshi and Bethea, as well as some of her key staff. The duty officer who had made the initial report was there though she looked a bit wilted.

Pipra with Abby and a dozen other managers filled one leg of the table. Captain Drago just happened to drop in and sit himself down next to Admiral Furzah, along with Penny and Masao, Amanda and Jacques. On the far wall, the representation for the colonials included not only Granny Rita and Ada but also the Speaker for the Association of Associations, if Kris wasn't mistaken.

Even the birds are learning to go to meetings, Kris thought, and called the meeting to order.

"While we've been developing things like 22-inch lasers and crystal armor, it appears the aliens have come up with a few tricks as well. Admiral Kitano, please report on last night's developments."

Kitano passed the ball to the lieutenant who took a breath and launched into telling all these elephants that the cows had learned a new way to eat the cabbage.

"We have now identified thirty-eight alien suicide ships within our established warning network traced back to eighteen different systems. They don't appear to have a refined knowledge of the jumps. They're just hitting them at high speeds and seeing where it takes them. Two have arrived so far. Six have jumped past us. The rest are still en route."

"That seems like an awful waste of life and resources,"

Admiral Kitano said. "Three misses, maybe more, for every arrival."

"It's worse. Three have blown up," the lieutenant added.

"Someone doesn't count the cost," Pipra said, darkly.

"No," Kris said. "Their Enlightened Ones are only interested in killing us. The ships are of hasty construction: one reactor, weight for the hit, and a small crew. They seem willing to throw as many at us as it takes to get a hit."

"We'll need an alert defense at the jumps into our system," Kitano said. "They haven't thrown atomics through the jump ahead of them yet, but it's only a matter of time. As I see it, we can only adjust the lasers up or down fifteen degrees. If we want to keep our ships anchored and rotating for gravity, we'll need to synchronize twelve ships at each jump. Twenty-four at both of them. Allowing for relief, that could tie up our entire fleet."

"So we don't," Admiral Benson said. "There's nothing written in stone that says lasers can only adjust through thirty degrees. Yes, for a fighting frigate that has to defend itself, you don't want too much of a hole in your bow. However, to defend our own jump points, we could damn near park a barge out there."

"Wouldn't a rotating station be a bit much?" Admiral Kitano asked. "What if the jump moved?"

"I'm not talking about a true barge, but we could knock together three ships out of merchant hulls, arm them with leftover 20-inch lasers, and allow the gun cradles to rotate sixty degrees."

"That would only cover half the rotation," Kris said.

"Not if we anchor the ships in threes and rig the bow guns to shoot around the mooring lines."

"Can you do that?" Captain Drago said.

"We rig the lasers outboard of the moorings."

"We have nine empty freighters," Admiral Tirpitz offered. "The Apple Blossom class has two reactors. If we merge the nine into six, you'd have reactors to charge lasers but not a lot of armor."

"We don't expect these jump guards to have to fight, just shoot," Kris said, and wished she had some wood to knock on. She might be making a terrible mistake, but she needed her frigates ready to fight, not rotating through static-station-ship duties at the jumps.

"I can get you a good three dozen 20-inch laser systems to mount on them," Benson offered. "What about crews, Admiral Tirpitz?"

"Out of the nine, we ought to be able to put together six good sailing crews. But we don't have anyone to man the lasers. Certainly not in a twenty-four/seven mode."

Benson grinned. "Have I got some birds for you?"

"Mixed crews with the Alwans," Tirpitz said. Clearly, she'd acquired Admiral Yi's low opinion of the locals.

"You might want to talk to Admiral Cochrane," Kris said. "We'll likely steal a few from his ships to crew your jump guards."

"I've also got a few colonials and birds to work on your yard, if you'll take them."

Tirpitz worried her lower lip. "Do I need Admiral Yi's authorization for these changes?"

"Do you need Yi's permission to convert the freighters into fighters?" Kris asked.

Tirpitz shook her head. "Three of the freighter skippers came to me this morning. They'd heard about the fight at the jump points and wanted to know if they could have lasers mounted on their ships. Two others will likely want in on the fight. Of the rest, I just don't know, but they are civilian and not under Navy authority. Although I'm not sure Yi agrees with that."

"Admiral Miyoshi," Kris said, "you see to it that Yi understands that we are going to do this. You might also tell him that his task force should be here on the Cannopus Station with the rest of Second Fleet. Admiral Bethea, I'm moving all of your ships to Gosport."

"There won't be a lot of them. Most of my ships are deployed."

"Still," Kris said, "I want you on Gosport Station. We might as well bite whatever bullet we have to."

"I'll tell Rear Admiral Yi he's moving," Vice Admiral Miyoshi said.

Kris nodded. Yi was a hardcase, and having his former

subordinate, and a woman, tell him he was moving out of his familiar stomping grounds was likely not the best way to go.

*Managing people—*Kris sighed—*was as much of a pain in the butt as killing aliens.*

"Okay, it looks like we can guard the jump points without tying up the fleet," Kris said. "Now, how fast can we grow the fleet?" she asked, staring straight at Pipra.

"No doubt, faster than I want to, but slower than you'd like," she answered, and they began to dicker.

43

The sense of ease that had gripped the fleet, station, and workers, whether on the moon or the asteroid mines, was gone. The yards worked around the clock, now with immigrants, colonials, and Alwans.

There was no talk of low morale.

The courier boats were the first to flow out from the yards. *Hermes*, *Mercury*, and *Apollo* were hardly finished before they jumped for the three squadrons watching the approaches to System X. They returned just as swiftly to report that there was nothing to report.

No aliens had shown up in their systems to either peel off warning buoys or try fast jumps to Alwa.

The same couldn't be said for Alwa itself.

Rarely did Kris rise in the morning to find fewer than fifty aliens somewhere in the picketed zone. Many missed on their way to frozen hell, but more were incoming, hunting for that right combination of speed and location that would give them a chance to dash themselves against Kris's defenses.

That was the thing about a suicide mission; hit or miss, it never reported back. The handful that did find the lucky numbers died in seconds.

But that didn't stop them from coming.

Kris watched this tragedy unfolding before her, and like the rest of humanity, shook her head.

It was now clear that eighteen systems were launching these one-way attacks. Kris eyed the map and gnawed her lower lip. Should she take the bait and go for one of them? Would she find a base ship, or a few dozen huge warships if she did?

She called in her key staff.

She stood before them as usual. Only now, her left hand had a tendency to brush the growing bulge beneath her heart.

What great commander ever took that stance? the joker inside her chided.

They'll have to find room for it in the Longknife legend, she chided right back.

"I do not like sitting here while the aliens take potshots. We've slapped down everyone that got through, but I refuse their right to the initiative."

"So, what do you *want* to do?" Jack asked.

"I don't know what I *can* do," Kris answered, "until we get a look at what's out there."

Penny smiled. "So you want someone to go take a look. Do I have to volunteer?"

"I'm thinking of someone else," Kris said, "though the job is the same: go, look, run home quick. The buoy tenders aren't doing anything. If we need to replace a jump buoy, I'll likely send a division of frigates."

"A scout will need at least three reactors," Penny said.

"So we merge three of the tenders into one," Kris answered.

"If I don't get the job, who does?" Penny asked.

"There's a former frigate commander running the guano mines," Kris said.

"The one who couldn't take no from one of his prettier Sailors," Jack said.

"Yes. He'd be commanding a bunch of birds."

"He'd still have some Navy types and colonials," Penny pointed out.

"So he gets a chance to keep his nose clean, or he gets to shovel the bird shit," Kris said.

"Make sure he has a good XO," Jack said.

"I will."

It was tempting to give him an all-male crew, but it didn't work out that way. Kris asked for volunteers for a dangerous mission. This time she wasn't flooded; too many were already on dangerous missions. As it turned out, his XO was a woman, former second officer off one of the freighters that was now a jump-guard ship. His engineering officer was a younger woman also from the Merchant Marine. They were about the only experienced hands he got. The rest of his crew were colonial or birds; his entire gun crew were Ostriches.

Kris personally told Commander Hanson of his mission and the makeup of his crew for the USS *Challenger*.

"Are you giving me a second chance or a suicide mission?" he said, evenly.

"I have better use for you, your crew, and your ship, than throwing you away on a suicide mission," Kris said. "You aren't doing bad, running the guano mine. I have need for as many ships and as many trained people as I can lay my hands on, so no, this mission is exactly what I'm telling you it is. I want to know who's sending suicide ships at me. Are their bases weak or strong? Am I up against two, three, or a dozen base ships?"

Hanson nodded. "I heard about the mission you sent your intel officer on, going out to get a peek at what turned out to be the alien home world. I take it you want me to get a peek and report back. Do I just go to one launch site or more?"

"We've laid out a course that should run you by three of them. You'll be using the fast jumps we've found that the aliens don't know exist. Needless to say, that knowledge is something we can't afford to fall into the alien hands."

"Understood. I run like hell, but if I can't escape, we blow ourselves to kingdom come."

"In that respect, we're just like the aliens," Kris said.

"Okay, let me have a look at my ship and crew," Hanson said, then he paused. "Thank you for this second chance, Admiral. I won't screw up again."

"Make sure you don't," Kris said.

He saluted. She returned it, and he departed.

Jack had come into her day quarters halfway through the meeting but kept silent. He returned Commander Hanson's salute as he left, then went to take the now-vacant chair beside Kris's desk.

"You're giving him a second chance?"

"Yes, we need experienced ship drivers."

"Do you trust him to do what you're ordering him to do?"

"I have no doubt that he will. Besides, most of his crew are locals, colonials or Ostriches. I can't see them letting him get away with anything flaky."

"No, I don't see an Ostrich doing that," Jack agreed. "Okay, answer me this question. He's getting a second chance. What about Sampson? She's an experienced ship driver, too."

"She got her second chance, and a third," Kris said, patting the little one on his or her head. Or rump. She was never sure which end was up. "Sampson got sent to the yard and stole a ship. We gave her brain surgery, and she dreams up this scheme to get me pregger and unfit for command. As I see it, that's three strikes, and she can shovel shit until . . . well, I don't know when, but certainly for a lot more time than I'm thinking of today."

"Seems fair to me. You want to come dirtside with me tomorrow? We're standing up the Second and Third Divisions, Alwa National Guard. There may be several Rooster militia battalions marching in the review as well. It should be quite a show."

"You now have three divisions under your command?" Kris said, raising an expressive eyebrow.

"Don't you go making me a corps commander. If anyone gets three stars, it should be Hayakawa. He's the man commanding the troops dirtside. He certainly deserves more than the brigadier star he's got."

"Give me a report on who's commanding what down there with your suggestions for ranks, and we'll see what tomorrow's parade looks like."

"Please don't go promoting folks before the parade starts," Jack said. "They've only got the ranks they're wearing. We don't have a BX with loads of spare eagles and stuff."

"Thank you, Husband, I will keep that in mind," Kris said.

NELLY, CAN YOU MANUFACTURE SOME EAGLES, SINGLE, TWIN, AND THREE STARS FOR ME WITHOUT ANYONE THE SMARTER?

I MAY NEED ABBY'S HELP.

I THINK I CAN TRUST HER.

So Jack presented Kris with a promotion list for the two new divisions. At the top of it was brevet Brigadier General Hayakawa with a recommendation for three stars and overall command of all troops stationed on Alwa. Kris signed off on colonelcies for the regimental commanders, which, she noted included Abby's Sergeant Bruce, and two stars for the two

Marine officers who had come out a few short months ago from human space as company commanders.

There was risk there, but if they didn't turn out, she'd sack them and give some other jumped-up company skipper a crack at the job. And she'd likely be doing it based on the recommendation of Lieutenant General Hayakawa.

But did she want him outranking Jack?

Kris mulled that one. She solved it by promoting Jack to Lieutenant General, Commander of the Alwa Expeditionary Force, Alwa system, with the Commander, First Corps, Alwa Defense Force reporting to him.

She signed Jack's promotion before she went to bed and Hayakawa's the next morning.

Jack didn't seem at all surprised when she called him front and center before the parade next day. Hayakawa must have been warned as well; a certain young colonial woman was standing close by and did the honors of pinning his three stars on his red uniform. The rest of the officers were read their new promotions but paraded in their old ranks. There was a lot of pinning going on as soon as the two divisions were dismissed.

Two reinforced divisions did march by. Three regiments of over three thousand, plus an artillery brigade of mortars. It was extremely light, but it was a fighting force, and marching in between the regiments of colonial and Rooster units were battalions of Ostrich militia. They held their rifles smartly and even got the cadence close to right.

"They take it for a dance," Granny Rita whispered to Kris as the first militia battalion marched by.

"Can they fight as well as they march?" Kris whispered back.

"God help us if we ever have to find out." Rita made it sound like a sincere prayer.

Kris got back from the dirtside honors just in time to make a quick visit to the *Challenger* before she sealed locks and headed out.

"Have you read your orders?" Kris asked Commander Hanson.

"I read them to the entire crew and got a cheer for it. I notice I've got three 20-inch lasers pointed aft and three forward."

"I'm as interested in you running as I am in you chasing,"

Kris said, and glanced at his XO. "Do you have a problem with that?"

"No, ma'am." She grinned. "I knew Captain O'dell. I'm amazed you got her to run away from a fight. Me, I like running. Better yet, don't get in a place you have to run or fight, that's me. Does this periscope really let us peek in the next system without having to go there?"

"Trust your boffin. If he says there are dragons in the next system, be assured, there are dragons, and you don't want to go there."

"Great," both Commander Hanson and his XO said.

"Now, off with you. Godspeed and a fair wind. A lot will depend on what you bring back, so come back."

"Aye, aye, Admiral," Command Hanson said, and Kris left them to get under way.

They cast off from the pier before she was off it herself.

Now all she could do was wait. Wait, and try to bring everything together.

The problem was, even if she could patch together a few ships here, an extra squadron there, she was still way too weak to take on three alien mother ships.

Who was she kidding? Unless there was another miracle in the Longknife bag of tricks, all of this was just the final act in a too-short play.

Baby took that moment to do some somersaults. *Yes, little one, I know you're there. How do I give you a chance to play in some lazy summer sun?*

Admiral Kris Longknife marched for her flag plot, perchance to find some hidden miracle.

44

A week later, the *Albatross* streaked in with a report from the B approach to System X. Rear Admiral Zingi and his squadron from Yamato had gotten their baptism of fire.

Zingi's squadron had arrived after the Battle of Alwa and he'd been left defending the system when Kris took two fleets out to nail the assassins. Still, he'd studied her reports, apparently better than the Earth admiral.

The aliens had sent him a full dish, thirty strong. Zingi surprised them; he defended in the fifth system out. There was no buoy in the sixth system to warn the bastards, and they sailed up to the jump in a loose formation.

Zingi had his periscope out; it warned him what was coming. He arranged his two divisions in squares behind the jump.

The first three aliens came through fat, dumb, and sassy. Not even firing. They died before they knew what hit them. The next three ships were at least shooting as they came through. The frigates took them full in their vulnerable sterns.

The last ship apparently had orders to return immediately and report. It was rotating even as 22-inch lasers slashed into engineering space, destroying containment fields and letting plasma loose in flaming streams. The ship came apart, pieces spinning off in every direction.

Six ships jumped in next; six ships died.

With no report, the alien commander must have wised up to his problem. Next through was a tiny atomic package. Zingi's ships nailed it before it could do anything.

And nailed the next ship as it came through and tried to twist around and return.

Thirteen ships and no report back.

The alien commander must have been sincerely pissed.

Three ships came through in rapid succession, firing everything at anything. But firing at a lot of empty space couldn't protect their vulnerable sterns with all the reactors and rockets that it took to propel a ship of four-hundred-thousand-plus tons.

Again, 22-inch lasers sliced into alien ships, reducing them to hot gases and wreckage in little more than the blink of an eye.

Having lost half his force, you would think that he'd cut his losses and go home. Apparently, "retreat" was no more in the alien dictionary than "surrender."

After a long pause, three more atomics came through, one right after the other. One managed a low-order explosion, but did nothing to the frigates holding in formation a hundred thousand kilometers back from the jump.

Then matters changed. A tiny vessel, little larger than a human longboat, appeared, flipped and made to head back.

It didn't make it through the jump before four 20-inch lasers pinned it in place. From the looks of the explosion, its antimatter containment field failed.

Ten seconds later, a second boat appeared. This time, only two lasers took it under fire. It didn't matter, it died just as fast.

In rapid succession, eight shuttles appeared, and eight shuttles died.

Apparently, the commander assumed the weak human frigates would have shot their few lasers dry. Three ships shot through.

And blew as frigates showed they could take out large and small targets and keep their lasers charged.

With nineteen ships lost, the alien commander didn't run but instead charged the jump, sending ships through at ten-second intervals.

Rear Admiral Zingi was ready for them. His Yamato frigates fired half broadsides from their bow lasers. Twenty-four lasers would bludgeon the stern of the first vessel. Ten seconds later, another twenty-four would slash into the second. Even as the forward batteries recharged, Zingi would flip ship, ready to take out the next ship with the four aft lasers on his eight ships, then flip again and use the half of his fully charged forward lasers.

Fire, fire, flip, fire. The drill went on for a minute before the

Enlightened commander's nerves broke. More atomics sailed through the jump, to be swatted down before they could do any harm.

Then nothing. Nothing at all.

Cautiously, Admiral Zingi sent his probe with the periscope up to the jump. It showed five ships in full retreat, accelerating away at their maximum of 2.5 gees.

Zingi pulled his ships up to the jump and formed a line. Once the fleeing alien was a hundred thousand klicks out, he ran his squadron through at five-second intervals.

Now the alien had no choice but to fight or flee. He lost two ships before he could make up his mind, then ordered the remaining three to flip and attack.

Now it was Zingi's turn to flip and run, but he ran with his stern 22-inch guns slashing at the alien. The three alien ships had been modified with a thick coating of volcanic rock. Under laser fire, the pumice boiled, spattered, and fell off in globs. A flip, and the forward batteries were burning off more rock. A second flip, and the eight human frigates danced away from the charging alien trio.

It went that way until there was no more stone to burn and lasers speared deep into the vulnerable innards of the ships.

One blew when a reactor along the central spine lost control of its demons. The second died as fire engulfed it faster than the damage opened it up to the quenching emptiness of space.

The last ship didn't give up the chase but hurled itself onto the combined fire of eight frigates. They cut it up but, for this one, there was no sudden end. Reactors went cold as more and more of the ship gave way under the pressure of human lasers and the heavy stress of 2.5 gees acceleration. For this one, the reactors went silent, not vicious.

It charged the humans until it had nothing left but its own momentum, and then it continued to drift at them, with one or two lasers still lashing out when they could be brought to bear.

This one died hard, but it died. And even as it drifted, helpless in space, no one sped away from it in a survival pod. No one tried to save themselves. Open to space, its crew died.

Kris found herself joining her staff in shaking their heads.

"They know how to die," Jack said. "If only they knew how to live half as well."

The report concluded that there was no observer on distant overwatch. "If the aliens sent these ships to find out what happened to their last lost ships, they have even more questions now," Rear Admiral Zingi finished dryly.

"So what will they do next?" Penny asked no one in particular.

"I'd send a Marshall forward under a branch of green to parley," Admiral Furzah said.

"They don't know how to do that," Kris said.

"In a hundred thousand years, none of them ever fought each other?" the feline asked. "Hard to believe that."

"Maybe not," Jacques said, an anthropologist in full lecture mode. "They have the entire galaxy to wander in. How often do you think two shared the same star system?"

"Hmm," the admiral purred. "How well do you think three of them will do allying to fight us?"

"A good question," Kris said. "A better question is do we send a copy of this report to the other two squadrons that we've got deployed and have them repeat the treatment if the opportunity presents itself?"

"Nelly, show me the other two approaches," Jack ordered. "Specifically, the two systems where our squadrons are operating."

Nelly did.

"Note how both of these, as well as Admiral Zingi's system, has more than one jump into it. Nelly, trace them back until you find crossroad jumps, jumps that would allow you to leave the approach the aliens have used and head for the system on another track."

Nelly did. It didn't take more than about eight jumps to sidestep one approach and slip over to another.

Jack turned to Kris. "If you want to suggest we try and nip off another dish, I'd go for it, but you might want to put a picket in these flanking systems to give your squadrons a warning if the aliens get smart."

"They always get smarter," Kris muttered, but she gave the orders to both set up the ambush and look out for a return of the favor.

It was well she did. Over the next two weeks, Admiral L'Estock's *Battleax* and other Sharp Steel Squadron ships got their chance to take out thirty alien warships from a second wolf pack in a near replay of Admiral Zingi's fight.

However, Admiral Shoalter had to pull his *Phantom* and other wild creatures back from his exposed position as sixty alien ships in two dishes made a move on his flank, using a different jump to enter his system. Without the alert from the jump buoy, he'd have been caught in a race to see who could get to the exit jump before the other.

The aliens from the Anton Wolf Pack didn't follow him though the jump. One dish set up shop guarding it, while the second dish jumped out and showed up a week later, again, flanking him.

Admiral Shoalter again chose discretion as the better part of valor and withdrew. Slowly, but surely, he fell back toward System X.

45

Soon the *Hermes* and the *Apollo* raced in to report that the Beulah and Clairissa Wolf Packs were conducting the same flanking maneuver on Kris's other far-flung ambushes. Admirals Zingi and L'Estock pulled back although Zingi risked splitting his forces. One of his divisions managed to give the aliens a bloody nose before turning to race them for the exit.

It was a close run thing at the start, with the aliens doing their best to nail them. *Idzumo* and her three sisters raced off at nearly four gees, leaving the aliens far behind as they struggled to push themselves past 2.5 gees. After a few salvos, there was little left to do but growl at each other as the aliens fell behind.

Kris had strong suspicions that the aliens were now communicating with each other. Those suspicions were confirmed when the *Challenger* returned. Commander Hanson made his report personally to Kris.

"We nailed one of their fast movers," he said, grinning from ear to ear, as he and Kris exchanged salutes. "We weren't looking for a fight, Admiral. We understood our orders," he said before Kris could even begin to form an opinion on his kill.

"We were coming up to a jump. We expected a nest of bastards to be on the other side, so we were slowing for a dead stop. One of those fast movers shot through the jump heading right at us. It only had one reactor, but our sensors identified two lasers charged and ready. We didn't attempt to talk to them, ma'am. We were in their laser range and in damn short range for our 20-inchers. Apparently, their gunners don't sleep by their lasers the way our Ostriches do. I ordered a shoot for the aft battery, and we hit them good. Then I flipped ship and gave them the forward guns. They never had a chance."

He paused for a moment. "Apparently, their single reactor vented somewhere other than at the ship, so there were plenty of chunks left when we were done with them. We retrieved pieces and turned them over to the boffins for analysis."

"I have the initial report," Nelly said.

"Don't keep us waiting," Kris said.

"The isotopic makeup of the metals are different from any ship we've encountered, different from this local arm of the galaxy. Likely, Admiral, we are dealing with another mother ship built thousands of light-years from here."

"Damn," Kris said. "Continue."

"We found three nests of alien warships. Each time we peeked into a suspected system, we found sixteen warships in a kind of rotating lattice structure. Apparently, their equivalent of our anchorages. The four- to five-hundred-thousand-ton warships had a half dozen or so single-reactor suicide boats laid alongside, getting ready to launch. But it was the design of the warships that told me we had something different here. While they all had three large reactors aft to power their rockets, instead of three identical reactors laid out along the keel line, there was one huge reactor, say, mother-ship size, situated forward. It's a very different design."

Kris nodded; she hadn't figured out how to handle three, and now she was facing a fourth monster coming in from a totally different threat axis.

I will not think this can't get any worse. I won't. I won't, because it likely will.

Kris forced herself to keep her rising panic down. Well down. Away from baby, down.

"Thank you, Commander, and well done. Have your crew get some shore leave. I'll be assigning the *Challenger* to the courier squadron. When a frigate command comes up next, I'll keep you in mind."

"Thank you, ma'am, I'd love one of the new frigates, but, with your permission, can I take the *Challenger*'s crew with me? They're good, ma'am. Very good."

Kris smiled. He was talking what she liked to hear.

"And if it's the same to you, ma'am, I'd like to take the *Chal-*

lenger out for another run. Me and my XO think we can find the mother ship. If she's not in the middle of the line, she has to be close to it. If you don't need us all that much running messages, we'd like to find where the queen spider is lurking in that web."

Kris glanced at her board. She had five of the couriers out with the retrograding forces. The *Kestrel* was just back with a report from Admiral L'Estock. The *Merlin* was already away to replace her on station.

It would be nice to have a third backup courier, but it would be better to know what she faced. The yards could knock together another courier. It didn't have to be armed.

No, that was a mistake. If the aliens were running couriers around armed, there was always a chance that they'd take a stab at cutting out one of Kris's message boats. No, the couriers had to have a fighting chance.

"Thank you, Commander. Yes, I would like to know what's out there. Refuel, resupply, and head out. Let us know your plan. If you aren't as lucky with this scouting cruise as you were last time, I'd like to know where to look for the wreckage."

"Don't you worry about us, Admiral. It's not luck that brought us back but seriously applied caution."

"Good luck and good scouting," Kris said, and made her dismissal salute sharp. He'd earned the honor.

Kris called in her staff. She briefed them quickly, then posed a question.

"The aliens are proving painfully quick studies. Without intending to, Commander Hanson picked off one of their courier boats. Once they realize it's missing, they'll know they've been scouted and they'll know there is an advantage to killing the messenger. Do we need to start patrolling our lines of communication?"

"Better yet," Admiral Furzah said, "when will they move from threatening your flank to trying to cut you off entirely? If they can figure a way to seize a jump between one of our exposed squadrons and Alwa, they can ambush you."

"I don't think we have to worry about being ambushed," Jack said. "We've got enough pickets out at each jump point. If one of our jumps goes silent, we know something hostile is going on when the connected buoys report back. No, they can't set up an ambush, but they most certainly can cut our most direct line of retreat and force a squadron to take the long way home."

Kris found herself patting her bulging tummy. The terror that she'd felt when Hanson reported the presence of a fourth mother ship, a ship she'd suspected but, apparently, denied deep in her bones, was rising again. She felt an almost uncontrollable urge to pack it in and run for home. She was breathing faster. Her mouth was dry. She'd known panic, and she was making its close acquaintance once more.

She gritted her teeth and forced her hand away from her belly. She laid both flat on the table. "Any suggestions?" she asked her staff.

"I've thought of putting Hellburners on some of the moons around the gas giants in System X," Penny said. "The problem is, even if we pick the right moon, without a maneuvering force to distract, they'd just shoot out the missiles before they got anywhere."

Jack shook his head. "How do we defend a system as huge as X from three base ships and all those damn warships? Three, four, maybe as many as five hundred."

"Let's not take counsel with our fears," Kris said, even as she struggled to take her own advice. "We don't know how many warships they have, and we've peeled off sixty, seventy, maybe eighty already."

"Ever the optimist," Amanda said.

"I try to be," Kris said.

"Sometimes she's even more successful than today," Jacques said.

"You'll excuse me for interrupting your little panic party," Abby said, dryly, "but you got me out of a nice warm bed, and I'm figuring you had some purpose. Mind sharing it with me?"

"We need to start patrolling our line of communications," Kris said, tackling the problem she could. It helped her ignore the monster challenge she couldn't. "How soon before we can see some more frigates?"

"Admiral Cochrane's new squadron is starting to take shape. The yards aren't spinning them out together. *Roger Young* is coming along as fast as they can push it. *Erwin Rommel* is only a bit behind it. *Vo Nguyen Giap* and *George Patton* are a bit behind the two lead ships. *Grant*, *Lee*, *Napoleon*, and

Marlborough are just starting to form. We're giving priority to the more complete ship whenever we can and only adding resources to the later ships when they aren't needed for the lead ships." Abby shrugged. "We figured four fighting ships now might be of more use to you than eight nearly complete ones later."

"Outstanding logic," Kris said. "Tell Admiral Cochrane that he better start exercising his crews full-time, blue and gold style. When those new ships come online, their crews won't have a hell of a lot of time to shake down."

"I have passed the word to him, Kris. He was already doing that, but he thanks you for the suggestion."

That brought a laugh from around the table.

"I guess that puts me in my micromanager's place," Kris admitted.

The meeting struggled on for a few minutes longer. The elephant in the room trumpeted silently while they ignored it. Finally, Abby sniffed that she had enough from them and needed to get some real work done, and one by one, the others followed her out, leaving just Jack and Kris to stare at the screens.

"You're trembling," he said softly.

Kris wrapped her arms around herself. She could feel the shaking. Try as she might, she could not still it. Jack came over and put an arm around her. In a moment, she turned to lose herself in his strong embrace. A few moments later, they were on the couch.

"I don't quite fit like I used to," she laughed as she struggled to find a way for her and baby to fit in his lap.

"You two fit just fine," he assured her.

She breathed in his masculine scent. Masculine warmth. Deep inside her, she knew that he was just as at sea as she was, but there was something about being held by him that made all the dragons nipping at her butt somehow more distant.

She accepted the illusion for the moment and let it warm her.

Slowly, she found the shakes taking their leave. Slowly, she found her center settling in place, on an even keel. Slowly, she felt less a terrified little girl and more the woman who was the terror of these aliens.

How many have I killed? How many billions? One

hundred? Two hundred? Two hundred billion dead, she repeated to herself. *Even if they win in the end, they've paid a hell of a price for our dead bodies.*

And we will have bought time for humanity and the Iteeche to make the blood price for them way more than these dogs can pay.

Done with the shakes, but not yet willing to leave the warmth of Jack's arms, she said, "You have any idea how we stop them next time?"

He shook his head. "From where I sit, it can only get worse. Why haven't they sent a ship through the jump backward? Accelerate it and flip it on the other side, let it come through the jump firing everything it has and boosting to go back through? Even if we do shoot it to crap, some of the crap will drift through, and they'll know it's an ambush."

"Ouch. Jack, I was hoping for something *we* could use. You're not supposed to be thinking for *them.*"

"Yes, but if we're not one step ahead of them, we'll be one step behind them, and you know what it has cost them to be a step behind *you.*"

"You say the nicest things *to* me, which means the worst things *for* me," Kris said, smiling up at Jack.

"What can you expect from the worst half of the human race?"

"I don't think you're the worst half of the race. I kind of like you."

"Thank you very much," he said, and kissed her. Not a peck, but one that felt all the love, respect, and value that he held for her. Considering that, at least for a few moments there, Kris was none too sure what use she was as an admiral, a woman, and a future mother, it was nice to feel that someone believed in her.

"Hm, keep this up and we'll need a shower," she said, breaking for air.

"And I have to check on ammunition production for our M-6s," Jack said. "We've been practicing a lot with the locals. If we assign Marines to ship defense, we'll need more ammo."

"Is it a problem?" Kris asked, putting her admiral's hat on.

"I don't think so. We've had a good supply of nitrates on

hand. The stuff was supposed to be for civilian use, but I don't think anyone will begrudge us Marines a couple of tons."

"You're robbing consumer goods for guns?"

"Yep."

"Thanks for telling me. I'll at least be ready when Granny Rita and Ada ambush me with their complaints."

"I'm only taking a little," Jack said, raising two fingers and spacing them only a bit apart.

"But that little bit," Kris said, raising her own fingers up, then using both hands wide apart to make her point, "will likely cause a big disruption."

"Such is war," Jack said, as Kris managed for her and baby to stand up.

"I think that has two meanings in the present situation," Kris said.

"Yep."

"You do your Marine thing, and I'll do my Navy thing. Maybe we'll even survive."

"Likely we will. You have a great track record. You and that Vicky Peterwald gal. I wonder how she's surviving without you around."

"Oh, so that's it. I'm all bloated and fat with your child, and now you start talking about Vicky Peterwald."

Jack laughed. "I figured mentioning Vicky would get you in a fighting mood."

Kris sighed. "Fighting for you and baby. Always. Now go. I've work to do."

Jack left, and Kris found herself staring at her situation board.

While Jack had been holding her, another suicide boat had found its way to Jump Point Beta. It had shot in at well over 1 million kilometers an hour. Very close to 1.5 million. It had been a test for the new jump guards.

The division of Hispania and Esperanto League frigates had been pulling full duty at the jumps; Kris couldn't risk two ships missing the speedsters. Defending the jumps had cost her an entire squadron. Those eight frigates had just been relieved by six ships designed specifically for guard duty.

The Bird class were compromises piled on top of halfway

measures. Nine Earth-built freighters had been molded into six gunships with three reactors each. To that mix had been added forty-eight 20-inch lasers made surplus by the up-gunning of five of Kris's frigates. The idea looked decent on paper.

As work progressed, its flaws became evident.

The hulls were thin; they kept space out and held in a mixed crew heavy with Ostriches and Roosters. Each ship had four lasers forward and four aft. The lasers' cradles had been modified to allow them to fire though an arc thirty degrees up to thirty degrees down.

On a regular ship, that kind of swing was to be avoided. It left a gaping hole in the ship's armor.

On these ships, it didn't matter. There *was* no armor. Not a stitch!

Nor was there much Smart Metal™ for hull-strength members. Someone did a workup of what would happen if the ships tried to make 3.5 gees, the normal fleet speed.

The computer simulation collapsed in upon itself like a tin can.

But, for a ship moored with two others and on constant guard for some suicidal maniac, it was good enough. Three of them had just proven it.

The extremely fast mover had shot through the jump going close to one and a half million kilometers an hour and adding to that with a 3.24-gee acceleration. It took it a second to locate Alwa but had started to swerve around to head straight at it.

That was the firing solution presented to the *Turkey*.

Kris had accepted *Ostrich* for the first one. *Cock o' the Walk* had been the best suggestion out of many for the second ship. *Eagle* and *Falcon* had gone to the next ones.

But *Turkey* had shown up repeatedly in Kris's suggestion box.

After repeated rejections, Kris relented, and *Turkey* was commissioned right along with *Egret*.

So, of course, it fell to the *Turkey* to have its forward battery pointed at the jump when the speedster shot through, intent on his death and millions of others.

Turkey got its first shot off within a second of the ship's appearance. It was a miss. The gunnery computer hadn't made allowances for the target's speed.

The officer with the conn, a colonial, wasn't about to let that first miss be *Turkey*'s only shot. She broke her ship out of mooring, sending the other two ships spinning off and wrecking their firing solution as she honked her ship around to follow the shooting star. They held their fire until they had a solid solution, then slashed at it with first one laser, then the next, finally the third.

All three hit although the last was firing on scattered chunks of hot metal. The reactor didn't turn it to gas, so all three ships bent to the task of making what was heading for Alwa into smaller, if speedy, bits of debris. In minutes, they had the wreckage sliced and diced into truly tiny portions.

Kris sent the division praise for a job well-done and breathed a sigh of relief. The Bird class had the best possible fire control computers for just this kind of fast mover. The aliens were nothing if not persistent.

And they were getting more persistent at faster speeds. This latest test showed that humans still had the upper hand. They had to. One slip, and there would be hell to pay.

Kris kept a division of ships at Cannopus Station always ready to get under way on an hour's notice. If a leaker got through the jump guards, they'd have to do their best to shoot them down close in. It would be harder, but it had to be tried.

Kris looked at what they had done today and found it good. Still, the birds would be a problem in a serious fight. Unarmored, they'd vanish at a single hit.

Kris shook her head and studied the sites that were launching against her. Eighteen of them.

If each had sixteen warships then that made for . . . too many. Say 272 ships in seventeen launch sites and the mother ship with a few more at the last one.

"Nelly, what launch site is it that the crew of the *Challenger* are so eager to check on?"

"The two in the middle. They figure one of those must have the mother ship."

"I'm looking at 272 ships at seventeen sites. You throw in sixty-plus with the base ship, and you've got over three hundred. Has a mother ship ever had three hundred warships?"

"The one that came at us in the Battle of Alwa had over two hundred, but some of those were survivors from the first wolf pack we took down."

"Yeah. Nelly, get a message to Commander Hanson. Tell him I'll bet him a case of Alwan whiskey that he doesn't find a mother ship behind either of those two middle jumps."

"Kris, he says he's sworn off the booze. He does stupid things when he drinks, and besides, that whiskey is undrinkable unless you're already drunk, but he'll take the bet. What two systems do you think he should check out?"

"There are eighteen nests. I'd pick the fifth in from each edge."

"Kris, I checked the jumps to all four of them, and the quickest jump sequence is to one of yours. He says he'll check it first."

"Tell him to pick what he wants to bet, and I'll see if I can match him."

"He says that's the problem with trying to bet around here. No one has anything decent to lose. He expects to be under way in less than four hours."

"Tell him I'll see him and his crew off. Nelly, remind me when it's time."

46

Kris missed wishing the *Challenger* off; it got away in three hours. "We'll find you those two base ships, Admiral. No need to see us off, we didn't use up all your luck from last time."

"I can't even get respect from guys I've keelhauled and given a second chance," Kris muttered, but she liked that spirit.

And she did want to know what was threatening her other flank.

She eyed her star map. Winning a battle depended on good ground and making better use of it than your enemy. If three base ships formed up at System X, they would be twelve normal jumps from Alwa.

Do I fight them at every jump? If I do, will they outflank me?

Kris studied the "ground" the jump points gave her and saw swirling battles as alien ships and her squadrons turned and twisted, each driving to catch the other overextended.

She'd lose that battle.

What if two more swooped in from a different flank? Kris shook her head.

"Do I defend here, defend forward, or damn it all and attack them now? Worse, is this battle plan coming out of my dreams about standing up to my mom and dad?"

Kris paused; she found herself smiling. It had always been mother and father before, never a familiar mom and dad like other kids. She patted the top of her belly. "Well, little one, there's not enough room in here for two kids. It looks like mom may just have to grow up. But does that make it the right way to fight this battle?"

Kris slept on her idea; her night was dreamless. She and baby slept soundly curled up against Jack's strong chest. Six million years of evolution trumped the reality of her situation. She was grateful for the comfort.

Next morning, Nelly passed the word to her admirals that there would be an 0900 meeting. To the fleet went out the preliminary order "Prepare to Sortie."

The admirals arrived looking cheerful. Kris pulled no punches.

"Betsy, I want you to take the rest of Third Fleet out to support Shoalter. Miyoshi, you'll take Second to support Zingi."

The Musashi admiral's face stayed unreadable, but Kris was pretty sure the idea of having half his forces made up of Yi and his questionable obedience did not make him jump with joy. "I'm pulling Yi's task force out of your fleet and replacing it with Cochrane's," she quickly added.

Now he gave her a feral smile. "A fight. Bonzai!"

Kris turned to her last fleet commander. "Amber, I've kept you back tending the home fires while I've gallivanted around having fun."

"I wouldn't call it fun, but you do have more miles on you than I do."

"Can you get the *Princess Royal* away from the pier today?"

"In four hours, I'm told."

"Then those are your orders. Take First Fleet out to support Admiral L'Estock. You can have Commodore Suluc's *Saladin* and the rest of BatRon 14 to bring you up to strength."

Kris paused to eye the grinning admirals she'd just given sailing orders. "Your orders are to delay the enemy by any means possible. In doing that, you are to be governed by the principal of calculated risk. You will inflict the maximum amount of casualties on the aliens while incurring the minimum amount yourself. I am sending you to bleed them, but to retain your forces intact for the coming battle, which will determine the fate of Alwa and all who live on it. Anything you can do to make them backtrack and look for another series of jumps to flank you is to be counted as a victory."

"We're playing for time," Admiral Kitano said.

"Exactly. They can afford to lose a hundred ships if it takes out one of your fleets. We can't trade them three ships to one. Thirty ships to one will still be a high price. We can never know when one ship will be the difference between the survival of Alwa and its destruction."

"You want no casualties?" Miyoshi asked.

"I can't expect that. The enemy has a vote," Kris said. "Bleed them. Delay them. Withdraw in good order. I expect they intend to concentrate in System X. When they do, withdraw to overwatch positions in the next system. Keep me informed by courier. I'll see about spinning out more couriers, but I want the yards to make me more frigates."

"Who gets to name them?" Betsy asked, sparkle in her eyes.

"Me," Kris snapped. "I'm tired of mythical beasts or dead men you have to research to see who they are and likely won't care much for what they fought for. I want something fitting like *Tenacious* or *Relentless* backing me up."

"You won't have much here," Miyoshi said, maybe a bit guilty for who he was and wasn't taking into battle.

"I've got what's left of Yi's task force. We've reorganized the Helvetican division, and I've got the trusty old *Wasp*. Or the new one. If the yards can get me another squadron, I'll have three at full strength, plus the Birds guarding the jumps."

"Good luck," Kitano said.

"And good luck to all of you," Kris answered them. "Godspeed and good hunting."

"The same to you," Kitano said.

"I hope not. I'm going to sit myself down and hold in place," Kris said with a chuckle. "I'm not going anywhere."

"I'll believe that when I see it," Betsy said as she took her leave.

"You can believe it. Someone has to hold the fort."

Quickly, they were gone, busy to get their fleets away from the piers. Kris headed off to see Benson in his yard superintendent's office.

"How's it coming?"

"I hear you're sending my ships out to fight aliens with us not in them," was his rejoinder.

"Yep, three fleets sortie today. We'll see how good a fleet

of thirty ships is at slowing down a wolf pack. They were getting too good at dodging around a squadron of eight."

"Well, what do we get to fight?" he demanded, but not all that forcefully. His feet were still up on his desk, and his eyes were flitting to the ship being spun out in the dock below.

"The next one you make after that one."

"Damn you, woman. I don't get the *Steadfast*. What am I going to end up fighting this time?"

"Well, I was thinking the next class might be the *Inflexible*. Doesn't that fit you?"

"Let's see, the *Inflexible*, *Indomitable*, *Invincible*, *Indefatigable*," he rattled off from memory. "It beats the *Fairy Princess* and *Mischievous Pixie*. But we need eight names. Tirpitz and her folks want a chance to fight for their lives. *Valiant*, *Vanguard*, and might I add *Vindictive* and *Victorious*."

Kris was none too happy to have him taking her naming prerogative, but she had to give him credit for some rather distinctive fighting names. "Don't you think *Invincible* is a bit optimistic?" she sallied.

"It did get blown up, but"—he shrugged—"sometimes you win, sometimes the dragon does."

"So, do I have to visit all the yards to find out how things are coming, or can I just ask you?"

"Tirpitz did very good. She managed to respin the Bird class while keeping her four main docks reserved for the *Tenacious*, *Persistent*, *Steadfast*, and *Relentless*. I've got the kernel of *Vigilant* started here, and the other yards attached to Cannopus Station have the *Insistent*, *Stonewall*, and *Unrelenting* coming along, too. Now that the new Earth squadron has cleared the yards, these are all we've got to work on. If you give me the go-ahead, we can start the Inflexible class as second priorities and put the Tenacious class into high gear."

Kris made a face. "What do you say we lay down the *Victorious* first and let that be the name ship for the class?"

"Only if I get to lay it down here and command it when we're done."

"You drive a hard bargain, Admiral."

"I'm stuck serving under a slave driver," he shot back.

They shook.

"I'll see if I've got any scraps lying around the yard I can call a keel."

"Why do I suspect you've been plotting this next class for at least two, three days?"

"Because I have. I can count the odds as well as you. I can also count the number of Sailors we have around here. You have yet to tap the crews of the repair ships. They got stuck dirtside last fight. They really want a chance to kill a few bastards this time."

"Thanks for reminding me. Now I've got to do some scraping and scrimping to put together crews."

"Go have fun. I understand Yi is really pissed about the officers, chiefs, and petty officers Pedro shanghaied out of his task force."

Kris grinned. "I signed the orders. I know everyone he lost. Hard to tell a man he can't accept a promotion, XO to CO, gunnery to XO, chief to Warrant, petty officer to chief. Admiral Cochrane didn't ask for a single lateral."

"He must have been dog robber to a really sleazy admiral back in his early days."

"No doubt," Kris said, and left Admiral Benson to work on his next miracle. Ahead of her was her second-most-difficult leadership challenge, right behind Sampson.

Admiral Yi was on his flag, the *George Washington*. He'd been none too happy when Kris ordered him to join Admiral Miyoshi's Second Fleet tied up to Cannopus Station. However, removing him from Gosport Station had given both Admiral Bethea and Admiral Tirpitz a chance to operate outside the poison he exuded. Not surprisingly, both flourished.

As for Cannopus Station, it had pretty much ignored the Earth admiral, and he'd returned the favor, in spades. Kris found Yi in his day quarters, a space larger and plusher than hers if much farther from the bridge.

"You didn't send me with the rest of Second Fleet," he said bluntly, as she entered his quarters. He also refrained from standing from where he was sprawled on a red leather couch.

Has he been drinking?

If he had, Kris could detect no odor.

"I'm holding your ships as the main strike force of Fourth Fleet."

"Who commands this new Fourth Fleet?"

"I do."

"Oh." He considered that for a moment. "And what do you intend to do with this new fleet?"

"It's holding the fort while the other three delay the alien wolf packs headed our way."

"Wolf packs. That's not a bad name for the bastards."

"They do fight in packs," Kris agreed.

"You going to steal more of my men?"

"Quite likely. I notice that you're adding colonials and Ostriches into your crews. Even a few Roosters."

"I'll take any that pass muster and keep their noses clean," he allowed.

"We're in the final stages of commissioning another squadron of frigates. I'll likely promote more of your officers to work with those crews. I plan on drawing down the crews of the repair ships, but I'll need experienced line officers and senior petty officers."

"And if I won't release them?"

"If *I* sign the order, you *will* release them," Kris said, evenly. Was he drunk enough to swing on her? That would settle a lot.

He examined the obvious for a very long time, then nodded. "Send me your written orders."

"You will have them this afternoon."

With that, she turned and left.

KRIS, COULD THAT MAN HAVE WALKED A STRAIGHT LINE?

I DON'T KNOW, NELLY. WHAT I DO KNOW IS THAT I'M GOING TO BE VERY CAREFUL WITH HIM.

47

NOW Kris waited. Battles were terrifying, but you were too busy staying alive to taste it. This waiting was gut-grinding, and there was nothing to do but do it.

So Kris did what she had to do.

The one thing she couldn't avoid was gestating this little inconvenience beneath her heart. She was entering her third trimester and all that energy she'd been enjoying for the last three months had gone AWOL.

Kris found her feet dragging . . . and swelling . . . even as she went about the desperate job of gathering support while her three distant fleets bought time.

Kris needed more scouts. She and Pipra had a knock-down, drag-out fight as they debated what ships could be passed out of the carrying trade from the asteroid mines and into Kris's scout fleet.

"We're operating at a bare minimum as it is," Pipra insisted. "You do want more Smart Metal and reactors, don't you?"

"Don't ask silly questions," Kris snapped back, trying to get comfortable and finding that she and baby were not getting along at the moment, and it would likely only get worse. "You know our lives depend on what your people make. I'm just asking if you can do more with less."

Pipra scratched her head. Kris was seeing more and more of that lately. A lot of folks were carrying tension in their scalps. "You've kept the freighters at single reactors to make sure none of them got it in their heads to run for home."

"Yes," Kris conceded.

"If we went back to two reactors, we'd be running half the ships back and forth, but they'd carry more than double the load, just half as often."

"Would that disrupt the flow of production?" Kris asked.

"Abby, what does your computer say?" Pipra said, tossing the bomb to Kris's former maid and now super project manager.

Abby spent a whole minute staring into space, communing with her computer, one of Nelly's kids, before she said, "We've got just enough of a buffer in our present inventory that we could take the hit of going to half the ships making half the runs but bringing in 235 percent each trip. But how long would it take the yards to respin two ships into one?"

"They're getting very good at that," Kris said, "Nelly, ask Benson."

"I've passed him Mata's schedule of ships in port and those coming in. He says they can respin two ships into one in as little as twenty-four hours. There's not a lot to do with a freighter. If they get the two ships orbiting the moon right now into the yard before noon, they can have one out by noon tomorrow." Nelly paused for only a moment, then added, "And that will give you fewer crew on the mining runs and some of the ship navigation and electronics for warships."

"Every scrap helps," Kris said, finally feeling comfortable in her chair.

"Kris, I'm working my people day and night. We've got people volunteering to work extra shifts to make sure some of the new hands don't screw up. I know your people are out there fighting for our lives, but I need you to know that we, back here, are fighting just as hard to get you what you need before you even ask for it."

"I know that, Pipra. Believe me, I know it."

"Well, it would be nice if you showed it."

"What do you want, a royal visit to your fabrication plants?"

"Hell no, that would just lose us production. But it would be nice if my folks knew you knew what they were doing and cared about it."

"Kris," Nelly said, "you've been looking at creating campaign medals for the First Battle of Alwa and an Expeditionary Medal against the Suicide Base."

"Yes. I should have signed off on those weeks ago. We'll need to add another for the Holding Campaign for System X."

"Why don't we issue a medal for industrial service in the

defense of the Alwa system?" Nelly asked. "There was a medal given back in the twentieth century. The King George Cross was awarded to the island of Malta for its people's courage under siege."

"We're certainly under siege," Pipra added, dryly.

"You want me to award a King Raymond Cross? Kris said. "I think Granny Rita might have something to say about that."

"How about a Princess Kristine Cross?" Pipra asked.

"I know I'm a cross you bear," Kris said, making a face, "but do we want to make it official?"

"Kris, I don't think you realize the impact you have on my people," Pipra said. "Yes, you're keeping them from running, but you are here, right beside them. Even six months pregnant, you haven't backed down. Kris, you may count on us, but we're counting on you, too."

"So something like the Princess Kristine Cross for Steadfast Support in the Defense of Alwa, huh?"

"Exactly. You have Nelly design you a ribbon to go with a silver medal sporting your face, and you'll give me just what I need to keep my workers in the traces until they drop or the aliens blast us to atoms."

"Please don't tell that to the troops," Kris said.

"It's just between us two. Do we really have a chance?" Pipra asked, all levity gone.

"I don't know," Kris said, letting honesty slip to the surface for a moment. "With what we have, we can't hold. With what we're trying to patch together . . ." Kris paused, then shook her head "Not against live base ships."

Kris took a deep breath. "There's supposed to be some secret weapon that they're putting together back in human space. The last group to come out heard about it but were warned to not even try to guess what it was, or they'd be booted from the relief force. Maybe if we hold out long enough for them to get it here," Kris said. "Maybe."

"So we're fighting for time and praying for a miracle."

"I'm afraid that's it, Pipra. That's all I can offer."

Pipra took a deep breath. "Then that is what we'll do. Now, if you'll get that cross officially knocked together, I'll arrange a five-minute break for people to look at a certificate with their name on it and cheer before I take the whip to them and get them back to work."

"I can have the template of the certificate for you in an hour," Nelly said.

A piece of paper and a prayer. Is that what we've come to?

But Kris signed the certificate, and Nelly distributed it to the shipyards, moon fabs, and asteroid mines.

Of baubles like that, seconds are bought.

48

Out beyond System X, Kris's fleets bought time the old-fashioned way, with blood and sweat and tears. The three wolf packs turned out to be a bit different, so each of the fights were, too.

Vice Admiral Bethea's Third Fleet had the toughest time with Wolf Pack Anton. Their Enlightened One hardly deserved the name. Or maybe casualties just didn't bother him.

Bethea deployed Third Fleet to make a stand two systems out from System X. It had two jumps in, so, of necessity, Bethea split her fleet to cover both jumps. Her situation was complicated because the eight frigates of the Esperanto League and Hispania still had the shorter-range 20-inch lasers. She split them, sending one division to each jump, then had to split up the Scanda Confederacy's squadron, sending the *Odin*, *Thor*, and *Frigga* to fight with her own Savannah Squadron while Admiral Shoalter's New Eden Squadron had the other three.

Fifteen ships each to hold two jumps.

Bethea's own Task Force 5 drew the bloody straw.

The periscope gave them warning that over sixty ships in two dishes were incoming. There was no chance to call for reinforcements. Shoalter's Task Force 6 had a dozen ships approaching his jump. Whether to force it or just fix him in place was hard to tell.

There was no question, the ships before Bethea's jump were coming at her with intent. Bloody intent.

Three ships came through at fifteen-second intervals, firing every laser they had. Three came, three died under a hail of lasers and antimatter rockets.

Then the aliens got smart. The next three ships came

through backward, their vulnerable aft end already flipped away from the eight ships Bethea had behind the jump.

But Bethea had fifteen ships and seven were deployed *in front of* the jump. They snapped off shots at the aliens' stern ends in rapid sequence and all three died just as dead as those that came through bow first.

Several small packages came through next, likely atomics. Quickly, they were lased to nothing.

A pause followed. Then the aliens began ramming themselves through the jump at ten-second intervals. Four- to five-hundred-thousand-ton behemoths shot through, alternating their facing.

It did them no good. Indeed, alternating them just made it easier for the two squadrons to shoot, recharge, shoot, recharge.

Twenty-four ships came through and twenty-four ships died.

After that slaughter came another pause. When it drew long, Bethea ordered the *Albatross* up to the jump. She did a quick four-gee acceleration and deceleration and slipped the periscope through.

"The other dish has had enough. It's withdrawing."

Bethea studied the picture for all of three seconds, and said, "Let's not let them go without a last dance, shall we?"

In ten minutes, she had her frigates arranged in a tight line at five-second intervals. There were advantages in going to war in fifty-thousand-ton frigates verses five-hundred-thousand-ton monsters.

Bethea led Task Force 5 through, her flagship *Lion* leading.

Into a target-rich environment.

Thirty alien warships were 120,000 klicks out, in a loose sphere presenting their hind ends. It was easy pickings for the 22-inch lasers that her big cats had been up-gunned with.

By the time all fifteen frigates where through, nine aliens were balls of gas, and the commander was just reacting to his danger. He flipped his surviving twenty-one ships, loaded with lasers and thickly coated with rock, and charged Bethea's two squadrons. Several tried to push themselves past 2.5 gees. One blew out its rocket motors and spun out of control.

Whether they made 2.5 gees or a bit more, it didn't matter. The human frigates flipped ship and backed away, hacking and slashing at them with their longer-ranged lasers while keeping well out of reach of the mass of lasers that might be good for lasing a planet from orbit but were totally outclassed against the humans' big 22-inchers.

Rocky armor blazed away in flaming chunks that gave only slight protection from the next incoming volley. Ships glowed and burned until there was nothing left but raw hull and vulnerable aliens inside.

Then ships died. Some died quickly as a reactor blew out and plasma ate them. Others died slowly as lasers sliced off chunks of ship and sent them flying off to trail briefly behind the ship before falling well away.

Damaged hulls collapsed under the pressure of the 2.5-gee acceleration; ships fell in upon themselves like a flower in some sort of reverse blossom.

Twenty-one ships gave chase to the humans. Twenty-one died.

Not one alien sought to save himself.

There were three exceptions to this slaughter. Three fast movers had broken away from the jump ahead of the main force and were well on their way for the nearest jump when Bethea ordered an end to her victorious flight.

When Bethea took stock of her ships, she found little damage to report. Both fights had been well out of range of the alien lasers. What hits they got were ineffective.

Like the French knights against British longbows, the aliens would have to come up with something different if they wanted to win a fight against 22-inch lasers.

Admiral Bethea held off her report until Admiral Shoalter had a chance to chase down his nuisance force. He jumped through and blew away six still close to the jump. The other six were already well away, accelerating at a full 2.5 gees.

Kris got the report less than a week after the fight. Coming in quickly on the heels of the *Kestrel* was the *Merlin* from Admiral Miyoshi's Second Fleet. The Beulah Wolf Pack had been more careful.

Miyoshi's Second Fleet had a tougher system to hold. It had three jumps in; he had to spread his ships more widely. Admirals Miyoshi and L'Estock's as well as Commodore

Zingi's squadrons each got a jump. The new BatRon 13 of Alwa-built frigates were added two or three to each jump.

That allowed for only five or six ships on each side of a jump.

It could have been tough fight, but the Beulah Wolf Pack's Enlightened One didn't seem to have the stomach for slaughtering his people with nothing to show for it. Each of the three jumps were tested with a trio of ships. The supporting dish stayed well back from the jump, and when nothing came back, immediately flipped ship and boosted away.

With so few ships to guard each jump, Vice Admiral Miyoshi chose caution and made no move to attack the withdrawing ships.

Two days later, the *Hermes* reported that Vice Admiral Kitano's First Fleet had rebuffed pretty much the same kind of attempt by Wolf Pack Clairissa.

"Nelly, can we hold along this line?" Kris asked.

"I'd like to say we could, Kris, but those fast-moving suicide boats tell me that the aliens know how to make long jumps. There are several jumps that wouldn't require more than four hundred thousand klicks an hour to take them into the jumps behind those systems."

"And we'd end up with a couple of dishes defending the jump we need to go through," Kris muttered.

"We could use a long jump to get out of that trap, Kris, but it might take our ships a while to get back to Alwa."

"Give me a list of the jumps, Nelly. We'll picket them. With luck, we can pick off their scouts, and they won't discover we've got a trail behind our Thermopylae."

"I didn't know you remembered that battle, Kris."

"Nelly, I do have a meat part of my brain that I use occasionally."

"I keep forgetting that part of your anatomy."

"Is that because you're only thinking about that parts of me that Jack likes?"

"Kris, I don't know if I should continue this fun game of pretending what I do and don't think about your physical makeup or whether I should get back to something serious."

"Nelly, if you want to be just one of the girls, you need to sound like us."

"But I am not now, nor will I ever be, one of you girls," Nelly sniffed.

"Well, it was fun thinking you were for a moment. Now, yes, we are holding several 'Hot Gates,' but it looks like we need to hold a few mountain trails as well. Get the couriers headed back with that data just as fast as they can be made ready."

"They report that they are ready now, just give them time to refuel and resupply."

"They've got to be doing 3.5 gees or better."

"A check of their vitals shows you're right, Kris, but the skippers are already taking on fuel and frozen meals."

"See if you can get them some decent box lunches from the station's restaurants and tell them the chow's on me."

"Done, Kris. I'm telling them what's available for take-out. These meals may be a bit spendy. They're ordering the most expensive stuff on the menu."

"They earned it."

Kris took a deep breath and eyed her board. Three suiciders had come through to impale themselves on the guard ships' lasers. The number had gone from one every couple of days to one a day, then two. Today was the second in a row with three.

Kris shook her head. "I may finally get to see what happens when two ships try to use a jump at the same time. I hope they're both suicide boats and not one of ours."

Then Jump Point Beta coughed up a normal warning buoy, followed a few moments later by the *Challenger*, and Kris found herself with a whole new set of problems.

No, a challenge. Not a problem, but an opportunity. She smiled.

49

"We found the alien base ships that are spawning the suicide boats right where you expected," Commander Hanson reported.

Kris grinned; even a Longknife liked it when they guessed right. Even a tired, pregnant, Longknife. She put her feet up on her desk, relaxed into her chair, which she had Nelly adjust until it fit her and baby as well as could be expected, and stared at the wall screen that showed the spread of systems spawning ten-thousand-ton boats that could make a very big hole in Alwa if they got through.

So far, the Birds had stopped every one.

Kris should be happy they were content to throw away their people in such an easily defeated way.

Instead, Kris eyed the screen.

She hated doing nothing, even if the aliens were doing little better than nothing.

"Nelly, talk to me about the two systems with the alien base ships."

"Kris, you aren't thinking of doing something to one of them, are you?"

"Nelly, thinking about something isn't doing something."

"I know many philosophies that say to think about a sin is the same as committing it."

"Since when did you take up philosophy?"

"Since it dawned on me that if you die out here, I and my children will die with you."

Kris patted the bulge at her waist. "Motherhood does things to you, doesn't it?"

Nelly said nothing.

The door to Kris's quarters opened, and Jack entered. "Nelly tells me you're examining options."

"Nelly is a snitch."

"Well, she only snitched to your husband and security chief."

Kris kept her feet up. "I just got comfortable. Pull up a chair, and we'll talk if you insist."

He pulled up a chair. "You planning on doing something wild?"

Kris mulled that over. "I haven't decided. I want to look at my options, Jack. Every girl grows up being told to sit there like a good girl. Hell, I'm a knocked-up girl. I didn't get this way by being good."

"Your husband might hold a different opinion," Jack said with a happy grin.

For once, Kris ignored him. "So, is there any weakness in the alien suicide array? They've scattered themselves over eighteen systems. 'He who tries to be strong everywhere is strong nowhere.' Didn't Colonel Cortez tell me that a while back?"

"If he didn't, a whole lot of other people might've said the same," Jack allowed.

"The *Challenger* checked on three systems and found sixteen ships in some kind of dock spawning suicide boats. Nelly, what's in the systems with base ships?"

"One base ship has sixty-eight warships guarding it. The other has eighty-four."

"So two or three dishes," Kris said.

"But you'd have to come through a jump and close the distance to the base ship," Jack pointed out. "They could be running away the whole time. You planning on doing a hammer and anvil on them? I don't see much of a hammer and damn little of an anvil at your disposal."

"We'll talk about what I can lay my hands on later. For now, let's look at the nut I might be tempted to crack. Nelly, put one of the systems up on the nearest screen and make it big. I'm comfortable, finally, and I don't want to have to waddle over to get a good look."

"You do not waddle, wife of mine."

"If I say I'm waddling compared to the dainty way I used to mince around, I'm waddling, husband, and you will agree under pain of losing way more husbandly points than you can afford at the moment."

"I will only stipulate to your opinion of your gait if I may enter into the record my delight in your glowing countenance."

"I'll give you a 5.9 for your save, lover boy. Now, foreplay complete, let's see if there's any way I can blow another base ship to hell. What have you got, Nelly?"

"What I will call System One is a mess. Three suns. Six jumps. Lots of gas and rock crap wandering around them in odd obits. The alien is close to one jump. That makes it easier to get the suicide boats running for it. There's another jump fairly close by, but it wouldn't help all that much if you wanted to use it for a pincer movement. The base ship would have a pretty easy run for any of the other four jumps."

Nelly made the system large and easy for Kris to follow as she walked her through it. Kris shook her head.

"Nothing nice there. What's the other one like?"

"This one is a simpler situation. One nice yellow dwarf. Three normal jumps. The aliens are orbiting a gas giant close to one of them."

"Nelly, you said three normal jumps. Does that mean there's a fuzzy jump?" Jack asked.

"Two of them," Nelly said, and showed them.

Both were close to the gas giant the aliens orbited.

Kris whistled. "We got a back door right into their nice party, and they don't even know it's there."

"Kris, we've been keeping those fuzzy jumps a secret," Jack said. "Is now a good time to show we can pop out of thin air?"

"You're assuming that they'll have any survivors to report what happened," Kris pointed right back.

"You think you could fight a battle of annihilation? How many warships does this one have, Nelly?"

"This is the larger force. One honking big mother ship and eighty-four of her huge kitten warships."

"And what have you got to take a shot at them?" Jack asked. Most likely he knew the present count of ships in port or fitting out, but he was leaving it to Kris to put her best spin on them or settle for a lower count.

"We don't have the Birds," Kris said. "They stay at the jumps and keep swatting suicide boats. I've got the good old, no, new *Wasp. Triumph, Swiftsure, Spitfire*, and new *Hotspur* from Helvetia now with 22-inch lasers. I've got that darling Admiral Yi and the twelve Earth frigates he didn't throw away on our last shoot."

"Assuming he follows orders better than last time," Jack said.

"Are any of his Marines talking to your Marines about his maybe having a drinking problem?"

"None within my hearing. Sorry. Do you think he does?"

Kris winced. "I have no proof."

"Can't you just relieve him because you've, what's the wording, 'lost confidence' in his leadership or ability to command or fight or something?"

Kris chuckled bitterly. "It does say that somewhere in the book, but it also says that coalition warfare is the pits. You can't just go around firing officers other people have put in charge."

"And if it wasn't for a coalition, we'd be mighty weak," Jack added.

"Exactly. If there were a senior Earth officer out here I could go to, I would. But Yi *is* the senior Earth officer. That complicates things. And no, I will not go to his subordinate officers and ask them for a vote of confidence in him. That's no way to command."

"I didn't suggest it."

"Correct, you didn't, and thank you, but I felt the need to clear the air. Nelly, get me Admiral Benson."

"Yes, Your Problem-ness."

"How is the *Tenacious* squadron coming along?"

"The first division is making a gentle tour around the moon. The last four are in the final stages of fitting out. Be warned, some of the locals on those ships are pretty raw. Pipra and I are holding on to our more experienced folks at the moment. Something about production being priority one, or so I'm told."

"And the *Victorious* squadron?"

"Just starting to quicken, Admiral. Likely we'll need a week before one of them can risk getting away from the pier. Tirpitz just laid her last one down a few hours ago. Can I ask why you're joggling my elbow?"

"I'm thinking of taking a few ships out for a spin."

"How long a spin?"

"The aliens have a mother ship sixteen jumps out, as the crow flies. I'm thinking of making a few fast jumps and seeing how they take to surprises."

"I'm wondering how I take to surprises. Would you mind if I dropped by? Maybe brought Admiral Hiroshi with me?"

"Feel free to. Jack's trying to talk me out of this jaunt even as we speak."

"Jack. Good man, even if he did marry a crazy woman."

"Be careful. That crazy woman may be throwing crockery by the time you get here."

Silently, Kris mulled the screen with Jack. Silently, she tried to imagine how a mere twenty-five frigates could take on eighty-four huge warships and one honking big mother ship. Not just take them on, but wipe them out. Leave no one to tell the tale of how it happened.

The smart thing would be to stay home.

Home here, or home on the other side of the galaxy? Kris answered herself.

The two admirals arrived and seemed to have somehow caught up Abby in their wake. They eyed the screen, then silently took seats around Kris's desk. Being comfortable, and baby presently engaged in doing backflips on her bladder, Kris stayed with her feet up, knowing very well this would have to end soon when she made one of her frequent trips to the head.

Nelly briefed them on the potential target.

"You going to drive them to the nearest jump?" Benson asked when Nelly was finished.

Kris shook her head. "I was thinking of something like a wild highland charge. Pop in on them from the nearest fuzzy jump, barrel at them with all I've got, and take them by surprise."

"Kris," Nelly said diffidently. "Even if you jump in at four hundred thousand klicks an hour and brake at four gees, they'll get a good six hours' warning, and you'll still be braking as you hit them."

"I was thinking of flipping ship, going through them fast, and using an orbit around that gas bag of theirs to sling back at them."

"And if they charged right at you? Through you and off to who knows where?" Benson asked.

"I've never known them to run from us while there was still any chance they could kill some of us."

"She has a point," Jack admitted.

"But she's basing her plan of attack on the enemy's not having learned a lesson. If I heard right about those latest fights out on the picket line of System X, some have learned to tiptoe away when we slam the door in their face."

"Those were probes looking for a weak spot. This is a fight for their mother ship. That hunk of steaming hate can't run nearly fast enough to get away from an attack," Kris said, rubbing circles on her belly.

"Another point for my gal," Jack said.

"You keeping score, General?" Admiral Benson asked.

"No, but I am remembering a certain law that allows me to cancel any order a certain serving member of the royal blood gives if I consider it dangerous."

"You wouldn't," Kris said, giving her husband, and security chief, the eye.

"I would, honey. I would. Being out here is one huge danger. You'll have to go pretty far to rise above the background noise, but if I think this is a totally harebrained suicide stunt, I and a half dozen Marines will lock you in your quarters. Your Highness."

Kris eyed Jack hard. He did not flinch.

"Totally harebrained suicide stunt, huh. That gives me a lot of rope."

"We are on Alwa Station," he said with a shrug.

"Okay, let's look at what we have. Admiral Benson, what's the status of the *Tenacious* squadron?"

"Not too bad now. They'd be better after a week of shaking down. Damn good and up to Alwa Station standards by next month. But you aren't asking me about next month, are you?"

"Two days. Three at the most. Nelly, how fast can we get out to this target?"

"Accelerate through Alpha Jump, use the fuzzy jump in the next system with plenty of rpms on the hull, pass through another fuzzy jump and drop right in on them. Four days, ten hours, thirty minutes from Cannopus Station to that system."

"A day of fighting in the system, then four and a half days back. Ten days away from here. The aliens are hunting for a less deadly pass around the blocks we've set up. I've got courier ships taking orders out to the pickets to outpost their flanks so the aliens don't steal a march around them. I want to be back here before things get too hot out there."

Kris paused to take the measure of the men who would judge her. "I want to move on this now or not at all."

"Why must you move at all?" said Admiral Hiroshi, sometimes retired from the Musashi Navy, and always superintendent on the Kure Docks on Cannopus Station.

"The three wolf packs attacking toward System X will likely sweep in from there to hit our Beta Jump. The two wolf packs that have so far been content to throw suicide boats at us could hit us through our Alpha Jump. Need I say anything about the problems of fighting an assault coming at us from both jumps at once?"

"So you wish to launch a spoiling attack to push them back."

"To let them know that they can't hit us without us biting a chunk out of their hide," Kris said. "We are not a tethered goat waiting for them to ring the dinner bell."

Admiral Hiroshi nodded. "This is not a foolish vanity. Many generals and admirals in history have done just as she wishes to do. Marty, is there any chance we could finish some of *Victorious* squadron and join her in this gallant ride?"

"Don't I wish, Hiroshi, don't I wish," Benson said, "but I think she's kind of counting on us to provide some sort of backup to the Birds out on the line. Am I guessing right, Your Highness?"

"The sooner you can have some sort of reserve force laid up at your yard but ready to go to space on a moment's notice, the happier I suspect Ada and my Granny Rita will be."

"The *Victorious* is coming along fine. Building all these ships to a single design is letting us just spin out the kernel and plug in the furnishings that we're getting from those moon fabs. Which brings us to the point, Admiral. I'd suggest that you visit each of the new ships in the *Tenacious* squadron. Those officers have come along mighty quickly, and some of the crew aren't all that far from the bird farm."

"You think a chance to see their admiral might help?"

"It can't hurt."

Kris eyed her belly. "You sure of that?"

"If you don't think so, then maybe you shouldn't be taking the fleet out," came in an even voice. There was no flinch behind it.

If I can't face those I'm leading, then I shouldn't be leading them.

Kris nodded. "That's what I'll do tomorrow."

50

Kris made one last pit stop. Resting a hand on top of baby, she whispered, "Be good for Mommy, dearest. This is only the first of many fights we will no doubt be in," she said, and smiled at the memory of her and her own mother duking it out in her teen years.

If I could see myself now, would I have been a little happier with my lot in life then?

An old question, no closer to an answer than it had been ten years ago.

First, Kris marched for *Wasp*'s Forward Lounge, there to meet her senior officers. Those ranged from Admiral Yi down to division officers on her new frigates, like gunnery and engineering.

Kris was struck by just how young they were. Take the skipper of the *Tenacious*. Becky Kaeyat looked like she should hardly have the family car keys. But Nelly explained as she shook her hand that Becky had come out as gunnery officer for the *Congress* and had handled her job well during the first Battle of Alwa. She'd gotten XO of the *Resolute* when promotions to flag opened up a vacancy and had fought her well during the expedition to take down the first suicide base. Now she not only commanded the *Tenacious*, but was brevet squadron commander.

She carried the burden of command cheerfully and with a firm handshake.

If she was bothered that her commanding admiral was bulging, she didn't show it.

None of the officers did, but met her eye to eye with confident handshakes. Kris called each by name as Nelly passed along where they'd come from to get these new ships into fighting trim. Many of them were promoted to their jobs from Yi's own battle squadrons.

Kris went through BatRon 16, then started with Yi and went down his ships. While few of his captains had been promoted after the dismal showing during the last expedition, many of the ranks below them showed men and women promoted to fill in behind. Kris even shook the wing of an Ostrich that was now the gunnery officer for the *Admiral Yamamoto* and a Rooster who had come from the reactors on Cannopus Station to take command of the *Franklin D. Roosevelt*'s engineering department.

Yi might have had to be dragged kicking and screaming into accepting locals, but given the choice of leaving empty billets aboard his ships, he'd adjusted.

Done with going eye to eye and hand to hand through her officers, Kris marched to her place at the head table, where Penny and Jack were holding the fort.

But Kris didn't sit down. Neither did she stand her troops at ease.

"We have won victory after victory here on Alwa Station. We had to. Victory meant the alien bastards died. Defeat means we die and everyone on the planet beneath us. As we stand here, three fleets from our station are harrowing the alien wolf packs, pushing them back from the system they have chosen as their rallying point. That point from which they will all advance on Alwa with murderous intent.

"Even as they defend us on their far-flung stations, from the other side of space, two alien base ships are hurling venomous suicidal attacks at Alwa. Attacks we have defeated one after another. Attacks we must defeat or see a horrible price extracted from those below.

"So far, all we can do is sit here and hit them as they come in. However, the aliens have gotten sloppy. They apparently think it is their job to strike out and ours to take it. They've spread themselves out to cover sixteen launching systems. They've left only a handful to guard their base ship."

Young officers leaned forward, eager for what would come next. Kris felt the energy in the room charging her. Even as she took that in, her eyes fell on Admiral Yi. He alone was standing hunched over, staring morosely at the table in front of him.

Kris felt the energy sink that was that admiral and made a note to talk to him afterward.

"We will show them that they can never count on Alwa Station to take what they hand out and not slap the hand that gives it."

The room took in a breath.

"We will make that base ship pay for its reckless disregard for its own defenses."

"Yes," came as a low hiss from her gathered officers.

"We will show those aliens the risk of turning their backs on an armed human."

Now the "Yes" was more than a hiss. Now it was a vow and a promise.

"We sail at 0900 tomorrow. Make ready for a fast cruise and a hard fight. Good hunting to us all. Dismissed."

The room filled with the cheers of hunters who saw the prey and were ready to take it down. They knew they faced a hard job but went at it with a will.

Fighters looking for a fight.

In an isolated island stood Admiral Yi. Beside him, his chief of staff looked almost as worried as Kris felt.

She made her way through the happy throng to Rear Admiral Yi.

"You ready for a fight?" Kris asked.

"Of course. Of course I'm up to a fight," he said, almost stuttered.

Kris glanced at the chief of staff.

"We'll be right with you, Admiral," Captain Nottingham said.

"Good. I'll have a council of war this afternoon to brief the senior officers down to squadron leaders."

"We'll be there, ma'am," the chief of staff said when Admiral Yi failed to answer.

The Forward Lounge had begun to empty as officers hurried off to make sure their ships would be shipshape and battle-ready. Kris rode the ebbing tide out until someone hollered, "Make a hole for the Admiral." Then she walked as quickly as she could, both to let them be about their duty and because baby was tap-dancing on her bladder.

51

The final jump was coming up fast—360,000 klicks fast. But then, the entire operation had been fast.

Kris's brief to her command staff had been quick; there was little to go on. To her surprise, Admiral Yi had been quiet through the entire meeting. She put that down to keeping her tiny fleet in one compact strike force.

Apparently "Don't divide your forces" was all he'd learned in his Navy.

The course Nelly laid in had been obtuse to say the least. The first jump had taken them 750 light-years toward the center of the galaxy. The speed and rpms Nelly laid in for this next one took them back out to the edge a good 350 light-years from Alwa and directly into the system with the alien mother ship.

While the trip so far had held to below 1.5 gees, things would get rather wild on the other side of this jump. Jack was naked, helping Kris out of her uniform.

He paused to caress her baby bulge. "You sure you're going to take good care of her?" he asked.

"Nelly promises me that she's fine-tuned the egg to take very gentle care of us both," Kris assured him, holding him close, skin to skin.

If only we had more time.

But time was fast running out, so she stepped into her egg and Jack helped the two of them settle gently within the confines of the Smart Metal™. He gave her a final peck and quick-stepped to his egg.

"Seal the egg, Nelly."

"Is it too tight?" Jack asked.

"It's fine. It's better than fine. If baby starts doing the can-can thing she does on my bladder, I can just let the egg take care of things. It saves me running to the head every hour."

"Always the optimist," Jack said.

Kris motored into flag plot. Admiral Furzah was already there, along with Penny and Masao. Kris had left Amanda and Jacques behind. There wasn't a lot here for an economist or anthropologist.

Kris studied her array. All twenty-four ships of the Fourth Fleet were in line behind *Wasp*. She and Jack had gone around and around about where *Wasp* belonged.

"The flag should not go first. You don't know what's out there," Jack had argued.

"You're right, Jack, we don't know what's out there, but we're going to be headed for it at over three hundred thousand klicks, and there's no way to peek through the jump or turn around and come back. We're committed."

"What if there's something there? A suicide ship or some-thing?"

"Jack, the fuzzy jump is well away from the direct path to any of the normal jumps. There's no reason for anything to be there."

"But you don't know anything about that system. Where the enemy is? What they're doing? Anything!"

"Correct, Jack, and as soon as I'm in the system, we can begin planning the actual move to contact. Any ships that jump through ahead of me will just have to twiddle their thumbs until I get there and start giving orders. I go through first, check things out, and holler orders as they come through."

"I hate to agree with her when she's in this kind of mode," Penny said, "but she has the better of this argument."

"I know. I just want to make sure we haven't overlooked something."

"I see no better way to go about this than the one she has laid out," Admiral Furzah said. "We cannot leap a twenty-foot-wide chasm with two ten-foot hops."

With that settled, Kris had the fleet in line, five thousand kilometers apart. Still, at the speed they were going, they'd be hitting the jump at five-second intervals. In two short min-utes, they'd all be through.

Trailing *Wasp* was the Helvetican Confederacy's division of four ships. Captain Zermatt's flagship *Triumph* led *Swiftsure*, *Hotspur II*, and *Spitfire*. Directly behind them came BatRon 16 with Commander Kaeyat's *Tenacious*, followed by *Persistent*, *Steadfast*, *Relentless*, *Vigilant*, *Insistent*, *Stonewall*, and *Unrelenting*. Last through the jump would be Rear Admiral Yi's Task Force 7, with twelve Earth ships, three to each reduced division.

Kris hoped she wasn't making a mistake leaving Yi on one side of the jump after she'd led the way to the next.

The chronometer in front of Kris reached 00:00.00. In place of the usual hint of dizziness was something closer to the nausea Kris had experienced from that tiny passenger she bore beneath her heart.

One screen showed the stars ahead. It went blank, then re-formed a distinctly different view. They waited.

"We made the jump to our target system," the navigator reported.

"Admiral," the captain reported, "we have evidence of alien reactors in system, but no specific location yet to report."

"They are supposed to be in orbit around that nearest gas giant," Kris let herself say.

"Yes, Admiral," Drago answered, "but we've got no direct line of sight on anything."

"Did we catch them on the other side of that planet?" Jack asked.

"You may be right. So, when will they come back around?"

"Your guess is as good as anyone's," Jack said.

"Fleet, begin a four-gee decceleration. Captain Zermatt, form BatDiv 40 to *Wasp*'s right, low. Commander Kaeyat, form BatRon 16 on my right, high. Admiral Yi, form Task Force 7 on my left."

Wasp, and Helvetican and Alwa ships immediately began the deceleration as they formed up. The same could not be said of the Earth ships.

The *George Washington*, and the ships behind it, failed to begin the deceleration burn and shot past on the left of *Wasp*, narrowly missing her.

"Admiral Yi, report," Kris demanded.

"Admiral Yi is not available," came in a calm voice. "This

is Captain Nottingham, Chief of Staff, Task Force 7. Admiral Yi is indisposed. Wait one while I follow your instructions," and the line cut off. The Earth task force did, however, begin a deceleration burn that quickly built up to a bit over four gees; the four Earth divisions formed into a square of triangles. To Kris's right, the other ships formed a triangle of squares. It was a compromise formation, but it fit the different tactical grouping Kris was stuck with.

"Please excuse my abrupt cutoff, Admiral Longknife," came a moment later. "I regret to inform you that Admiral Yi froze up just as we made the jump. He lost his lunch as well. The ship's surgeon has assisted him from the bridge, and he is under sedation."

"Are you prepared to lead Task Force 7?"

"Commodore Pavlenski of BatRon 11 is senior officer present. I have contacted him, and he has declined to take command but will conform to the flagship's movements."

Kris had often complained about the chain of command that she fought with. Just now, she had to wonder what the Earth fleet was going through as it sorted itself out. After this battle, she would clean house, but for now, she had a battle to win.

"Fine, Captain Nottingham, you have the command," Kris said, and clicked off.

"What was that all about?" Penny asked no one in particular.

"I should have followed my instincts and replaced Yi before I got us out here."

"We live and learn," Jack muttered, not quite under his breath.

For the next hour, they decelerated hard. Kris wanted to be slow enough to either go into orbit around the gas giant or to swing around it and head out to wherever her enemy was running.

She also wanted to be able to flip ship and present them her bow guns and armor if it came to a fight.

Of course, to have a fight, she needed an enemy.

"Captain Drago, are you surc there are alien reactors in this system?"

"We have a solid signature from them, both background

noise from the plasma and noise from the electronic gear. As best we can tell, the gas giant ahead of us is masking them."

"For how much longer?" Kris asked.

"The noise we have is nondirectional, Admiral." *You know that as well as I do,* was left unsaid.

Kris gnawed her lip and tried to keep her worried mouth shut.

Just when she was about to lose that battle, the aliens presented themselves for battle.

The entire bunch, gigantic mother ship and eighty-four huge warships, swung into sight. They must have seen Kris just as she spotted them. The ponderous mother ship rolled over and began a deorbital burn.

"They're moving," Jack observed.

"But are they charging us or running?" Admiral Furzah asked.

Kris eyed the screen and waited. It would be easier for them to head for the nearest jump. She would have to change her plan, turn her deceleration toward the gas giant into a pursuit swerve. It would take more reaction mass, but she had mass to spare although she'd have to refuel before she headed home.

An hour later, it became clear the aliens were not running. The mother ship hiked up her skirts and went to 1.35 gees, as the whole swarm headed straight for Kris.

"They're charging," Kris said. "Good."

"They charge us. We charge them," Admiral Furzah said. "It has always been that way among us."

"Yes, but we have gravity and inertia to worry about," Jack pointed out to the feline Sasquan. "In space, we battle with more dimensions and different forces than on a planet."

"Ah, I see. If they charge through you, and you charge through them, it is not so simple a matter as bringing yourself to a pouncing halt and turning on your heels."

"No," Kris said. "Inertia must be canceled, or redirected, or they must keep going. Nelly, are there any jumps behind us that they can see?"

"It's just empty space, Admiral. They'll need to make a major course adjustment. Both of the nearest jumps are inconvenient."

"Very interesting," Kris said, mulling a most complex set of variables.

"Kris," Penny said. "These folks have been sending out suicide boats. Is there any chance they intend to ram you?"

"Ram someone in space?" Masao said. "Space is huge. You can't just nose up to a ship and run into it. Not at the closing speeds we've got."

"But they are heading for us and we for them," Penny said, standing her ground.

Masao opened his mouth, then thought better of it.

"I admit that the odds are against ramming," Kris said, then went on, thinking as she spoke, "but they do look ready to trade their lives for ours."

Slowly, a smile crossed Kris's face. She knew it was not a pretty one. "Let's see how this goes. Nelly, send to fleet. Prepare to close up to five-hundred-klick lateral intervals."

"At this speed?" came from Captain Drago. "Are you crazy, Kris?"

"No more than usual. Do you see a problem?"

"None other than the obvious. We're doing over three hundred thousand klicks. It won't take much for a small problem to become a big one."

"Do you foresee a problem in our future, Captain?"

"None other than that we're following one of those damn Longknifes."

"Then I'm sending an execute order."

"Five seconds is all we'll have to dodge, but okay, Your Highness, they're closing up on us."

The frigates nudged in closer. Kaeyat's two divisions to Kris's right and below formed themselves into two lines of four. Zermatt's four ships formed a square close above their top.

The Earth squadrons to Kris's left formed two lines with the triangles pointing above and below. *Wasp* was sandwiched in rather tightly.

"I'm not even breathing," came in a half whisper from Captain Drago.

An hour later, the bastards reacted. Sixty of the warships formed one huge dish, but it was a tightly woven array with ships at little more than a five-hundred-klick distance, possibly less.

Two warships paid for it when one lost control for a moment and crashed into its neighbor. Both fell out of the dish. One exploded.

From the reserve around the base ship, two ships accelerated to fill the hole.

Sixty ships in a tight dish boosted out a good hundred thousand klicks ahead of the mother ship and the twenty warships that swarmed around her.

They were all headed straight at Kris.

Kris grinned. "This is going to get interesting."

For the next several hours, the two forces hurtled at each other. Kris reduced her fleet's deceleration to 3.5 gees, then down to 3.25. As much as she wanted to be at a reasonable speed when the two fleets met, she wanted to conserve her ships and their engines more. On her boards, some of the engines on the Earth ships had crept into the yellow.

Now, every ship was comfortably green.

As they drew to within five hundred thousand klicks of the aliens, Kris brought Nelly into her plans.

At three hundred thousand klicks, she informed the fleet. "We are about to do a starburst maneuver at four gees. Captain Zermatt, you will assume command of Task Force 8 and pass above the hostiles, keeping outside their hundred-thousand-klick range. Task Force 7, you and *Wasp* will pass below their dish. My computer is sending you your sailing orders now."

"Received," both Nottingham and Zermatt reported. On Kris's board, each ship blinked twice as it acknowledged its orders. "We will execute as we hit the two hundred-and-fifty-thousand-klick mark. Open fire at two hundred thousand klicks and fire at will. Try to concentrate on targets by divisions or sections. Good shooting," Kris said.

"Execute starburst . . . now!" Kris ordered.

Ships swung around. Now, instead of decelerating toward the enemy, they were blasting laterally. Their momentum still carried them toward the waiting alien warships, but now their rockets shot them off so they'd pass above or below them.

Kris waited to see how the aliens' Enlightened One would react.

She hadn't long.

The alien dish came apart as half changed their acceleration vector down and the other half aimed up. The warships
that had been holding to the same 1.34-gee acceleration as
their base ship now jumped up their power settings to 2.5. A
few went even higher.

As Kris sought to pass wide of them, they scrambled to
get into her way.

Wasp slipped over to join the division with Yi's flagship,
George Washington, turning the triangle with the *Franklin
D. Roosevelt* and *John F. Kennedy* into a square.

As the range closed to two hundred thousand klicks, *Wasp*
and her division mates picked one of the closest aliens and
concentrated their aft batteries on it. Sixteen 22-inch lasers
pinned the closest ship.

It glowed. It burned as it shed flaming globs of rock. It
burned, but it did not break.

As one, the division flipped to bring its forward batteries
to bear long enough to empty them.

And Kris got a big surprise.

The alien ships came apart. Correction, they separated.

Where one ship had been, now a half dozen or more ships
were hurtling out, trying to reach for the human frigates. In
place of the thirty ships that had begun to drop down, following Task Force 7, almost two hundred blips filled the screen.

"They've launched suicide boats," Nelly reported. "We
can clearly identify the single small reactors on the additional
ships."

The spawning of the suiciders was frightening to behold,
but it did not go smoothly.

Several of the smaller craft had been damaged by the
initial volley from the frigates. One exploded almost immediately, shoving its mother ship almost into the ship next in
formation. Another careened around wildly before impaling
itself on a huge warship. The two of them vanished in one
gigantic explosion.

Still, as Kris's ships fired their forward volley, they had
to aim with care to get their original target and not its suicidal offspring.

They also had to fire the forward battery quickly and flip

back around to get their sterns pointed at the aliens and boost away from them.

While her ships blasted on course and recharged their lasers, Kris studied what her fleet had accomplished so far.

The aliens were still out of their range though they struggled mightily to change that. Kris's ships had concentrated their first volleys on seven alien warships. Five were gone, vanished in vast explosions. Two tumbled powerless, out of the fight.

With the one that the suicide boat had been kind enough to kill, Kris still faced fifty-two warships.

By the time the aft capacitors were reloaded, they were within 150,000 klicks of the closest ship.

Her divisions did not fire on Kris's orders, but rather on the command of their division captains. Kris watched as they fired, then flipped, fired, and quickly flipped back.

This close, the 22-inch lasers were murder. Six more warships vanished. It would have been seven, but a suicide boat interposed itself between the targeted warship and absorbed enough laser energy to save it.

As Kris's ships accelerated out of the enemy's main vector, the alien suicide boats settled in between the two fleets.

"They're trying to absorb some of our lasers," Jack observed.

"They're suiciders, not stupid," Penny said. "But they sure look crazy to me."

"Yeah," Kris agreed. "Nelly, show me course projections," and her screen now showed her ships with blue vectors, the alien with red.

If the courses and accelerations held true, the next volley from Kris's fleet would be almost at a hundred thousand klicks. The aliens would likely be firing every laser they had, hoping, even at extreme range, to damage some frigates.

"Begin Evasion Plan 4," Kris ordered. "When we fire our forward batteries, do not flip until we are out of range of the dish."

"Aye, aye, Admiral," came from her two task force leads. Ships blinked their acknowledgments.

Seven alien warships burned under the close-range hits of the aft batteries, then blew up when hammered by the forward guns. Twenty-one alien ships were gone, but the remaining thirty-nine lased the space around Kris's ships. Their laser fire was attenuated and blooming; still, they shot.

Kris's ships took the weak lasers in with their crystal armor, slowed them to a stop, then radiated them back into space.

"I imagine that is causing some jaw dropping out there," Jack said dryly.

"Let their jaws drop, just so long as I don't have to go to funerals," Kris muttered, half to herself.

Now the alien warships in the leading dish were speeding out of range, but the twenty ships of the rear guard had more time to react to Kris's deployment. They also spawned dozens of suicide boats; some had slammed themselves into three-gee accelerations, climbing high to meet Task Force 8 and diving toward Task Force 7.

"Take the little boys with your secondary batteries," Kris ordered. "Apply the main battery to the warships."

Twenty warships came at Kris. You could doubt their sanity, but not their courage. Twenty died under three volleys from Kris's frigates. A dozen suicide boats that got to within fifty thousand klicks of the frigates were burned by the 5-inch lasers.

They died, but they kept Kris from getting a single shot off at their base ship. The behemoth waddled by them, doing a good 1.35-gee acceleration away from the gas giant while Kris decelerated toward it.

They shot past each other with neither side attempting to communicate.

Maybe a few humans thumbed their noses at the aliens. What they did back at the humans was anybody's guess.

Once the Fourth Fleet was out of range, Kris checked with Nelly. "We will make orbit, won't we?"

"You can drop deceleration to 1.5 gees and let folks have a break. We'll need to check for things like mines left in orbit around the gas giant, but space is huge. Do you want to refuel?"

"We might as well. A stern chase is a long chase. Tell the fleet to prepare to deploy pinnaces for a quick refueling run as we swing by."

"Order passed and acknowledged."

Kris eyed the now-departing aliens. They'd actually cut their acceleration to .5 gee. Did they want her to chase them? That was her intent, but if it was what they wanted, maybe she should rethink her strategy.

Then again, 1.34-gee acceleration was the most Kris had ever seen a mother ship do. Maybe they needed time to mend and fix. They were aliens. There was no telling what they thought.

Kris took a deep breath and assigned herself a five-minute break.

NELLY, CAN YOU MAKE THIS EGG A BIT BIGGER? I'D LIKE A FEW MINUTES WITH MY LITTLE ONE, IF I COULD.

CERTAINLY, KRIS.

Kris's egg took on a clear baby bump and she found her hands free to rub her belly and pat baby on the head . . . or rump . . . she still had trouble figuring out which end was up.

I brought you safely through this, and I'll keep you safe from all the bogeymen.

When her serious side tried to raise doubts, Kris mentally shut it down.

I will keep you safe. I will. That's what mommies do. And when this is over, I will find you a safe place were Mommy and Daddy can do regular jobs and come home to baby like regular parents. I will. Somehow, I will.

When Kris came out of herself, she found the battle timer had advanced eight minutes. She gave baby one last pat, let her hands make one last loving circle of her swollen belly, then thought, NELLY, TIGHTEN UP THE EGG. IT'S TIME TO WORK.

YES, KRIS.

"What have our erstwhile friends been up to?" she asked.

"Not a lot," Penny answered. "They're going away from us at a slower acceleration. The warships and little boats shut down entirely, and the mother ship has overtaken them."

"So the warships are between us and the base ship," Kris said.

"The warships and the suicide boats," Jack corrected.

"Admiral Furzah, does your history include a situation where one side had an advantage in projectile weapons over the other and could select the range?"

"Yes. The only solution that ever worked was to invent a better projectile weapon. That, or come up with, ah, something to ride that could cover the killing ground faster than the throwing weapon could kill you."

"Heavy cavalry charging archers," Penny offered.

"Oh, so you had them, too."

"The solutions to the problems we give ourselves while trying to kill each other seem to have the same answers no matter what world you're on."

"Yes." The feline's grin showed lots of teeth . . . and no regret for her bloody history.

"We have the range, and we have the speed," Kris said.

"So they die," the feline admiral said with finality.

"How can they either close the range faster against us or get greater range from their weapons?" Kris asked.

"I imagine several Enlightened Ones and their Black Hats are gnawing at that problem for all they're worth," Jack said.

"Yes, I imagine they are."

52

Kris's Fourth Fleet swung around the gas giant. It had over a dozen moons and something of a ring. A dozen suicide boats shot out from one moon. More hid among the rings.

Their reactors gave them away. They died long before they could do anything.

Several packages with radioactive signatures were shot out of space before any frigate came close.

"Which begs the question," Jack mused. "Were they expecting to defend this supply depot, or are they starting to leave these kind of calling cards wherever they hang out?"

"We'll find out soon enough," Kris said.

When they swung out from behind the gas giant, sensors took the measure of the alien battle array.

"They've set a course for the nearest jump point," Nelly reported, "but they'll need days to reach it, assuming they follow a sensible course of accelerate, decelerate, and approach the jump at dead slow."

"But if they're desperate to get away and don't care where in space they end up?" Jack asked.

Kris nodded. "No bet, but for now, the base ship is plodding along at .55 gees with all the surviving warships and little boats trailing behind. I know a hopeless situation, and they've got hopeless stamped all over them."

"But cornered rats can fight without hope and with nothing held back," Admiral Furzah said.

"Exactly."

"Necessity being the mother of invention, I think we can count on these folks to be real mothers," Penny said.

"May I point out," Masao said, "that we do not want any of

them to survive to report how a human fleet appeared out of nowhere in their space."

"Point well taken," Kris said. "Let us get about the execution of those poor damned souls."

Kris's fleet accelerated away from the gas giant at three gees; they'd decelerate to approach the enemy fleet at a decent closing rate. The mother ship pulled up her skirts and put on a full 1.34 gees. She held it only a few hours, then began to slow: 1.31, 1.27, 1.21. She was losing acceleration fast as Kris came up on the rear dish.

The alien suicide boats had also slowed. The first one Kris's fleet came up on suddenly went pedal to the metal and tried to ram the lead frigate.

Tenacious shot it out of space at fifty thousand klicks using her 5-inch lasers.

Space came alive with a killing rage.

It wasn't just dormant suicide boats, but smaller stuff, like Kris had faced on the expedition to take out the first suicide base ship. There were small craft with space for only one or two men. Some had matter-antimatter drives that gave off a signature the sensor suites could track, but others were ancient chemical rockets that drifted quiet as a rock before suddenly coming as fury incarnate.

A surprising number had atomic warheads. The tiny leak of radiation gave them away.

It got worse as they closed on the defending warships. The space between Kris's fleet and the diminished dish was littered with all kinds of junk.

Some of it was just rocks.

Too much of it was space-suited aliens with small maneuvering units and explosive packs. The *Steadfast* took a hit from one. It didn't do a lot of damage, but if the fellow had had an atomic . . . ?

"We need more close-in defense," Jack said. "If you can order up some firing slots on the hull, I'll have my Marines man them."

"I've got a better idea. How many of those twenty-five-millimeter automatic grenade launchers does each ship's company have?"

"Half a dozen," Jack said. "We try to have one in each fire team."

"Get them to the hull. Nelly, I need a fire control system and a cradle to slave those launchers to the ship's defense."

"The Army has something like that to take down air vehicles," Nelly said. "I'm passing this along to the fleet."

The hasty installation came none too soon. A single-man unit that did have an atomic package got winged close to the *Stonewall*. He caused minor damage when he blew himself up.

Kris reduced acceleration. She had the enemy; it was only a matter of time. If they wanted to turn their execution into a slow one, desperately resisted, Kris could live with that.

Live with it was the key term. They were going to die. Kris would not lose any more of her crews in this fight.

The fleet plowed its way through the wreck and ruin of men, tiny rockets, and small suicide boats.

Slowly the aliens gave ground as they died by the hundreds. By the thousands.

Soon enough, they'd be dying by the tens of billions.

Tenacious got a bit ahead of the fleet. One alien warship went to almost three gees, aiming itself at Commander Kaeyat's flagship. She did the smart thing, firing her forward batteries, then held steady as her squadron mates came to her aid, pinning the charging warship with their fire until it gave itself up to the ravages of its runaway reactors.

Only then did the *Tenacious* flip ship and zip back to the cover of the rest of the squadron. They held in place as three more of the alien warships tried to emulate their mate, only to meet the same immolation.

Carefully, in ones and twos, the alien warships died. Slowly, by the twos and threes and fives, the suicide boats burned.

By the tens and scores and hundreds, individual drifters tried to blow holes in frigates with their own deaths but died as Marine rockets blew them to bits.

The fleet was meticulous and slow as it went about this, not as a fight between two equals but rather as an execution where one would die while the other would definitely go out for a beer when all this was over.

In the end, the mother ship was left without defenders. All the warships were dust; all the suicide boats had failed and gone to whatever reward they had been promised.

Or not.

Now the fleet began the measured slaughter of a ship nearly as big as a moon.

Killing something of that size did not go quickly, not without Hellburners.

The Enlightened One tried to dodge his fate, sending his ship first in one direction, then another. As it waddled back and forth, it shot lasers at the nearest frigates and spewed small craft and space-suited figures into the void.

For a moment, Kris thought some of the suits might seek to live. Then sensors brought up a solid picture of four of them: suit, tiny propulsion system, and a big pack of explosives.

"Shoot anything that gets close," Kris ordered.

The circling frigates did not get close. The mother ship's lasers were dangerous out to 100,000 kilometers. They might do some damage at 120,000. Kris held the fleet at 140,000.

At that range, the 22-inch lasers hacked into the base ship. They slashed rocket motors, sending the moon-size structure shooting off in unintended directions, with the hull spinning and twisting in ways never intended.

Lasers carved the structure of the gigantic craft, weakened main strength girders that caved in as the ship did its own destructive dance.

Here and there, a laser struck a reactor, shutting down the magnetic containment field and letting loose plasma that splattered metal and flesh with the temperature of the sun, incinerating the lucky and leaving fire in its wake for those condemned to a slower death.

The frigates fired, flipped, fired, recharged, and flipped again. Their 5-inch secondaries cut down anything that got near, and what they missed, the Marines bagged.

In Kris's flag plot, Penny watched the butchery and shook her head. "Not one message. Not one word. They are helpless, but they will not beg for life. What kind of insanity are we fighting?"

Then she turned to Kris. "What kind of insane will we

become before we either annihilate them or finally beat them to a pulp that will talk to us?"

"I don't know, Penny," was all Kris could say.

Penny and Masao left flag plot.

"You don't have to stay for the end of this slaughter," Jack offered. "I can see it through and call you if anything comes up."

Kris shook her head. "I will watch what I have ordered."

In the end, the reactors did more to the ship than Kris's lasers ever could. Plasma got loose, leaping from one reactor to the next, until fire ate the ship from the inside. Hatches popped open as people chose the cold kiss of space to the burning fire they had lost mastery of. Men and women, some with children in tow, pushed themselves out into the vacuum.

Kris fought not to vomit.

"It is done," Nelly finally said. "There is no sign of life on the mother ship. I guess we could check it out, but I don't think you want to waste the time."

"No," Kris said. "Even if there are a few hidden away behind a bulkhead that still holds, they won't have air for long. Nelly, give me the fastest course for Alwa."

"We can go back the way we came."

"Make it so, Nelly. I'll be in my quarters if you can keep the acceleration down to one gee for a while. I need a shower."

"I think we can arrange for one hour of one-gee acceleration. We'll need to go to four after that."

"Then advise the fleet we have one hour to catch our breath. Jack, are you with me?"

"Always."

Four days later, Kris found out just how close she had cut it.

53

"I'm glad you're back," came from Admiral Benson even before Kris got back to the Alwa system. "We got trouble."

Kris's Fourth Fleet was decelerating in the next system out, planning on hitting the jump into Alwa at a good fifty thousand klicks. She listened as Benson explained.

The aliens were getting smarter. With three wolf packs meeting opposition on different approaches to System X, they did what any human commander would do.

They concentrated their forces on a single weak point.

Admiral Miyoshi's Third Fleet was holding the pass against Beulah, the middle wolf pack. To defend a three-jump system, he'd split his ships, assigning ten or eleven to each jump. It had worked. He'd beaten back attacks on all three jumps, destroying scores of warships.

Suddenly, the jump periscopes at all three reported a base ship with a full escort of nearly two hundred warships bearing down on each jump!

He did what anyone would. He sent off couriers hollering for help and backpedaled.

Worse, the aliens had a new weapon. Among the warships rushing across the system at 2.5 gees were three strange-looking ships. Miyoshi found them different enough that he ventured a frigate through to get a good signature on the things.

Each of the three wolf packs had several.

The gravity anomaly detectors said they were dense. Likely tens of meters of thick basalt and granite. There were also lasers deep down under all that stone and water. The reactors were smaller and spread well apart. They were likely shielded with more rock.

How long the frigates would have to fire at these heavies to blow away one that just blasted through a jump was a test Miyoshi would not leave to his small divisions.

Admiral Miyoshi gathered his data on those battering rams and checked out the other approaching warships. They, too, were heavier, with more and denser rock. Done, he ordered retreat.

Bethea and Kitano arrived just in time to join him in abandoning the system.

They were holding now, one jump out from System X. Unless Kris had orders to the contrary, they'd withdraw as soon as the mother ships and battering rams came up and were ready to force the jump.

Kris examined the data and sent an order for Admiral Benson to send to Kitano by the fastest courier. "Admiral Kitano, you take command. Continue the withdrawal. Imperative the fleets not be lost."

"So, now, what do we do?" Kris muttered, as Jack peered over her shoulder at the ugly-looking situation board. "Here I'd been thinking of taking a break. Giving shore leave to my fleet to throw a bash, drink some beer."

"It never slows down," Jack said.

Kris shook her head. "And now the aliens can force any jump. It's only a matter of time before they outflank us, surround us, and wipe us out."

Jack said nothing.

Kris shook her head. "Against one of them, we win. Against three, maybe four if they finally pull in the one I didn't go after, I have no idea what we do."

"Well, it looks like we better start doing it."

"Yeah."

They docked on Cannopus Station just as the *Mercury* came through Beta Jump. "Kitano is withdrawing the fleets to System X. What are her orders?"

System X had too many ways out that led to the Alwa system. Once the aliens got there, there would be plenty of resources for them to refuel, restock, and maybe build more warships, fast movers, even battering rams. The survey of the system had identified asteroids rich in uranium, something mentioned in the old stories of forbidden atomics.

Kris would have given her right arm to keep the aliens from System X, but she could think of no way to stop them now.

"Tell Kitano to picket the four jumps out of System X that lead to Alwa with a division each and bring the rest of the fleet home. They've been run hard and fought well. They need some yard time before we take our next swing."

"I'll carry that word," the skipper of the *Mercury* said, swung around the nearest gas giant, and headed right back out.

Then it got worse. The jump buoys two systems out from Alwa reported reactors. Lots of reactors. Reactors off the buoy's scale.

"Four wolf packs, and they're getting reinforcements!" Kris wanted to weep.

"Even the aliens' fast suicide boats haven't jumped ten picketed systems," Jack pointed out. "Let's say we don't panic until we see whether they're getting reinforcements or we are."

"Nelly, how long before we get better information?"

"A day, Kris."

"Okay. I don't panic for twenty-four hours."

It was like waiting for Christmas. Only this Santa might have presents for her . . . or a death warrant.

Kris checked in with Doc Meade to verify that her gallivanting around the universe at four gees hadn't harmed her or baby.

"I wouldn't have thought those high-gee stations were that good," Doc Meade observed.

"I and my children were constantly observing each of the pregnant women on *Wasp*. We adjusted them in real time," Nelly said proudly.

"I hope the *Princess Royal*'s and *Lion*'s pregger detachment are as well taken care of."

"I passed my app to their main computer before they sailed. If those computers had enough excess capacity, they should."

"Why didn't you tell me?" Kris and Doc Meade asked at the same time.

"You two had enough to worry about," Nelly answered.

"The women were free to ask for shore duty," Kris said.

"I wonder why none have," Doc Meade said.

"I don't think they want to leave their shipmates in a jam," Nelly said. "I'm a computer, but I understand loyalty."

"Yes, you do," Kris agreed.

"So, I hear we got company coming," the doc told Kris.

"Which company?"

"We all know about System X. It's the next system over that has everyone abuzz. Anything you want to tell your doc?"

"You know more than I do. All I know is the tiny bit that's official. No doubt the grapevine knows more."

"No doubt. Is it true that the jump buoy can't make hide nor hair of the reactors?"

"Some of them," Kris admitted. "I'm told that some of the reactors have a signature close to ours, but none of them fit anything we've got. Or had when the last ship headed this way."

"You think it's that something new I heard about?"

"That something new that you shouldn't have heard about?" Kris asked right back.

"Yeah. Good grapevine. If only I could turn it into decent wine."

"You get enough whine out of it," Kris said.

"And she complains about my jokes," Nelly complained.

"Enough, I've got more patients than you, and I need to see how our future moms made out on this bad trip. Nurse, help the admiral to get her feet back on the deck."

"Coming, Doctor slave driver," came from the hall.

"You get that sort of lip, too?"

"We never should have abolished the cat-o'-nine-tails," the doc said.

Kris's next stop was Admiral Benson. "Thanks for holding the fort while I was out blowing shit up."

"You're welcome, though for a while there, I was afraid someone was going to have fun blowing my shit up. It looks bad out around System X. I hear you did good."

"Another base ship gone, but only eighty-two of the warships. No doubt the rest will sign on with the other base ship, and trot around to System X to stand in line to force us back."

"There have been fewer suicide boats the last few days. You think they'll fold their cards and try something more conventional?"

"Even when they stand up and fight, they're using suicide tactics. Did you see my report about Marine grenade launchers taking down boarders? At least I'm thinking of them as boarders, though I assume if they get aboard, they'll just blow a hole in the ship when they blow themselves away."

"Don't bet on it. If they can blow a hole in the ship, they can get inside. Your Marines may earn their pay the old-fashioned way."

"Yeah. Tell me, how are your new frigates coming along?"

"We got two of the Victorious class fitting out. I've laid down *Courageous* and *Illustrious* in the docks they vacated."

"You're not closing up shop?"

"Why should I? The mines are still shipping ore. The fabs are still sending us what we need for ships. I intend to be hatching ships right up to the minute you tell us to down tools and fight those ships for our lives. Any idea when that will be?"

"Everyone wants to know. Would it bother you if I admitted I don't know?"

"Nope, though it might worry me to think there is an honest Longknife in the batch."

"I was born under a dark moon," Kris said. "The black sheep of the family."

"We all must bear our crosses. Speaking of which, I've got work to be attending to. Call me if you need me."

"Don't I always?" Kris said, and made her way to the meeting she dreaded.

She presented herself unannounced at the quarterdeck of the *George Washington*, but she doubted she was unexpected. The Officer of the Deck turned her over to an ensign, who headed off as if she already had specific orders for when the fleet's admiral showed up.

Kris was glad for a native guide. While all the Rim-built frigates were laid out to a common scheme, Kris could have easily gotten lost among the *George Washington*'s twists and turns. The ensign brought Kris not to the admiral's quarters, but to a door with CHIEF OF STAFF, TASK FORCE 7 painted on it. The ensign rapped once, was told "Enter," and opened the door for Kris.

"Admiral commanding Alwa Sector, sir," she said, waiting while Kris entered, then firmly shut the door behind her.

"Admiral, thank you for coming," Captain Nottingham said, standing. "Computer, create a comfortable chair with leg support."

The captain pointed Kris at a recliner that formed itself to her shape and began gently massaging her feet as she sat.

"The chair is patterned after one my wife liked when she was expecting," the captain said, retaking his own seat. "I understand swelling of the legs is a bitch."

"And was she a bitch?" Kris asked, remembering Admiral Yi's own comments.

"My wife was the best thing that ever happened to me. Unfortunately, she died of a stroke shortly after our daughter's birth."

"I'm sorry for your loss," Kris said, hating the automatic way the words came out.

"I likely would not have volunteered for this duty if she were still waiting for me at home, but you aren't here to talk to me about my problems, are you, Admiral?"

"No."

"He's not a bad man, Admiral. Admiral Yi is a good administrator. He got this fleet into the shape it is. The shape you fought it last week. They're good ships. Good crews."

"Then what went wrong?"

Now it was the captain's turn to lean back in his chair. "Jim is very knowledgeable about ships, war, and how they've been fought for three thousand years of human history. He used to talk to the wardroom for hours, dissecting this or that battle down to the slightest detail upon which victory turned. His knowledge was impressive."

Kris nodded, allowing the man to praise Caesar. This could not go on forever.

"We talked about the Battle of Hastings just before our first battle. Do you know it?"

"I have a sketchy idea. The Norman conquest of England back on Earth?" Kris said.

I CAN GIVE YOU A FULL BRIEFING, Nelly thought.

DOWN, NELLY, IT'S THE CAPTAIN'S STORY.

"Hastings turned on the Norman heavy cavalry riding down the Saxon heavy infantry. The infantry mistook a feigned retreat by the horsemen for a full retreat. They came off a strong position and were ridden down by the heavy horse for that mistake. Jim thought we were the heavy horse, and we could ride down the weaker alien ships. That was what he was doing. He'd charge them, they'd break, then we'd slaughter them in the rout. Hastings all over again."

"But our alien 'heavy infantry' were not on bad ground and had more fight in them," Kris pointed out.

"Yes, Admiral. Jim was . . . dismayed at what happened. He managed to hold it together through the fight, but he got more silent as the days went by."

Kris had wondered who held Yi together. Still, she would not fault the captain his loyalty.

"He hardly said a word after your briefing," the captain said.

"He didn't say a word *at* the briefing," Kris pointed out.

"None of us did. We know our desperate situation. If the aliens were foolish enough to split their forces and overextend themselves, you wanted to cut out a section that was overexposed. I was all for it. I assumed Jim was, too. It bothered me he didn't mention that the aliens had split their forces, but I figured it was more of the thoughtful face he was giving us.

"His silence got worse as we followed you. When it was time to order the task force through the jump, he just waved his hand. Once through, he only stared at the screen. When you gave us our orders, he leaned over and lost his lunch. I knew then that I had to do something. I gave orders for the task force to deploy as you ordered, then called Commodore Pavlenski and told him the admiral was indisposed. If I didn't know him better, I'd say there was panic in Paulo's voice. He said, no, he couldn't take command as we were going into battle. The task force expected the flagship to lead. He'd follow my orders."

Kris ventured an "Interesting."

"Pedro Cochrane and Yusuf Suluc are young and hard charges. I'm not surprised they asked for two more divisions and a task force of their own. Paulo was always happy to stand in Jim's shadow."

"And when Admiral Yi's shadow vanished?" Kris asked.

"I think he found the sunshine blinding."

"You say Admiral Yi is a good administrator. Would you say the same for Commodore Pavlenski?"

"Yes. If they'd stayed on Earth, both would have retired with four stars."

"And no battle experience," Kris said, dryly.

"Regretfully, yes. It's been a long peace."

"So I've heard. Would you have a problem taking command of BatRon 10?"

"No, ma'am."

"Do you have any suggestion for command of BatRon 11?"

"I'd reach down to the skipper of the *King George V*, Admiral. All of the division commanders are good men. They'll follow orders, but if they have to *make* them under the pressure of battle, I would not expect the orders to be good."

"We just had a battle," Kris pointed out.

"Once you made the initial deployment and call to charge around them, not through them, like I expected, like I think Jim expected and was terrified of, it was not so much a battle as a rout. An execution."

"My thoughts, exactly," Kris admitted.

Kris eyed the overhead, seeing her very thin chain of command. Captain Hans Zermatt had fought in the First Battle of Alwa, but as a division commander. His division had been broken up until recently, leaving him doing admin legwork for Admiral Benson. Commander Becky Kaeyat commanded her ship and squadron well, but she was green.

"Captain, I'm promoting you to commodore as of now. Nelly, cut the paperwork. You've got command of BatRon 10. Who gets Task Force 7 is something I'll need to think about before we sail next, and rest assured, we will sail before too long."

"What will you do with Admiral Yi?"

"I think we can find an administrative position for him. God knows, we need more of a shore establishment than we've got."

"You won't regret that, Your Highness."

Kris weighed the switch from admiral to Your Highness, and decided the man from Earth likely meant well. Maybe a Rim princess was worth more than she gave herself credit for.

Kris had the chair cough her up. "Would you mind passing that app to my computer?" Kris asked.

"I got it when he created the chair," Nelly said.

"Good, I'll be seeing you around, Commodore."

"I suspect you will," the new commodore said, and bent his head back to his desk.

Outside, Kris found the ensign waiting patiently down the hall, across from two Marines. That door said ADMIRAL YI, COMTF 7.

Kris returned all three salutes and gave the corporal on duty a slight nod. He opened the door. "Admiral Commanding Alwa Sector," he announced.

No voice answered.

The day quarters were elegant to the point of being out-of-date by a couple of centuries. The floors looked to have expensive Persian rugs. The walls seemed wood-paneled. The entire place was overstuffed . . . and empty.

Kris went to the night quarters and knocked on the door.

"Go away," answered her.

"Admiral Yi, this is Admiral Longknife, and I have a job for you," she said, and opened the door.

The room was only dimly lit. The admiral was in bed; he wore a rumpled nightshirt.

"I'm not well," he said weakly. "They've got me on meds that make it worse."

"No doubt. But I have a job for you. At least as soon as you feel you're fit for duty."

"What kind of a job?" he spat. "Shoveling bird shit dirtside?"

"No. My base establishment is threadbare. We didn't know we had a logistics problem until it bit me on the butt. I need someone to help Admiral Benson stay ahead of our logistics and look at our total admin lash-up. We're putting it together with spit, glue, and baling wire. I've looked at your file, and I think you're just the man to get this thing shipshape."

"I could do that," sounded almost human.

"I think Pavlenski would be a good man to work with you, assuming you want him."

"He knows his stuff," Yi agreed. "I could do worse."

"Think about it and let me know when you might be ready

to hit the ground and what you think your work might look like. We don't have much for you to go on, so you'll be pretty free to put your own stamp on things."

"Will I report to you?"

"No, I'm establishing a Commander, Base Forces Alwa Sector. You'd report to him. He'd report to me."

"That would work," he agreed.

"Then I'll be on my way. Things are moving fast. Take care of yourself and get well."

"I'm feeling better already," Yi said.

I wonder how Rear Admiral Benson will be feeling when I tell him.

"You're putting me in command of what?" was his expected reply.

"Commander, Base Forces Alwa Sector. That will also make you Vice Admiral, Commanding Reserve Fleet," Kris added this time.

"What's the reserve fleet?"

"However many ships you can get out of these yards with however much of a crew you can patch together."

"We're working on the next squadron. We've been spinning out eight ships at a time. Tirpitz is getting her workers up to speed. Now that they're building to our design with none of the junk they put on those Earth-built ships, she thinks she can get four out. Let's see. Eight by the end of next week. Twelve two weeks after that and another twelve in a month. Hell, between our yard birds, the colonials, and real birds and some of the fab workers, we'll be ready to answer bells anytime you call."

"That will keep you busy. I'm getting you some decent admin support. Rear Admiral Yi. Make sure he doesn't get us so overadministered that we can't fight."

"Don't worry. I brought out a good deputy superintendent. If I don't let him have the job I'm holding, he's going to go sour, or full-time farmer, or ask to have a ship. Anyway, I'll give him the yard. If I'm right, Hiroshi has someone like that at Kure Docks. Could I have a deputy?"

"So long as he's not Yi."

"You give me Rear Admiral Hiroshi as my right arm, and I'll keep Yi and anyone else in line even if I have to rip off their arm and beat them over the head with the bloody stump."

On that note, Kris left Benson's office to cut papers for a whole lot of promotions and reassignments.

Thank heavens, Jack came home horny, because she was not about to die without jumping his bones another couple of times.

Tomorrow's problems would come soon enough.

54

Or not.

"Hey, Kris, cancel the panic party. This is Commodore Phil Taussig, commanding Wardhaven's Frigate Squadron 16 on the new and improved *Hornet*. Wait until you see what followed me home."

Since the message, sent through Beta Jump buoy, was a visual, she could see what he had. Beside his command chair stood a woman and a boy of maybe four. She was in the uniform of a lieutenant commander. The boy wore a bright red shipsuit. Kris suspected that declared to one and all that he was not to be trusted near delicate equipment, nor much of anything else.

Phil was true to his word. He'd brought his family out.

God help all such fools, Kris fervently prayed.

She was surprised to discover how much she meant it.

She patted her belly. *Baby, are you making mommy religious?*

Or just desperate? the snide part of her shot back.

Let's see what else Phil brought, Kris thought, cutting off her argument with herself.

The poor instrumentation on the jump buoys continued to go bonkers over the incoming ships.

"Some of the readouts were just plain unbelievable," Nelly sniffed. "The sensor teams are pulling their hair out. Even the weaponry on the ships isn't right."

"Is it wrong?" Jack asked.

"It's something," Nelly answered.

"So, we wait," Kris said. "I trust Phil with my life. He would not lead an alien sneak attack. Meanwhile, tell Admiral Benson to get the shipyards working even faster, if they can.

And tell Commander Hanson of the *Challenger* to meet me at Admiral Benson's office at 0900."

Kris found herself back with the former superintendent of Cannopus Docks. "Marty, I know you wanted the *Victorious* for your flagship, but I'm giving her away."

"Who gets my pride and joy?" the newly promoted vice admiral demanded.

"I'm sending Commander Hanson back out, and I figure he and his crew deserve something more than a patched-together scout."

Admiral Benson took the measure of the commander standing at stiff attention in the presence of the two admirals. "You cleaned up your act, son?" the crusty old Sailor demanded.

"Yes, sir."

"You going to stay squared away?"

"I was stupid, sir. I am not an idiot. I've learned my lesson. Besides, if I screw up again, I know Admiral Longknife will have me shoveling bird shit, not bossing those shoveling."

The old admiral laughed. "I doubt she'd let you have a shovel, either. She is one of those damn Longknifes."

The commander made no answer, but from the look in his eyes, Kris was pretty sure there stood a man who would follow *this* damn Longknife into hell, with or without a map.

"Okay, Commander, you can have my flagship. What you going to use for a crew?"

"I was hoping to transfer over *Challenger*'s, ma'am, if I might," he said to Kris.

"You'll need more. I'll put a draft on the Earth task force to get you about a quarter of your crew. The rest will have to be green colonials and birds. We don't dare pull the best of them out of the yards or the fabs."

"I understand, ma'am. Sir, when will the *Victorious* be ready?"

"She's ready now, Commander. All she needs is a crew."

"I assume you have a job for us," Commander Hanson said, turning to Kris.

"I want you to check on that other mother ship that's spawning suicide boats. There's been a drop-off of incoming crazies. I need to know whether they have given up on this idea and are moving to join the others. A new mother ship and wolf pack's worth of warships will be a major reinforcement to those at System X. If that's happening, I need to know."

"I assume my mission is to go, see, and run away fast even if you are giving me a shiny new frigate," the commander said.

"You got your orders in one."

"Then, ma'am, if you'll excuse me, my crew and I have a job on our hands. If possible, Admiral Benson, I'd like to have the *Victorious* away from the pier by this time tomorrow. Day after that at the latest."

"Godspeed and a following wind," Benson said.

The commander saluted, did a smart about-face, and marched with pride for the door.

"Young fool," Benson added when the door had closed behind him. "He's going to do his shakedown cruise on a course straight for the enemy."

"You think I should have sent him back out on *Challenger*?" Kris asked. This guy had been Navy when she was still in diapers.

"Hell, no. In the fix we're in, his cruise will likely be one of the more peaceful. Still, it gets you right here, or wherever an old pelican like me has a heart, when you see the likes of him. I'm glad you gave him a second chance."

"He deserved it, and he's earned his new frigate."

"Damn right. Now, what can you tell me about what Phil is bringing in?"

"Not a damn thing. We didn't put the best of sensors on the jump buoys. They're pickets and likely to get popped by any passing bastard. They were programmed to spot the difference between our reactors and theirs, and identify several of the different signatures we've got on file. What they're eyeballing is not in the database."

"So I heard. Well, if you don't mind, ma'am, some bossy admiral gave me a whole new set of problems, so if you'll get your backside out of my visitor's chair, I'll get to work."

"I treasure the courtesy you show me," Kris said, and hauled herself and baby out of a rather comfortable chair, and noticed as she turned for the door that the Smart Metal™ chair got a lot more utilitarian now that it wasn't cradling her and baby.

She said nothing but went to see what chores she'd missed.

Abby and Pipra were waiting in her day quarters to go over production figures that would have been astounding a month ago. "We think we can get some parts for the lasers from the light fabs. It will cut down on the flow of consumer goods to the locals, but they can just suck it up."

"Abby, have you told Granny Rita and Ada about this?"

"Hell, Kris, Ada and Granny Rita were the ones who suggested it. That suck-it-up idea came from Granny. That old girl is in full battle mode. God help any old bird that gets in her way, she'll fry him up for a turkey dinner just by looking at him."

"So it's that way dirtside, huh?"

"They know we're outnumbered, outgunned, and in deep shit. That don't mean we're outclassed. Outclassed? Never!"

"That Granny Rita?"

"Hell no, Kris. That's pure me," Abby said.

"We've got reinforcements coming in," Kris said.

"So we heard. They going to be any good?" Pipra asked.

"I have no idea. There's something different about 'em, but whatever it is, they aren't talking, and I'm not asking."

"Then, if you don't mind, we'll be on our way."

"One thing," Kris said, as a thought crossed her mind. "The Earth frigates brought out the crystal armor. We haven't had any frigates from the Rim with it. Is there any chance you could jack up crystal production?"

"We could use light fabs for that," Abby said. "It'll mean more birds squawking."

"Do it."

"We're on it."

Kris found she'd done about all she could for now. That seemed to be the job of a senior admiral. Get everyone running off in forty-eleven different directions, then sit on your butt until some came back with a new collection of snakes.

"Baby, I think there's time for you and me to have a nice slow bath." It wasn't as nice as when Abby ran the water and turned Kris's hair washing into something luxurious and nearly sinful, but it worked out fine for the two of them.

The *Victorious* made it away from the pier late that night, without alerting Kris. They did four gees to Jump Point Beta and got through just ahead of the incoming fleet.

Seeing that fleet up close and personal must have been something near religious.

It was quite a sight to Kris watching from her flag plot.

She had her full team: Jack and Admiral Furzah, Penny and Masao, Amanda and Jacques. Even Abby managed to show up.

It was a show worth going out of your way to see.

Phil's *Hornet* led a squadron of Wardhaven frigates: *Courageous*, *Furious*, *Glorious*, *Formidable*, *Illustrious*, *Implacable*, and *Powerful*. All had the weird reactors, but the reactors were only the start of the strange.

"They've got twenty lasers," Nelly reported. "Double our number with different capacitors. Chief Beni is driving the sensor crew crazy trying to figure them out."

"Do they have crystal armor?" Kris asked.

"No."

Kris scowled. Had Earth held on to the secret . . . or were the moneymen arguing over who got how many bags of gold for the patents? It didn't matter, she'd fix that.

"Abby, tell Pipra we'll need that extra crystal."

"I already did."

Four support ships followed Phil. The next warships were from New Birmingham, and the names said it: *Birmingham*, *Milun*, *Essen*, *Pittsburgh*, *Manchester*, *Newcastle*, *Yawata*, and *Jamshedpur*. Each name of an industrial city of that planet. Most had been founded as New-Something, but the new wore off years ago.

All had the new reactors and lasers but no crystal protection.

Abby made another call to Pipra. The industrialist's shout of dismay came loud and clear through the commlink.

"Nelly, advise Admiral Benson that we've got ships coming in that need to upgrade their armor. Tell him to get with Pipra about any ideas he has to make that go faster."

"He's been following the show. He has his folks working on it."

"Good man."

New Birmingham's squadron was trailed by what looked like a repair ship and six freighters. They'd hardly cleared the jump when a mixed squadron started popping in. The first division was from Woolomurra. The flag *Warumungu* with the *Arrenrente*, *Canberra*, *Toowoomba*, *Te Mana*, and *Te Kaha* made for a six-ship division. The next division was five. From Tillamook came the *Ammanoosuc*, *Maawaska*, *Nashaminy*, *Popmanoosuc*, and *Wampanoag*.

"What kind of names are those?" Jack asked.

"I have no idea," Nelly confessed. "Tillamook is famous for their light footprint on the planet. If I were to guess, and a computer never does, I'd say those are either the names of rivers or the larger of the small villages. Tillamook refuses to be mapped. If you want to travel, you hire a native guide. Some of you people are so strange," Nelly concluded.

"Well, where did they get the ships?" Penny asked.

"I suspect, like Woolomurra, they bought them and provided the crews," Kris said. "Interesting what that says about our support back home."

"Very interesting," Jack said. "They didn't send four but rather five or six. Does anyone else want to hear the story of how they ended up with extra ships?"

"I suspect it is something totally human," Nelly said, with a strong hint of a sniff.

"More ships," Kris said, to end that. Four freighters and a repair ships followed the reinforced squadron, assuming Tillamook and Woolomurra were working together.

More frigates showed up; Kris actually clapped her hands. "Hikila has sent ships!" The lead ship was the *Hikila*, followed by *Port Stanley*, *Keokuk*, *Port Canterbury*, *Pukaki*, *Port Canberra*, *Taupo*, and *Port Adelaide*. Kris smiled. "Half named by islanders, half by folks from the big island. All likely built and crewed from Hikila."

Six freighters and a repair ship followed.

Two huge ships followed the Hikila squadron. Kris didn't panic this time. She was familiar with the stations they'd sent out. The first one identified itself as *Kiel* out of New Birmingham, the next as the *Gdansk*, from Sawa. Both quickly began to spin out piers.

Behind them were two equally large ships that Nelly

promptly identified as factories in flight, the *We Can Have That for You Yesterday* and the *Sacrificial Lamb My Ass*.

"Who came up with those names?" Penny asked no one.

"I don't think we'll have to tell them they aren't going back," Jack said.

If the last four ships were huge, the next ship through dwarfed them and brought everyone in the room to their feet.

"That ship must be double the size of one of the alien warships," Penny said. "It has to displace a good million tons if it weighs a gram."

It squawked as *Conqueror* from Wardhaven.

"An optimistic name," Kris said.

"The sensor crews are going bonkers," Nelly reported. "It's got a dozen reactors the size big cities have, all located amidships. There are a lot of battleship-size ones aft for rocket motors. Kris, that ship makes no sense. I'd say it was a portable fabrication plant, only there's no heavy machinery, and there's something on the bow that doesn't fit anything I've ever seen."

"They said they were working on a surprise," Jack said.

"Well, they surprised me," Nelly shot back.

Hardly had that anomaly cleared the jump than a second came through.

"The *Ultimate Argument* from Savannah," Kris said. "What kind of name is *Ultimate Argument*?"

"Cannon is the Ultimate Argument of kings," Nelly answered back.

"*Conqueror. Ultimate Argument*," Jack said. "Someone sounds awful confident."

Then a third one, just as huge and full of question marks, jumped in. "*Opening Statement* from Pitts Hope," Kris read from her board.

"The bastards will not talk to us, so we have an opening statement and an ultimate argument," Masao said slowly.

"I don't know what they are," Kris said, "but I think folks back home expect them to settle someone's hash."

"I can't wait to see what they are," Jack said.

There was one final squadron, providing rear guard for the fleet. From Hekate came the *Diamond*, *Emerald*, *Garnet*, *Opal*, *Ruby*, *Turquoise*, *Sapphire*, and *Topaz*. All with the powerful guns. None with the new armor.

Kris did the tally. Forty-three new frigates. Three anomalies, a pair of factories to drop down on the moon, and two more station ships.

"Nelly, tell Admiral Tirpitz to prepare to have two docks mate with her station fore and aft of her present position. If she has any questions, contact Admiral Benson on the drill. Ask Admiral Benson how many of the new arrivals can dock on Cannopus Station. It's my preferred place for them. I'll need to brief them on our situation, and they sure as hell need to brief me on what they've got."

"Doing it, Kris."

"Oh, and send to Phil on the *Hornet*. 'Please report with family to my quarters on *Wasp* soonest upon your arrival. I want a briefing on what followed you home.'"

"It's on its way."

Kris found she had stood about as long as her legs wanted. "Nelly, make me one of those comfortable chairs." One appeared at the foot of Kris's table, near the screens. She settled into it as her team found chairs and, together, meditated on what they had now.

"Abby, what can we do about crystal production?" Kris said. "Coordinate with Admiral Benson. I want to take Phil's squadron directly into the yards for installation. Nelly, send to Phil. 'What are the *Hornet*'s dimensions at Condition Zed? Are the other frigates the same?'"

"Sent, Kris."

"Okay, crew, let's think. What are we missing that we could do now before seconds cost blood?"

The conversation lasted half an hour and added nothing. The others went to do what needed doing and Kris found herself alone with Jack.

"You headed off for Marine stuff?"

"I don't like the bastards attacking with small units and individuals. My Marines need to practice repelling boarders."

"You go do that."

"What will you do?"

"I think it's time for me and baby to take a nap. It's been an exciting morning."

"I think the two of you have earned a break," Jack said.

He gave her a kiss on the forehead, then baby a kiss on whatever end was up at the moment, and left.

"Nelly, does this thing recline as well as get my feet up?"

"How much do you want?" Nelly asked.

"Not that far," Kris said as she found herself almost laid out flat. Slowly, Nelly brought the back up. "There, and take the lights down. Not on the boards, I want to see them," Kris said, as the overhead lights dimmed.

Kris eyed her four fleets. Or was it five? How many squadrons would she have? That would depend on how soon the aliens made their move. Would they wait for the suicidal bastard to join them? That would get Kris more time.

It would also give them time. What would they do with it?

Kris found her eyelids heavy. She closed them, and slowed her breathing.

She was young again. At least everything at Nuu House was so much bigger than it had been the last time she was there. Her mother was a giant, nearly twice as tall as Kris.

And Mother was crying. Crying for Eddy.

Kris remembered this moment. She'd felt so lost. So guilty for being alive when Eddy was dead. Kris remembered going into a corner and crying.

It seemed that all of them, Father, Mother, Brother, and she had gone into their own separate corners and wept alone.

It was all Kris knew how to do. Mother and Father did it, so she did, too.

Now Kris knew that was wrong. Now Kris knew they should have pulled together and shared their grief. Now she wished they had.

In her dream, Kris found she wasn't nearly small enough for that corner. She had to move furniture to get up, but she did. Funny, Kris was pregnant now in her dream, but still she managed to get up and make her way to Mother. She found herself hugging Mother, something she'd never done. Hugging her and patting her hair. "Now, now. It will get better. This will pass."

Of course, alone, separated from each other, it had never gotten better.

But in her dream, Kris found herself sitting in the rarely used rocker, holding her mother in her lap, a mother that was suddenly so much smaller. She rocked her mother, soothed her.

"We can get through this, love. We can't see it now, but we can," she said softly to her weeping, shrunken mother. "Trust me. If we go out and meet this, we can get through it."

Kris came awake, but the last words of her dream echoed in her head. "If we go out and meet this, we can get through it."

What am I trying to tell myself? Is this one of those dreams Doc Meade warned me about? Am I just trying to resolve my life for me and baby? Or am I seeing something clearer here?

Kris's eyes went to the screen that showed the star chart. System X was twelve jumps out from Alwa, two if you used the fuzzy jump in the next system and went directly into System X. Was that a bad idea, to have an entire fleet show up were the alien could see no jump?

"It depends on what we can do if we do it," Kris said, rubbing baby gently as she thought.

"What are those monsters they've sent us? Nelly, are any of the new frigates from Wardhaven carrying Hellburners?"

"Let me check. No Kris. They did not bring out a new supply."

"Interesting. Very interesting," Kris said, and patted baby. "What is your great-great-grandfather shipping us for Winter Faire?"

As much as Kris, both the young one and the older version, hated it, she'd just have to wait to find out.

55

"**You** wanted us to report as soon as we got in," Commodore Taussig said as he saluted, the grin on his face pure joy.

A woman with lieutenant commander's stripes stood next to him, saluting with one hand while the other held the pudgy paw of a four-year-old who struggled manfully to stand at attention and salute, too, while fidgeting only a little bit. His white sailor suit showed evidence that he'd managed to find dirt even on Kris's pristine ship and station.

Well, that was what four-year-olds do, find dirt. Kris found herself rubbing baby even as she returned their salutes.

"Sit down. So, you asked your wife, and she came. Tell me that you're risking your family because what you brought will make it safer for us all."

"It will, Kris. You won't believe what they've done."

"Try me."

"You remember that question you raised when they briefed us on the Hellburners. 'Can you bring out the thing that chips stuff off neutron stars and use it to shoot stuff at the bad guys?'"

"I seem to recall that question," Kris said. "I also recall it would take a huge chunk of a planet's energy budget."

"Energy as we humans produce the stuff."

"We humans?"

"We never asked the Iteeche how their electric plants work," Phil said, beaming. "When your friend Ron took the Emperor the full report of what faced us, the old palace got hopping. Then we gave them Smart Metal. It was a huge trust issue and King Ray took a major hit. Some tried to impeach him.

"They might have, too, but Ron showed up at our side of the demilitarized zone with a ton of their own science. Now we know how they managed to spoof our sensors during the war. Even better, we know how to get more energy out of the same power plant. Five times for a small ship reactor. Ten times for a huge city-size power plant."

"And someone remembered the experiment that gave you the Hellburners," his wife added. "I'm Bahati, Admiral, and this is Little Phil."

"Hello," the youngster said.

"And hello to you," Kris said before returning to Phil.

"Those things can knock a rock off a moon or something and send it shooting out at, what's the speed?" Bahati said.

"About .05 the speed of light," Phil said. "Call it fifty-four million kilometers an hour, give or take a few millimeters."

"Nelly, show that in comparison with the Alwa system."

The number sounded huge, but a star system still dwarfed it. "They'll see it coming," Kris said, "and dodge."

"Yes, but a whole lot of stuff can make dodging hard."

"Yes," Kris said, but she was looking at System X. It even had a neutron star right there waiting for them, not all that far from a fuzzy jump. It was quite a bit farther from a regular jump.

Something to think about.

Phil Junior was getting more of the fidgets. "Nelly, can you make a toy frigate for this little starship captain?" Kris asked, and just as quickly little Phil was squealing with glee.

"Phil won't let us use Smart Metal to make toys for the kids," his wife said.

"The kids?" Kris echoed.

"Several of the crew from the old *Hornet* brought their families with them. Some of the old chiefs complain the ship is as much a day-care center as a warship," Bahati said.

"When we went on the Voyage of Discovery," Phil said, "no one said we weren't coming back, so yes, the old *Hornet* had a lot of family men expecting to be away for a couple of months. Now they want to settle down here."

"Will you be going dirtside?" Kris asked Bahati.

"I'm an Information Systems specialist. Frigate systems are my specialty. I've made arrangements with one of the wives who is an elementary-level teacher to care for little Phil while I'm away." She glanced at her husband. "Phil wants me assigned to the Cannopus Yard. I want to stay on the *Hornet*. I've helped her work up."

"It would be a hard day for little Phil if I lost another ship with us both on it," Phil said. There was a darkness behind his eyes that Kris chose not to plumb.

"There are plenty of ships that need crews," Kris said. "Jack's still on *Wasp* most of the time, though."

"Yes," Bahati said.

"We'll talk about it more later," Phil said.

"Well," Kris said, sensing the subject needed changing, "what is it with your frigates? You say your reactors are good for five times the power of mine. What's all that good *for*?"

"Five times the hitting power," Phil said, beaming at the chance to praise his new ship. "The main problem is applying all that power. They're working on a 24-inch laser, but they're got teething problems. Anyway, the new *Hornet* has twice the lasers, so we can fire one while the other is recharging. Each laser has twice the capacitors. Instead of a two- or three-second burst, we can hold the beam for five or six seconds. I've held it for almost seven seconds by feeding juice in the back while firing it out the front. We have twice the power cabling from the reactor and cooling for the lasers, but we're firing them just as fast, every fifteen seconds. We fire off the top battery for five to seven seconds, then fire the bottom battery. By the time they're dry, the top is just about ready."

"If you flip ship and fire the aft battery, the front will definitely be locked and loaded," Kris said.

"Yes. Hit them hard and hit them often."

Kris walked with them to the Forward Lounge, where she met the key staff from the new warships and addressed all hands over the net. The briefing went pretty much to form. The folks who came out this time, even the merchant ships and factory workers, knew this was a one-way voyage until matters were settled. This time Kris announced that there would be Articles of War signed by all hands: Navy, Marines, and civilians.

"Make no mistake, you sure look like the old-time cavalry arriving just in the nick of time. There is a fight for our very lives coming. But it is a fight we will win!" Kris finished, to a cheering room.

"Now we make it happen," Jack muttered to her as she stood beaming back at the confident new arrivals.

And they did.

It was a well-ordered drill. Freighters parked their cargos for Alwa or the moon base in a trailing or leading orbit. Kris kept them as twin-reactor ships, and several headed out to the asteroids with new miners and their gear to kick production into higher gear.

The two composite factory ships dropped down to the moon. They were set up according to the latest survey near water and better access to aluminum and iron. It took a week, but their fabs were in production just as the extra loads of minerals and other resources arrived from the mines.

Gosport Station doubled in size. The first assignment for the new yards was to spin out six more Bird class guard ships to relieve the six that had been on duty for a month. That ate up nine of the newly arrived freighters, but with Smart Metal™ flowing out of the factory ships as they used rock, iron, and aluminum to replace it in their outer structure, these new Birds were closer to frigate standards.

Frigates and battlecruisers, that was the word around the stations. The newly arrived ships with their twenty 22-inch lasers certainly looked more like battlecruisers than frigates. They were cycled through the yards; there were now sixteen slips in the eight yards. Rather than respinning freighters, they were occupied by battlecruisers as yard personnel went over them with rigs designed by Benson's crew, coating newly arrived battlecruisers with crystal armor.

All this took time.

As it turned out, the aliens were willing to give Kris time. They were working on a few tricks of their own.

Commander Hanson brought the *Victorious* back with news; the other suicide-spawning mother ship was gone. He checked two more systems. The alien warships had vanished; their dock now spun empty.

"The clans are gathering," Jack whispered.

The number of arriving suicide boats dropped to nothing. Kris kept a pair of the new Birds near each jump, but sent the others to outpost jumps away from System X that weren't being guarded by the fleets. The original Birds were docked and up-armored.

As soon as the first sixteen frigates were up-armored to battlecruiser standards, they were dispatched to the three fleets. They relieved frigates to return to Cannopus Station and be refitted with the Iteeche power system, upgrading them to battlecruiser standards. They might not have twice the lasers, but they halved the time needed to recharge. The lasers would heat up; the yards added extra refrigeration to the guns.

All the training and practice of a lifetime was now on the line. Yard managers reached deep into their heads, their guts, their very hearts and came up with designs that had to work the first time, every time.

While Admiral Benson and his crews worked miracles, Kris sent Hanson and the *Victorious* to observe System X. She expected the aliens to move as soon as the fourth wolf pack showed up.

His report, dispatched as soon as the *Victorious* jumped back into the Alwa system, left Kris wondering if, when the aliens came, she'd be able to stop them.

The aliens were learning.

Not far from the gas giant they were fueling from was a tumbling rock of a planet. They were slicing huge slabs off it and lifting them to orbit, where they cut them to fit the outer hull of their giant warships.

Kris had expected that.

What surprised her was the growing fleet of smaller ships. Their three reactors were only slightly larger than those on frigates. From the sensor take off them, they were getting warship-size lasers, maybe bigger, set in their bows.

"They're building frigates," Jack said.

"We knew they could build a few fast movers," Penny said.

"But their fast movers were never very good," Masao said. "Many blew up or broke down."

Kris nodded. "We'll see if they solved their quality control problem. I figured the huge number of reactors and lasers on their ships was their way of getting around sloppy maintenance or construction standards. You can afford to have two or three reactors off-line when you have a hundred. Not so much when you only have three."

"But if they have fast cavalry, as fast as your own," Admiral Furzah said, "you will not have so much freedom to maneuver."

"Exactly," Kris agreed. "We beat them over the head with our advantages, and they learned the lesson."

"How fast are they knocking those small ones together?" Penny asked.

"I don't know," Kris said. "We need some ships on the other side of the jump, so they can observe everything while it's happening."

"Will they let us?" Jack asked.

"We are vermin," Penny reminded them. "They want us to know fear even as they slay us. I'll give you five to ten they don't do anything so long as we stay well away from them."

"I won't take your bet," Kris said, "but I'll try it. Nelly, tell Commander Hanson that I'm promoting him to captain of a division. He'll take *Victorious* and *Valiant* back to System X, Jump Gamma, anchor there, and observe. He's to sail as soon as we upgrade his sensor suite to the best available. If he needs anything off *Wasp*, he's got it. Boffins as well. I want him to fingerprint those new ships, track their production and shakedown process."

Kris was sending him back out again. Him and his crew. They were turning into a good team. Too bad that meant she would likely use them up.

The reward for a hard job well done was a worse job.

56

Time passed.

The aliens made use of their time. Kris used hers.

Kris wanted to see the *Conqueror* in action. Becky Kaeyat got her commodore's star after the last fight; Kris ordered her to take BatRon 16 for a run to the closest gas giant both to get a load of reaction mass and to give the gunners a shoot. Her squadron got away from the pier a half hour ahead of Earth's BatRon 10 with *Wasp* and *Conqueror*.

Without explanation, Kris ordered the *Relentless* and *Stonewall* on a high course.

At five million klicks from a large asteroid, Kris turned to Nelly. "Kindly have *Conqueror* knock a chip off that rock. Something the size of a small frigate and aimed well above the plane of this system to avoid trouble. Then alert the high frigates that they'll have a target soon."

"Done, Kris."

There was a pause, much longer than Kris expected. Apparently, *Conqueror*'s crew were just along to sightsee. Ten minutes later, sensors reported something going on aboard the big boy.

Two minutes later, a beam shot out from the huge ship, hit the asteroid, and a big chunk of the place took off like a billiard ball.

"Now let's see if they can it hit," Kris said.

Both frigates used a shoot, shoot, look, shoot, shoot, look approach to the fire control solution, or so they reported later. They only had to shoot, shoot, and look to see that the fifty-thousand-ton stone bullet was a cloud of dust.

Admittedly, it was dust moving at .05 percent the speed of light.

"Advise *Relentless* and *Stonewall* good shooting and well done. Advise *Conqueror* they were a bit slow, and the stone bullet they produced is not going to do much damage to the alien ships. We need to come up with a better plan."

"Sent," Nelly reported.

Kris sent Commodore Kaeyat's squadron on to the gas giant for more fuel. She returned with the *Conqueror* and the frigates. They'd be next to have their reactors upgraded.

As it turned out, Benson had figured a way to rework the frigates to battlecruisers without running them through the yards' graving docks. Those were reserved for the ships he intended to command. Instead, his teams brought a barge around to the pier where a frigate was moored. Using the flexibility that Smart Metal™ allowed, they'd slit open the hull first around one reactor, then the next, and finally, the last, doing what needed doing. The laser cooling didn't even take that much of an invasive effort. A tiger team would come aboard with a ton of extra Smart Metal™, pour it into the hull near the lasers, then program it into piping to cool the lasers and carry the heated reaction mass back to the reactors to feed the plasma.

The superconducting cabling to move more power to the capacitors took more work. It had to be manufactured, not squirted out, but it turned out you could have Smart Metal™ swallow the stuff, like a snake, then draw it through the ship to where you wanted it.

Kris was making good use of her time.

Then she got the next report back from Captain Hansson and the *Victorious*'s sensors. They had sent a pinnace through the jump with a full week of observations. It was downloaded to the *Alarm*, a new courier ship respun from one of the newly arrived freighters. It raced back at four gees acceleration.

Kris was grateful for the speed. She was none too happy with the report.

The alien cruisers were maneuvering in sections of fourteen, close enough to her squadrons of eight as to make no difference. They formed a small dish of three, four, four, and three. For larger units, they'd form those fourteen into formations of two, three, three, and two, for a task force of 140.

"That's a lot of fast movers," Jack said.

"And the mother ships seem to be in some sort of contest to see how many they can knock out. They're turning out eight or ten a day."

"They intend to bury us," Jack said.

"Drown us in our own blood," Kris repeated the threat of the old woman she'd sent back to human space. She'd asked Phil how that had gone down.

He's shrugged. "I got there. This force was ready to sail. They asked me if I wanted to go back. I said I'd go if they renamed a ship *Hornet*. They did the next day. I can't say my wife was all that happy about being rushed aboard and off across the galaxy. Her folks were left with the job of packing up our apartment and putting it into storage. I suggested they sell it, but they insisted we'd be back. Three days after we arrived, we were boosting back. I suspect if we hadn't aimed for Wardhaven, we'd have missed the whole thing."

"And Captain O'dell?"

"She said she'd come back with the next fleet. She had some things she wanted to do. She also had a fortune in media interviews. That's another sore point with my wife. She wanted me to take some of that money. I told her there was no place to spend it here." He paused for a thoughtful moment. "She has a lot of reasons to be unhappy with me. I owe that woman, big-time."

"We all owe folks big-time."

"Or we will if we can figure out how to make what they gave us work. I saw the report on the *Conqueror*'s test. Not so good."

"Not so good at defending this system," Kris said. "But there are twelve systems between here and there. As well as a neutron star in System X."

"But if you go out there, could they get between you and Alwa?" Phil asked.

"Could they? We know the fuzzy jumps. They don't. Would we really risk that much if we did?"

"I'm glad I made commodore, but I'm even gladder you're the admiral."

"Thanks a lot."

"You're welcome a lot."

On that, Phil left. Kris continued to cycle ships out to the fleets picketing System X. She'd up-armor one group and up-engine the other. Admiral Benson kept adding to his "reserve fleet," that he knew quite well would be in the front with the rest. The numbers were reaching toward 184 plus the up-armored and gunned Birds.

That sounded like a fantastic number . . . until Kris got the weekly report from Hanson. The fourth mother ship had arrived; the number of the huge warships was over a thousand. Counting was impossible; they kept moving around, docking on base ships, then shooting off.

Of the new cruisers, the count was 560 in four of their ten segmented dishes plus more forming up into blocks of fourteen.

There were now eighteen battering rams and six more building.

In the last month, Kris had doubled the number of ships at her disposal.

The aliens had done the same.

She'd upgraded the quality of her ships.

The aliens had added an entirely new class that did its training hidden from prying eyes in the next system out.

They had their surprise. Kris set out to examine hers.

She ordered the three *Conquerors* to follow Kris's augmented Fourth Fleet. BatDiv 40 led the way with the *Triumph*, *Swiftsure*, *Hotspur II*, and *Spitfire*. In their wake was Commodore Kaeyat with Alwa's own BatRon 15's eight battlecruisers. Right behind them came the twelve Earth battlecruisers of Captain Nottingham's Task Force 7. All had upgraded armor, reactors, and improved lasers. The three huge beam ships, or death stars, depending on who was talking, followed them and *Wasp*. Providing the rear guard was Phil Taussig's BatRon 17, with its upgraded crystal armor.

All of Kris's ships had been in the yards for one reason or another. Now she would find out if that made a difference.

They accelerated at a constant 1.5 gees, hitting Jump Point Alpha at a good three hundred thousand kilometers an hour. At Nelly's recommendation, they put on 17.6 revolutions per minute as they approached the jump.

The screen in Kris's flag plot went hazy, then three new stars appeared.

One was a dead neutron star, swinging rapidly around a dull red dwarf. "Nelly, contact Professor Szilard of the *Conqueror* and advise him the fleet will conform to his movements. He is to approach the neutron star as close as he considers necessary and test fire all three of his ships. He is to demonstrate how fast they can fire and how well they control their aim."

"He says the captain of the *Conqueror* recommends we make for an orbit around the neutron star's closest planet, one-third of an Astronomical Unit out. He would prefer we not exceed the present 1.5-gee acceleration or deceleration."

"Advise the fleet, Nelly, though I would like to know just what those big babies can actually handle. Didn't anyone test them?"

"Kris, from what I have been able to find in the data provided, they spent all their time testing the equipment, not the ship they put it in."

"That sounds more like a science project," Penny said.

"And one put together by people who never fought for their lives with their nifty new toy," Kris growled.

A day later, they went into orbit around a burned and blackened rock one-third of the distance from the neutron star that Earth was from old Sol. Kris had her ships anchor to each other, which left *Wasp* balanced between *Tenacious* and *Relentless*. The three beam ships moored likewise with their gadgets aimed toward the star for at least part of their rotation.

Then the testing began.

All three took several long minutes to fire after Kris gave the order.

They were supposed to slap a bullet off the neutron star and slam it into the red dwarf.

All missed.

The advertising said they could fire once a minute.

The *Ultimate Argument* got a second shot off three minutes later. *Conqueror* took nearly five minutes. The *UA* had gotten a third shot off before the *Opening Statement* managed its second.

"This remind you of something?" Penny whispered behind her hand.

"Yes, but I can't relieve scientists and ship them off to shovel bird shit," Kris growled.

Kris held on to her patience for another ten minutes while the three ships got off six shots between them. Three for the *UA*, two for the *Conqueror*, and just one from *OS*.

"I knew there was reason I asked Professor Labao to join us for this little walkabout. Nelly, get the professor up here. Tell Captain Drago that I want him to accompany me to the *Conqueror* along with Captain Taussig."

"Begging the admiral's pardon," Nelly said, "but Captain Drago points out that the longboats are not as hardened for space as *Wasp*. He strongly suggests that the admiral attend this meeting by teleconference, and if she argues with him, he suggests that her security chief lock her up."

"The longboats aren't hardened?" came from both Kris and Jack.

"My mistake," Kris said. "Captain Drago, I understand those monsters are being operated by contractors, both operational and scientific. Would you kindly go over there and find out if any of them know which end is up? You will act as my broom. If necessary, you may bribe, coddle, or kick butt. Your discretion."

"I'm not sure that's possible," Captain Drago said. "Operating reactors we can pretty much do. Operating those monsters and getting the lead out of their fire teams, I'm not so sure."

"Well, tell me what you can. We will not win any fight with this level of performance."

"Understood. Let me do some nosing around. I've gone down the crew list for those oversize tubs and I know a few of the folks. I'll be back in a couple of hours to tell you what I've found."

"You going to take Professor Labao?"

"Yes, if for no other reason than for him to talk boffin to the boffins and keep them out of my hair."

So Kris found herself and baby sitting safe on *Wasp* while her former contract captain went off to talk contractor with those running the show.

"You don't have to do everything yourself," Kris lectured herself as her temper cooled. "Just so long as you know someone who can do it better."

Four hours later, Captain Drago was back with proof he did indeed know how to do it better.

57

"This will likely come as no surprise, but it's a mess over there," Captain Drago reported dryly. "Scientists are running things like one fun experiment. Contractors treat everything like a nine-to-five job and don't want to do anything too quickly. Safety first, second, and last. You wouldn't believe the checklist the reactor boss on the *Opening Statement* had. The deputy reactor chief on the *Ultimate Argument* is now running the *Opening Statement*'s kettles."

Drago paused to glance at his wrist unit. "I knew several of the contractors. Some were good Navy once. A few weren't, and they haven't gotten any better. How they got this job, I don't know. I brought a boatload of them back with me and promoted a lot of people on the spot. There were a few who questioned my authority. By the way, Jack, thanks for the loan of the Marines. I think even the slowest finally got it through their thick skulls that they are in a combat zone, and I work for the Goddess-of-Damn-Near-Everything."

"Who is willing to show them what a pregnant bitch can be," Kris said, in full grump. "Grampa Ray sent me that collection?"

"In his defense, each *planet* sent you that collection. I get the impression that just like each of those ships is operating its own show, several of the planets back home think they can go their own way on a lot of things. Listening to them made me glad I'm out here."

"When can we try our next shoot?" Jack asked.

"I promised everyone eight hours to mend and fix," Captain Drago said. "The problems over there are more software, or meatware, than hardware. It's a good design, or so I'm told by folks I trust. They just haven't thought of it as battle drill.

By the way, I instituted battle stations. I'm none too sure they'll know what it means, but they will hear it next time."

"Captain, could we sack half of them and put our folks in?" Kris asked.

"Assuming we could do their job, Kris, there are five thousand people on each of those monsters. How many frigates would you have to lay up to find eight thousand hands?"

Kris flinched.

"You don't want to put an Ostrich just off the plains on one of those ships, Kris. There are KEEP OUT signs every two meters. That really is the highest tech that we and the Iteeches have. By the way, I ran into several."

"Iteeches! Don't tell Granny Rita," Kris said with a dry chuckle.

Briefing finished, Kris settled down to a nap. She didn't actually fall asleep but spent her time studying her boards and meditating on different solutions to her many problems.

Thus, she didn't notice the quiet in her head that meant Nelly was busy elsewhere.

Two hours later, Nelly roused Kris. "Your Highness, I and my kids have an idea."

When Nelly started being respectful, Kris knew she was in for some nasty surprises.

"Yes, Nelly," Kris said, coming fully awake. "What's this idea?"

"Mimzy, Sal, and I have been reviewing the contents of the data files on the *Conqueror*, *Ultimate Argument*, and *Opening Statement*. We've noticed several things."

"And what might those be?"

"Before we begin, Kris, we don't want to seem disrespectful of the work done by the people who built the beam ships or the scientists who worked so hard to get this project up and running."

"Okay, Nelly, you've shown that you've learned tact. Now spit it out. It's just us two girls here."

"I know we don't need to be so tactful with you, but we needed the practice. Kris, we think we can make better use of the beam weapons. The scientists are delighted to just chip a neutron star. Getting the chip to go where you want it was never a high priority. Yes, there were those pointing that deficiency out, but it was a lower priority than getting the system working. No one holding the purse strings asked the critical question. 'Can it hit what it's aimed at?'"

"It's shiny and goes bang," Kris said dryly, "it must be good, huh?"

"Something like that."

"So, we have a really whiz-bang toy that can't hit the broadside of an alien mother ship."

"At the present time, yes," Nelly answered. "However, we can fix that. It will take hands-on work in real time, but if we adjust the frequency of the beam and the way we generate it, we think we can get a bullet that will hit what we want."

Kris reviewed what she'd just heard. "Real time?" she said.

"Yes, Kris. We have to be on the ship, or very close, and we have to work the actual generating devices. There are a lot of things that can go awry. We will have to suppress them as they develop."

"One of you per ship?" Kris said.

"No, Kris. Based on what Mimzy, Sal, and I have seen, it will take three of us on each ship to make this happen."

"Three per ship?" Kris said, feeling a cold chill down her spine.

"Yes, Kris. I remember the last time we deployed me and all eight of my children to do something that was impossible for anyone else. I lost three of my children and you lost three good friends retrieving enough reaction mass for *Wasp* to make it home."

"Yes," Kris said, and found her hands massaging baby. "Can you test your theory from here?"

"Yes. You won't need to go aboard one of the beam ships for now. We three can do the test from here although we may not achieve the accuracy we want."

"It will be close enough for proof of concept."

"Kris, there is also a good chance we can come up with a way to confuse the aliens when they try to evade our bullet."

"How, Nelly?"

"We need more time. Let us work on it for a bit before I say too much."

"Do it your way," Kris said, and felt the emptiness in her head that told her Nelly was off on her own.

Seven hours from Captain Drago's return, the *Ultimate Argument* announced that it was on schedule for further testing in one hour. The other two were a bit slower.

"That's fine. We can only work on one ship at a time," Nelly reported, dropping back into Kris's head, then vanishing quite away again.

One hour later, the *Ultimate Argument* reported itself ready for a shoot.

"You may fire when ready," Kris said. "Target the center of the red dwarf."

"Yes, Your Highness," came back.

At Kris's elbow, Captain Drago grinned. "I did put the fear of one of those damn Longknifes in them, didn't I?"

"Or at least of a princess," Kris muttered, none too sure how she felt about being known as a princess damn Longknife to those across the way.

Fifteen seconds from Kris's order, the beam ship fired. A slug from the neutron star shot out . . . to wing the upper-right-hand quadrant of the target.

Just barely.

Kris, we're ready to take over aiming the beam, Nelly reported.

Wait a bit more, Nelly.

"How soon can you get your next shot off, and can you improve your accuracy?" Kris asked.

"One minute, Your Highness. Yes, we can improve our aim."

Kris waited patiently for fifty-seven seconds before the *UA* spat out a beam. This time the slug missed the red dwarf entirely, sailing below and left of the star.

"Sorry," came back immediately. "We'll try again."

"*Ultimate Argument*, I have a computer over here that would like to have access to your fire control system. I think it can improve your shooting."

"Nelly?" came back, not quite incredulously.

"Yes, the Magnificent Nelly," Nelly said from Kris's collarbone.

"Do we want a strange computer in our system?" came from a different voice. Someone had an open mic.

"We've missed twice," said the first voice.

"I have been in your system for the last eight hours," Nelly said, dryly. "You haven't had any problems with me there."

THEY DIDN'T EVEN NOTICE ME.

DOWN, NELLY. REMEMBER, TACT.

YES, TACT AND BUTTER-CAN-MELT-IN-MY-MOUTH NICE-NESS.

"Your Highness, if you wish to risk the systems on the *Ultimate Argument* to this unauthorized access of a computer that's not test qualified to the system, you may."

"How's that for covering your ass?" Captain Drago whispered, but not too softly. More than one could play the open-mic game.

"This will not be an 'unauthorized access,'" Kris responded. "I am authorizing it. Nelly, please do what you think necessary to put the next bullet in the middle of that star."

AND KEEP IT SIMPLE, NOTHING FANCY. WE'LL SAVE THAT FOR LATER.

YES, YOUR HIGHNESS. KIDS, MAKE ME PROUD.

RIGHT, MOM, came in Kris's head in two-part harmony.

"*Ultimate Argument*, you may fire when ready."

"We're ready now. Initiating primary ignition."

And a beam reached out to slap the neutron star. A chip shot off from it and quickly covered the distance to the star next door.

And splatted it right in the center of its disk.

"Spectacular shooting," came in awe from the *Ultimate Argument*.

"That was just lucky," was again on an open mic.

"We should be able to check that out," Nelly said, "as soon as you get another shot ready. What do you say you knock ten seconds off your recharge time?"

"We'll see what we can do," came back at Nelly.

"Initiating primary ignition," came back in forty-eight seconds.

Again, the center of the sun's disk took a hit. If it wasn't the exact same spot, it was close enough to make no difference.

"Wow," was in several-part harmony from the live mics on the *UA*.

"Do we need to do that again, or can I try an experiment?" Nelly asked.

"We know all about experiments," the *UA* answered. "Bring it on."

"Kris, we are pretty sure we can put a spin on the bullet. That should make it more accurate for long-distance single shots. What we want to do is score the surface of the bullet so that the spin will cause fragmentation along its trajectory. That way, the aliens may start to evade only to find themselves dodging more than they expected."

"Try it, Nelly."

"We'll need to aim this bullet out farther."

"Pick your own target."

"How about that rocky planet on the other side of the suns?"

"Go for it."

The beam was reloaded in thirty-nine seconds. They fired and watched as a single bullet sailed out from the neutron star. "It will be seventy-three minutes before we see if we hit it right," Nelly reported. "Shall we try another ship?"

For the next hour, the three ships took turns firing under Nelly's control. They also worked on getting their battle drill down, aiming to fire every fifteen seconds.

The *Ultimate Argument* managed to get off six shots in two minutes before a problem arose, and they had to drop out to fix it. After that, they were only able to manage a shot every thirty seconds.

"We'll need to make a permanent fix. It will take the better part of a day to do that."

"Do it when we're done," Kris ordered.

The other two ships never managed to get more than three shots off in two minutes and usually held to one every sixty seconds.

"You will get together with the fire teams on the *Ultimate Argument* when we are done here and see what they are doing that you aren't."

Sixty minutes into the shoot at the planet, Chief Beni on sensors announced in something only slightly lower than a shout, "The neutron bullet just split apart."

"It should be in four sections," Nelly said.

"Four it is," Chief Beni answered.

"Yes!" Nelly exclaimed. "Now let's see how we do."

Thirteen minutes later, the four sections impacted in the exact center of the planet's four quadrants.

"Bull's-eye," Nelly said, presenting a target she'd generated before and overlaying it on the planet's now-dust-marked face. If there was a difference, you'd need a computer to spot it, and Nelly wasn't talking.

"Very good, Nelly. Outstanding."

"Thank you, Kris," Nelly said, and you could almost hear her taking a bow.

"Let's head back for Alwa," Kris said, and the fleet lifted anchors and departed.

"You have a plan?" Jack asked, as they lay beside each other that night.

"I'll have a plan to run by you and the staff when we get back," Kris said. "Now, make me forget I'm an admiral planning a fight, but do it carefully. My breasts are sensitive and I think they're starting to leak."

Jack was very careful but very thorough.

58

Kris let her eyes rove down the table. Her entire staff was here.

Jack sat to her right. Alone of those here, he knew what was coming. He'd helped her make this plan the best she could.

Admiral Furzah sat to Jack's left, followed by Captain Drago and Abby.

To Kris's left were Penny and Masao, Admiral Kitano, Amanda and Jacques.

At the foot of the table, on a hookup, was Commodore Rita. It might be eighty years since she had led BatCruRon 16 into battle, but she still had the steely eye of one of humanity's most-fighting captains.

"We have to defend forward of Alwa," Kris began. "Any fight should be as far from Alwa as we can make it. Alwa is their target. From what we've seen of their suicide attacks, we don't want them close to Alwa. There is a second reason. Our most powerful weapon is worthless in this system."

The screens on both sides of the room lit up with the same scene. The *Conqueror* knocked a chip off an asteroid. It shot out for several hundred thousand kilometers only to be converted to sand by the *Tenacious* and *Relentless*.

"Nothing in this system is hard enough to form the bullets needed to smash base ships. If we fight here, we will lose," Kris said with finality.

"So, we don't fight in my backyard," Commodore Rita drawled, sounding way too much like the Granny. "Where *do* you fight?"

"In their backyard," Kris said. "They've set up shop in System X, been exploiting it for resources and building a new, fast wing for their fighting force. We fight them there."

Kris paused; the screens now showed System X.

"Here we have a neutron star, ammunition for the beam ships. The aliens are far enough away that we can make their approach march a grueling battle of attrition."

"You will need that," Admiral Furzah purred. "Surely you have learned that the ratio of the forces in a battle is the square of their size. You have two hundred ships. They have sixteen hundred at last count. By my reckoning, they outnumber you not eight to one but two hundred and fifty-six to four. Sixty-four to one."

"We know that rule, Admiral Big Cat," Granny Rita said, "and we're going to beat them. Thank God that ex of mine is good at getting the best stuff pushed forward to where the fight is. You can always count on him for that."

"But won't the aliens dodge these neutron bullets if they see them coming?" Admiral Kitano asked. "I know I would be opening up my formation to let them pass. Incoming always has the right-of-way," she added with a chuckle.

"Can you dodge a machine-gun volley?" Jack said softly.

"Machine gun?" Kitano asked, with a raised eyebrow.

"If the beam ships fire a bolt every fifteen seconds, that means a shot every five seconds. Nelly has a way to make the fifty-thousand-ton bullets splinter into four darts. Try dodging that."

Admiral Kitano thought for a long minute, then shook her head. "That sounds great, assuming these three beam ships fire as fast as you say they can. Can they?"

"Someone read our report," Kris said.

"Every inch of it. Out loud," Kitano shot back.

"Okay, yes and yes. Yes, when we took the beam ships out for a test run we found they were still in the experimental stage, so we kicked butt, replaced personnel, mind-set, software, and hardware." Kris paused to let that sink in.

"Right now, the repair ships *Vulcan*, *Arasi*, and *Artifex* are tied up alongside each beam ship. Those Navy hammer and screwdriver types are going over the ships, reviewing where the breakdowns occurred and toughening them to battle standards. We've got the fabs on the moon knocking out tons of critical spare parts. We will mate the repair ships permanently to the beam ships. In the coming fight, if they need something fixed, those Sailors will have what they need to get it working in Navy time, not civilian time."

Kitano considered that. "What about armor? Those beam ships are big targets."

"I've talked to Admiral Benson about that. He says there's no way to cram all that high-tech kludge into anything like Condition Zed."

"Can we load them up with more Smart Metal?" Amanda asked.

Abby shook her head. "We'd be blending local Smart Metal with what they came with. That's something we've avoided. And when we finished, they'd weigh so much, they likely couldn't get under way. No, folks, what you see is what we fight."

"Any delay," Kris said, "would have the aliens charging into the Alwa system, where we'd be fighting with our backs to the wall."

"My wall," Granny Rita drawled.

"Glad I won't be fighting in those big eggs with a target painted on them," Jacques said.

"Unfortunately, you will be," Kris said. "Everyone who has one of Nelly's kids will be forming three-person teams to manage the fire control systems on those battlewagons."

"Oops," Jacques said. "Honey, you've been lusting after this computer around my neck. How about I give it to you?"

"I was lusting after the body under your computer, lover boy, and I'll be right there beside you."

"So I get to be the courageous warrior, but I don't get to kiss you good-bye and go off to do fun guy things, huh?"

"Kiss me all you want, but never good-bye," Amanda said, and leaned over and gave him a kiss that went way longer than a peck.

There are problems having civilians in war counsels, Kris thought, not leaning over and giving Jack just as long a kiss, though she longed to.

"Moving right along," Abby said. "I take it that me, Colonel Bruce, and Cara will have a beam ship of our own."

"Yes" Kris said. "I know this will disrupt the colonel's regiment dirtside, but if this works, they won't have to fight."

"And if it don't, there likely won't be much chance of their winning. I suspect the aliens intend to sanitize Alwa right down to bedrock, like they did that first planet."

"I'm getting that impression," Kris admitted. "Those fast suicide boats didn't mean to leave much standing."

"Who does that mean I'll be going out there with?" Jacques asked.

"Jack, Penny, and I will be on the *Conqueror*. You, Professor Labao, and Chief Beni will be on the *Opening Statement*," Kris said.

"Retired Chief Beni who came out here to fight them that killed his boy? All three of us who got the new computers to replace the last three of Nelly's kids that got killed in a three-way hookup."

"I'm afraid so."

"Honey, kisses or no, you stay here."

"Kisses or no, I'm going out there with you," Amanda replied.

"I'm being drafted into this."

"And I've got a reserve commission that I'm sure the nice princess over there will activate if I bat my eyelashes at her husband a few times."

"Activate her, Kris," Jack said. "Torture by batted eyelashes terrifies me."

"Consider yourself on active duty," Kris said, smiling fondly at Jack.

"Foolish woman," Jacques said.

"Foolish man," Amanda said. "Now, if there's nothing we can add to this meeting, I have a few words I want to exchange with this warrior of mine."

"I doubt there will be words exchanged," Admiral Furzah purred, as the two left.

"What have we got left to check out, Kris?" Granny Rita said. "You will defend far forward. That's settled. What next?"

"How do we enter the system?" Kris asked. "The aliens don't know that we can use fuzzy jumps. They don't even know they exist. There's a nice fuzzy jump near the neutron sun. The nearest standard jump is much farther away. Using that jump would have the advantage of getting them committed and headed our way before they have to face the full fury of our neutron bolts. However, using that jump would also cut down on the time we have to hit them with those bolts."

"Why not use the closer fuzzy jump?" Admiral Kitano asked.

"What are the chances we can annihilate every ship in the enemy horde?" Jack asked back. "Any one of them gets away, and the next alien ships will know we have some way of appearing out of space they don't know about. At best, they get nervous. At worst, they go looking for the fuzzy jumps and discover a fast way around the galaxy. A fast way to the human side of the galaxy."

"Not good," Captain Drago said. "I, for one, vote for a normal entrance. The O club on Cannopus Station has the silhouettes of four base ships with a nice bright red line through them. When we finish these, I expect to add another four. Still, that leaves thirty to forty."

Those around the table nodded agreement.

"We use the normal jump," Kris said, ending that discussion.

"What next?" Admiral Kitano asked.

"This will be as much your decision as mine," Kris said. "I will be commanding this fight from the *Conqueror*. You will have tactical command of the battle line. As I see it, that will consist of all four of the main fleets. I'm adding one of the newly arrived squadrons to each of the existing fleets, and one to Admiral Benson's Fifth Fleet in reserve. Do we send it with you to make the interception or hold him back with the beam ships?"

"We're going to have a hell of a fight on our hands, what with a thousand of those warships of theirs now having six hundred of their fast movers to outflank us," Admiral Kitano said slowly. "I'd like to have Benson with me. Sorry to strip you down to just about nothing."

"I'm leaving four Bird class guard ships at Alwa. The other eight will escort the beam ships," Kris said.

"I'll try to have a decent-size fleet when we rally to your position," Kitano said.

"The beam ships should attrite the aliens for you before the fight."

"When do we move?"

"There's no use in further delays," Kris said. "The yards have finished up the last of the battlecruisers. Even if they were to lay down another squadron for us, I'm none too sure we could find crews. We head out day after tomorrow. Sortie at 0900."

"How are you going to get on the *Conqueror*?" Amber asked. "I noticed you sent Captain Drago over to kick butt and take names when the beam ships screwed up."

"Yep. Baby and X-rays do not mix. They're taking me over in *Wasp*'s pinnace. It's hardened enough for orbit. They're also jacking up the hardening on the *Conqueror*. It should be a piece of cake."

"You're setting your pretty ass down on the biggest target, and you call it a piece of cake. Admiral, you've got a skewed perspective."

"No doubt I do. I'm a Longknife," Kris said, with a chuckle.

The two went to study the order of battle on the wall of Kris's flag plot. Jack stood at Kris's elbow, Admiral Furzah and Captain Drago at Kitano's.

"Who commands Fourth Fleet?" Kitano asked. "You took it out last time."

"I'm short flag officers," Kris admitted. "Captain Zermatt of the Helvetican never fought more than a squadron. Commodore Nottingham fought the Earth task force when Admiral Yi funked out on us. There is one captain who might fit a three star slot."

"Who?" Kitano asked.

"Captain Drago," Kris said.

"What?" the mentioned captain said.

"You were an admiral once upon a time," Kris said. "A damn good one, I hear. You left a desk job to keep a certain princess delinquent out of trouble, which got you into enough trouble and fights to satisfy any fighting man. We're heading into a desperate fight. I won't be commanding a fleet from my old flag. Why don't you take Fourth Fleet out for a spin?"

Captain Drago stood silent for a long minute. "It sounds like an honor I can hardly refuse," he finally said.

"You have any problem with this?" Kris asked Kitano.

"I'd say you've been underutilizing this man for a long time. I'd be glad to see him back in the saddle."

"Nelly, cut the paperwork," Kris said.

"It's on Admiral Longknife's desk," Nelly said with glee.

Kitano retrieved the certificate. Kris signed it, and handed it to her longtime friend. "You better go find some stars."

"Thank you, I think. Wouldn't you know I'd get a fleet with just days to get ready."

"What do you expect from one of those damn Long-knifes?" Kris said.

Admiral Drago saluted. "Now, if you'll excuse me, I've got a rather tough job at hand."

"You want to keep *Wasp*?" Kris asked.

The freshly minted admiral shook his head. "I think having *Wasp* and *Intrepid* with those Birds will be the least I can do for you."

"Thanks. Let's hope I don't need them."

"Yeah, right," Drago said with a smile, and exited.

For a long moment, Kris and Amber continued gazing at the screens. Both gravitated toward the one showing System X. Kris measured and remeasured the distance between the alien base at one end of the system, her neutron star toward the other, and the jump she'd use to enter.

"You think they'll charge you once they take a few hits?" Amber asked.

"But will they charge in without decelerating or come in slow and light on their feet to dodge?"

"I'm ordering the ships on blockade duty to refuel on their way to the rally point. I'll have the ships here take on double their normal reaction mass load. If they don't use it, they can dump it, but if they need it . . ," Amber left unsaid.

"Nelly, calculate a Condition Zed for the battlecruisers with excess reaction mass."

"How much excess?" Nelly asked.

"I don't know."

"You're no help," Nelly growled.

"There's no way to tell until we get there," Amber answered for Kris.

"A fat lot of good all that nice crystal armor is going to do you if you've got reaction mass bulging out love handles."

"Love handles, Nelly?" Kris yelped.

"You know, those things you get . . ."

"Yes, I know how you get then," Kris said, cutting Nelly off, and patting her own very bulging "love handle."

Amber was polite enough to almost stifle a laugh at Kris's computer's image of her fleet. Or Nelly's discomforting of Kris. Kris didn't ask which and changed the subject.

"Anything more we need to do?" Kris asked her Navy deputy.

"Yes, would you mind promoting Rear Admiral Hawkings to command the First Fleet so I can concentrate on leading all of them?"

"The Battlecruiser Fleet for you," Kris said. "The Battle Fleet for me."

"Something like that," Kitano said, nodding.

"Nelly."

"The paper is already on your desk," Nelly answered.

Kitano retrieved it; Kris signed it. "I wish I had more ships for you," she said as she handed Amber the promotion for her subordinate into her place.

"We took on the first alien base ships with what, thirty-four frigates with only 20-inch lasers. Now look at us. You're sending me out with five fleets as big or bigger. What's that, two-hundred-plus battlecruisers? How will I handle all of them?"

"You'll find a way."

"God help the aliens. If they're still thinking of us as vermin, they won't know what hit them."

"You did read the report that they may have longer-ranged lasers on those fast cruisers. Maybe some on their warships."

"I read it. I'll keep them at arm's length. I'm no Admiral Yi. My religion strictly forbids doing crazy charges. But we've got the 22-inch lasers and crystal armor. I'll use it all—cautiously."

"Good. Godspeed, good hunting, and sink them all."

Admiral Kitano saluted. Kris returned it. Admiral Furzah, Penny, and Masao followed her out. Kris was left alone with Jack.

"You really that confident?" he asked.

"Hold me. Feel my trembling," Kris said, folding herself into his arms.

59

Most of the fleet was already on station, guarding three exits from System X. Word went out to pull back from Jumps Alpha, Beta, and Gamma and rally at Jump Eta.

A pair of courier ships were left at each jump to keep an eye on what the aliens were up to. At last report, they were still orbiting that gas giant, busy making more ships.

Three days later, every human battlecruiser this side of the galaxy was one jump out from System X. Kris joined the *Conqueror*, using *Wasp*'s pinnace. It had been strange, sailing with Commander Pett. She was a competent woman, well versed in Kris's need, but she was not the friend Drago had become.

He had taken *Unrelenting* in Captain Becky Kaeyat's division for his flag. Kris had issued a lot of promotions in the last three days. She would not send young people into bloody battle wearing junior rank for the job they'd do this day.

Admiral Furzah calculated the odds against them at sixty-four to one. She, the ever-optimist cat, had transferred with Kris, Penny, and Masao to the *Conqueror*. They would provide her key staff for the coming fight.

With the newly respun *Falcon* and *Harpy Eagle* keeping watch on the far side of the jump and reporting no activity from the aliens except in their own little corner of the system, Kris decided to risk a fast entry into System X. The *Conqueror* and her sisters would go through the jump at forty-eight thousand kilometers an hour. Keeping eight hundred kilometers between them, they'd make the jump a minute apart.

The battlecruisers coming out from the Alwa system were all under Admiral Kitano's direct command. She had them tucked in closer, at a hundred-klick interval; they'd jump every ten seconds. Tight, but not likely to dent any hulls.

None of this would have been possible if the aliens had deployed even the most rudimentary pickets. They hadn't even chased the *Victorious* away but left it to report on matters until Kris ordered it withdrawn as her beam ships approached the jump.

The *Victorious* and *Vanguard* waited patiently fifty klicks from the jump. Kris could only wonder how Hanson was taking the word of his promotion to commodore and command of BatRon 16 in Benson's reserve fleet.

The jump went smoothly. Kris watched from her flag plot, reestablished in *Conqueror*'s core. *Wasp* had even brought over her desk, leather couches, and chairs. More importantly, they'd brought her screens. Nelly attached them to the very good sensor suite aboard the beam ship, necessary for targeting even if the designers hadn't been nearly as committed to hitting something.

Kris and Nelly would see that changed.

Once through the jump, *Conqueror* set course at 1.5 gees for a burned cinder of a planet orbiting the neutron star. The other beam ships followed.

Immediately, battlecruisers began to shoot through. Thirty-five minutes later, the fleet was sorting itself into a cross of four task fleets, each with four or five squadrons. Admiral Benson trailed in reserve with four squadrons.

Wasp and *Intrepid* caught up with *Conqueror* and took station well ahead. The eight Bird class frigates, *Ostrich, Cock o' the Walk, Eagle, Falcon, Heron, Osprey, Kiwi,* and *Kookaburra,* came up the rear. Slower to join were *Merlin, Hermes, Apollo, Atalanta, Diana,* and *Artemis.* Unlike the Birds, they had four reactors instead of three. That gave them speed but only four 20-inch lasers to the Birds' six. Birds could fight but not run. Merlins had better run rather than fight.

Kris had no idea which class would help her the most, but they were all she had. Beam ships could hardly run.

Hours later, the aliens answered Kris's gambit. Every alien ship, warship, fast cruiser, and mother ship, took off for Kris's side of the system. The mother ships accelerated at 1.3 gees. Most of the warships pulled ahead at 1.75 gees, then slowed to 1.5 gees. The cruisers had also bolted at first, at nearly two gees, but were slowing to keep close to mother.

Only the door knockers stayed in orbit. Interesting, that.

Kris ordered the battlecruiser fleets to slow to one gee and intercept them halfway across the system. That done, she urged the beam ships to lay on more acceleration, but the skippers of the three big round balls were reluctant. "Remember, we have to slow this steaming hunk of cow turd, Princess. If we lay too much energy on, we might not slow down, and then what?"

NELLY, ARE THE STRUCTURAL AND ENGINEERING LIMITS OF THIS CONTRAPTION AS LIMITING AS THESE FELLOWS THINK?

KRIS, I CAN TELL YOU THE REACTORS ARE STRESSED AT 1.5 GEES AND THE HULL IS MAKING ODD MOANING SOUNDS. I THINK HE MAY BE RIGHT. I DON'T THINK THE DESIGNERS OF THESE THINGS REALLY UNDERSTOOD WHAT BEING IN A WAR MEANT.

THANK YOU, NELLY. "Okay, Captain. Keep me informed."

Jack smiled at her. "That didn't hurt, now did it?"

"I guess I'm spoiled. The first *Wasp* gave us everything it had. The last two *Wasp*s didn't leave me with a complaint in the world."

"And now all your vultures are coming home to roost."

"Something like that."

"Why don't you and baby take a nap?"

"Damn it, Jack, I hate being this tired," Kris said, but through a huge yawn.

"It's not time to fight yet," Jack said. "Nelly, make her one of those nice chairs. Lean back, dear. I'll get you and baby a blanket."

"And what are you going to do? Watch me drool?"

"You don't drool, love. But I need to check *Conqueror*'s Marine detachments. It's got a lot of colonials, even a few Ostriches. I think the scientists are a bit taken aback to see a bird in Marine green. I don't want any chest bumps to break out."

"You do that. Baby and I will wait for you."

She blew him a kiss. Instead, he trotted over and gave her a gentle kiss on her forehead.

To Kris's disgust, she was asleep before the door closed.

60

Kris came awake before *Conqueror* flipped to decelerate toward the burned-out planet that would be their base for this fight. About a third of an Astronomical Unit from the neutron star, the distance from Sol to Earth, the rock was in easy range of the star, but far enough away for the ships to avoid the worst of the huge magnetic waves coming off it.

Somewhere on Kris's desk was a report marveling at how lucky they were that the two stars here were separated by nearly half of an AU, some seven million kilometers. If they'd been closer, they'd be dealing with a red dwarf being robbed of its substance by the neutron star and all sorts of nasty stuff.

Kris patted baby and told her how lucky she was.

The aliens had settled onto a solid course while Kris slept. The mother ships were in a diamond formation, one high, two middle, one low, some hundred thousand klicks behind the battle line. Their acceleration had slowed to one gee.

The warships had formed up into a huge battle array. Each mother ship had seven dishes of thirty ships ahead of it. This trip out, the dishes were arranged in groups of two high, three middle, and two low.

This only accounted for some eight hundred warships. The others seemed to swarm in no particular pattern around the base ships.

It was the fast cruisers that bothered Kris.

Their smaller, fourteen-ship disks had started out in ten dishes of four that extended the warships' box out, giving one very high, two wide in the middle, and one well below the warships' diamond.

But the cruisers weren't staying put. They kept spreading

out or pulling back in, edging ahead of the warship line a bit, then slowing until the more ponderous warships caught up.

Those cruisers added an unknown that unsettled Kris's stomach and likely weren't doing Admiral Kitano's digestion any good, either.

What was clear was that any way you organized that mob, they could swallow up Kitano's fleet and not even burp.

"We'll have to be very careful," Kris muttered, patting baby, who seemed at the moment to still be asleep.

In all of this there was no doubt that the aliens were making for Kris's battlecruiser fleet.

"Nelly, when we start shooting neutron bolts, it will be a deflection shot. Will that be a problem?"

"Regrettably yes, Kris. Not the deflection, that's a piece of cake. The problem is calculating where the ship will be ten hours from now when the bolt arrives. In that time, the alien fleet may have accelerated or slowed down. Our bolts could sail by them unnoticed."

"So the enemy gets a vote and our best laid plans can take off for left field," Kris concluded.

"Yes. I can tell you that the aliens have been holding steady since halfway through your nap. If they keep this up until we get to that cinder planet, we just might have something we can bet the farm on."

"Nelly, your colloquialisms are getting very pleasant and right on," Kris told her computer.

"Thank you, Kris. I'm doing my best to sound less like a cold computer and more like a flesh-and-blood person. I think you humans are more comfortable with that. I do hope I will have time to do more studies of you humans."

"We all want more time," Kris said, patting her unborn child.

"Yes."

They stared at the boards, massaging that thought and the enemy's predictability for some time.

This was the part of the battle Kris had learned to hate. The waiting. She'd done all she could. Nothing more would improve their chances of coming out of this alive. The last thing the fleet needed was a commander dithering and joggling the elbows of those who would do the fighting.

Kris wished she could take another nap, but she was all napped out, and baby had awoken and appeared to be jumping rope on Kris's bladder. Not being in the eggs yet, Kris had to take care of that matter on her own. Returning from the head, she eyed the boards again.

Nothing had changed. The aliens were building up one strong head of steam. They were headed at Kitano's fleet at a wild charge, ignoring Kris and her beam ships.

Big mistake.

Hopefully.

Kris tried to extrapolate what a wild, high-energy charge would be like between those two battle arrays. How many collisions could the aliens manage to steer themselves into? Could Kris lose her entire fleet in one big, head-on crash? Space was large and ships just didn't smash into each other very often.

Still, with closing vectors of a million klicks an hour or more, dodging would have to be done in a blink and jinking out of the way with that much inertia on a boat would be a bitch.

Kris wouldn't put it past the aliens to try.

Then Kris spotted the upside of that strategy for the aliens. They'd be headed for the jump out of the system toward Alwa, and what was left of Kris's fleet would be headed away from their base.

Maybe this crazy charge wasn't that crazy after all.

Kris noted that Kitano had dropped the acceleration on her fleet from one gee to .8. No surprise, Kitano had spotted it, too.

Then Kris smiled. "I wonder how long that charge will hold up when I start taking potshots at their precious mother ships from over here. I do my thing, you react and do your thing. Now I do my thing again." She blew the enemy Enlightened Ones a poisoned kiss and settled into her comfortable chair to watch developments.

Jack came back from his Marine duties to take Kris to dinner. *Conqueror* had five different restaurants. Kris settled down in a comfortable chair in a spacious and quite nice Japanese restaurant. She ordered tempura but passed on the sushi after giving a thought to how long it had been since this "fresh" fish swam in some sea.

Kris couldn't help but look around and frown. "When the fighting starts, will all this stay like this?"

"Afraid so," Jack said. "I've looked at the plans, Kris, and *Conqueror* should be called the 'spaghetti factory.' No one really knows what's behind this bulkhead or that compartment. They were finishing it as they sailed. From what I'm getting from my Marine detachment skippers on the other ships, each is an individual work of art. I've got nanos mapping this ship just like we did the alien ships that fell into our hands."

Kris winced, then thought it through. "I know this is tough for you, but imagine what shape we'd be in if they took the extra time to standardize the design."

Jack nodded.

"Besides, who knows, the difference in one ship may keep it shooting when the others have gone silent for a problem in their design."

"That's not a happy thought," Jack said.

"You want an unhappy thought, think of me. No sake tonight. Not even tea. Just plain water."

"Oh, you can drink the tea," Jack said. "I jogged by this place earlier today and told them I'd be bringing you and asked if they had some noncaffeinated tea. That's chamomile tea. You and baby will sleep like, well, a pair of babies tonight."

Kris lifted her teacup in salute to her husband. Dinner was delightful, and she did sleep like a baby with the little one letting her sleep as well.

Next morning came early as *Conqueror* went into orbit around the cinder. *Ultimate Argument* was a thousand klicks right behind, with *Opening Statement* trailing. Kris intended the ships to enter a highly elliptical orbit that would bring them almost a hundred thousand klicks above the cinder before plunging them back to make a fast graze past the planet before rising high again.

This orbit would give them the maximum time in a firing position before the planet blocked their fire, but only for a brief twenty minutes. Hopefully, they wouldn't be down there when anything crucial happened.

In orbit, the beam ships anchored themselves together.

Once stabilized, Kris ordered battle stations. The familiar "Bong, bong, battle stations, all hands to battle stations, bong, bong" lasted a lot longer than Kris wanted. It was a full fifteen minutes before the Klaxon cut off, and Kris's board showed *Conqueror* manned and ready. Again, *Ultimate Argument* had beaten the flag.

Kris shrugged. It might be her flag, but she hardly considered *Conqueror* her ship.

"You may commence primary ignition at will. The targets are the alien base ships." If she took them out early, there was no telling what the aliens might do, but at least she'd have them gone.

UA fired immediately, *Conqueror* next, and, as expected, *OS* was last. After four firing sequences, *UA* fell into a fifteen-second rhythm. *Conqueror* came up to speed a bit later. *Last Stand*, as Kris was thinking of her ever-tardy third ship, took a half hour to get into a steady habit of knocking bolts off the neutron star every fifteen seconds.

"I've got the darts just the way I want them," Nelly reported. "The front end is only three millimeters square and formed like a regular pyramid. That should deflect radar, especially with it rotating at 900 rpms. They're about seven millimeters long. I expect them to spin off into four darts only a million klicks short of their target, say, one minute shy of the mother ship. It will be interesting to see what happens."

"Yes, it will, Nelly. Now, we wait for nine hours."

"Less, Kris. The aliens have been closing on the battle-cruisers at a steady one gee."

"You're leading the targets?"

"The first round are. We're varying the assumptions for the later bullets. Some ahead. Some behind. Some right on. We've shot enough bolts that we can afford to allow for Kentucky windage."

"You like that phase," Kris said, remembering how Nelly had sniffed at Phil Taussig's suggestion that the Magnificent Nelly might need some.

"It's a helpful turn of phrase when dealing with you humans," Nelly answered.

Kris waited; she smiled at the thought. Being a lady-in-waiting for the last seven months had done nothing for her patience, but she'd learned there was nothing for it but to wait.

Even baby seemed content. Kris knew she was awake, but there were no somersaults or jump rope or other things baby tended to do when she was excited.

Together, Kris and baby waited out the bolts as more and more of them joined the long line of death headed for the unsuspecting aliens.

61

"We should start seeing hits any time now," Nelly said.

Kris came awake. "This chair is too damn comfortable," she grumbled.

"I thought I might as well let you sleep, Kris," Nelly said. "It's going to get lively here soon."

"Yes," Kris muttered as she heaved herself and baby out of the comfortable chair and waddled her way to the head. Baby might not be dancing on her bladder, but she was sure taking up room.

Done, Kris got back to her chair, eyed it like an enemy, then settled back into it and felt it conform to her ever-changing bulk. "Nelly, don't make it too comfortable."

"Yes, Kris."

But Kris didn't notice the chair change.

Oh, well, no doubt trillions of women have wished for what I've got.

But what I really want, little love, is a safe place to put you while Mommy goes out and kills what would hurt you.

"It's happening," Nelly said, ending Kris's internal dialogue with the life beneath her heart.

This had happened hours ago, but, thanks to the speed of light, Kris only saw it now.

The horde had maintained a steady course and acceleration for its collision with Kris's mobile fleet.

They likely would not make that mistake again.

A warship exploded. Then another, followed rapidly by several more. But even as the enemy's main battle dishes were taking punishment, darts were slipping past them to hit the mother ships. One took a hit, then another and another.

It looked like all four were trying to sidestep the barrage

coming their way, but jiggering a small moon's course was no easy task.

The least damaged ship flipped itself around and dove down ninety degrees from its base course.

It still took hits as it edged away from the others. Or maybe warships had taken hits intended for her. Back at the battle line, it looked like a Lander's Day fireworks display as more warships and cruisers blew up.

The enemy formation was coming apart as ships jinked to avoid nearly invisible darts on their screens or to just not be where they were.

The enemy fleet was hard stung. Two mother ships lost all acceleration and were just coasting. "Nelly, will that work for them?"

"I don't think so, Kris. I'm not sure where all the spun-off quarter darts went, but we aimed a lot behind the base course."

Even as Nelly spoke, one of the drifting mother ships took another hit. This one sparked reactors to lose control of their plasma demons. The ship burned.

The ship that still had weigh on took a hit, too. Only the diving ship managed to miss the bolts aimed for her. "Lucky bastard," Kris muttered. "Nelly, cease fire, give the bolt ships a rest. We'll need to wait until we see what they do before we send out a new volley."

"Yes, Kris. I ordered a stand-down on the beam ships four hours ago, just after you dozed off."

"You did, did you?"

"As you have noticed, there was not a lot we could do just then, and some deficiencies had begun to make themselves known in our systems."

"They had? And you didn't wake me?"

"Kris, an admiral with a screwdriver has got to be even more dangerous than an ensign with one. The repair ships did their jobs. What do you say you do your job, and I do mine?"

Kris considered reprimanding her computer for both letting her sleep and exercising her four star rank while she slept, then decided to let it slide. Kris was feeling more rested than she had in several days, maybe several weeks. And Nelly had gauged her targeting and the systems-maintenance needs just right, which was to be expected of a computer.

"Well done, Nelly," Kris said.

"Thank you, Kris."

Kris eyed the alien fleet on screen. Two mother ships were rolling lazily in space, drifting as inertia took them. One was making maybe a quarter gee, zigging and zagging.

"Nelly, are the beam ships ready to go back online?"

"Yes, Kris. I've received several requests to test the systems."

"Let's fire a couple of bolts toward the drifting mother ships. Don't bother splitting them into quarter bolts."

"You want to hit those ships with a full fifty-thousand-ton shot?"

"Yep. Let's see what happens when we really hit one of those bastards."

"It will be like slicing watermelons with a sword at full charge," Nelly said.

"Likely."

"What if one of the warships gets in the way?"

"Do you think a five-hundred-thousand-ton ship can slow down a fifty-thousand-ton neutron bolt?" Kris asked.

"No doubt the scientists and Navy types will be interested in the results."

"Do it. Scatter fragmentation bolts around the one that still has weigh on."

"Yes, Kris. What about the fourth one?"

"Ignore it for now. It's too unpredictable. But those others? Slam them hard."

"The bolts are on their way."

Kris leaned back in her chair, got comfortable, and watched developments.

As expected, the one fighting alien mother ship zigged and zagged, changing acceleration as it went. Someone was seriously into unpredictability.

"Nelly, you see any pattern?"

"No. Their Enlightened One is being most erratic, but the base course is for us."

"Yes," Kris agreed. "This one learned fast."

Ahead of the lone mother ship still headed for Kris, the battle dishes had spread themselves out, massively upping the distance between each ship to well over thirty thousand klicks.

Each ship did its own little jig within its space. Some of the late-arriving bolts would occasionally pick one off, but culling the herd was harder now.

They were also on a new course, headed straight for Kris.

The cruisers had suffered less from the bolts, being out of the line of fire to the base ships. They spread out but held their position as wings to the diamond battle array.

Now, everything was aimed at engulfing Kris's three beam ships and their tiny escorts. Kris patted baby and tried not to think about her and the little one's being the center of the bull's-eye for a very big arrow.

Her eyes went to Kitano's Mobile Fleet. Amber had upped her acceleration to 1.5 gees on a course to intercept the alien warships. Now, instead of the aliens being spread wide like a deadly flower set to engulf her fleet, the aliens were edge on to Kitano's battlecruisers. The aliens were spread out too widely to offer mutual support.

Kitano would hit one of the cruiser groups, cut through it and into the flank of one of the warship disks of disks. Assuming Kitano could arrive at the meeting engagement with the right vectors to run parallel with the warships, she'd be in a perfect position to chew them up one bite at a time.

"Nelly, calculate from Amber's present position an intercept that lets her come alongside the aliens."

A vector appeared, one that started at 1.5 gees now and included some intense braking.

"Does the fleet have the fuel for this?" Kris asked.

"It will be close, Kris, and they are likely to use much of the spare fuel you took on, but, yes, it can be done."

Kris smiled to herself and patted baby on her head. "You've got a smart mommy, if I do say so myself."

Kris eyed her boards that showed the standard availability of the eighteen frigates and couriers. There was nothing on the three beam ships. "Nelly, how are the beam ships doing? Could you give me some visual that tracks them if they fall below optimal?"

"A couple of reactor readouts should work. The weapons are very peculiar, but I can knock together something. Hull integrity is easy to gauge. Jack is worried about boarding parties. Should I have a symbol for boarders?"

"Why not? Though how the aliens will manage it is any-body's guess. Can you show me where they are? It wouldn't do to walk out of here for a bite to eat and run into one."

"I'll see what I can do," Nelly said.

Kris eyed the board. It was like watching a train wreck, as the old saying went. The aliens were on a direct course for her. Kitano was on a direct course for them. They might as well have been on a space elevator's rails for all the chance they had to avoid the inevitable.

"Nelly, toss some more bolts out there to keep the aliens honest. I wouldn't want them to relax. Say, one fragmentation bolt per ship per minute. Can they meet that schedule for the next hour?"

"I think so," Nelly said.

So Kris watched. One screen showed a visual of the neu-tron star. Every twenty seconds, there would be a bright flash, and another tiny bolt of fifty thousand tons would head off at a fraction of the speed of light. "It looks like my ships have got their rhythm," Kris said.

"It does," Nelly agreed.

Kris curled up in her chair, got comfortable, and watched, gently rubbing her belly and baby.

62

The carnage began to get serious.

First one, then more fifty-thousand-ton bolts smashed into the two gravely wounded mother ships. One began to blow itself apart as it took hits at thirty-second intervals. The first two hits on the other apparently took it on one flank and sent it spinning. Later hits threw huge sections off. It didn't so much die, as fall to pieces as huge chunks shot away.

"It must be hell there," Penny whispered softly.

"Yes," Kris agreed.

The third small moon struggled to stay under way, to follow the alien horde as it sought Kris's blood. Kris's anger caught it.

First one 12,500-ton fragment hit, then another, then a third. The bullets drilled into the ship, shattering structure and smashing flesh and blood. Inevitably, some of what they smashed were reactors. The ship began to burn. The alien captain tried to turn the huge thing, to work it out of the incoming barrage. However, there was no escaping. Not now. Not after he'd spent the last seven hours heading straight down Kris's throat.

More darts slammed into the ship: 12,500 tons hitting at over eighteen thousand kilometers a second. The ship burned from the inside and blew huge jets of plasma from its reactors out into space. It started forward and worked its way aft as the bow became nothing but a burned-out wreck. Later, bolts shot through from bow to stern, where the propulsion reactors made for easy hits and lethal consequences. The fire burned and the ship glowed before yielding itself up as one huge fireball.

"Three down," Kris said, feeling nothing even as her mind

calculated the deaths of 150 billion intelligent beings. The number was just too big to grasp.

The one surviving Enlightened One was quick to react to the slaughter of his three associates and all the people they held in thrall. Two detachments of cruisers, half of what he had, took off for Kris at 3.5 gees.

"I guess they don't like us," Kris said, counting the fast-moving cruisers and coming up with 280. "Nelly, let's put some bolts across their path. They're bound to run into some of them."

"A lot of them, if we intend to survive," Jack said dryly.

"I've advised the teams on the beam ships to increase the rate of fire to two bolts a minute," Nelly said.

"Good. Divide them between the fast cruisers and the rest of the horde, say, one to two."

"We're on it."

The neutron star began to sparkle at ten-second intervals as more chunks off its hide got kicked off at one-twentieth the speed of light. It would be hours before they saw the results.

Apparently, Admiral Kitano saw the same development. Admiral Benson's reserve fleet had been trailing the four fleets, in reserve as his name, and the training of his crews, implied. Now they beat on four gees and aimed themselves on an intercept course for the fast-moving alien cruisers.

Out in space, less than four AUs from where Kris stood, the bullets snapped out six or seven hours ago began to slash through the alien fleet.

Most missed. Space was huge, and the ships were jinking as much as their huge size allowed. But the aliens had committed themselves to a course right down Kris's throat. That made them predictable within their randomness.

That fraction of predictability, that they wanted to kill Kris, meant she could kill them.

Bolts pierced through ships, sending them spinning out of control. Bolts slashed into reactors and left a hot, expanding ball of gas in their wake. Some ships survived the encounter with a bolt, only to fall off their course struggling with cascading catastrophes, leaving their formations with gaping holes.

Kris tasted the rage of these dying aliens, unable to come to grips with their tormenters. This didn't have to be.

"Nelly, we've sent them enough messages in hard neutron star. Raise me Jacques."

"I'm here, Kris."

"Compose a message. Tell the alien Enlightened One that this slaughter does not have to continue. He can stop it by ending his quest to kill us. He can save his life and the lives of everyone following him if he turns away from this slaughter and makes for open space."

"You know I can't say that exactly."

"Send the message that will carry the freight, Jacques."

"Give me five minutes."

Kris counted five minutes, and thirty more bolts before Jacques was back. "I've composed the message. Do you want to hear it?"

"No, just sign my name and fire it off."

"The *Last Word* has sent it."

"So its crew is calling the *Opening Statement* the *Last Word*?" Kris asked, grinning despite the weight of the day.

"Yep. They are holding up their end of the deal now, but they're keeping the nickname."

"Humans," Nelly said, but there was a smile in her words.

"Aren't we wonderful, just a little less than the angels?" Penny observed.

Kris turned back to the boards. The surviving alien base ship was accelerating at 1.25 gees, zigging and zagging right and left, down and up by swerving its hind end around and letting the bank of huge rocker motors steer the ship. So far, it had managed to avoid any bullets. It had to be luck. Nothing could explain how he got something that big through all the bolts in space.

Ahead of him, the alien warships re-formed themselves into one huge set of dishes, three layers thick in front of their last surviving base ship. On the side Admiral Kitano was coming up on, the cruisers formed up well away. That would force the humans to fight their way through the fast movers before they'd get a chance at the warships or have a go at the base ship.

Behind them, the 150 or so warships that had been

protecting the three destroyed base ships organized themselves into a fighting force. They accelerated to 2.5 gees and aimed themselves at Kitano's flank.

"A fight's coming, and it will be brutal," Kris muttered.

"It will also come in waves," Jack said. "They've lost their unit cohesion. We may have to fight eight times as many ships, but we'll fight them in dribs and drabs. This is a fight we can win."

Penny nodded. So did Admiral Furzah. "They are fools, these aliens you fight. They are throwing away their advantage."

"We haven't won yet," Kris reminded them.

The aliens died in ones and twos as darts found them and took them apart. With the cruisers slamming themselves forward at 3.5 gees, hell-bent on driving themselves down Kris's throat, it was impossible for them to swerve when a bullet came at them. The smarter ones angled their course a bit away from Kris. The ones that didn't died in five or six hours as Nelly spotted their folly and sent a bullet out with their name on it.

The smart ones kept up their 3.5-gee acceleration, but varied it a bit up, a bit down, a bit to right or left every half hour or twenty minutes.

They lived while the others died.

Too many lived.

It was the same among the seven hundred warships. Those who came straight at Kris paid the price as 12,500-ton darts six millimeters long and one in diameter harpooned their ships like whales of old, leaving them bleeding, burning, vomiting out their life until they gave up the ghost and blew themselves up.

"I hate this business, Jack," Kris said after watching five ships go out in different ways in less than a minute.

"Yes."

"I don't want to do this again."

"I know."

"But I've got to see this through, don't I?"

"There's no way out but through," Jack agreed.

"Nelly, Kitano will be tackling the outriding cruiser task force in six hours. Have some of them gotten predictable?"

"Yes, Kris. They've only been getting the strays from the other targets. I think they doubt we can hit them."

"Show them the error. Concentrate two out of three bolts on them for the next fifteen minutes."

"Can do, but the systems on all three beam ships are showing wear. They need a break to let the repair crews fix and mend."

"Pass the word. In fifteen minutes, we will shut down for maintenance, but let's create some holes for Kitano."

The star sparkled as bolts were chipped off and sent on their way. Fifteen minutes later, with fast movers heading down their throat and other ships about to come to blows, the mightiest weapons forged by humanity fell silent as mere men struggled to fix what they had made.

63

The beam ships were down for four hours. Interestingly, *Last Word* came back online first, and quickly built up to four shots a minute before settling down to a steady throw of three.

Conqueror was its usual steady second. *UA* was conspicuous by its absence for an entire half hour. Kris sent a congratulatory message, and a princesslike thank-you for all the hard work of both the operators and maintainers when all three were back up.

Out in space, the bolts sent out earlier still had a ways to go. Jack ordered takeout from a Chinese restaurant, and Kris's staff ate without taking their eyes off developments.

It was surreal. As they ate, more darts slammed into alien warships and cruisers. More aliens died. It was like some bad movie that had only one plot and no development. Kris ate, and patted baby, and watched as aliens died doing all they could to kill her and her child.

Kris ordered more shots sent out at the one remaining base ship. "Maybe if we get it, they'll go away," she said, more a hope than a real thought.

Sometimes, five minutes would go by without a ship dying. Then three would vanish in the blink of an eye.

It went that way for much of a day and a night. Three times they paused the bombardment to allow the beam ships time to fix and mend before something got out of hand and did damage to those huge machines.

"Those fast cruisers, headed straight for us, I don't think they're going to flip," Penny pointed out.

"One wild charge at an unthinkable speed," Admiral Furzah

purred, and seemed jealous that the aliens got the wild ride while she was stuck on the receiving end.

Kris studied the situation. If the cruisers didn't flip and begin deceleration, Admiral Benson would have a tough call. He could keep his thirty-two battlecruisers accelerating—and end up, like the cruisers, doomed to die in ships that couldn't slow down.

"Nelly, send to Benson. You will decelerate even if the alien cruisers do not. Make orbit and prepare to render assistance."

That done, Kris ordered more bolts for the fast-approaching cruisers. "Nelly, do you think you could fragment those bolts more, say, eight or sixteen bits? Seems that six thousand, even three thousand, tons ought to vaporize a cruiser."

"I'll see what I can do, Kris. No promises. We'll be testing this on the fly, if you'll excuse the pun, and we will not know the results until we see what happens when it happens."

"Do your best."

"That is what I and my children always do."

Again, Kris felt the strange absence of Nelly in her skull. Nelly insisted she and her children needed their humans. Kris had no idea what the strange symbiotic relationship was between her and Nelly. Still, Nelly was loath to distance the two sides of the bargain. Where Kris went, Nelly went, and, if like today, Nelly needed to be close to *Conqueror*'s fire control computers, Kris was here so Nelly could be.

Someday, when things slow down, I'm going to figure this out, Kris swore.

But for now, Nelly worked her miracles, and Kris eyed the boards in flag plot.

The final moments of approach were working out between Admiral Kitano's Mobile Fleet and the aliens' cruiser wing. Two hundred and eighty cruisers formed into two groups, one high, one low, each with ten divisions of fourteen cruisers were closing rapidly on Kris's four battle fleets. Not bad odds compared to what Kris had faced the last times out.

That cruiser wing had gone untouched by the darts from the neutron star. They might have gotten lazy. They paid for it now.

Fragments of 12,500 tons shot into their midst. The angle of attack was not head-on. Here darts gashed cruisers, breaking their backs and leaving them twisted wrecks in the wake of something unseen. A few got off easy; darts took them through the reactor, and they vaporized in one huge burst of light and gas.

Death flashed through their midst for fifteen minutes as they struggled to come to grips with the human battlecruisers. They were 280 strong when the invisible came their way. There were barely 150 when the neutron hailstorm passed them by.

Then Kitano's battlecruisers opened fire.

Whatever the range of the new cruisers' lasers, it didn't have the reach of the 22-inchers on the battlecruisers. Cruisers took hits. Some folded. Some exploded. Unarmored, the cruiser force took the scourging, but the survivors held their course to close with the humans.

Admiral Kitano faced two tough choices. Eight hundred or more large alien warships, four to five hundred thousand tons each, were bearing down on Kris's beam ships. They had to be defended.

But at the moment, Kitano had these alien cruisers heading in, committed to closing to hand-to-hand range, desperate to get their hands around Kitano's throat.

If Kitano bore away to keep the range open, the huge fleet of alien warships got to increase its lead in the race to Kris's slug throwers.

Kitano chose to let the cruisers close and fight it out all along the line.

An alien cruiser fleet got to go toe-to-toe with an equal number of human battlecruisers.

The cruisers did have longer-ranging lasers. They made human ships glow at 140,000 klicks. They lit a few up, but at a horrible price.

The 22-inch lasers ripped at them.

At first, it was one-to-one, and many thin-skinned cruisers died. Battlecruisers then concentrated their fire two, three, or even four on one. The more the humans concentrated, the faster alien cruisers died.

"What does that mean to us and the two hundred and eighty headed our way?" Kris muttered

"Kris, that number is down to one hundred and ninety-two," Nelly reported. "Several suffered reactor failures. More found neutron star not to their liking."

"Good," Kris snapped.

"Kris, I think we have a problem," Nelly said.

"I'm listening," Kris grumbled, finding that she was getting tired of having problems. All she really wanted was to have this kid born safe and sound with ten fingers and ten toes.

"There were a hundred and fifty alien warships heading for Admiral Kitano's flank. They were the guard ships for the three base ships we destroyed. Fifty of them have changed course. Instead of bearing down on Kitano's fleets, they are heading for the jump we came through."

"Oh, shit," Jack muttered.

"We only have a pair of courier ships guarding that jump," Penny said.

Kris found herself juggling ships in her mind's eye. She didn't need Nelly to run a full analysis to know that Admiral Kitano was committed. There was no way any of her ships could reverse course. All Kitano's energy was aimed at engaging the huge fleet in front of her.

Kris glanced at *Wasp* and *Intrepid*, as well as the eight Birds and eight couriers she had guarding the beam ships. Except for the two large frigates with their ten 22-inch lasers, the others were 20-inchers and totaled only eighty at that. Kris had bet the farm that this would not happen. Apparently, she'd been too good and left the aliens so enraged that they'd risk anything to get at Alwa. Now they had a handful of ships in place to do just that.

"Damn," she finally said. "We will concentrate on the ships facing us. As soon as we finish this fight, we will turn what we can around and chase those bastards. Hopefully, a few fast jumps will put us ahead of them. For now, we concentrate on what's in front of us. Nelly, send these orders to Kitano from me. Attack what's here. We'll chase the others later."

"Sent," Nelly said.

Kris looked at her staff. They did not meet her eyes.

"Kris," Nelly said, "would you like me to make an estimate for time and movement to see where we will intercept the breakaway alien fleet?"

"No, Nelly. Any estimate you make will not reflect damage we suffer or fuel expended. All the gas giants we can refuel from are either on the other side of the system, or in the next system. We will tackle that problem when we finish with this one."

"Spoken like one of those damn Longknifes," Penny spat. "For God's sake, Kris, that's Granny Rita out there."

"Penny, take a walk," Kris ordered. "Masao, go with her, please."

For a moment, Penny and Kris stood face-to-face, Penny's an angry red, Kris cold and committed. Her gut was another matter. No doubt, baby was not enjoying sharing space with the venomous void that passed for Kris's stomach at the moment.

For a moment they continued to lock eyes . . . then Penny broke for the door, and her friend followed in her wake. Still, as he closed the door behind them, his eyes met Kris's. There was dismay at what he'd seen.

Then the door was closed, and Kris turned back to her screens.

"Tough call," Jack said, coming up to rub her aching shoulders.

"God help us all if we don't have enough fuel when this is done to at least make it back to a gas giant. Back to a gas giant and fast passage to Alwa," Kris whispered.

"And you will see what you see when it's there to see," Jack said.

"Yes. Jack, I can't worry about what I can't do anything about. I've got to fight the battle I've got before I chase down a new one."

"I understand, Kris."

"I know you do, Jack. I know you do. Just don't call me Ray. Okay?"

"Never."

"You have made a hard but correct call," Admiral Furzah said.

"Thank you," Kris said, and hoped she meant it.

"The other hundred warships have altered course to join the fifty headed for Alwa," Nelly reported.

"I expected they would," Kris said. She patted baby. That was all she could do.

64

"What the hell," Jack said, unusually venting surprise.

Kris was busy grabbing for something to hold on to. "Nelly, drop this footrest."

Around her, the *Conqueror* was doing some kind of bump and grind. Then it went sideways, and all gravity fled. Kris held tight to the table and tried to protect baby.

"The *Ultimate Argument* has blown out a capacitor," Nelly reported. "They've got a fire on board. One of the reactors is out of control, and they're venting it to space. Its feedback is affecting four more. They may have to dump them. The *UA*'s skipper broke his ship out of the mooring. *Conqueror* and *Last Word* have also cut loose and are distancing themselves from the *UA*.

Kris waited as the skippers and crews did what they had to do to survive. That did not include sending any darts at the approaching enemy.

It was an hour later before the captains of the *Conqueror* and *Last Word* reported they were ready to anchor again to each other and commence firing.

Kris ordered *UA* to make for the distant Zeta Jump Point. She'd suffered five hundred casualties, killed, wounded, and missing.

What would have happen to *UA* if they didn't hold the line was not worth thinking about.

Kris ordered *Conqueror* and *Last Word* to limit their fire. "One shot a minute. Let's make sure everything is ship-shape."

It took an hour to work up to two shots a minute.

"That long firing sequence *Last Word* used," Nelly said.

"They've gone over it again and are using half of it. It's still twice as long as *UA*'s."

Kris eyed the incoming attack waves. "We may have no choice but to go back to rapid fire, but we can put that call off a while."

The first wave of eighth- and sixteenth-size bullets were approaching the onrushing cruisers. The ships charged headlong into a trap that rapidly turned marvelous works of high tech into wrecks and ruin.

A dozen cruisers vanished in the blink of an eye. More the next minute. In the face of onrushing death, cruisers tried to evade, to dodge after days of 3.5-gee acceleration. The inertia on the thinly built speedsters was brutal. Two ships bent in the middle. Since one took a pellet a moment later, it likely was doomed either way.

For fifteen minutes, the onrushing wave of barbs devastated the cruisers. They died in twos and threes. Once, six blew out in a single second.

"I think I got the fragmentation pattern just right," Nelly said, but she did not crow. A deadly pall hung over flag plot. This was not so much battle as murder.

Of course, if these murderers got half a chance, they'd make a suicide dive right down the humans' throats.

Kris ordered the beam ships to aim more pellets at the onrushing cruisers. She also ordered *Wasp* to lead her last-ditch defense squadrons out to make a quick orbit around the neutron star, rising high and passing low to stay out of the line of fire, and to come up along the path of the incoming cruisers. No doubt the speed difference would give them little time to shoot, but they'd have more time to aim than holding formation with the beam ships.

"There's a risk," Kris told *Wasp*'s new skipper, "that you'll be in heavy traffic when you come back at us: cruisers and the wreckage of cruisers as well as our outgoing shots. We'll try to give you a good idea of where that is, so you can dodge, but we can't make any promises."

"Admiral, we knew the score when we shipped out. Give us targets. That's all we ask."

"Good luck," Kris said, and cut the link.

She turned to Jack. "Hold me."

He did.

What kind of a woman am I, sending so many out to die? What kind of an admiral am I, needing a man to hold me?

No doubt, a lot of generals and admirals needed some human comfort when things got bad, Jack answered on Nelly net.

What?

You were thinking it rather loudly, Nelly answered. Maybe I shouldn't have passed it along to Jack. You can sue me later, when all this is done.

Kris let Jack hold her. She felt the buzz in her bones, not shaking like before but something different, as if every bone in her body had taken on a resonance. Slowly, in Jack's arms, it died away.

"Thank you," she said, stepping away.

"Can I come back in?" came plaintively from the door.

"Certainly," Kris said, "although I've just sent our last defenses out to make a quick swing by our local star and come back up, possibly in neutron traffic, to get the best shots they can at the incoming cruisers."

"I was going to suggest that," Penny said, coming gingerly back into flag plot. "Kris, I'm sorry. I was out of order. It won't happen again."

"Yes, it will, Penny. That's why I have you here. We both knew that was the only order I could give, but neither one of us liked it. You had to say it. I had to do it. Now get caught up and let me have the benefit of your thoughts."

Penny studied the board for a bit, then turned to Kris. "You remember when you told me you wanted *Endeavor* to run away, not fight?"

"Yes. Someone suggested I turn in my Longknife 'Do or Die' merit badge."

"I was wondering. Is there any reason we have to stand and fight these cruisers? Could we maybe duck out when they get here?"

Kris slapped her forehead. "Right. We spend fifteen minutes every twelve hours behind this cinder of a planet. Why not spend the few minutes they're in range hiding there?"

"With all the energy they have on their boats," Masao said,

"there is no way they could bend their course to an orbit. They are coming at us hell-for-leather. Let them eat hell."

Kris found herself hugging her friend, not a hug for her, but a hug for joy. She even planted a kiss on Penny's cheek. "You are a genius, woman. A defensive genius. Nelly, calculate what changes we need to make to our orbit to accomplish this."

"If we make a minor adjustment this orbit, we can make a second adjustment an hour before they pass through, and yes, Penny is right. From the lead ship to the last one is less than five minutes."

"Nelly, advise the captains of the change in orbits. Also, adjust our targeting. The cruisers still get one shot out of ten. We don't want them to think we're ignoring them. Nelly, are the ships headed for the Alwa jump holding a steady course?"

"Yes, Kris."

"Are you thinking what I think you're thinking?" Penny asked.

"Why not? Nelly, the next ten minutes, we concentrate on the wayward detachment. Give them one-sixteenth pellets. They're far enough out that any damage is better than none. Then, once the original storm is on its way, they get one shot in five. That leaves seven shots in ten for our friends out Admiral Kitano's way. By the way, Nelly, advise Kitano of both our plans to dodge the cruisers and the bullets we've sent at those who skipped out on her. We need to keep her in the loop."

"Done, Kris."

Kris glanced around her flag plot. A few minutes ago it looked like a funeral. Now it was more like the early stages of a victory party. Kris knew this could change, but it felt good for now.

She rubbed her belly and felt baby settle down with her to wait.

She hadn't long.

65

The aliens didn't wait for Admiral Kitano's battlecruisers to attack them. Instead, they wore away from them and invited Kitano to try the deadly space they'd been in.

Kitano declined the honor, instead leading her ships up and over the clouds of racing neutron fragments.

Kris studied the situation and decided it was too ambiguous for her long-range fire. She ordered the beam ships to slow fire, one round every minute, and send three out to the far force headed for the jump and one at the cruisers. Again, Kris advised Kitano of developments and that she'd have clean space to fight five hours from now.

Before her, cruisers died. What would happen to the far-flung forces would be a long time coming.

Jack took Kris out for a candlelit dinner at an Italian restaurant. Kris was again struck by a surreal feeling as the waiters went about their business and off-duty workers sat at tables, chatting as normally as any day while ships did battle and people died only a few Astronomical Units away. Of course, those units were measured in millions of kilometers. Still, in Kris's flag plot, they fought a battle.

Here, they dined on veal parmigiana and a truly unique and very fresh Caesar salad.

"We grow the lettuce aboard ship, Your Highness," the waiter said as he set the plate before her.

"This is not relaxing," Kris told Jack after the wine waiter retreated with no order.

"I know, but imagine the report these other diners will take to their shipmates. 'I ate with the princess at Luigi's. It can't be all that bad.'"

Kris winced. "Is that the message we want?"

"When all hell breaks loose, it will be soon enough to worry. For now, everyone does their job, and things will work out," Jack said, saluting Kris with a water goblet.

Kris saluted back. "Leave tomorrow's evil to tomorrow, huh?"

"Unless you can send some neutron slag at it, yes," Jack answered.

Kris left half her delicious meal on the plate. Between baby taking up so much room and the nervousness that she could not shed, her stomach had little interest.

They walked, hand in hand, back to flag plot. "Anything pop while we were at supper?" Jack asked as soon as they stepped through the door.

"Just the usual," Penny reported. "Is Luigi's as good as they say?"

"Very good," Kris said, "assuming you don't have a baby shoving your stomach up into your throat."

"Mind if Masao and I take a break?" Penny asked. "I'm a bit hungry."

"With gratitude for watching the store while we did," Kris said, and sent her friends on their way.

With Admiral Furzah, she studied the boards.

"Is it as strange for you as it is for me to watch this slow-motion battle?" Admiral Furzah asked. "In our histories, there are stories of sieges that lasted for years, but this. This is strange."

"The time for terror will come."

"Hmm. I think the time of terror is coming to your Fast Fleets," she said.

Kris had noticed that. While she'd dined with Jack, the neutron darts launched hours ago had been racing through the empty space that both the aliens and Admiral Kitano were carefully avoiding. Soon, their battlefield would be clear; Kitano was already edging closer to the aliens.

They had spread out, loosening their dishes to let ships dodge. Many hadn't. "Nelly, what's the count on alien warships?"

"We've destroyed a hundred and twenty-three. There are six hundred and ninety-seven left, Kris. Oh, and while you were out, Lorna Do's *Churchill* didn't quite dodge. A dart winged her. She's still holding out space, but her crystal armor got knocked off, and her lasers are questionable. She's trailing the fleet."

"We knew the risk when we laid on this battle," Kris whispered.

The battle began to develop. The aliens were in a diamond array, each corner made up of six dishes of roughly thirty warships each. Here Kris got to see the difference between the Enlightened Ones. One array was an open, six-pointed star. The next was two columns of three. The third was a pentagon with one dish in the middle. The last was more a swarm with six loose formations that constantly changed shape.

"That's got to be a bitch to control," Jack said.

"Are you sure it is controlled?" Admiral Furzah asked. "It looks like no one commands there."

"She may be right," Kris said. "I think Kitano will try that one first."

Kitano's four fleets were in a diamond formation of their own. Admiral Drago's Fourth Fleet held a bit back, facing three of the alien dishes as Kitano slipped the other three down to engage the loosely formed enemy.

That alien commander must have seen what was coming. Either he gave the order to charge, or his skippers got it into their own heads to do so. However it happened, nearly two hundred warships flipped over, aimed themselves at the approaching battlecruisers, and charged. They'd been maintaining 2.5 gees for days. They had a lot of energy on every ship, all headed for Kris. Now they bent their course with anywhere from 2.6 to 3.1 gees straight at the battlecruisers.

Kitano saw it coming. She slowly pulled back, not letting the aliens get too much of an advantage in acceleration, then she gave them a blast from the forward batteries, flipped, and took off at three gees, giving them a taste of the aft batteries.

Now the aliens gave chase, doing everything they could to catch the battlecruisers. The humans reloaded their aft batteries every five to seven seconds, depending on whether they were the new ships with eight guns aft or the upgraded battlecruisers with four.

Once, Kitano ordered a flip and let them have it with the

forward batteries, six or twelve for a full five seconds, then flipped over again.

The alien charge was mad, wild . . . and erratic. The faster ships were the first to die as Kitano concentrated on them. Then the next wave and the next. Warships might be five hundred thousand tons of anger coated with slabs of granite and basalt, but they were mortal, and could only take so much from 22-inch lasers.

"The battlecruisers are concentrating two or three lasers on the same point," Nelly reported. "Five seconds worth of that from 22-inch lasers will burn a hole in anything."

And it did. Kris had to remind herself that what she saw was hours old. Warships surged ahead and died in fiery explosions as lasers slashed them. Some battlecruisers took hits; they glowed their response.

Battlecruisers glowed and cooled as alien warships burned and vaporized.

"When will they learn this is suicide?" Penny whispered.

"They know it is," Kris said. "That Enlightened One is willing to send them to their deaths. Why?"

The aliens played the suicide card again. Smaller boats launched from the larger warships, aimed for the nearest human ship. Secondary batteries slapped them down. Big warships burned, and little suicide ships sparkled in death. Smaller explosions lit up.

"That rocket-launcher defense is working," Jack said.

"Did we mount any rocket launchers on this big target?" Kris asked Jack.

"No, this huge target has no secondary armament. No defense at all."

Kris's eyes grew wide.

"And yes, I've had all the Marine rocket launchers we brought aboard mounted on the hull. They'll have to be operated by Marines on line of sight. The huge sensor suite this tub has is all aimed at targets way out there. Nothing for right at your elbow."

"Nelly, can you do anything about that?"

"No, Kris. Jack already raised this with Sal. My kids are smart, Kris, but we need something to work with. These sensors can't track anything as close as a million klicks."

"Oh, brilliant," Kris said. "I should have spent a week crawling over this monster, getting a feel for what they'd given us."

"You were rather busy, my loving Admiral," Jack said, "and we did have to dock these monsters two hundred clicks ahead of the station to make sure ships didn't run into them. There wasn't time."

"No, we couldn't delay this attack," Kris agreed.

"Let's just pray they don't get near us," Penny said.

"Prayer is not a strategy," Admiral Furzah said. "At least, not a winning strategy."

Kris said a hearty amen to that.

The battle of the first array resolved itself while they talked. While one corner died, the others did not sit idle. The three remaining arrays, in their different formations, closed on Admiral Drago's Fourth Fleet, trying to get in range of him and do to him what the rest of the fleets were doing for their brothers.

Drago backstepped slowly, giving ground while burning the closest warships under concentrated volleys. They burned, but one of his was caught by an atomic explosion. The *Vigilant* was Alwa-made and had a green crew. They must have missed something. It cost them dearly.

Now ships were coming in from three different directions: warships, suicide boats, and a few fast cruisers that the one surviving mother ship had apparently saved back. Drago's ships were hard-pressed. The *Bismarck* followed the *Vigilant* into an expanding radioactive ball.

Drago turned fleet and began a serious retrograde.

Kitano brought the three other fleets through the wreckage of the alien dishes and took one alien array on the flank.

Drago had held the bridge long enough for Kitano to eradicate one-quarter of the alien force. Now she was back on the battlefield, taking large chunks out of the alien commander who'd arranged his ships in a pentagon.

"That's got to hurt," Jack said, as the two outer dishes of the pentagon vanished in little more than a blink.

What was left of that array became chaos as it fell apart and sought to merge itself to the other two. All except one. The center dish charged straight into Kitano's fleet, blossoming like a flower with suicide boats and smaller craft.

Thirty against 150 were lousy odds. Kris had fought them and knew it for a fact. The alien ignored that, and died too quickly to obtain enlightenment. His warships died, then secondaries mopped up the smaller stuff.

The alien attack failed, but it had taken another battlecruiser out. The newly arrived *Maawaska* from Tillamook let a suicide boat with an atomic get too close.

Whoever commanded the two remaining arrays took in what they'd seen and appeared to learn a lesson. At least they tried.

The remaining fifteen dishes rearranged themselves. Two dishes higher, three dishes next, five in the middle, then three and two to the bottom. The middle dishes advanced on Kitano's ships slowly, the upper and lower ones faster.

"Finally, they are using their superior numbers to engulf us," Admiral Furzah purred. "They can learn."

"But so can we," Kris pointed out.

Kitano's fleets spread out, leaving a hole in the middle facing the enemy's refused center. Then the fleets dashed up and out, each one taking on all or parts of two wing dishes, thirtyplus battlecruisers against fifty to sixty huge alien warships.

It was not a fair fight.

Again, the long-range lasers galled the stone-clad warships. Again, the warships broke into ragged charges, desperate to close with the humans. Once more, the alien dishes gushed forth a flood of vicious little boats, some tipped with atomics, all striving to get close enough to kill.

The aliens fought, and the aliens died.

But while eight dishes were engaged, seven were free to get into mischief. An alien commander saw it and put it to good use.

Now the center put on acceleration, swept forward and down, trying to take Miyoshi's Second Fleet on its flank. Five dishes strove to slam into his exposed flank even as the two dishes he was attacking charged in as well.

Miyoshi was sandwiched. His ships began to glow, then burn, even as more aliens exploded into vapor.

Drago's fleet was on the other side of Miyoshi. Suddenly, he found his targets falling back as fast as they could. He pursued.

As Kris and Drago had learned, a pursuit through recently vacated space was dangerous. Still, Miyoshi was suffering, so Drago plunged in, secondaries sweeping the space in front of him.

Poor *Hotspur*, second of that name to serve under Kris, stumbled onto a suicide boat with an atomic on board and vanished away to dust. The newly arrived *Te Mana* suffered a near-similar fate. It must have winged the attacker at the last minute. The battlecruiser from Woolomurra managed to hold together and fall out of line to lick its wounds.

The other fleets closed in as fast as they could dispose of the warships in front of them, in pursuit as Miyoshi's ships gave ground grudgingly. The *Asahi* from Yamato paid the full price as six warships got her range. They burned through her crystal armor to the reactors inside. She exploded.

The *Roger Young* from Alwa suffered the same fate, as did the *Essen* from New Birmingham and the *Tone* from Musashi. Other ships glowed but fought back, blowing their assailants into vacuum.

First Fleet closed on the alien formation, fighting its way up from the bottom through space seeded with suiciders in both boats and smaller getabouts. The *Daemon* from New Eden took an atomic and vanished. The *Resolute* from Wardhaven took a near miss and limped out of the line. Wardhaven's new *Formidable* didn't see the suicider who got her and blew up, leaving only a few survival pods to show where she'd been.

If Kris was sickened as she lost first one, then another battlecruiser, the alien commander must have gnawed his guts as his own ships vanished by the dozens.

Battles do strange things to time. Even here, far from the wrack and ruin, Kris felt time dilate as seconds stretched into hours, and hours vanished in minutes. It was as if she'd been standing at the boards for hours, but the timer showed only thirty minutes gone as the last warship made a dash for the *Atago* and blew up under fire from the entire Musashi squadron.

"Thank God that's done," Penny breathed.

There was a flash, and *Saladin* vanished into radioactive dust.

"Nelly, send to Kitano. 'Well done. Stand clear of the battleground.'" Kris paused for a moment, her eyes flitting across the system from the now-won battle to the alien base ship with its fifty escorts still bearing down on Kris's position, to the 150 making for Alwa.

"Begin deceleration to set the most economical course to make a sustainable orbit around the red dwarf. Stay clear as much as possible of the direct line of fire between my flagship and the last alien base ship. When you are set on course for the dwarf, concentrate all available fuel on the least damaged ships and have them modify their course to swing around the dwarf star and back to Jump Eta. I will commence the pursuit of the hostile fleet breaking for Alwa using Admiral Benson and forces at hand. Any reinforcement from you will be appreciated. Longknife sends."

Kris sat down in the comfortable chair, had Nelly raise her swollen legs and recline her back a bit. "Now we fight our own little battle. Let's see how your brilliant plan works, Penny."

"God help us," her longtime friend said.

66

The Battle of the Cinder was a study in vectors and angles. *Wasp* led the handful of ships Kris had around the neutron star and fell into a course nearly parallel to the racing alien cruisers.

Even with their faster reloads, they only got off two volleys as the aliens shot past.

The beam ships sent as many tiny bullets their way as they could, but the angle rapidly got impossible. For the last twenty minutes the aliens were on approach, there was nothing Kris could do to hit them.

She wondered when the aliens realized that the beam ships had adjusted their orbit enough to put the burned-out planet between them.

Wasp's skipper kept a live camera on what happened next and passed the feed to Kris as soon as she cleared the cinder. The aliens hammered their ships with even more gees, accelerating to try to catch Kris before she slipped away or decelerating in an insane attempt to make an impossible burn into orbit.

Ships slammed into the planet. Ships broke in two. Two ships collided and one of them banged into a third. "It was a mess," *Wasp*'s captain reported, a big grin on her face.

But the alien wave passed, and Kris breathed a sigh of relief.

Well out, the last mother ship and her fifty warships bent on an extra fraction of a gee and headed straight for Kris.

"Let's send her a few reminders that she's got a lot of space to cross," Kris ordered. "Nelly, fill the space in front of them with three-thousand-ton fragments. Let's see if we can wing that lucky bastard. If we hurt her, maybe we can send something solid for the kill."

"Should I take the beam ships up to three rounds a minute to surprise them with a decent-size wave?" Nelly asked.

"Are the ships good for it?"

"For at least five minutes, Kris. Then we'd better back off to two a minute. The fifteen minutes we were behind the planet gave everyone a break, but not enough to do any major maintenance."

"So we'll need to rest in a bit."

"Yes, Kris."

"Pass the word. Thirty minutes from now, they can take four hours off."

"Done, Admiral."

So the battle slowed again. Slowed enough that Kris found she had a minute to look behind her. *Ultimate Argument* was slowly boosting toward Jump Zeta at a half gee. Despite Kris's best effort, allied with the aliens own desperation, a half dozen cruisers were headed fast in her general direction.

Nelly noticed it first. "Kris, we have a problem."

"Another one!"

"One of the cruisers is bending its course toward *Ultimate Argument*."

"Damn," Jack said. "Don't they ever give up?"

"I haven't noticed that in their character," Penny said, ever the helpful intelligence officer. Even Masao joined the rest in shooting her a dirty look. "Well, I'm just saying."

"Nelly, has *UA* noticed the problem?" Three of Nelly's offspring, along with Kris's friends Jacques and Amanda, Chief Beni, and her science chief were on that ship.

"I am sending a warning."

"They've got nothing to shoot at that bastard," Jack noted.

A minute later, it became clear *UA* had noticed its peril. Now she accelerated at a right angle to her previous course. It was a very close run thing. The alien cruiser gave it everything it had, but at the end, its engines faltered just enough. *UA* took one laser hit in a section already damaged.

The cruiser went on its mad way. The huge beam ship wobbled in space for a bit before settling back on course for the jump. An hour later, the cruiser blew itself up rather than face a slow death in cold space. Over the next hour, dozens of cruisers who had survived so much gave themselves over to their reactors' plasma.

"Victory or death," Kris said.

"I think Jacques would tell you, destroy the vermin or surrender to your fate," Penny said.

"It seems that way," Kris agreed.

Kris slept during the four hours the beam ships devoted to preventive maintenance. Even baby seemed exhausted by the battle. Kris woke after the first wave of neutron fragments swept through the general space of the alien mother ship.

"I recorded it," Penny said.

Kris watched for fifteen minutes, nibbling a bran muffin and drinking chamomile tea as warship after warship was stung by tiny three-thousand-ton pellets. It was harder to make out their impacts on the small moon of the mother ship, but it began to waver in flight. For an entire minute, it steered off course before catching itself and bearing around to face Kris again.

"We hurt them. The mother ship's acceleration is down to .86 gees. Five warships aren't there anymore, and a dozen can't maintain the fleet's acceleration."

"Nelly, how much are they zigzagging?"

"They're not holding one course for more than two minutes, now, but that's actually putting them in a smaller volume of space. They are also closer. When the beam ships are back online, I'd recommend a half hour of three slugs a minute, spinning to maximum fragmentation. Three thousand tons seems to be a deadly hit."

"Let the crew know our intention," Kris said.

A minute later, the ship's announcer let everyone know, "Maximum primary-ignition effort in thirty minutes. We're going for the last mother ship, the mother."

There may have been more to the message, but it was garbled.

So they sat back to wait and watched the show as more bolts shot out at their last target.

"Kris, are we going for total annihilation of these four alien clans?" Jack asked.

"I don't know," Kris said. "Are they all out here?"

"Where are those door knockers?" Penny asked. "The stone-clad battering rams to force a jump."

"I haven't seen them," Masao said.

"Nelly?" Kris asked.

"They have not been present during the fight," she said. "There are a group of reactors back at the gas giant the aliens used as their base. They have been just sitting there at low power. They appear to have just powered up. Kris, it is likely they are on the move, but I cannot yet say to where."

"I'd hate it if they followed the wolf pack headed for Alwa," Kris said. "They'd sure make it harder for us to hold a jump point. Still, if they take off for points unknown, the rest of these bastards will know that we beat four of them and how we did it."

"If the others find out about this, will they run for cover or run for us?" Penny asked.

"Anyone's guess is as good as mine," Kris said, patting baby.

"Kris, I've been meaning to ask," Jack said. "Who leads the last-ditch defense of Alwa with what fuel we can scrape together?"

"Who do you think?" Kris said.

"I was afraid of that," Jack said through a stormy scowl.

"I am responsible for Alwa's defense, and the *Wasp* pinnace will be drawing all the spare fuel from the Birds and couriers. She can pick me up."

"I'll go tell the Marines to pack it up, we're moving out."

"Nelly, ask Kitano to name a commander for the defense of this system. While we'll be taking all the reaction mass we can find from the fleet, the beam ships can refuel some of the Bird class to get fuel from the next system and bring it back. It may take a while to get the fleet moving again, but they shouldn't be totally dependent on the success of me and Admiral Benson's forlorn hope."

"Sending it, Kris. I have a message from Kitano. Roughly one ship in four will be chasing after your Forlorn Hope. Kris, it's heavy with division flags. Taussig's *Hornet*, Kaeyat's *Tenacious*. Admiral Drago is bringing the Earth's *Churchill*, and Admiral Nottingham has the *George Washington*.

Miyoshi's Second Fleet is lightly represented. They took a pounding, but Admiral Zingi's *Mikasa*, Cochrane's *Nelson Mandela*, and Suliu's *Genghis Khan* will make it. All told, twenty will be following you."

"Is Kitano staying?"

"No, Kris, I should have mentioned the *Princess Royal* first."

"Which of my admirals is not on the list?"

"Miyoshi."

"A good man."

Kris eyed her board. Admiral Benson's reserve fleet, which had missed most of the fight since he was detached to try to protect Kris, would arrive just in time to make one swing around the neutron star and head back to the jump. That would give her four squadrons, thirty-two ships, but most of them were crewed by yard workers, colonials, and birds. It would be their home they'd be defending, but they sure hadn't had a lot of time to learn to fight their ships.

Kris shrugged; she had what she had, which included baby. She smiled and patted its head, or rump or whatever she was presenting for mom's attention. She would fight this battle as best she could with what she had.

So far, that had been enough to attend to the slaughter of hundreds of billions of aliens.

Kris shivered.

"Tell Kitano to organize her detachment. I'll be looking for her." *If things go wrong, it will be Kitano's job to try to save Alwa.*

67

The alien skippers were getting smart. The thirty around the mother ship still hovered, but at a greater distance from it and each other. The 126 racing for Eta Jump were spread out. The drumbeat of neutron hail had their attention.

Fewer died as the pellets raced through their formations, but ships were stung. Some blew up.

The mother ship held its course for Kris's flagship.

Kris watched as the long-distance battle worked itself out. Kitano's fleets wore away from the lone mother ship as they tacked to reach the red dwarf. As soon as undamaged pinnaces had redistributed the fleet's reaction mass, twenty ships detached themselves from the rest, decelerating hard to swing themselves around the dwarf and use the neutron star for more braking before heading back toward Jump Point Eta.

Yes, Kris would use the same jump the aliens were aiming for. With the door knockers still watching from across the system, Kris had to.

She and Nelly had examined the aliens' acceleration. They'd hit the jump at over a hundred thousand klicks. That would throw them several jumps inward toward Alwa. Kris would have to hit the jump at less than fifty thousand klicks to stay in the system, do a quick swing by the nearest gas giant, then head for the fuzzy jump and a direct jump to the system just out from Alwa. She'd be there when the aliens jumped in after doing two shorter jumps.

The only question was if she could get to the jump into Alwa before the aliens. If she failed, the aliens would have a free shot at Granny Rita and company.

It would be a close run thing. "Nelly, let's get some more darts out at the Alwa-bound fleet."

"Kris, both the skippers of the beam ships and their science officers have asked me to inform you that you need to go easy on them."

"They don't want to talk to me, Nelly?"

"It seems so."

"There are some disadvantages to your reputation," Jack said.

"Do tell," Kris answered. "How, easy, Nelly?"

"One round a minute for half an hour, then an hour off for maintenance."

"Is it that bad?"

"Yes, Kris."

"Do we need to cut back even further?"

"No, Kris. I think they've got things under control."

"Okay." Kris eyed the two targets. The mother ship was closing fast, not attempting to brake, and the warships closing even faster on the jump. "One round a minute from each ship. Three for the Alwa-bound ships, Nelly, one for the inbound mother ship."

"I have passed along those orders."

Kris sat in her chair, feet up, patting baby and eyeing the flow of the battle. She was used to battles playing out at breathless speeds. A battle where time stretched out as ships covered distances measured in tens of millions of kilometers while traveling at tens or hundreds of thousands of kilometers per hour was hard to get the mind around, and even harder to adjust the flow of adrenaline for. At times, baby had been jumping rope and doing headstands, and Kris gladly would have done the same. Other times, she and baby sat as placid as on a summer's day.

"What a way to fight a battle," Kris whispered.

"Our time will come," Jack said, reaching for her hand. They settled down, her in her comfortable chair, his hand on hers, and watched the fight develop.

"You hungry?" Jack asked.

"Kind of," Kris admitted.

"Want a hamburger and fries?"

"A cheeseburger with all the fixings, maybe double pickles, but no onions. Hold the onions. I don't think baby likes onions. Oh, does anyone want half a cheeseburger?" Kris added. "I don't think I can handle a whole one."

"I'll take it," Penny said. "I usually leave half of mine."

Jack headed out to get chow, with Masao at his elbow, leaving the two women alone. Even Admiral Furzah left to see if there was any fresh meat that hadn't been burned.

"I'm sorry about my outburst," Penny said as soon as they were alone.

"No need, Penny. It was a miserable thing I did."

"But you're working on setting it straight. I should have realized you'd find a way to work this out. Worse, you were right. There wasn't a damn thing anyone could do about it at the moment. The aliens saw an opening and grabbed it."

"I don't know," Kris said. "Maybe I should have left the reserve fleet there. Heaven knows, I've just had that poor fleet flying back and forth and wasting good reaction mass."

"Can you read minds or see the future?" Penny asked.

"Not this week," Kris said. "I think this gestation thing is messing up my crystal ball."

"No doubt. How do you intend to work the intercept?"

"Carefully. Very carefully. I have no idea how long it will take us to refuel or how fast they dare take the jumps. We'll just have to play this one as it develops."

The cheeseburgers returned. Even the feline from Sasquan had found a couple of pounds of freshly ground beef. They munched their burgers as fragments of a neutron star, chipped off six hours ago, hammered ships for the next twenty minutes, leaving them torn, twisted, or wrecked.

The one-sided battle continued as the aliens strove to get their revenge for their murdered brothers . . . and themselves.

"Kris, the alien warships will be approaching the jump soon. That is one place we know they will have to go."

"Any suggestions, Nelly?"

"It would be nice to hammer the jump. Could I ask the beam-ship management teams about some rapid fire just as the ships reach there? They will probably try to go through at ten-second intervals. It won't do us any good to fire the same because all we'd have to be is off by a second, and all our darts would miss. Still, if we were to try for an eleven-second interval . . ." Nelly left the rest hanging.

"Nelly, get me the captain of the two ships."

"Kris, for this you will likely need the captains, chief science officers, and superintendents of reactors."

"Get me all of them."

Kris's screens changed to show six heads. Most were gray- or white-haired. Two were women. None looked happy to face Kris.

"In six hours, the aliens will be sending their warships through the Eta Jump headed for Alwa," Kris began. "It would be nice if we could make them share that space with a lot of neutron darts."

"How many?" the gray-haired man in a gray Merchant Marine uniform with four stripes on the shoulder boards said.

"They will try for ten-second intervals. They have been known to risk five-second intervals, but not at this speed. We, of course, won't know when their ten-second intervals start. I was thinking of getting off a dart every eleven or twelve seconds for fifteen minutes."

"So each of us would have to have primary ignition every twenty-two seconds," the other captain, this one in blue, said.

"Something like that."

"But there would be no *guarantee* that we'd make even *one* hit."

Kris couldn't remember whether this speaker was a chief scientist or in charge of reactors. Then it hit her. There was no weapons officer in the whole bunch.

I've got to make some changes when this is done.

"There hasn't been an aimed shot from your weapon system this whole battle," Kris pointed out. "We put the neutron darts out there and the aliens are kind enough to run into a few of them."

"That's an interesting way of thinking," another civilian said.

"That is how battles are won and lost," Kris answered, as evenly as she could manage.

The six looked at each other, from screen to screen. Kris had the distinct feeling they wanted to say no, but none had the courage to say it to her.

If they hadn't the guts to say no to a princess, what are they doing out here?

Kris took the bull by the horns. "So, in thirty-two minutes will you be ready to begin a rapid fire sequence?"

"Ah," came from six mouths.

Kris gave them her most placid face. Maybe with a Mona Lisa smile.

"I guess we can do it, Your Highness," one of the civilians finally said.

I wonder if Grampa Ray gets this kind of solid support, Kris thought, and bit her lip to kill a wry smile.

"Thank you very much. You have the thanks of a grateful world."

They rang off.

"Did you get the feeling they didn't want to do this?" Penny asked no one.

"I didn't see any resistance," Kris said, wearing her sunny smile.

"Yeah, right," Jack muttered.

Thirty minutes later, the beam ships began a rapid-fire staccato. Beneath them, the neutron star sparked every ten, eleven, or twelve seconds.

Then Kris heard a crunch through the hull of the *Conqueror*.

"Kris, *Conqueror* has suffered a failure in one of its capacitors. It has been taken off-line and the power lines to it cut."

"Are we in for a catastrophic failure?" This sounded too much like the failure that took *Ultimate Argument* out of the fight.

"No, Kris. The potential failure was spotted in time and the system taken off-line quickly. Also, power requirements were reduced gracefully. There was no backwash into the distribution system."

Again, Nelly was using that passive voice. Kris considered digging deeper, then thought better of it. If Nelly wanted to be coy, it was best to leave her alone.

There was no report from the captain, but the flashes on the neutron star continued, now at the rate of five every minute or so.

With five minutes left in the shoot, *Opening Statement* took a third of its systems gracefully off-line. The last shots went out four to a minute.

When that was done, Kris authorized a four-hour stand-down for maintenance.

She got some rest while the beam ships were down. When she awoke, the alien base ship was closing fast. The two sections of Kitano's fleet had pulled well away from them. Admiral Benson had jacked up his deceleration to cut the time needed to make orbit and was now joining *Wasp* and *Intrepid*.

It was time for Kris to make some hard decisions.

Once again, she talked to the double troika. "The alien base ship is twelve hours out. We'll again adjust our orbit to dodge them. At their speed, they can't make a major change but no doubt they will try. You can't fool many people twice."

Now it was their turn to eye her blandly.

"The best way for you to keep the aliens from slitting your throat is to nail them during the next nine hours. I'm thinking the best thing you can do for your insurance companies is to fire off a dart every minute. Can you do it?"

"One primary ignition a minute for nine straight hours?"

"Or less if you nail him," Kris said, helpfully.

"Could maybe one of us go down for a few hours? We could spell each other?" a civilian asked.

"I don't know. How many hits have you been making?"

"I don't know," seemed to be the consensus.

"By my estimate, maybe three out of a hundred hit," Nelly said.

"We're only getting *three* percent hits!" came from several throats.

"Not bad, all considering," Kris said. "These aren't guided weapons."

"Oh," the captain in blue said, nodding.

"So, I think darts spinning out four fragments at this range should do very well. One a minute from each ship. If you have to take a maintenance break, feel free to do so, but remember, you only have nine hours to hit them before they'll be too close."

The six began to talk among themselves; Kris rang off.

Over the next nine hours, Kris spent most of her time

preparing for the next battle as the Battle of the Neutron Star ground its way down to a bloody end.

Kris transferred her flag to *Wasp*, leaving Abby, Cara, and Colonel Bruce to control both of the big ships. *Wasp* joined Admiral Benson's Reserve Fleet and, without waiting for Kitano's reinforcements, boosted for the distant jump.

The alien ships came on, their course limited by intent and speed. The slow beat of the neutron bullets slammed alien warships and the base ship. Warships blew up. The base ship took hits, faltered, but bore in.

It was a bedraggled few that survived to watch as the beam ships again adjusted their orbit. Or tried. *Conqueror* suffered an engineering failure as it made a burn. Despite Kris's best plans, it did not disappear soon enough behind the cinder of a planet. Every alien ship that could bring its fire to bare aimed for it in the few seconds they had her in range.

Conqueror took hits. She burned and shed skin. Kris expected her to explode any second.

Beside her, Penny's face showed a hard smile. "I talked with her first officer," she whispered. "I told him how you could move Smart Metal around to shield where you were vulnerable. I think he listened to me."

"I think he did," Kris said.

Hit, skin blazing as it steamed off into space, *Conqueror* held together even as its orbit took it out of harm's way. The desperate Enlightened One wore ship trying to follow only to have the base ship clip the tip of a tall mountain on the dead planet. With as much energy as the small moon had on it, the collision was catastrophic. A quarter of the base ship splattered itself across airless waste. What was left of the Enlightened One's domain ricocheted off, took out three warships, and headed out, spinning wildly, into nowhere.

New stars appeared and disappeared quickly as warships that had survived the battle thus far chose to end it quickly rather than face their cold future.

Twenty minutes later, the beam ships came back in communication with Kris. Reports from *Conqueror* were bad but could have been worse. Despite all her punishment, she was still holding air pressure for her crew and machinery. There was no question that she would never again fire a neutron slug.

"We're still here," her captain reported. "And my first officer says to tell that staff gal of yours that he learned a thing or three from her or else we wouldn't be."

"The next time you go into battle, we'll see that you have some defensive officers and a few lasers of your own."

"Oh, please," he said.

Kris turned her gaze toward the jump ahead.

"Once more, into the fight," she whispered to herself and baby.

68

Admiral Benson's flag, *Temptress*, led the fleet through the jump at 50,000 kph and began braking, bending its course toward the near gas giant. *Wasp* came though, at the tag end of Hanson's BatRon 16. In another three minutes, the rest of the reserve fleet was in system and braking for a refueling stop.

Of the aliens that had gone through the jump many hours earlier, there was nothing. They had definitely used it for a long jump and were well on their way to Alwa. Time was critical.

Kris would have to hold the refueling pass to one partial orbit, grazing the giant's atmosphere before taking off for the fuzzy jump.

"Nelly, can we take a battlecruiser down for a refueling pass?"

"It won't be good for the crystal," Nelly answered. "It's designed to slow down light, not transfer heat."

"Nelly, ask anyone you can what we can do to protect the crystal and get a fuel-capturing arrangement on a battle-cruiser."

Ten minutes later, *Wasp*'s ship maintainer, an old friend of Kris's, L. J. Mong, the chief of the boat, and several other chiefs were in her day quarters.

"Ma'am, the whole idea of the pinnace was to keep the frigates out of a gas giant's atmosphere. However, thanks to some calculations by your computer, we do have an idea," he said. Behind Kris, a new view opened up on the screen. On top, *Wasp* was almost as small as Condition Zed, but with her crystal armor buried under several centimeters of cooling Smart Metal™. Below, the poor ship bulged out worse than Kris, with a huge maw open to take in reaction mass.

"You think that will do?" Kris asked.

"We don't know for sure, ma'am, but we don't think we'll lose any ships. We just aren't sure what kind of shape we'll be in when we're finished."

Kris thought for a moment. "I'm willing to take on the hostiles with sixteen ships. Will this foul up more than half the fleet?"

Senior Command Chief Mong eyed the other chiefs, then glanced at the lieutenant commander in charge of maintaining the *Wasp*. "I don't suppose so, ma'am."

"Then pass that schematic to the fleet. If anyone has suggestions, they can talk to me anytime."

"Yes, ma'am," the chiefs said, and they followed their officer out of Kris's day quarters.

"Sixteen ships, huh? Against how many?" Jack asked.

"About a hundred at last count. We got a third of them. Maybe winged more."

"We'll see what we see."

The close pass to the gas giant left one ship unable to reorient itself afterward. The *Opal* out of Hekate couldn't change its configuration back. This might have been as much a problem with the Smart Metal™ as the pass.

Looking very much like Kris felt, the *Opal* was ordered back to System X to deliver its reaction mass to the ships coming along behind. She would also pass along the idea for capturing reaction mass without slowing down.

Twenty-four ships accelerated for the fuzzy jump. Their next stop would be the system one out from Alwa. The aliens would very likely jump into that system, their third jump to Kris's second.

Of course, they'd be coming in a different jump from Kris. That would make matters very interesting.

69

Wasp cleared the jump, snug in the middle of Admiral Benson's Reserve Fleet. Benson's *Temptress* had come through first; he'd bent his course toward the Gamma Jump as he decelerated. With luck, the battle fleet would cruise up to the jump the aliens would use, take up defensive positions, and shoot up the aliens as they stormed through.

It was a nice battle plan.

It didn't survive contact with the enemy.

Kris's fleet was halfway there, decelerating all the way, when the jump started spitting out alien ships, also decelerating. They were at a bit over 200,000 kph; they'd need to slow down if they wanted to hit the next jump at 50,000 kph or less.

Any more, and they'd vault over Alwa to some other system.

So they decelerated, their bows with all those lasers pointed where they'd been, their vulnerable rocket motors pointed where they were going.

Admiral Benson ordered the fleet to flip around and change their vectors to slow them and get them across the aliens' course.

Kris leaned back in her egg. Most of her flag plot was unfamiliar. Her gear, even including her screens, had been left behind. Kris was offered the screens from the chief's mess.

"We won't have much use for 'em, ma'am, until this fight is over," Senior Command Chief Mong had said.

Now the screens showed the aliens running down their base course, like a space elevator on a rail, slowing steadily at 1.72 gees as they headed for the Alpha Jump into Alwa system.

Benson's course would have the Reserve Fleet pull up on

their port side about three-quarters of the way across the system. They'd have the last quarter of their cruise to the jump to fight it out.

Kris doubted it would last that long.

"Nelly, what do you make of the alien ships? How much damage did we do?"

"Several are hurting, Kris. At least six are not holding to the 1.72 deceleration. That leaves ninety-two."

Kris studied the system and the likely encounter ahead. She and Nelly could find no option better than what Admiral Benson was doing.

For a long day, the two fleets held to their approach courses. Each bore down on the other with the slow finality of death.

"This waiting is hell," Penny muttered.

"It was like this when navies were under sail. The wind might die with the two fleets close enough to hear each other talk but not shoot," Nelly told them. "They talked of iron men on wooden ships. No women were allowed. They must have been very strange men."

"They were different times," Kris said. Then eyed the clock. "Or maybe not that different."

The approach wore on. Kris kept one eye on the enemy and the other on her fuel state. It would be close.

They had to make the jump at under fifty thousand klicks or risked being thrown into some distant system with a huge amount of energy on the boats but not enough fuel to brake. And if the system had no gas giants to refuel from, or they were out of range of their depleted tanks . . .

That thought was on every mind.

The aliens might very well lose this next fight, but the humans could lose as well.

As they closed to within two hundred thousand klicks of the aliens, Kris said, "Nelly, please send a copy of the message Jacques composed for the alien base ships."

"It is sent."

"I don't believe the Enlightened One responded," Jack said.

"No, not a word."

"You think this will be any different?"

Kris shrugged. "Nothing beats a try but a failure. Sooner

or later, we have to either learn to talk or kill each other. I've had enough killing today." She found herself reaching for her belly in the egg. Without an order, Nelly expanded the egg to give Kris room to pat baby.

"If we can't end this, this little one will grow up to fight the same fights again and again."

Jack nodded. Even in an egg, you could see that simple expression.

They were at two hundred thousand klicks. Kris would order her ships to fire in only a moment. Unless the aliens had a trick up their sleeves, this would be another massacre.

"Kris, I have an answer from the aliens."

"Yes."

"'It is better to die than eat vermin shit.'"

Across the way, eighty warships suddenly veered around, their engines going from decelerating them toward the jump point to ramming them toward Kris's battle line.

Kris snapped out her orders. "Fire volleys by squadrons. Squadron commanders, select the closest ships for targets. Fire and flip as needed by squadrons. Open fire now."

The aliens were charging Kris's line. Again, they charged at whatever acceleration they could lay on: 2.6 to 3.12 gees.

Kris's battlecruisers cut their deceleration burns. Then, by squadron, flipped to bring their forward batteries to bear. For five seconds, the six lasers struck out at the aliens. In tight salvos of three lasers, they pinned the foremost alien warships. Each stone-protected warship took the full force of forty-eight lasers concentrated on only sixteen points. The lasers, powered by the upgraded reactors, burned the alien ships for five seconds.

Burn through was inevitable.

The four leading alien ships took their hits, burned, and blew up.

Three of Kris's squadrons then flipped ship, poured on three gees to open the distance from the alien charge, blew away another three ships, and accelerated away for another five seconds while all lasers recharged.

The seven ships from Hekate did a different dance with death. They continued to drift under no acceleration as their second forward battery took a different alien ship under fire, pinned it, and destroyed it. Then they flipped, jacked up their acceleration away from the onrushing aliens to 3.5 gees, and let both of their rear batteries pin two ships, one after the other.

One ship was hit hard but survived.

Then, like the other divisions, the Hekates repeated the process again.

Alien warships took battlecruiser salvos. They lit up, burned, and exploded.

One managed to get to within 160,000 yards when the human frigates were turned, stern on. Its new lasers got a lucky hit on the *Invincible*, slashing into its engineering spaces and damaging a laser. The *Vince* struggled to get out of the line of fire. Its squadron mates immediately gave the alien their full attention and burned it, but not before the battlecruiser with the unfortunate name began to eat itself. The *Vince* blossomed with survivor pods as its crew took to the cold of space rather than face the fire of their own ship.

The *Lucky Leprechaun II* also took a hit, but she proved luckier than her predecessor. This skipper dodged out of the enemy fire with a fortunate jink, then quickly mended the ship before more damage could be done.

Kris's ships suffered, but the aliens burned.

Ten warships had stayed steady on course, decelerating for the jump, intent on using the sacrifice of its brothers to get at the system that had defeated them for so long.

Kris fought the fight with one eye on her fuel gauges and the other on the tack she'd need to cancel out all this dancing away from the course to the jump.

"No more running," she finally had to order. "Set course for the jump. We fight it out on this course."

The fleet, obedient to her orders, brought their engines around to face the jump. Now they presented their broadsides to the aliens. Battlecruisers could only fight from their bow or stern.

Now the rhythm of the fight changed.

Battlecruisers coasted, faced the enemy, fired, flipped and fired again. Then, while they reloaded, they went to 3.5 gees deceleration.

"That can't be good for the engines," Jack muttered from his egg.

"No one's screaming."

No one but the aliens.

They had the humans where they wanted them, but of the eighty that had started the mad charge, less than a dozen survived. And while they heated up the battlecruisers, and made hits on the vulnerable sterns of the *Persistent* and *Enterprise*, they did not make the critical hit they aimed for.

Battlecruisers glowed under laser fire that would have blown them away a month ago. They glowed, but held their place in line and hammered the last of the alien charge to dust.

Done, Kris brought her ships back into something like a formation even as she eyed the twelve ships that had held back.

Did someone over there order the charge? Why those ten?

"Nelly, send the surrender offer again."

"Done, Kris. We'll be in range of those twelve ships in five seconds."

"Then they have five seconds to reply."

"'I will be your slave,'" Nelly snapped. "That is the message from them. 'I will be your slave.'"

"Tell them to dump their reactor cores," Kris ordered.

"I'll try," Nelly said.

"We can't let them get into the Alwa system while they're under power," Jack said.

"We can't let them get close to us while they've still got power," Kris said. "They go dead in space, or they die."

Kris's ships passed the two-hundred-thousand-klick mark. There was no word from the aliens.

"Nelly, tell them we need to see their bellies. That's what dogs do when they surrender."

"I sent that. There is no word from them. They just repeat, 'I will be your slave.'"

The fleet decelerated toward the jump. They closed to within 180,000 klicks of the aliens. The aliens continued to decelerate.

"Can we order them to abandon ship, to get into life pods and get out?" Penny asked.

"I doubt they have any." Kris thought for a long moment on

how to get "Surrender your ship" across in a different language. "Damn, we need Jacques. Nelly, tell them to stop decelerating and give us their ship."

"I sent it Kris."

They waited as they came up on the 170,000-klick mark. "Any answer?" Kris asked.

"They just say the same, 'I will be your slave.'"

"So, they remember slavery," Jack said.

"Apparently," Kris said. "Send to fleet, prepare to take the last alien ships under fire. Fire by divisions."

Kris's board showed acknowledgments.

They passed the 165,000 mark and were quickly coming in range of the new alien lasers. Kris considered letting them get the first shot off, do something to prove their treachery. She patted baby one last time. It was doing jumping jacks on her bladder from the feel. *How do you like Mommy's adrenaline, little love?*

"Jack, you asked why I had to be here."

"Yes."

"It was for this," Kris said, then added. "Fire."

Twenty-nine ships, all the undamaged ones, went to zero deceleration, aimed their bows at twelve alien ships, and lashed out at them with every laser they could bring to bear.

Aliens glowed, burned, and blew out into expanding balls of flame.

Battlecruisers flipped to bring their aft batteries to bear and hit those that still lived.

There were no more aliens headed for Alwa.

It was a near thing, but every ship of the Reserve Fleet made it through the jump, barreling through at just below 50,000 kph. They immediately bent their course for the nearest gas giant.

They had hardly entered the system when Admiral Yi reported they had traffic in the next system out. A fast-moving fleet had jumped in and was slowing down. More reinforcements had arrived.

Still in her egg as *Wasp* made a hard reach for orbit, Kris breathed a sigh of relief. She was pretty sure the new largesse from human space would not have arrived soon enough to stop the aliens' last try to blast Alwa, but she didn't ask Nelly for a check.

As it happened, Kris was out of her egg and back in uniform when the new ships began coming through. The screens from her flag plot were back on the walls in the CPO's locker so she had to go to the bridge to get The Word.

It left her stunned.

"This is Grand Admiral Santiago with orders for Captain Kris Longknife. I am to relieve you forthwith and you are to return to human space soonest. I will explain more when we can talk in private."

"Hasn't she said enough?" Jack said.

"I need to sit down."

Someone else kept a count of the new arrivals. Kris found herself seated in her day quarters, staring at the overhead.

It never quits. They just never quit. Longknifes suck bilgewater. Through a straw.

Kris had recovered by the time *Wasp* caught the first tie-down and pulled into her place on Canopus Station. Kris's fleet made it in an hour ahead of the *Thunderer*, Admiral Santiago's flag.

Kris was saved from having to pay her compliments to the newly arrived grand admiral by Santiago's message that she would instead meet Kris in her quarters.

"Strange and stranger," was all Kris said.

Kris stood in her spiffiest maternity blues, which was to say the least lumpy. The stripes of an admiral still etched her sleeve as Sandy Santiago walked in. She'd been an admiral when Kris was a freshly promoted lieutenant. Kris had given her daughter a reference for her academy application.

What was the situation between them now?

It was hard to say which one saluted which. Maybe Nelly could have measured it.

"You've done an outstanding job, Kris, from everything I've seen."

"We're still trying to retrieve the last of our scattered ships. I sent a squadron of battlecruisers back loaded as tankers. Should I have asked your permission, Grand Admiral?"

"Oh, right. Oops. Sorry Kris, and it's Sandy among us admirals. I had specific orders to make that announcement, right from King Raymond. He wants you back soonest, and he figured the best way to get you moving would be to let everyone know right at the get-go that I had orders to relieve you, and you had orders to depart immediately."

"Immediately," Kris said, sweeping a hand over her rather large bump.

"Ah, right, I did hear something from Captain O'dell that

there had been an epidemic of pregnancies. I didn't think you'd be one of them."

Kris pointed at Jack. "May I introduce my husband, Lieutenant General Jack Montoya."

"How many Marines are out here?"

"I command a division afloat and a corp of Alwa National Guard ashore," Jack said.

"The Alwans are under arms?"

"I think your brief may be a bit out-of-date," Kris said, and began to update her replacement. She ended, an hour later, by laying down her own specifics.

"I am not traveling this pregnant. Not at the accelerations we have to use to go leaping across the galaxy. I will stay right here. I will have my baby right here. I will not travel until the doctor says my baby can travel."

Grand Admiral Sandy Santiago nodded agreement. Even a grand admiral knew when she'd been trumped by a Longknife.

72

"Here you go, General, your latest little recruit," said Doc Meade as she laid the cutest tiny bundle in Jack Montoya's arms.

He held that miniature miracle with awe and the utmost of care. He couldn't help but stare at the fingers. Just like his, right down to the fingernails, but so much tinier.

Deep blue eyes stared up at him, under a shock of black hair. Then the perfect mouth formed an oh-so-large yawn for such a little face. The eyelids blinked, then closed for the moment.

"It's normal for a newborn to fall asleep after it's made a study of its new world," Doc Meade whispered to Jack.

He smiled a thank-you.

"Well, don't I get to see what my labors have wrought?" Kris asked from where they had made her comfortable, at last. Jack still shivered at the last couple of hours. No question the human race would have died out long ago if men had to do what his loving wife had just done.

The tiny bundle in his arms made it all worthwhile.

"Mrs. Longknife, may I introduce you to Ruth Maria Brenda Anne. Your latest adoring fan."

"Whom you have put to sleep," Kris said, but she was reaching for her daughter. Gently, Jack made the transfer. Now Ruthie lay on her mother's breast. Jack joined Kris in fondly caressing their daughter with his eyes.

"We've come a long way, little one," Kris said. "And you will go a long way soon enough, but for now, baby, you belong to Mommy and Daddy and we belong to you."

About the Author

Mike Shepherd grew up Navy. It taught him early about change and the chain of command. He's worked as a bartender and cabdriver, personnel advisor and labor negotiator. Now retired from building databases about the endangered critters of the Pacific Northwest, he's enjoying some fun writing.

Mike lives in Vancouver, Washington, with his wife, Ellen, and close to his daughter and grandchildren. He enjoys reading, writing, dreaming, watching grandchildren for story ideas, and upgrading his computer—all are never-ending.

He's hard at work on Kris's next story and on *Vicky Peterwald: Rebel*.

You can learn more about Mike and all his books at his website mikeshepherd.org, e-mail him at Mike_Shepherd@comcast.net, or follow Kris Longknife or Mike Moscoe on Facebook.

From *New York Times* bestselling author
MIKE SHEPHERD

Kris Longknife
TENACIOUS

There's no rest for a Longknife—even if you're a newly-wed. Vice Admiral Kris Longknife's honeymoon gets canceled when she hears that the space raiders' home world may have been discovered. Finding where the raiders came from could be the key to saving humanity. If only uncovering their secrets were that easy...

As Kris returns home, she ends up tangling with a mutinous crew determined to take off alone. The dissident group leads Kris straight into a new mess—a system filled with strange, deadly enemies poised to wipe another sentient civilization out of existence. Kris and her squadron are ready to prevent total annihilation, but the mutineers have other plans...

• • •

mikeshepherd.org
facebook.com/AceRocBooks
penguin.com

From *New York Times* Bestselling Author
MIKE SHEPHERD

. . .

The Kris Longknife Series

MUTINEER
DESERTER
DEFIANT
RESOLUTE
AUDACIOUS
INTREPID
UNDAUNTED
REDOUBTABLE
DARING
FURIOUS
DEFENDER
TENACIOUS
UNRELENTING

. . .

Praise for the Kris Longknife novels

"A whopping good read . . . Fast-paced, exciting, nicely detailed, with some innovative touches."

—Elizabeth Moon, *New York Times* bestselling author of *Crown of Renewal*

mikeshepherd.org
penguin.com

M905AS0815